A Body's

Just as

Dead

a novel

A Body's

Just as

Dead

Cathy Adams

SFK
PRESS

To Julian "JJ" Jackson, who makes me laugh every day.

Prologue

Summer, 2008, Drayton, Alabama

Pete-O *always said he lost his legs, but he didn't actually lose* them. They were cut off by a doctor when his diabetes got so bad he didn't have a choice. Jack and his mother, Lilith Ann, who was Pete-O's sister, went with him because that was what family was supposed to do when somebody had major surgery. Despite Lilith Ann's tempting invitation to join them, Jack's older sister Magda and his brothers Robert and Josh didn't take her up on it. Jack thought they would get to watch Pete-O getting his legs sawed off like in TV shows when people stand way up above somebody in surgery in a glass room so they can look down at what's happening. The thought of seeing a man's legs getting sawed off made the twelve-year-old Jack pretty excited, so he told all his friends he would get to watch. When it turned out they didn't get to see anything and had to sit in plastic chairs in the waiting room, he was pissed. For about an hour he sat there fuming at his mother, even though she hadn't actually lied to him. She never told him they'd see his uncle's legs get cut off. He was just hoping.

Losing his legs left Pete-O angrier than he'd been before, and he was usually in a bad mood even when he had both legs. Lilith Ann, Norva, and Jack went over to his house a lot because Pete-O couldn't do much for himself, and he was so mad at everybody and everything, he didn't want to try. "You just got to stop feeling sorry for yourself," Lilith Ann would say, and then their sister Norva would say the same thing: "Yeah, you got to stop feeling sorry for yourself." Whatever Lilith Ann would say, Norva would repeat, until Jack wondered if Pete-O was going to start crawling on the floor just to get away from the two of them. He was sure that was what he would do if he

had sisters like that instead of Magda, who ignored him most of the time. Jack could run outside in the yard when people started getting on his nerves, but Pete-O had to just sit there in his wheelchair—or worse, lie there in his bed and listen to his sisters driving him crazy. One thing Pete-O did like about having his sisters there was all the food they cooked for him. Lilith Ann got her hands on a diabetes cookbook, and for the first time in his life he was eating healthy food, which he enjoyed more than he dared admit.

Pete-O had to get help doing every little thing, and that was what Lilith Ann and Norva were there for, plus some nurses who came by every day to help. Jack didn't really know what they did, because he always went outside as soon as they came around. It was one day when they were there that he found the puppy. He was solid brown and fat, and his feet were muddy as if he'd walked a long way before showing up under a yellow bell bush in Pete-O's yard. Jack knew all the dogs in the area, and this one didn't belong to anybody. He figured somebody dumped him on the road, because the dog was scared and shaking when Jack crawled under that bush to get a better look. He talked softly to the little puppy and petted him until he could ease his hand underneath the dog's belly and pull him out. At first Jack thought he'd take him home, but Lilith Ann was always threatening to shoot the three they had already for getting into her flowers, pulling sheets off the line, and chewing up her gardening shoes. This puppy was warm, he liked having his ears scratched, and he smelled like bologna. He needed a home, so Jack decided Pete-O should have him.

At first Lilith Ann frowned when Jack held the puppy up to her and told her it was a present for Uncle Pete-O. "Now Jack, that dog's probably full of worms," she said.

"Uh-huh, probably got worms," said Norva, pointing a finger at the dog.

"He ain't got worms. Lookit how fat he is," said Jack. Lilith Ann didn't look like she was going to change her mind. Jack had to think fast. "We got wormer at home. I'll give him some and he'll be fine."

"Who's going to let him outside to pee? That dog'll make a mess of Pete-O's carpets," said Lilith Ann.

"A real mess of the carpets," said Norva.

"Jack! Bring it here," said Pete-O from his bedroom. That shut Lilith Ann and Norva right up.

"Put him down here a minute. Let me see him," said Pete-O, when Jack presented the puppy. He pushed himself straighter against his pillows and leaned forward to take a look. The little dog took a few steps towards him, leaving dirty paw prints on the clean sheets Lilith Ann had put down the day before. Pete-O put a meaty hand on the dog's back and rubbed his fur. He began nodding. "Go get that wormer and get him cleaned up."

That settled it and the dog was his. Pete-O named him Daryl and the dog soon became his favorite companion. Pete-O told everybody that Daryl was his guide dog, and later, when Pete-O got himself a second-hand wheelchair accessible van and started driving himself around town, Daryl was with him everywhere he went. Most people knew Daryl wasn't really a guide dog, but nobody said anything. Jack discovered later that Pete-O had told a few people he had lost his legs in the Gulf War, and besides that, he always wore a "God Bless America" cap with a flag pin stuck in the side. Nobody was going to tell a man who'd had his legs blown off in Afghanistan that he couldn't bring his dog with him into Waffle House or Kroger's. Jack got him a "Proud to be an American" bumper sticker for the back of his wheelchair just to shut people up.

Pete-O liked to spit out the window of his van when he was driving, and sometimes he had crumbs in his beard from the Little Debbie cupcakes or orange waffle cookies that smelled like cardboard he snuck when he went out with Jack. He made Jack promise not to tell his mom and Jack swore it was their secret. Jack spent a lot of time looking out the window of the

van when Pete-O was talking to him, just so he wouldn't have to see his face up close. But Pete-O was the only uncle he had who would take him anywhere he wanted to go, so Jack hung out with him. Besides, Daryl was always with them and Jack loved being with Daryl. He ate the same things Pete-O did, and sometimes he had orange crap hanging from his mouth, too, though it didn't seem so disgusting on a dog.

Pete-O bought a double-action autoloader, and Jack was so enamored he could hardly take his eyes off it. Pete-O let Jack go with him after school on Thursdays to the shooting range and taught him how to use it. Lilith Ann and Norva were just glad their brother had taken an interest in something and was getting out more. Jack's mother even decided Daryl hadn't been such a bad idea. Pete-O and Jack would leave Daryl in the van with the windows rolled down so he wouldn't overheat, and he'd bark like a fool at the shooting until they were done. Jack got pretty good at hitting the target, even better than Pete-O, who would always tease him with, "Eh, you ain't so hot," whenever Jack got a bullseye. Jack would answer back, "You ain't so not," which didn't make any sense but it made them both laugh anyway. Jack figured Pete-O was having some eye problems because his diabetes was getting worse, but he loved to go shooting more than anything. Pete-O would sit up as tall as he could in his wheelchair, take aim with his left eye squinted and say, "Here's yours, you son-of-a-bitch," right before he squeezed off a few rounds. One day Jack asked him who he was talking about, and he said, "Jack, there's a new one every week," and then he started laughing. Jack laughed with him because he thought he was supposed to, but he didn't know what Pete-O thought was so funny.

On the Thursday when it happened, they stopped at Walmart like they did every week after the shooting range so they could both get a Coke slush. They weren't really made of Coca-Cola, but that was what Pete-O called it, and it was their favorite treat after an hour or two of target practice. Jack liked the green and purple flavors mixed and Pete-O liked the orange. His lips turned orange when he drank it and he dribbled some in his beard. He bought Daryl a wiener from the hot box on the counter and put it on the table to cool. All Daryl could do was stare like it was the last thing he was ever going to eat. His whole body quivered and he kept licking the slobber from his lips. "Look at him," said Pete-O, smiling. "Nothing he likes better than a wiener." He reached down and stroked Daryl's back as the dog wolfed down the meat. Pete-O picked up his drink, shook the ice, and sucked hard on the straw until there was nothing but air. They were nearly through when the man approached their table. His hands were on his hips, and for some reason it made Jack think of his mother, the way the man was standing there with his lips all curled in like he was going tell him to go pick up the dirty clothes on his floor or clean up the kitchen counter where he'd left a mess from making a sandwich. Later Jack decided it had been a stupid thought, but it had been the first thing that crossed his mind.

"Sir, I'm afraid the dog will have to go outside," said the man. He wasn't wearing one of those vests like the other Walmart employees, the one with the smiley face on it. He was wearing a white shirt and a tie, and he had a company nametag that said "Jerry." His hair was combed over his head real neat like he had just gotten it cut. He was a manager, and from the look of his clean nametag, he must have just been promoted because Jack had never seen him before.

"Maybe you're not paying attention," said Pete-O. He pushed his wheelchair away from the handicap-accessible table a little and let Jerry see his legs, or where his legs used to be.

"Yes, sir, I can see your situation, but dogs are not allowed in the store."

"My what?" Pete-O chuckled and his plaid shirt shook over his belly, but it was an irritated chuckle. "Did you say 'my situation'?"

"I sympathize with your handicap, sir. My own brother was

in Iraq and came back without his left hand, but be that as it may, the dog has to go."

"Well, be that as it may," mocked Pete-O, "my dog happens to be a guide dog, and your policy says that he can be here."

"That policy is for trained service dogs, and this dog does not have proper identification," said Jerry, dropping his hands from his hips.

"Proper identification?" This time Pete-O did let out a laugh, and Jack did, too. "You hear that, Jack? This guy thinks Daryl oughta have identification, like he's some kind of police officer or something." Daryl had been sitting back on his haunches until then, but the conversation was getting loud and he must have figured something wasn't right because he stood up and got real still.

"Service dogs have vests and their owners have papers," said Jerry, his voice growing terser.

"Well guess what?" said Pete-O, his voice rising. "I don't have papers. All I got is this," and he pointed to his head. Jack wasn't sure if he meant he had a brain or if he was pointing to "God Bless America" and the tiny flag pin on his cap. "And this is all I need. We still live in a free country, or at least we're supposed to. But all people like you can do is to take our rights away one by one that men fought and died for, and you think we'll just sit back and take it."

"Sir, we are not the government. We are Walmart. And that dog has to go outside," said Jerry.

Two women had entered the snack area and loitered near the next table, listening.

"It's a sorry state when a crippled vet and his dog can't even sit in a Walmart and have a cold drink," said Pete-O.

"You ain't no vet." Jack hadn't meant to say it. The words just came out, and from the way Pete-O glared at him, he was sure his uncle was never going to take him shooting again. He was as ashamed as he'd ever been in his life. He knew Pete-O was lying, but saying what he did like that in front of everybody made Jack want to throw up his Coke slush.

Pete-O was still glaring at Jack when he answered the manager. "It don't matter one bit if I'm a vet or not! My dog is as much a service dog as any blind person's with one of those fancy vests. He can bring me a magazine and he even knows how to turn on the faucet in the bathtub."

Jack was pretty sure Pete-O was lying about the turning on the faucet part, but one time he had seen Daryl pick up a *Guns and Ammo* magazine off the floor and carry it to Pete-O. He found his chance to try and make Pete-O less mad at him about the vet thing. "That's right, and he can even hit the buttons on the telephone." Pete-O looked a little surprised, but he didn't try to contest. The part about the phone was a lie, a big lie, but Jack thought this guy Jerry deserved it, and he couldn't wait to tell his mother the story. She'd think it was funny. Everybody would. He smiled as he thought about telling the story to everybody as soon as he got home.

"If you don't leave with the dog, I'm going to have to call the police," said Jerry.

"Is that a fact?"

"Yes, sir, that's a fact."

Pete-O's lips pressed together as he reached into his pants pocket. He fumbled around for a second, and then he pulled out his pistol, which pointed straight up at Jerry. All the air in Jack's mouth got sucked down his throat and he couldn't let go of his Coke slush. "You want to call the police," said Pete-O, "you go ahead and you tell them my name is Pete-O Hemper. Those'll be the last words you'll ever speak."

"Now, now, just a minute. . ." Jerry took a step backwards, his hands out in front of himself as if he thought this would shield him from a bullet.

Pete-O cocked his pistol. "Here's yours, you son-of-a-bitch," and fired.

Blood spread over Jerry's stomach like a big red flower. There was screaming, but it sounded like it was coming from far away.

Jack's whole body went numb, and he watched Pete-O put his wheelchair in reverse and back away from the table. Pete-O was saying something, calling his name, but Jack couldn't hear him. He just sat there while Jerry fell to the floor where Daryl had been standing a minute before. Or at least it seemed like a minute to Jack. Pete-O turned his wheelchair around and started rolling away, Daryl trotting along behind him. Jack watched the two disappear down the aisle of Halloween costumes and candy. He didn't know how long he sat at that table, squeezing his cup until it burst open in his hand. He just knew the screaming didn't stop the whole time.

When Jack finally caught up to them, it was all over. Pete-O was in handcuffs, still sitting in his wheelchair. Police were all around him, and there was a wall of people trying to get a look who were being held back by more cops and employees with smiley faces on their vests. He heard from somebody later that Pete-O had handed his gun over to the police without a word. Pete-O must have spotted Jack because he called his name and everybody looked over at Jack. "Take Daryl," Pete-O called, and then the police started pushing his wheelchair toward the big entrance doors. Somebody had put a leash on Daryl, and one of the police officers was holding it out to Jack. Daryl had that same scared look he'd had the day Jack found him under the bush. He put his hand on the trembling dog. Pete-O turned his head right as they pushed him out the big sliding doors. He was smiling the way he did at the shooting range, like he was in charge of everything and somebody was going to get his.

Chapter 1

2013, Drayton, Alabama

Ray Allen was on duty the night Baxter Hemper walked through the door of the T&A Lounge wearing a raincoat. It was August, and it had not rained for the past three weeks. Ray Allen never saw it as odd that a man would come in wearing a blue plastic raincoat with pink lashings and a lace-trimmed hood. Baxter took his coat off, revealing another jacket underneath, and then sat down.

"What can I getcha?" asked a young woman in a T-shirt with a V-neck that looked like it had been cut with scissors. The "V" stopped halfway into her cleavage, and a tattoo of Speedy Gonzales was clearly visible on her left breast.

"I would like Amish beer," Baxter said, hesitating slightly after each word.

The waitress stopped chewing her gum and dropped a hand by her side. "Amish beer? Am I supposed to know what that is?"

"It's holy, like water."

She studied his face a moment, and then began nodding her head. "Yeah, I think we got some of that. You want the regular or the light version?"

"I want Amish beer."

"Amish beer," she muttered to herself, turning to go.

Baxter pushed his hand up the side of his head and smoothed his hair down. It was the slowness of the movement that gave him away. Any other man would seem like an everyday guy performing an everyday motion. Baxter never got the speed of anything right, especially when he was off his medication. He was always either too fast or too slow, and his inability to execute subtlety, to blend in, got him stares everywhere he went.

"Here you are. One Amish beer." The waitress in the V-cut T-shirt placed a Löwenbräu in front of Baxter.

"Who is that young lady?" Baxter pointed to the woman dancing on the second riser of the multi-level stage in the center of the bar. She was the only dancer on the stage, and she kept her eyes somewhere beyond the front door. From Baxter's seat, a Band-Aid was visible on the back of her left foot, just above the purple ankle strap of her four-inch heels.

"That's Juicy Fruit Janeeca," said the waitress.

While Baxter watched the young woman dance to a Bob Seger song, the waitress went behind the bar and said something to TP, who nodded. Baxter placed the blue plastic raincoat on the chair next to his with gentle deliberation, like letting down a fallen comrade on a battlefield. Two men from the next table stared.

Baxter stood, walked to the riser where the young woman danced, and slid his hand inside the breast pocket of his coat. He caught the dancer's eyes, and her movement slowed to a grind when he presented a flat, crisp twenty-dollar bill. He didn't reach for the bright green thong she wore, but bowed his head and laid the bill at her feet. Then, he rose like a meditating monk, his eyes closed, and his hands respectfully by his sides. The dancer gave him a half-mouthed smile and deepened her grinding thrusts.

"Hey, horseshit, get outta the way!" shouted a large man from a table right in front of the stage. He held a half-finished Budweiser, and when he laughed he showed a missing tooth.

Baxter turned by adjusting his feet like a toddler about to change direction. "You should learn some respect," he said.

"Who you supposed to be?" said the man. "You act like that guy on *Kung Fu*. Don't he?" He nudged the younger man sitting with him. "Hey, you remember that show from when we was kids?"

Baxter was already on his way back to his table, ignoring them completely.

Janeeca's dance set ended, and she was replaced by a blonde in a pair of leather shorts. Stepping off the stage was hazardous in four-inch heels. The younger man at the *Kung Fu* table jumped up to assist her and was crestfallen when she kept going. She put a hand on Baxter's chair and bent forward until wisps of buttercup blonde hair fell across her face and grazed the top of his balding head. They loved that. They all did.

"You mind if I sit down for a minute?" she whispered close to his ear.

"You're welcome to join me," he said.

Slipping into the seat across from him, Janeeca gave him a smile. "Thanks for being so generous. There's not a lot of tips like that in this place. I've never seen you in here before. What's your name?" She let her breasts graze the perpetually cold Formica tabletop. It was a sure motivator for hard nipples, a trick she had learned from the other dancers. She figured she could probably get another ten dollars from him.

"I'm Baxter Hemper." Baxter's eyes stayed on her face.

"I hope you're enjoying the show."

Baxter didn't respond.

"So, Baxter, what do you do?"

Baxter's eyes dropped to the table, and he waited a moment before answering. "A mediator."

"Oh, that's like working with metals and stuff, right?"

He hesitated. "No."

"I used to think I wanted to work in a laboratory," Janeeca said. "Not like Frankenstein or anything like that. But one of those places that invents lotions and bath oils and perfumes and stuff like that. I've always had a real sensitive sense of smell. But then I read somewhere that they tie rabbits down and drop stuff in their eyes to see if they're allergic, and they cut the vocal cords on monkeys so they can't scream when they experiment on them with eye shadow and stuff. I think that's awful. So, there's always stripping," she said, and then, "I love animals."

"Of all God's creatures, dogs are the most pure of heart,"

said Baxter.

"That's beautiful. Did you just now make that up?"

"Yes, yes I did."

"I used to have a dog named Mitzy, a little terrier. She was so small she could fit in my purse. Sometimes I'd carry her into the grocery store in my coat pocket."

"What happened to her?"

"My ex-husband dropped her out the window and broke her back." For a moment, Janeeca's eyes turned pink, but then she smiled again, shaking her head.

"He sounds like a terrible man," said Baxter.

"That's why he's my ex-husband. Daren was such a jerk. Once I planted a whole row of rose bushes down the edge of the yard next to the driveway, and he backed his truck—" She took a breath and forced a smile again. "Hey, you're not here to listen to sad stories like that. I'm sorry. Do you have a dog?"

"My brother has a dog, but he's in prison."

"Oh." Janeeca was unsure what to say next.

"You are a lovely girl," said Baxter. He wasn't smiling, and he had not yet looked down at her exposed breasts.

"Thank you." Janeeca drummed her fingers on the table, searching for a new direction to take the conversation.

"I have magic inside me," Baxter said.

Janeeca wasn't sure she heard what she thought she heard, and she remained quiet for a few seconds. "I thought I'd prune my yellow bells tomorrow. It's supposed to be sunny. I put four of them along the front porch. Can't nobody run over them in front of the porch."

"There is a river that cascades in purity and coolness right through the soul of me," said Baxter, his hand splayed over the center of his chest.

The music changed and the blonde began to unzip her black leather shorts. She must have been five pounds lighter in the hips when she bought them, because despite all her wiggling, she could not work them down. She attempted to incorporate the wiggle into her dancing, but the grimace on her face gave away her dilemma.

"I'll be right back," said Janeeca. She walked to the stage, her butt cheeks jiggling to the delight of the two men at the *Kung Fu* table right in front. She slipped her fingers inside the hems of Lora Nell's shorts and tried to work them down the dancer's legs from the bottom while Lora Nell wiggled her shoulders in time to the music.

"Hey, give us some girl-on-girl!" shouted the large man. Janeeca jerked hard on the shorts and Lora Nell nearly lost her footing.

"You girls need some help with that?" said the younger man at the table.

Janeeca turned and gave him an acid-sweet smile. "You boys let us do the stripping, all right?" When she turned back to Lora Nell, her eyes were slits. She knew her behind was close enough for one of the men to reach out and grab. "You're going to have to be still a minute and quit dancing so we can get these off," she hissed.

"I can't quit dancing. Alton's looking," said Lora Nell.

"They won't budge. How'd you get them on?"

"I laid down on the floor," said Lora Nell, her exposed belly gyrating behind the unzipped shorts.

"How about if I get some scissors and cut them off you," suggested Janeeca.

"Hell, no!" said Lora Nell, talking through clenched teeth. "These are real leather."

"All they are now is real stuck. Nobody tips strippers who don't strip, and Alton is looking mad," said Janeeca, sneaking a glance back at the bar.

"Screw Alton!" said Lora Nell, seductively pushing her fingers down the front of her shorts as she rotated her hips in a circle.

"You girls going to discuss the price of corn up there or are we going to see some ass?" shouted the large man, the one who had insulted Baxter.

Janeeca whipped her head around. "You're looking at mine, aren't you?" Any sober idiot could have picked up on the hateful tone of her voice. She didn't see Baxter step behind her with a gun barrel sticking out of the blue raincoat with the lace-trimmed hood that he held at his waist.

"Shit," said the younger man at the *Kung Fu* table. He and the large man jumped up and began backing away with their hands up in surrender. The one who had insulted Baxter dropped his half-finished Budweiser on the table, sloshing it across Janeeca's naked stomach. He turned from the table, muttering something to Baxter, his feet tripping in his drunken run to the exit. Lora Nell ran shrieking from the stage, the unzipped front of her skin-tight leather shorts flopping. The men at the other tables couldn't see what the issue was until Baxter turned around, and then a second wave of feet hit the door. Creedence Clearwater Revival played on the speakers and the lights were set on a low blue-purple hue, making it all but impossible to see exactly what was happening from Alton's position behind the bar. He gave an angry look toward Ray Allen's empty seat, and then he took a baseball bat from behind the bar and stormed over to Baxter, where Janeeca was frozen to the floor beside him.

Alton shouted over the music. "What the hell trouble you—"

Baxter turned and aimed his gun at Alton's crotch. "Whoa! Hey, put that down." Alton's hands were up in surrender, but he held fast to the bat. He cast another glance at Ray Allen's empty seat, and then cursed TP, who had gone to the office in the back. "Come on now, buddy. You don't want to hurt nobody. Whatever trouble you got, it ain't with me." He flicked his eyes helplessly on Janeeca, who stood with her mouth open.

"Spirits speak in my soul and I cannot help but listen," said Baxter. "They are shouting! Can't you hear them?"

Alton eyed the gun, wondering if he could take it away before this crazy guy castrated him. "Maybe you should go outside if they're so loud. Sometimes this place gives me a headache, too," he said.

The speaker system bleated a warning that there was a bad moon on the rise. Baxter clenched the gun butt closer to himself and squinted as if his head hurt badly.

"Mister, please put that gun down," Janeeca said in a squeaking voice.

Baxter motioned to the door with the gun. "Both of you, go outside."

Alton shot one last look toward the back office where TP had gone, probably with one of the dancers. "Shit," he hissed under his breath. No one was left in the place except the three of them. Lora Nell had jumped in her Toyota Camry, unzipped leather shorts and all, and spun out in the parking lot along with the customers. The other dancers had probably done the same when they heard her screaming through the exit.

Baxter, Alton, and Janeeca paraded in a line outside and stopped in the middle of the gravel lot. The T&A Lounge neon sign, a purple figure of a topless woman, hung above them on the front of the building. The bar still owed two payments of $149 on the sign, and already one of the neon breasts had burned out. Because TP had refused to purchase the maintenance contract, it would cost them extra to get it working again. Now they had a purple-faced woman with what looked like one oversized jelly doughnut on her chest. The dancers hated the sign—the breasts were bigger than the woman's face, so they were delighted when one of them burned out. Alton suspected one of the dancers had done something to it, but TP said none of them was smart enough to figure out how to sabotage a neon breast.

"You see that?" Baxter shouted. "Can you hear what it's saying?"

"I hear a little hum, but all those signs—"

"Shut up!" said Baxter. Alton backed up a step when Baxter's hand tensed on the gun. "That sign is sending me messages."

"That sign's a big ole titty. It's designed to send a certain message," said Alton.

Janeeca stood beside him, her hands stiff at her sides. In nothing but a green thong and purple heels, she was suddenly very conscious of her nakedness out there in the dark with two men, but Alton's eyes were only on the gun, and Baxter kept pulling at his hair with his free hand and squinting up at the sign.

"If you don't like the sign, how about we take it down? First thing in the morning, my partner and I can take it right down, and you won't be getting no more messages. If you'll just put that gun down I promise we'll take care of it," said Alton.

"People who lay with dogs get up with fleas!" said Baxter.

"That's a fact, sir. My mama used to say exactly that. She did, and she was a good lady, God rest her soul. I loved my mama. I did. She—"

"Shut up! For crying out loud, shut up!" Baxter took a step toward the sign and shot a hand toward it. He moved the gun safely on his far side. "Do you honestly mean to tell me you cannot hear that?"

Alton's eyes jumped between Janeeca and Baxter. "Uh." He rubbed the side of his nose with his index finger. "I do believe I, uh—yeah, I believe I hear it. You hear it, don't you, Janeeca?"

"I hear it," she said.

"What is it telling you to do?" asked Baxter.

A cold wash of sweat poured over Alton's brow. "I think it's telling us to be calm." He took a step closer to Janeeca and pulled her in front of his body.

"What the hell are you doing? Let me go," she hissed.

"Agents of darkness have been sent here," said Baxter. "They want to consume our souls. They huddle in this place like snakes in a cave, waiting to swarm. And that sign is Satan's beacon!" Baxter raised his gun and Alton pushed Janeeca toward him.

"Oh-ma-God! Don't kill us!" Janeeca begged.

But Baxter wasn't aiming at her. He squeezed the

trigger—*thunk!*—and then lowered the gun from his shoulder, pumped it, and shot again. This time the *thunk!* was followed by a *ping!*, and the nipple of the remaining lit breast went dark. He pumped one more time and aimed. Alton opened his eyes at the sound and looked at Baxter. *Thunk!* The rest of the breast went dark, and Baxter dropped the gun to pump again.

"A Daisy? You got a damn Daisy pump BB gun? I can't believe this!" Alton shoved Janeeca aside and she landed on the gravel, scraping her hips and hands on the rocks. "I'm gonna tear your head off, you crazy bastard!" He grabbed Baxter's shirttail and yanked him backwards, reaching for the gun. Baxter gripped the barrel, and his feet ground into the gravel as he and Alton scuffled with the gun. Alton got a hand around Baxter's forehead and squeezed his fingers into the bone, but Baxter's body was tense as steel and he held onto the gun.

"Give me that gun, you sonofabitch!" Alton said, spittle flying onto the side of Baxter's face.

"You are full of their venom," said Baxter.

The slam hit Baxter and Alton so hard that both men's feet were lifted from the ground before they were knocked backwards onto the gravel just inches from Janeeca. Alton couldn't see anything because the man's chest was pressed into his face. A gold nugget medallion necklace struck Alton's front teeth, breaking one in half as his head struck the ground. As the three of them rolled over, Alton's chin popped the back of Baxter's skull, and Alton blinked his eyes trying to maintain consciousness. He had sucked the tooth down his throat in the fall and his hand went to his mouth.

"I got him! I got him!" Ray Allen Coswell, the man responsible for making sure no one got into the building with a weapon, confiscated the BB gun from Baxter. He jumped up with the Daisy, his breath in frenzied spurts. "I got him, boss! I got the gun!"

Alton couldn't see Ray Allen's dot-sized pupils or even tell that Ray Allen was cranked up on speed. He rubbed his tongue over the nub of throbbing broken tooth and lunged at Ray Allen with a guttural scream, sending the strung-out man skidding across the gravel. Tiny rocks shredded into Ray Allen's back and his shirt became bloody from the raw flesh. Alton grabbed the Daisy from Ray Allen and smacked him across the face with it.

"You have got to be the dumbest sonofabitch I've ever seen. It's a damn BB gun! Can't you see this? I nearly had it and you knocked my goddamn tooth out over a BB gun!" Before getting up, Alton punched Ray Allen in the mouth for good measure. Baxter remained on the ground looking up at the sign. Only a pair of red lips and the T&A remained lit.

"I thought he was going to kill you, boss. Honest! I was just trying to save your life," said Ray Allen, his head jerking quickly.

"Aw, look at that. Look at the sign. It's ruined," said Alton. He put a hand up to his face again as if he were about to cry.

TP came running outside. "Where the hell is everybody? I come out to the floor and there ain't a soul in there!"

"Naw, TP, we were all out here in the parking lot having ourselves a picnic 'cause it's such a beautiful night!" Alton grabbed the barrel of the gun and began smashing the butt into the ground. After three strikes it splintered, leaving him holding a metal tube and a pump.

"What happened?" asked TP.

Alton went through a two-minute spiel from the outburst in front of the stage to Ray Allen's tackle. He concluded by sitting down on the gravel and cursing his aching tooth. He pointed first at Baxter and then at Ray Allen. "You are paying for the sign, and you are paying for the tooth."

Ray Allen's eye muscles twitched and he sat quietly. TP handed Janeeca his jacket and she slipped it around her shoulders.

"I try to establish a place with a little class, some ambience, a real gentleman's club, and look at what happens," said Alton. "I end up getting my teeth knocked out by one of my own people in the parking lot, and my sign that we hadn't even paid for yet is SHOT TO HELL! You can't aspire to nothing around this place. A man with drive just gets his teeth knocked out." He pointed at Baxter. "You keep that guy right there. I'm calling the cops." Alton chucked what was left of the BB gun to the ground and started back inside. "I got to have me some Percodan."

At the mention of cops, Ray Allen got up and headed for his car. "Alton's pretty mad. I got to go."

"Cops? What are you thinking, man? We don't want cops around here." TP gave Alton a pleading look.

"They're not coming inside, dumbass. Just keep him out here and it'll be fine." Alton was dialing 9-1-1 on his cell as he entered the building.

TP and Janeeca stood over Baxter, who looked at the darkened sign and showed no interest in confrontation or even getting up from the ground. His back was covered in gravel dust and he had a few cuts near his waist.

"You hear how quiet it is?" he asked.

"You just keep your mouth shut," said TP.

Janeeca smiled at what was left of the sign. "I think I like it better with just the lips, too," said Janeeca.

"What would you know? Looks like a piece of junk now," said TP.

"It's quiet," said Baxter, his voice low and calm. He crossed his legs and hugged his arms around his knees. "It's not speaking."

"The cops'll be here any minute, so you just can it," said TP. He kept putting his hands on his hips and pacing around like a bride waiting for the groom at a shotgun wedding. "Looks like this night's shot to hell. It's only 11:35 and we're dead. Word gets out that people are coming in here pulling out guns and shooting up the place and all the decent folks stay away."

"It's a strip bar in Alabama, TP. Since when have the decent folks ever come here?"

"I know what it is, pinhead! I own this place. You don't have to tell me what it is. Decent folks is the ones who got money to spend. Travelers. Conventioneers. Salesmen. People like that."

"Only folks I ever see in here are the ones who live here and sometimes college boys who drive over from Gadsden. Look at where we are. Out in the middle of nowhere! If I ever saw a conventioneer come through here I'd probably fall off the stage," said Janeeca.

"Last April we had a whole bunch of tire salesmen from Minnesota come through here one night and they spent damn near $1,500 dollars," said TP.

"That was because their van broke down up the road and they all walked here waiting for the TripleA folks to come and get them," said Janeeca.

TP gritted his teeth and shook his head furiously. "This place has got real potential. And once it takes off we're going to get us some classy women. Some pretty women who've taken dance lessons and don't just get up there and flounce around. You'll find yourself out of a job then," he said.

"You're breaking my heart, TP," said Janeeca.

Alton returned with a baseball bat in one hand and a rope in the other. "The dispatch says they can't get a car out here for another twenty minutes. They had a fight out at the tractor pull tonight and everybody's still tied up over there."

"A tractor pull! I dang near forgot that was tonight. No wonder we're so dead," said TP.

"I could have told you that," said Janeeca.

"Hush your mouth! I can't figure why we didn't get some of their traffic after it ended," said TP.

"Because when you go to a tractor pull, you take your family. When you go to a strip bar, you don't. It's not exactly a cross-over thing," said Janeeca.

"Well, Miss Marketing Major," said Alton mockingly, "after they drop their wives and kids off, what are they gonna do the rest of the night?"

"You ever hear of some men staying home on Saturday night with their families? Some folks do that."

"Now, that's not the kind of behavior we want to encourage, is it?" said Alton. "I'm outta here before the police get here. I've still got some unresolved business with those boys."

Janeeca rolled her eyes and pulled TP's jacket tighter around herself. "Writing bad checks again?"

"Won't you shut your mouth?" Alton grunted and put a hand to his mouth. "Damn, that tooth is killing me. Look here, I'm going to cinch Mr. Daisy Pump's wrists with this rope until the law gets here. Where's Ray Allen?"

"Soon as you mentioned the police he decided he had somewhere else to be," said Janeeca.

"Dadgum jerk."

"I think the words you're looking for are 'convicted felon'."

"I didn't exactly pluck you out of the Baptist choir to work here," Alton said.

Janeeca chewed the inside of her lip and said nothing while Alton tied Baxter's hands at the small of his back. He turned the rope one way, then another, and then he held it still as if in a momentary stupor. He blinked hard, his top lip pulling up and revealing a spot of blackness under his broken tooth.

"Janeeca, you keep an eye on him until somebody gets here. Then you come get me," said TP. "He gives you any trouble, you whack him good with this bat." He pointed at the bat on the ground next to her.

"What? You're leaving me out here to watch this guy?"

"I got something to do inside. Don't worry, we'll keep you on the clock," said TP.

"Like I got any place else to be," Janeeca muttered.

TP headed back inside the lounge, and Alton pulled his car keys from his pocket. His eyes were beginning to glaze over from a potent mixture of pharmaceuticals he'd found in the office desk.

"You'd think there'd been a mafia murder around here the

way everybody's taking off," Janeeca said.

"Just make sure he stays put. And when the cops get here, you let TP do the talking," Alton said.

"The first thing they're going to want to know is why everybody split."

"I got to get to an emergency room dentist. This is killing me. I'll make a statement tomorrow."

"You moron, emergency rooms don't have dentists!"

Alton ignored her and opened the door to his Monte Carlo with custom baby blue leather interior. He started her up and took off down the road, holding his cheek with one hand.

Baxter remained on the ground, his legs in the lotus position and his eyes closed.

"Looks like it's just me and you," Janeeca said, sitting down beside him. He kept his eyes closed. "Hey, before everybody gets here, I wanted to thank you for what you did. About those men and the sign and all. Nobody ever stands up for us dancers."

"I'm sorry I can't offer you a ride home."

"I have a car, but thanks." Janeeca reached over and flicked a piece of grit from Baxter's face, and he turned to look at her finally. "You just had some dirt there. . .on your cheek," she said.

"Thank you. Would you tell me something personal?"

"I guess. What do you want to know?"

"How did you get hurt?" He motioned with his head toward her ankle. Janeeca put a hand over the Band-Aid and sighed.

"That's nothing. I just got scratched when I was pruning some pyracanthas at the back of my house. It's been a long time since I talked to a man so polite."

A Chevy Impala pulled into the lot and a man hung his head out the passenger side window, staring at Janeeca and Baxter sitting on the ground.

"We're closed," Janeeca said.

"So give us a show out here! We'll pay!" The man eyed her long legs sprawling from underneath the jacket. She picked up the bat and stood, holding it in front of her with both fists.

"I said we're closed. There was a double murder tonight."

"Murder? You're kidding?"

"Yeah, two dumbasses in a green Impala didn't know when to leave, and one of the dancers smashed their skulls in with a bat."

The man hanging out the window said something to the driver, and they whipped around Baxter and Janeeca, tossing out a half-empty beer can. "Bitch!" Tires squealed as they made the U-turn from the parking lot to the road, slinging gravel behind them as they sped away.

"I killed thirty-one men," Baxter said. Janeeca lowered the bat to her shoulder. "In the Gulf War," he continued.

"Oh. Well, you were just doing your job." Janeeca dropped the bat to the ground, tucked the bottom of the jacket underneath her, and resumed her seat.

"I did it with my eyes."

"You killed thirty-one men with your eyes?"

"I have to be very careful," Baxter said.

"I guess so. You got any family?"

"I have a sister, Lilith Ann. My other sister, Norva, she died."

"Oh, I'm sorry. Was she sick?"

"She was embarrassed. Because of what our brother did."

"I don't think people can really die of embarrassment," said Janeeca, suddenly afraid of making him angry.

"He killed a man," said Baxter.

"With his. . .eyes?" Janeeca whispered.

"He used a gun. It was in the newspaper."

"But you, you didn't." Janeeca bit her fingernail, searching for something else to say. "You know you're not the only one who's had a problem with that sign. Sometime last year some folks from the First Baptist Church in Piedmont came out here and prayed right across the road there for three nights running. They said our sign was a siren for the weak of spirit. They set up a camp service under those trees and sang hymns and prayed 'til all hours. It near killed our business. Alton was so mad he wanted to pick them all off with a shotgun. It finally ended

on the third night when Alton closed up early and said we could all go home because there wasn't but about four people in the place. It was sort of my fault what happened. Dancers have to park at the end of the lot, and when I walked to my car I saw the Reverend Helms waving his hands over his head and singing. I yelled out, 'Hey there, Walter! Good to see you again!' You should have seen the faces of those women standing there with him. They stopped singing right in the middle of 'Trampling the Unwashed in the River of His Blood,' and they looked at him like he'd sprouted leprosy. I don't know what happened after I got in my car and left, but they never showed up again. Alton and TP thought I was a princess when they heard what I did. To tell you the truth, I felt right bad about it. I'd met him in the check-out line at the hardware store about a month before. He was standing in front of me with a flat of zinnias, so I struck up a conversation with him about fertilizers. He told me his name and said he was a pastor. He was real nice, and he invited me to his church, but I never did go. He didn't do anything wrong, but I guess in the end it didn't matter. People are more interested in what they want to believe about you than in the truth." She picked up a handful of gravel and let it drop through her fingers back to the ground.

"Sometimes when we try to do nice things we end up hurting people," said Baxter.

"You know, I don't think you're all that bad of a person. If it hadn't been for Alton and Ray Allen, nobody would have got hurt at all. I think it was sort of funny, the BB gun, and you shooting out the sign. It did look real the way you were holding it. I think the Reverend Helms would have been pleased."

"I heard voices. I had to stop the voices."

"You hear voices in your head?"

"Not in my head. From out there." Baxter looked toward the sign.

"What do the voices say?"

"They tell me what to do."

"I hope they don't tell you to hurt anybody."

"No, I don't hurt people. Bruce Lee used to talk to me, but not anymore."

"So you do karate and stuff?"

"No, I don't need it. I have the eyes," Baxter said.

"Oh yeah. I forgot."

"Now I hear from Alan Hale."

"Alan Hale?"

"The Skipper, from *Gilligan's Island*."

"Oh yeah, I remember that show. Hey there, 'Little Buddy'!" Janeeca laughed, but Baxter remained poker-faced. "Did the Skipper tell you to come here and shoot out the sign?"

"Of course not. He tried to talk me out of it."

"I see. So, is he kind of like the voice of reason?"

"The only voice of reason is the voice of no words," Baxter replied.

"Bruce Lee must have told you that."

"No, that was Sidney Poitier."

Janeeca threw a glance back at the club and thought a moment. "Hey, you know, I could untie you. I could tell TP you loosened the knot and hit me."

"I would never hit you," Baxter turned, and Janeeca could see that he looked genuinely hurt.

"Of course you wouldn't. I could see that right off. That's why I'll help you before the cops get here. They're going to put you in jail. You understand that, don't you?"

"Yes, I know. I expected as much."

"How about if I don't say that you hit me? I'll tell them I stepped over there across the road to squat in the bushes, and you got loose and ran away."

"I would never hit you."

"Come on! It doesn't matter. Just get going." Janeeca reached behind Baxter to untie the rope. She gave it one tug and the entire thing fell to the gravel. "Dang. Alton sure don't know how to tie a person up."

"I did it," said Baxter.

"Right, the eyes thing," Janeeca said, and then she considered him more seriously. "You mean you could have run off already?"

"It would have been rude to leave in the middle of a conversation."

Janeeca shook her head and laughed in disbelief. "You really are a piece of work." She pointed at the road with the bat. "Now take off. Get in your car and go."

"I walked here."

"Fine. Head for the woods, then. And don't show your face around here ever again. Alton may not be so stoned the next time he sees you," she said.

"The woods are lovely, dark and deep." Baxter stood and brushed his pants off with excruciatingly slow hand movements. Janeeca stood, too, and looked over her shoulder at the front door, shuffling her feet nervously. "Good night," he said. "It was a pleasure meeting you."

"Same here. Now you'd better go."

Baxter looked up at the sign and smiled at his handiwork.

"Go home and prune your yellow bells," Baxter said. He turned and began walking in the direction of the Reverend Helms's prayer camp. He disappeared into the bushes as the sheriff's car pulled into the parking lot. When Baxter turned to take one last look from behind a thicket of forsythia, he saw Janeeca standing with a young sheriff's deputy who couldn't take his eyes from the deep V of her coat. She held a limp piece of rope in her hand, shaking her head and shrugging her shoulders as the blue and red lights from the car turned round and round in the darkness of the T&A Lounge parking lot.

Chapter 2

Magda *looked in her closet, reached for the navy blue dress,* but then sighed and slammed the door shut again. She had tried walking out in a pair of jeans and a black sweater to the den where her mother waited in her Dark Blue Funeral Dress and Matching Shoes, but Lilith Ann had gritted her teeth in that way she always did when one of her children did not meet her standards.

"We're doing this for Viv, you know," said Lilith Ann. "She's so torn up about what happened."

"The whole thing's too weird if you ask me," shouted Magda.

"Nobody asked you, so get dressed and let's get going."

"I don't see why we have to do this every time."

"Funerals are for the living, you know that."

Magda opened her jewelry box and spied a pair of imitation pearl earrings. She flipped her hair back and held them up to her ears. They were just subtle enough not to look fake. "I don't know what to wear to these things," she said, admiring the earrings.

"I bought you a dress to wear to these things when your daddy died," said Lilith Ann. "Or whenever we have to go to court over something stupid your uncles do. Or one of your brothers."

Magda dropped the earrings on the dresser and stomped over to her closet door. She put her fist on it and pressed her forehead against the back of her hand. Her mother hardly ever mentioned her father's death, and when she did it was like hearing something obscene, something a little frightening coming from her mother's mouth. "This is not the same thing at all," she said.

"That doesn't matter to Viv," said Lilith Ann.

"It's not like it's a real funeral. Why can't I just wear my

interview dress?"

Her mother's voice was closer now, in the hallway. "It's real to Viv, so you'd better be nice," she said, and then stuck her head into the room. "Don't wear the gray, it makes you look fat. Wear the one I bought you."

"I guess one good thing about being locked up is missing this funeral. Robert and Uncle Pete-O can both be thankful for that." Magda turned her face toward her mother and sighed hard.

"There is nothing to be thankful for in being locked up."

"Mama, if there's one thing you've always taught me, it's that there is something to be thankful for in all situations."

For once, Lilith Ann clamped her mouth shut and said nothing.

Everyone in the family was at Josh and Viv's place except for Baxter, and of course Robert and Pete-O. Robert, Magda's brother, was locked up for disorderly conduct and some questionable activity with a gun. Pete-O was serving a twenty-year sentence, and Baxter was back at Stoney Brook Home for Mentally Disabled Adults. Just a few weeks after his dust-up at the T&A, he showed up at a liquor store and bait shop on the river, naked and covered with scratches, saying he had silenced the devil at last. The judge ordered two months of "observation," which meant Baxter couldn't leave the facility. "Just for safekeeping," Lilith Ann said of her younger brother, as if he were a valuable wristwatch that needed to be tucked away in a drawer. "We can't ever seem to have all the men in this family out from behind bars at the same time." She took a seat on one of the lawn chairs Viv and Josh had set out in the yard for the service.

The casket was white with gold trim. Josh had placed it on a folding table, and Viv had flanked it with two oversized ferns that looked out of place in the chill November air. The lid was up and each family member walked by, looking down and pausing long enough to satisfy Viv before taking a seat. Lilith

Ann and Magda sat on the front row next to Viv and Josh, who were in the places of honor. Kimmy and the five kids sat in the back, two neighbors who were there for the Italian Crème cake that was served after all of Viv's funerals sat to their left, and Jack stood next to a crab apple tree several yards away with his dog, Daryl. Finally, Viv refolded the handkerchief she always carried to her funerals and stepped with grim purpose to the table. She put one hand inside the coffin and began.

"I loved Forrest Gump as much as any mother loves a child. I loved him and his brother, Homer Simpson, like they were my babies."

Magda let out a snort and quickly recovered as Lilith Ann shot her a warning look.

Viv kept her eyes on Josh and pressed on. "And when Homer died, you all," she glanced across the crowd, "most of you all were here to help me send him on to heaven. And I believe with all my heart that Homer is in heaven right now, and when Forrest gets there, the two of them are going to fight over God's lounge chair just like they did over Josh's chair in our den." She paused, waiting for delighted laughter, but it came only from the two neighbors who were pulling their coats tighter against the frigid air.

"Is that really a baby casket?" asked Kimmy's second-to-oldest boy, Matthew.

"Shhh!" Kimmy reached over her baby's head and pressed a finger against Matthew's mouth. "I said no talking at the funeral."

"But it's a dog, Mama," Matthew whined.

"Shush! And I mean it," Kimmy hissed. "Or you won't get any cake."

Matthew grimaced but he shut up and stared hard ahead at his Aunt Viv and the tiny casket holding her dead terrier. He was definitely not going to jeopardize getting his share of the cake. That was the best reason for sitting through funerals, even though the only ones he had ever attended had been for dogs, courtesy of his Aunt Viv.

"Dayum, it's cold out here," Magda whispered to her mother.

"Hush," said Lilith Ann.

"Won't Kimmy's kids get sick out here in this weather?" Magda said a little louder.

"And when it's our turn," Viv said, in her best funeral voice and casting an eye at Magda, her sister-in-law, "to take that walk into Jesus's arms, I know that for me, those arms will already be filled with Forrest and Homer. And LaShonda and Princess Amber and Chappy, too. Amen."

The chairs were snapped shut and a line formed along the casket table so fast it took both Josh and Viv by surprise. Each person trailed by and expressed condolences. "He looks at peace, Viv. Just like he's taking a nap," said Lilith Ann, repeating the same words she had used at Homer's funeral eight months earlier. Those were her go-to funeral words. No matter who had died, dog, man, or woman, her words of comfort were always that whatever was in the casket looked asleep, which Lilith Ann quoted with greatest sincerity. She'd even said it the previous winter when Jack brought home a frozen kitten that Daryl had sniffed out behind the garage. The ground had been too hard to bury the kitten, so Jack climbed onto a ladder and placed the body on the garage roof, safely away from Daryl, and there it lay taking a nap for the next four months until Jack finally noticed what was left of it one beautiful May afternoon while he was mowing the lawn.

Jack was Lilith Ann's youngest, twelve years younger than his next sibling, Magda, and though his mother would never have admitted it, he was the "surprise" of her brood. Magda, Josh, and Robert were exactly two years apart, as if their parents had procreated on a schedule, and then twelve years later came Jack. His father, Linden Boyd, doted on him as if he were the first grandson, and when Linden died of heart failure when Jack was only eleven, Jack broke free of the family like a renegade dog. He never left, but he removed himself from the circle of older siblings, and Lilith Ann watched her youngest child wander the perimeters of both family and land.

First at the food table after Viv's latest funeral was over, Jack cut himself a generous piece of Italian Crème cake and headed to a corner to sit with Daryl at his feet. He waited for Magda to finish her mandatory disagreement of the moment with their mother and then caught her eye. He had something important to ask her. No, to tell her.

"I'm going to see Pete-O on Thanksgiving," he said, even before Magda could get into a chair. Before Magda could ask why, he jumped ahead. "Baxter still has about three weeks left at Stoney Brook, so I need for you to get him for Thanksgiving. You know nobody else will."

"Wait, wait," said Magda, trying to follow. "Why do you have to go and see Pete-O on Thanksgiving Day? Why can't you wait until the day after? Bring Baxter to Thanksgiving like you said you would, and then Mama won't even know."

"Because if I don't go, Pete-O's going to sit there all by himself, and that's just not right. Mama won't go and Baxter can't go. I'm all Pete-O's got left."

"Look, Jack," Magda searched for the right words. "It's nice that you want to make sure Pete-O isn't alone on Thanksgiving—"

"He's still family. Doesn't matter what he did."

"If we spent all of our holidays with the family that gets locked up, there wouldn't be anybody here to celebrate," said Magda. "I'm just thinking of Mama and how upset she'll be if you're not here."

Jack shoved the rest of the cake in his mouth, giving it the most minimal chewing before swallowing. "Mama's not the only one whose feelings count in this family." He shook his fork at his sister and leaned in. "You know they're letting him out by spring."

"Jack, there is no way they're letting Pete-O out that soon. Not after what he did."

"It's his health. State don't want to pay for sick inmates, and Pete-O's in bad shape. He told me."

"And you believe him?"

"You wait and see. He'll be back home by April Fool's Day, maybe even sooner," said Jack. At this, Daryl perked up his ears as if he understood just what Jack was saying.

"That'd be quite an April Fool's joke," said Magda, scratching Daryl's ears.

Chapter 3

When her uncle asked to drive the car, Magda could think only of *Rain Man*.

"Will you let me drive? I'm a good driver," Baxter said.

"You don't have a license," said Magda, keeping her eyes on the road.

"I'm still a good driver."

"I'm sure you are."

After Baxter's return from his stint in Vietnam, he spent time in a V.A. hospital before being referred to a home for people who were "not right in the head," as Magda's mother liked to explain. Baxter's thin, brownish-gray hair was shorn off in a chop job that Magda was sure he'd done himself and probably with no mirror. Everything he wore, even his shoes, was as beige as his skin.

She was twelve the first time Baxter was sent to live at Stoney Brook Home for Mentally Disabled Adults, and even then she'd felt in her gut that there was something very wrong with Uncle Baxter being put in a place like Stoney Brook. He was always kind to her, even when she behaved abhorrently toward him. One time when she was ten, she wore white knee socks to a church dinner, a crime she was not aware of until some girls laughed at her. Uncle Baxter took off his own socks and offered them to her, which made the girls laugh even more. Magda ran out the door, leaving her uncle standing in the hallway of the Sunday School wing, barefoot, socks in his hand. She could feel his eyes, earnest and solemn on her back as she ran out the door.

Uncle Baxter sat next to her in the car, and Magda could see that despite the bags that had formed underneath, his eyes were still as earnest and solemn. He counted no grievances and held no grudges. Yet he forgot nothing.

"Uncle Baxter?"

"Yes?"

"Do you know, the socks?" Magda did not look at him. She could not.

"Yes."

"I just wanted to tell you," she paused. "I'm sorry about that."

Baxter watched the oncoming traffic. "They laughed at you."

"I know." She turned her head and took in the side of his face. Though he was thin, his jowls hung low and slack, like a person who'd once been substantial but had somehow been deflated.

"They shouldn't laugh at you," said Baxter quietly.

Magda slowed at a stop sign, looked in both directions and continued. They were no more than two miles from her mother's house, and it was Thanksgiving Day. Uncle Baxter had been allowed, if not invited, to attend the family dinner. Magda was more patient than the rest of the family when it came to Baxter's "spells," like the time he sat on the floor of the Winn-Dixie, held his head between his fists and insisted he had a microchip in his neck, implanted by his dentist during a tooth extraction at the behest of the NSA.

Magda was coasting down a residential street lined with cheap houses and scantily kept lawns when she suddenly realized she was biting her lip. She had made up her mind. "Uncle Baxter?"

"Yes."

"Would you like to drive the rest of the way home?" She cast a quick glance his way.

"I'm a safe driver. I never go over thirty."

Magda slowed to a stop in front of a house with an enormous topiary of a dog in the yard, or maybe it was a dinosaur. It stood over six feet tall, its leafy green nose upturned and its tail docked short like a curved baton. Baxter got out of the car to admire it. "That's a Kerry Blue Terrier, the national dog of Ireland," he said. He proceeded to the driver's side of the car and got in before Magda had a chance to ask him how he could possibly discern a topiary dog breed. She shook her head, scooted into the passenger's seat, and belted herself safely in. Baxter did the same, and then put his hands on the gear shift, inspected the speedometer, steering wheel, and inexplicably, the windshield wipers.

"Are you sure you remember how to drive?" Magda asked, the seeds of doubt now creeping in.

"I'm a very good driver." Baxter twisted the knob for the windshield wipers, and they squeaked to life once more across the dry windshield.

"I don't think we need that," said Magda.

"If it rains, I'll need to know how to properly engage the wipers."

Magda looked up into the cloudless sky. "Yes, I suppose you would. That's good thinking."

Baxter twisted the knob in the opposite direction and the wipers eked to a stop. Pulling the gear shift to "D," Baxter let the car roll away from the curb in front of the house with the giant Blue Kerry Terrier. Baxter was as good as his word and for the remaining mile and a half to Violet Meadows Lane; they never exceeded the 25-miles-per-hour speed limit, a feat of personal restraint that Magda was sure no one else in her family had achieved in her lifetime. She was feeling quite satisfied with her decision to let her uncle drive, all the way up until he turned left onto the driveway and then swerved toward the yard, making no attempt to brake. Baxter drove her Honda straight into her mother's cement bird bath and braked just two feet from the porch steps.

"Good God in heaven!" Baxter's sister, Lilith Ann, was still chewing when she ran out onto the porch. "Look at my fountain! Look at what he—just look at this—just—I can't believe this!" She managed to swallow the helping of turkey she had shoved in her mouth at the very moment Magda's Honda ran smack into the bath, which now lay in three pieces atop the yellow and purple pansies she had planted in a figure-eight

design just the way she had seen in last month's *Better Homes and Gardens*. Most of the yellow pansies were crushed under the driver-side tire, and the purple blooms were gouged by the broken cement, uprooted in a raw wound of exposed soil. "Magda! This is your fault," Lilith Ann shouted. "You know Baxter's not right. He's got no business driving a hard bargain, let alone a car. I swanee, what a mess."

Magda stepped out of the car and laughed. The Honda was barely scratched. "That was pretty funny."

"Nobody's trying to be funny."

"Humor is a distancing mechanism for the emotionally insecure," said Baxter.

Lilith Ann pointed a finger at her younger brother. "You can just keep your opinions to yourself."

"Look, I'm sorry. I'll pay for the damages," said Magda.

"He coulda killed somebody."

"Well, he didn't."

"I would never hurt you," said Baxter, speaking softly to Magda.

"What if one of Viv's dogs was out here messing around? Or, Lord God," said Lilith Ann, putting a hand over her bulging eyes, "what if one of Kimmy's kids had been out here playing when the two of you came gunning across the yard?"

"Viv's got six dogs and Kimmy's got almost as many kids. If Uncle Baxter hit one of them there'd be plenty left over." Magda squatted on the ground and began trying to reset some of the pansies with stems that were still rooted in the soil.

"Magda Suzanne! You'd better take those words right back into your mean little mouth." Lilith Ann bent over and shook a finger in Magda's face.

Magda pressed the soil around a limp pansy. "Which words? About the kids or the dogs?" She pushed up from the ground and began slapping her dirt-encrusted fingers against her jeans.

Baxter had not moved from beside the car. He stood calmly, neither looking at the women nor the consequences of his driving. Instead, he watched a squirrel that was keeping a safe distance at the corner of the house and nibbling cautiously on something small and brown while the women squabbled.

"I just can't believe—"

Magda cut her mother off. "We're here. It's Thanksgiving. We'll fix your yard, now shut up, Mama. Just shut up. Nothing's going to go wrong this year." She bounded onto the porch and pulled the front door open without looking behind her to see her mother's angry face. Inside, the house smelled of cinnamon bread and a baking turkey, and not a soul was there. "Where is everybody?"

"They're not due for another half hour," said Lilith Ann, holding the door open and watching her docile brother, who remained by the car. Her lips pursed and released over and over the way they always did when she was angry.

"You told me to have Uncle Baxter here at 11:00," said Magda.

"That's because I didn't know what crazy thing he was going to be wearing or doing when he showed up, and it looks like I was right to think that." Lilith Ann's arms shot upward. "I didn't want the family to be embarrassed. For once I'd like to have a nice dinner without somebody shooting a pistol across the house, or throwing an ashtray through the TV just 'cause they don't like the football score, or rolling around in a fistfight in the front yard like last year."

Suddenly Magda felt sorry for her mother, whose upper lip was coated in sweat from the tension. "There won't be any of that this year," she said. "Rob's in jail and you know Josh can't have guns anymore after that thing at Pizza Hut. Besides, Uncle Baxter's the last one anybody ought to be embarrassed over. He never means to cause trouble. Josh and Robert are the ones you ought to worry about."

"I never knew Josh or Robert to wear a dress and bury Barbie dolls in the back yard," said Lilith Ann.

"He was wearing an apron, and I don't know why you think

burying old toys is so much worse than shooting a gun through the house. At least Uncle Baxter's never just about killed anybody." Before Lilith Ann could open her mouth to bring up the broken fountain, Magda cut her off. "And car accidents don't count."

"Whether it was with a gun or a car, it don't matter." Lilith Ann turned on her heel and went into the kitchen.

Magda sighed hard and pulled the front door open wider. "Come inside, Uncle Baxter," she called. "You can watch the football game."

Baxter had no interest in football or any other sport, but he was very good at sitting quietly and staring at the television for enduring lengths of time, as long as he was on his medication. If she asked him to sit in her mother's favorite chair and watch the blaring box, he would likely do it until they were called to eat, and say nothing to anyone. He made it to the porch just as Josh and Viv pulled up in their pick-up and honked the horn. "Hey, Mama!" Josh was shouting out the truck window before he even got the engine shut off. "We brought dressing! Damn, what happened to the fountain?" He pushed the driver-side door open and unfolded his long legs.

"An unfortunate accident," said Baxter.

"Magda forget to look where she was going?" Josh asked.

"It was my fault," said Baxter. "I was—"

"He was talking to me and I wasn't paying attention to where I was going," Magda blurted on her way back out the door. "What's that you got, Viv?"

All eyes turned to Viv, who was struggling out of the passenger-side door with both arms wrapped around a squirming lampshade under a blanket. "I know Lilith Ann's not going to like it, but Tebow is still not over his surgery and I couldn't leave him at home. He barks every time somebody moves too fast 'cause he can't hear what's going on, plus he has to have drops in his ears every two hours."

"Oh boy," said Magda, taking a peek at the grunting,

miserable terrier's head inside the big, white cone. "Once Kimmy gets here with the kids nobody'll notice Tebow."

Inside the house, Lilith Ann was directing final meal preparations in the kitchen, and looking at her watch anxiously as the hand ticked toward noon. She launched a series of complaints about how Kimmy was always late since Robert had been locked up, and Magda reminded her they had been late the previous Thanksgiving, and now that Kimmy was taking care of all six or however many kids they had by herself, she was not likely to become any more prompt.

"It's five kids, not six, and the only reason they were late last year was because Robert had to go back and get his gun."

"And we all know how that turned out," said Magda.

"If you had five kids to take care of, you'd make sure you had a gun with you at all times, too. It's called being responsible and taking care of your family," said Viv, pouring up a big pot of giblet gravy into a gravy boat.

"How the hell does bringing a gun to Thanksgiving dinner with your five kids running around constitute taking care of your family?" said Magda.

"We are not going to talk about that anymore. Now everybody get to the table. We're not waiting for Kimmy and the kids." Lilith Ann grabbed a platter of sweet potato soufflé, pushed the swinging door open with her behind, and plopped the dish onto the dining room table.

Viv stayed behind in the kitchen and lowered her voice. "You never know when somebody's going to try and hurt the people you love."

"With what, a bowl of gravy?" asked Magda.

"You never know what could happen. It's just so bad these days. You can't even go to the grocery store without taking a gun for protection in case some—"

"Like Pete-O?" Magda's words stopped Viv cold.

"I said let's eat," Lilith Ann shrieked from the dining room.

Everybody migrated to the table and sat down. Magda spent

most of Thanksgiving lunch imagining herself someplace else, someplace quiet where no one knew her, like Waffle House or France. She wished Jack was there because he was the only other person her mother was more likely to nag.

"Magda, you look lost in space," Lilith Ann said. "Eat your food."

"She could stand to lose a few pounds anyway," Josh piped up. He shoved sweet potato soufflé in his mouth, and Viv, beside him, nodded.

"Starting to get that 'secretary spread' from all that sitting at your computer writing those letters," Viv said.

Magda exhaled hard through her nose and stared at Viv. Like at every other winter holiday gathering, her sister-in-law wore a sweater with some kind of newborn lamb or puppy embroidered on it, as if the holidays were really all about furry animals with little bells around their necks. The year before, Magda asked Viv why didn't she wear a sweater with a Pilgrim getting his throat cut by an Indian or even an Indian getting his throat cut by a Pilgrim, depending on what revisionist view of history you wanted to take, but Viv just glared at her and asked why she had to always ruin everything that was godly and decent. Magda was recalling how the argument ended when Lilith Ann interrupted her thoughts.

"I said eat your food!"

"Mama, I'm not four years old. Don't tell me to eat my food."

"Hey," said Josh, putting down his fork, "you still thinking you're going to China?"

Magda had mentioned months earlier she could get a job in China and might just up and leave.

Viv giggled a little and covered her mouth with her napkin. "Well, if those Chinese want to come here and take our jobs, there's no reason why she shouldn't try to get one back for herself. Maybe if she did, she could stop all that nasty letter writing," she said, and then looked out the window and changed the subject entirely. "You'd think Kimmy could get the kids into hats and coats and get them over here before suppertime."

But Josh wasn't going to let it go. "Can you speak any Chinese yet?"

"Over 950 million Chinese speak Mandarin," said Baxter, who had been quiet since lunch began.

"Why you want to go all the way to China when there are jobs around here?" asked Lilith Ann. Of course the jobs she was referring to were cashier at Dollar General or Walmart, and baker's assistant at the Piggly Wiggly. "I know you've got yourself a college degree, but your daddy and I didn't pay for it so's you could take it all the way to China."

Magda had no idea where she wanted to take her college degree, but she knew it wasn't going to be to the Dollar General, or Walmart, or the Piggly Wiggly.

"You know it's against the law to be a Christian over there," Viv piped up.

"No, it's not," said Magda.

"I read where they put this guy in jail for preaching on a street corner."

"I thought Billy Graham made them Christians back in the fifties," said Lilith Ann.

"It's a big country," Magda said. "He may have missed a few."

"Don't you read the news, Mama?" asked Josh. "Nearly every one of em's an atheist."

Lilith Ann held her fork in the air a second before shoving it into her green bean casserole. "Well, all I can say is the United States of America is the only place I ever want to live. There's no telling what could happen to a young woman in a country like that."

"I would never let anyone hurt you," said Baxter. He had stopped eating and stared at Magda, his eyes hard and serious.

"I'll be fine no matter where I go," said Magda, smiling comfortingly at her uncle. "Besides, there're no guns in China."

Josh and Lilith Ann both began talking at once in response to Magda's shocking announcement, but their words were

interrupted by the sound of the doorbell ringing over and over.

"I don't know why they can't just open the durn thing," said Lilith Ann, dropping her fork and heading for the front door.

Three of Kimmy's kids darted into the foyer before Lilith Ann made it around the corner. Shouts of, "Hey, Grammy!" "Lookit what I got!" "We're starving!" and "Scott pooped his pants in the car!" all competed for attention while Tebow barked in desperation at the new commotion. Kimmy took one last draw on her cigarette and stubbed it out on the porch steps before rushing in with Jessica Ann perched on her hip and pulling Scott by the hand. "I'm sorry we're late. It takes a miracle to get five kids into clean clothes and out the door without them fighting every two seconds. And Scott here had a little accident. We've got to get him cleaned up."

"That's all right, hon. We already started 'cause we didn't know...shut that dog up, Viv!" Lilith Ann shouted. "I'll get the kids fed. You take care of that one," she said, waving Kimmy down the hall with the baby and the smelly two-year-old in tow.

"That weird guy's out again," Kimmy called over her shoulder as she entered the bathroom.

"You mean Baxter?"

"No, that little guy at the end of the street. The one with the big tattoo on his neck."

Lilith Ann hurried off to the kitchen to get the paper plates she kept especially for when Kimmy's brood came over. Ten minutes later, when Kimmy and the two younger children returned to the table, Cody, Matthew, and Rob Jr. were half-finished with their turkey and dressing, and each had smeared one or more foods on his clothes.

"Daddy's coming home for Christmas," said Rob Jr. He held his spoon upside down, licking gravy off the back.

"Getting out early, huh?" asked Josh.

"A Christmas present, and not a day too soon," said Kimmy. She sighed and put a bite of sweet potato in Jessica Ann's drooling mouth. "I know I'll feel better with him back in the house. Sometimes I don't feel safe."

"Something happen?" asked Lilith Ann. Scott had crawled into her lap and was trying to stick a finger in her gravy.

"No, it's just that, you know, with five kids. It's hard to keep an eye on everybody when three are in the yard, one's on the toilet, and two's in the kitchen tearing up a roll of paper towels."

"That's six," said Magda.

Kimmy mouthed something to herself, and Lilith Ann answered for her. "We know what you mean. There's nothing like a daddy."

"There's a mother." Baxter spoke with no inflection in his voice, and all the adults cast a glance his way.

"How long is he allowed out?" asked Viv.

"He's not locked up," said Magda. "He's served his observation time. He can come and go as he pleases. And you don't have to talk about him like he's not here."

"Baxter, we hadn't seen you since Homer Simpson died, I guess," said Josh.

"April 12, 2012. My sister Lilith's birthday," said Baxter. Josh and Viv grinned at one another and shrugged.

"Hey, where's Jack?" asked Viv.

Lilith Ann held up one finger. "Didn't show up and didn't say why."

Josh opened his mouth to speak when the oldest grandchild piped up. "Can we be escused?" Rob Jr. stood up from his seat and hopped on one foot.

"Already?" asked Lilith Ann. "All you had was a spoonful of turkey." She was about to protest, when the three oldest boys darted away from the table, with Kimmy calling from behind to stop running. Tebow began another barking tirade that didn't stop until Viv picked him up and put him in her lap. Baxter put his napkin beside his plate and slipped away without anyone noticing.

"That was about the longest I've had all of them at the table at one time since Robert got locked up," said Kimmy.

"Five minutes?" asked Viv.

"I'd have to duct-tape Rob Jr. down to keep him in his seat. His teacher says he has the OCD and the HDHD. I think Cody and Matt's got it, too, 'cause they jump around like they're on fire all the time."

"Must be contagious," said Josh.

"Ain't there a pill for that?" asked Lilith Ann, taking Scott's hand from her plate and offering him a pinch of her dinner roll.

"Yeah, but you know we don't have insurance," said Kimmy. "Robert said he wasn't going to have that Obamacare the government forced down his throat. Said he'd rather pay the penalty than have the government telling him what to do." Kimmy sat back with a smug expression.

"And that's exactly the attitude that put him in jail," said Magda.

"He's not in jail over that Obummercare," said Viv.

"So Robert refused to buy something that his family needs that he couldn't afford before Obamacare made it available just so that he can say he's not going to buy it? And now you can't get the medicine you need for your kids? Do you hear how asinine that is?" said Magda.

Kimmy's face wrinkled up, and it was clear she was trying to sort through the logic. "Well, I have been so jumpy lately myself." She pushed her hair off her forehead and stared down at her plate, "Sometimes I just think. . ." but she didn't finish her sentence.

The table was quiet a moment and then Josh spoke up. "I remember when Mrs. Barns duct-taped me down to my desk in fifth grade. She had my mouth taped shut, too, so I couldn't even ask to go to the bathroom. Nearly wet my pants."

"I think that's illegal now," said Magda.

"Sometimes a little discipline's what a child needs," said Lilith Ann.

"Or maybe Ritalin," said Magda, "if they've got insurance."

Feet scuffled in a mad rush to the dining room, and Cody

and Matt stopped at their mother's lap. The two faces were flushed, and the four eyes darted nervously.

"What?" asked Kimmy. "What is it? Don't just stand there looking at me like that!"

"Kimmy," said Viv cautiously, "they're not doing anything."

Kimmy stood up abruptly from her seat and shifted Jessica Ann to her hip. The two boys took their cue and ran off ahead of her and back down the hall where they had been only moments before. Kimmy followed at a fast trot.

"Is it just me or does Kimmy seem like she's about off her gourd today?" asked Viv.

"Oh my God, put that thing down right this minute!" Kimmy's shriek made everyone at the table jump up and scramble down the hall toward Lilith Ann's bedroom. Lilith Ann plopped Scott on the floor before following the rest. Screaming in protest, he toddled along behind her and was nearly caught up with the crowd when Viv screamed and Tebow howled in her arms. Everyone gathered in a bunch at the bedroom door.

Grinning, Rob Jr. held his grandmother's Smith and Wesson in both hands, pointing it up at his mother. "I mean it, Rob," said Kimmy. "That is not a toy. I'm holding your little sister in my arms, now put the gun down."

"Shit," Josh muttered, frozen in the doorway. Magda stood back, holding Viv by her shoulders. The squirming dog's cone bumped against Viv's face.

"Oh, for crying out loud," Lilith Ann said as she shoved past Josh, who remained inert in the doorway. She gestured at Scott, who whined from the floor behind everyone's legs. "Would somebody get that baby and shut him up?"

"Mama, don't!" Magda shouted.

Lilith Ann made a little humph sound before stepping up to Rob Jr. and twisting the gun out of his fists with one hand and slapping him hard across the side of his head with her other. "Maybe if I'd a done that to your daddy more often he wouldn't be where he is now."

"Mama, are you out of your mind? He coulda killed you," said Josh.

"He couldn't have killed nobody 'cause there ain't no bullets in the gun. I took them out and hid them up in the top of the closet that night after what you done at the Pizza Hut."

"How was anybody supposed to know that? Give it to me and let me check it. There could still be a bullet in the chamber."

"I've known how to handle a gun since before you were born, which is more than I can say for you," said Lilith Ann, handing the gun to Josh.

"Lots of people say that just before somebody gets shot," said Magda. "Mama, what are you doing with that? When was the last time you shot a gun?"

"I know how to shoot a gun if somebody comes through my bedroom window in the middle of the night," said Lilith Ann.

Josh smacked the cylinder shut. "No bullets, thank the Lord. But she's right. Mama needs a gun in the house for protection." He gave his younger sister a stern look. "This gun could save your life," he said. "And don't you even start with all that crap about being more likely to get shot by your own gun."

From down the hall, a door closed but everyone ignored it because almost immediately Kimmy's hand shot out and slapped Rob Jr. across the head even harder than Lilith Ann had, surprising everyone, not the least Rob Jr. Kimmy's face trembled, and her eyes turned hot and red. "You pointed that gun at your mother! Don't you ever do anything like that again. Don't you ever. Do you hear me? Never!"

"Yes, ma'am," came Rob Jr.'s startled soft reply.

"You could have killed me." Kimmy broke into sobs. "My own son."

"All right now, everybody's fine. Nobody got shot," said Lilith Ann. She put an arm around Kimmy, whose eyes suddenly got bigger. "He's not gonna shoot his mama, are you Rob Jr.?" asked Lilith Ann, bending her head toward her grandson.

"No, ma'am," Rob Jr. croaked.

Kimmy went limp and let Jessica Ann slide from her hip onto the floor. "I'm about at my end. I really am." She covered her face with her hands and sat down roughly on the bed, her thin shoulders shaking.

Lilith Ann picked up the baby, who was mesmerized by a wad of carpet fuzz between two of her fingers. "I remember when your daddy was as big as you," said Lilith Ann, casting an eye at Rob Jr. "He used to run up that tree there every time he got himself a whooping for acting up." She looked out the window at the sycamore that towered over the back yard. "I knew just as soon as your granddaddy got the belt put back in the loops that Robert would be halfway up that tree. He'd sit there smartin' for a bit, but then he'd come on down after a while."

Rob Jr.'s eyes were focused out the window, high in the tree as though he were looking for his dad somewhere in the naked branches.

"I remember that," said Josh. "Seemed like every time Robert got mad about something he ran up that tree."

"When he was up there was the only time he couldn't get into any trouble," said Magda, and everybody except for Kimmy laughed a little.

"I just want him home," sobbed Kimmy. Lilith Ann put a hand on her back, patting it gently.

"If he was—" Kimmy stopped and stared over Lilith Ann's shoulder. She made a huffing sound like she could no longer breathe and pointed past her family. Everyone turned at once and saw him.

A young man held Scott with one arm wrapped around his waist. The other hand held a screwdriver to the boy's temple. Viv fainted on the hardwood floor with a *thunk!*, and with her, Tebow hit hard enough to knock the bark out of him for a moment. Magda was closest to the man, and she could clearly see the tattoo on his neck of a dragon biting through a winged, naked woman.

Scott hung limply, his wide eyes staring back at his mother inside the bedroom.

"I don't want to hurt him, but I will," said the man.

"What do you want?" asked Lilith Ann.

"I just need money. And that gun. Gimme the gun."

"You put that baby down." Lilith's Ann's voice was calm and low. She took a step forward next to Josh, who clutched the gun in both hands.

"Don't make me hurt him," said the man. Kimmy made a mewling sound.

"Put down the baby," Lilith Ann said again. She took the gun from Josh's frozen hands and held it out in front of her. Magda shrank away and bent over Viv, who was murmuring back into consciousness. "Here it is," said Lilith Ann, extending the gun outward by the barrel. The young man was sweating profusely. The skin on his face above the dragon was pocked with red sores and scars, and his head was shaved. His thin legs shook as he shuffled backwards and forwards with Scott dangling like a marionette against his chest.

Lilith Ann pushed the gun closer. "Put him down so you can take the gun."

The man kept clutching Scott and shifting his glance nervously from the old woman standing calmly before him to the gun in her hand. He sniffed and began nodding his head, muttering something to himself. In a moment, he slid the baby down slowly to the floor and then snatched the revolver from Lilith Ann. She gave an audible sigh when he pointed it at her. "Now, put the screwdriver down. You don't need that no more."

He gave out a little laugh of triumph and tossed the tool over his shoulder.

"Don't I know you?" asked Lilith Ann. "Aren't you Marlene's youngest boy from the end of the street?"

"He's one of those meth heads," said Magda, still leaning over Viv. "Look at his face."

"I ain't on meth," the young man said angrily. "I just got bad skin. Now shut the hell up before I shut you up." He gestured the gun toward Magda. Scott began crawling toward Lilith Ann who picked him up and held him on her hip, checking over his face and body for injuries.

Then, the recognition set in. "Peevis? Peevis McMahan?" said Magda. "I went to high school with you."

"Yeah, and you was a stuck-up bitch then, too. Now you know who you're talking to."

"Why don't we all just go back to the table and have some more lunch? Peevis, I reckon you can have a plate, too, until the police get here," said Lilith Ann.

Peevis cocked his head and aimed at Lilith Ann. "Lady, you got the Alzhiner's? I got a gun."

"I know that."

"I want everybody to put their money on the floor. I know you got money."

"You're not getting any money because I'm calling the police right now," said Magda. "And if you were smart you'd take Mama up on that offer for some lunch." She rushed past Josh and Lilith Ann to the phone next to the bed.

Peevis smiled wide, and his gray teeth shone like wet pebbles as he squinted toward Magda's back. "I always thought somebody ought to shoot you."

Lilith Ann screamed, "No!" just as the blood spurted all over her hallway. Behind Peevis, the bloody, broken piece of fountain cement still clutched in his fist, was Baxter. Peevis collapsed and settled in a heap, his eyes gaping at the ceiling as blood pooled on Lilith Ann's pine-paneled floor and inched toward her feet.

"I wouldn't let anyone hurt you," said Baxter, still clutching the broken chunk of cement.

Chapter 4

A fter Pete-O went to prison, Magda moved into his house and stayed there for two weeks, and then she insisted the place smelled like rancid cooking oil and moved back to her mother's. Then, for about five months when Robert was out of work and Kimmy was pregnant with their fourth child, the five of them lived in Pete-O's tiny house until Kimmy threatened to burn it down if Robert didn't find them a bigger place. Lilith Ann rented it to two "hippies," a term she used because both had beards and one of them played a guitar, for a year and a half, but she kicked them out because one day when she went to check on the water heater, she thought she smelled something "funny." Despite their explanation that they were making artisanal soaps, a kitchen covered in soap-making ingredients, and the evidence of three dozen boxes of wrapped bars of soap marked Sage Forest Soap: A product of the Enlightened Generation Bath Products Company, Lilith Ann decided they must be up to no good.

Not long after their departure, now sixteen, Jack moved in and brought Daryl with him. He began renovating the place as he earned money from part-time jobs. He had been in the middle of repapering the bathroom when he got the confirmation letter from the state about Pete-O's impending release. He put aside the wallpapering job and began working on the most important update the place needed, replacing the rotted wheelchair ramp. No one in the family knew of Pete-O's release. Everyone's energy and attention had been on Baxter.

Depending on which newspaper or Internet story one read, either Baxter had saved the lives of his entire family by taking down with his bare hands a crazed intruder who had just threatened to murder a baby with a screwdriver, or a crazy uncle had smashed the head of a man who was holding an

empty gun on ten people who could have easily knocked him down and called the police. According to whether the reporter was talking to relatives or friends of the deceased, or friends or relatives of Baxter, Peevis McMahan was either a sweet boy who never hurt anyone, always remembered his mama's birthday and loved NASCAR, or he was the reason incarnate that all decent, Christian Americans should fight to keep Barack Obama from trying to take their guns away.

Magda pulled into the driveway of Pete-O's house, where Jack was busy putting the last touches of gray paint on the ramp railings. The paint on the ramp matched the newly painted shutters of the house, and a row of azaleas had been recently planted along the side of the ramp. Daryl lay under the ramp, his paws resting comfortably on the fresh dirt around the azaleas.

"They're supposed to give a verdict today," said Magda, leaning on the open door of her Honda. "I think you ought to be there."

"Got a lot to do," said Jack, dipping his brush into a paint can.

"Fixing up your house can wait," she said.

"It's not my house," said Jack, keeping his eyes on the brush, moving it methodically back and forth on the underside of the railing.

"Jack, you know Pete-O's never going to come back to this house. He'll never live out that twenty-year sentence."

"I know what they gave him."

"Baxter is the one who could use his family's support right now."

Jack never took his eyes from his painting. "Verdict'll be the same whether I'm there or not."

"You didn't miss a day of Pete-O's trial and he was guilty as shit. The least you could do is give the same courtesy for your other uncle, who isn't guilty as shit."

"He bashed a guy's head in," said Jack. He dropped the trim brush in a Mason jar of paint thinner and stood up to inspect his work. "I used to play army with Peevis down by the creek when I was a kid. He always wanted to be the American and I was the Nazi. He let me shoot his BB gun because Daddy took mine away after I shot at Robert. Said I might hurt somebody with it. Ain't that funny?"

"The man who threatened to jab a screwdriver into your little nephew's head let you play with his gun?" Magda stepped out from behind her car door. "That's a real heart-warming story. Why don't you come down to the courthouse and see if you can tell that story on the witness stand so everyone will know what a great guy Peevis was?"

"Look," said Jack, walking toward Magda. Daryl crawled out from under the ramp to follow. "I went through Pete-O's trial because I was the chief witness, and it was the worst five weeks of my life. I was just a kid. I went to Robert's trial, and I even went with Mama to bail Josh out last time when he pulled that shit at the Pizza Hut. I don't give a damn about Peevis, and besides, everybody knows Baxter is going to get off. They'll probably throw a parade for him through downtown Drayton and call him a hero. I'm just tired, Magda. I'm sick to death of all of it. I'm sick of reading the latest Hemper or Boyd story in the newspaper and having every store manager look at me funny when they see the name Jack Boyd on the job application and then say they'll 'be in touch' but the call never comes. I've got one last thing I need to do here, and then I want to leave this place. I want to go somewhere that the names Hemper and Boyd don't mean shit."

"Putting all your money into this house just doesn't make any sense if you're leaving, and you know Pete-O's not coming back," said Magda. Daryl went to her and pushed his head into her hands, wanting a rub. She scratched at the soft skin behind his ears and he smacked his lips appreciatively.

Jack had the letter in the inside pocket of his overcoat. He could show it to Magda, but no matter how many times he made her promise not to tell Lilith Ann, he knew that within a half hour the entire family would know that in two months Pete-O, the Walmart shooter, would be back in his hometown of Drayton, Alabama, and there'd be no end to the family conflicts over his release. Jack brushed his hand over his pocket and returned to his painting. "Tell Baxter I'll bring Daryl by to see him soon as the trial's over."

Magda held Daryl's warm head in her hands while he stared up at her with pleading brown eyes. "You're the only one in this family that's got any sense," she whispered. She scratched his chin, returned to her car, and headed toward the courthouse.

Jack was right about the hero part, though no one threw Baxter a parade. WBRC-TV sent reporter Ziggy Boyle, who proceeded to interview interested onlookers outside the courthouse. A young woman with freshly bleached hair and hoop earrings that reached her shoulders identified herself as Janeeca Williams as she smiled widely into the camera. "Baxter Hemper is a special person who risked his life to save the people he cares about. Maybe he hears things other people don't hear, but he's a gentle person, in his heart, you know?"

"What America needs is more people like Hemper who will defend their families, and if all they've got is a rock to do it with, then God bless our rocks," said a man named as John Smith. He refused to remove either his hat with "Redneck Jihad" in red letters or his mirror sunglasses.

A red-haired young man wearing a heavy silver cross around his neck, and a T-shirt featuring the outline of a large gun and the line "COME AND TAKE IT" spoke next. "This just goes to show how important our Second Amendment rights are, and how we have to fight to keep the government from taking those rights away." The television camera, too tightly focused on his head and shoulders, missed the one-fingered salute he gave at the end of his short speech. On the underside of his bicep was a tattoo of a flying eagle clutching in its talons an automatic weapon; when the young man held his arm up in "salute," the bird faced downward and looked as if it were hanging from a dismembered tree branch. A smattering of applause could be heard off camera.

When the verdict of "Not Guilty" was handed down, spontaneous cheering sounded throughout the halls and outside the courthouse. Baxter was released from the courtroom into the custody of a sheriff's deputy, who was to escort him directly back to Stoney Brook where he would remain under observation for six more weeks. Apparently the judge was not comfortable with unconditionally releasing a man who insisted The Skipper from *Gilligan's Island* sometimes conversed with him, even if it was to work out his problems. Magda, Lilith Ann, and Josh flanked Baxter and the deputy as they cleared the courthouse doors. Ziggy met Baxter on the marble steps and shoved a microphone in his face.

"How does it feel to be a free man after your ordeal?"

Baxter's court-appointed attorney broke in before Baxter could reply. "Mr. Hemper is looking forward to spending Christmas with his family."

"It's too bad he won't get to spend it in the can with his brother, the other killer in the family," shouted an old man. A few members of the crowd stepped back to reveal a sickly, unshaven man with a shriveled arm. His jacket was too skimpy for the cold December weather, and his right hand shook with palsy. He raised his good fist at Baxter and tried to speak again, but his voice was trapped by feeble rage in his throat. Whatever else he was about to say was cut short when a sheriff's deputy pushed him back and called for the crowd to keep moving.

"Who was that?" asked Magda.

"Peevis's grandaddy," said Lilith Ann, shouting over the din. "Peevis was his only grandson." She shook her head in pity as she looked back at the old man trying his best to shout in his thin voice over the crowd even as a deputy held him back with a single hand. "I ought to take him some soup."

The next morning's newspaper ran Baxter's acquittal as front page news, with a color photograph of Baxter being led down

the steps with his attorney, Lilith Ann, and Magda next to him. The mostly cut-off, smiling face of Juicy Fruit Janeeca Williams was a blur in a corner of the photo. "Hemper Murder Trial Ends in Acquittal."

For the next few days Lilith Ann did her best to toss out every newspaper she came across that said anything about her brother or Peevis McMahan or, as reporters liked to refer to it, "the heroic defense" or "the Thanksgiving Day attack." All she could do was fume when she arrived at Kimmy's for Robert's release party and saw a stack of papers going back to the day after Thanksgiving arranged in chronological order so that Robert could read the entire account of how his Uncle Baxter took down a crazed killer who had threatened his son's life. Lilith Ann stood over the stack and put her hands on her hips.

"Uncle Baxter's been in the paper like fifty times," said Rob Jr., holding up the top newspaper to Lilith Ann. "My name's in there, too."

"Let's hope it's the last time until you graduate high school," said Lilith Ann as she sat down in Robert's lounge chair to watch the local news. She pushed the newspaper that Rob held away from her face and sighed.

"If there'd been bullets in that gun I would have shot that Peevis McMahan right between the eyes," said Rob Jr., making a gun with his hands and shooting into the air.

"I told you there would be no more talk about anybody shooting anybody," said Lilith Ann. "And don't you forget what I told you will happen to you if you touch my gun again."

Rob Jr.'s face flinched a little.

"You remember, don't you?" Lilith Ann's voice was low and deadly. She snatched at Rob Jr.'s "gun" and squeezed it until there was nothing there but two flattened hands.

"Yes," said Rob Jr.

"Yes, what?" Lilith Ann hissed.

"Yes, ma'am," he said.

"Now, you give your grandmama a hug." Rob Jr. cocked his

head and meekly slung his arms around his grandmother. "See, that didn't hurt so bad, did it?"

Lilith Ann had begun the afternoon helping Kimmy out with the barbeque and then the potato salad in the kitchen, but since Thanksgiving she found her nerves quickly became frayed and she had to sit down frequently to clear her head. She could hardly bear to be around more than one grandchild at a time. Since the day she saw Peevis holding a screwdriver to her grandson's head, Lilith Ann's nerves had been like out-of-tune piano wires that jarred with every new movement. On that day she had been calm, so calm she was the one who answered all the police officers' questions, quieted down the hysterical Kimmy, broke up an argument between Magda and Josh, and then fixed coffee for everyone after Baxter had been taken into custody for further questioning. She was the one who made the final decision that they would let the court-appointed lawyer represent Baxter because she was certain the only people who would convict Baxter would have to be twelve people loonier than he was, and since there were not twelve people in Rayle County loonier than Baxter, that was that. When everyone finally went home and Magda shut herself in her room, Lilith Ann went into her own bedroom, locked the door, sat down on the far side of the bed and cried for a full half hour not only for the vision she carried in her head of her youngest grandson in Peevis's murderous arms, but for her oldest son in jail, for his own stupidity, and even for her brother, Pete-O, the most guilty one of the bunch.

"Magda's here!" shouted Rob Jr., making Lilith Ann jump. "And Uncle Baxter! Mama, can I plug in the tree now?"

Lilith Ann put her hand over her eyes and rested her head against the back of her chair. The afternoon would be a long one, and Robert would be the star of this show despite Baxter's first appearance at a family gathering since his court appearances had ended.

Rob Jr. crawled behind the Christmas tree and grabbed the

conglomeration of extension cords Kimmy had created when she bought four new strands of fast-blinking colored lights at Walmart earlier in the week. He fumbled a minute before he got the plug into the wall socket, and the room lit up like a bypass motel lodge on prom night. Red, blue, yellow, and green flashed in fast random motion, sending a blast of color around both sides of the double-wide.

"Good night, Rob Jr.! I feel like the police have pulled me over," said Lilith Ann, shielding her eyes.

Kimmy appeared in the door of the den, drying a plastic bowl, beaming. She wore a short bright yellow dress with matching suede ankle boots. The effect, with the addition of the lights, was that of a deleted extra from *The Wizard of Oz.* "I got a whole bunch more lights this year. Last year Scott chewed through two of the cords and only the top half of the tree had any lights. I wanted everything to be perfect for Robert when he gets home."

"It's sure an eye-popper," said Magda, "but I'm afraid it might set off seizures in the kids. Can't we tone it down somehow?"

"I can make the lights go slower," said Rob Jr., crawling once more to the back of the tree. For a few seconds the lights actually flashed faster, but after some playing around with the switch he reduced them to a slow fade.

Baxter, who had remained silent and still in the doorway, exhaled noisily. "That's much better."

"You can sit down if you want," said Lilith Ann, motioning to an empty spot on the end of the sofa. Baxter sat down and looked at his grand-nephew. "Don't stare too much at those lights, Rob Jr. They can do things to your eyes."

"Colored lights can't hurt your eyes," snapped Rob Jr.

"If they did, all the police would be blind," said Magda.

"I like 'em and Daddy's gonna like 'em, too, as soon as he gets home," said Rob Jr., tugging at one of the red plastic balls hanging high on the tree. No ornaments graced the bottom third of the tree, in order to keep the youngest children from a glitter and tinsel feast when Kimmy's back was turned, as had happened the previous year. There was also not a single gift under the tree. This year, Kimmy had hidden the gifts in the shed behind the trailer and told the children she had seen a wolf with a bloody face and fangs sneaking around outside, and they were not to go near the shed until their daddy was back to eliminate the wolf with his .22. It had been a whole week since Kimmy told the children this story, and Cody had taken the terrifying image of bloody fangs to bed with him each night, imagining how he would survive until his father could safely dispatch the threat that lurked right there in their back yard.

"I'd say that's enough tree for the whole extended family," said Magda. "That's a cute dress, Kimmy. Is it new?"

Kimmy ignored the question. "Don't you have yours up yet?"

Magda gave her mother a look. "Nope."

Kimmy put on a look of shock. "Lilith Ann! You always have your tree up way before ours."

"Not putting up a tree this year," said Lilith Ann.

"The kids'll be so disappointed," said Kimmy. "They'll think Santa's not coming to your house."

"He's not."

"You should at least put your manger scene in the window."

"I'm not putting up a single piece of tinsel or peppermint this year," said Lilith Ann.

"Well then," said Kimmy, "I guess you'll just be helping the War on Christmas win."

"Whatever I don't set up before Christmas is something I don't have to put back in the attic after Christmas." Lilith Ann sat with her arms crossed over her lap, staring at the news. "If that makes me part of a War on Christmas, then so be it." There was a popping sound behind the sofa just as the lamp on the table beside it flickered off, and then a baby began to cry.

Lilith Ann jumped up and reached behind the table. "Why it's Jessica Ann," she said. "I didn't even know she'd crawled in here."

"She's at the plug again," Kimmy said wearily. "Oh, honey, you've got to stop doing that. Mommy's told you and told you you're going be electrocuted if you keep chewing on plugs. I swear it's like having a puppy in the house."

Lilith Ann settled back into her chair with the sniveling Jessica Ann in her lap.

"Magda, why don't you help with putting up a tree? You're not working right now. You ought to help your mother with stuff like that," said Kimmy.

"She been busy lately with that writing business she's got going," said Lilith Ann. "Since what happened with Baxter, more people have been hiring her to write those threatening letters, and they're not just for people breaking up anymore. One man wanted her to write an eviction letter, and most of them want her to put her own name on the letters just so they'll see Boyd on it. I guess everybody knows she's related to the Hempers. Craziest thing I ever saw."

"Can't you can put aside your hate mail-writing business long enough to put baby Joseph, Mary, and Jesus in your window?" asked Kimmy.

"That little 'hate mail business,' as you like to call it, has earned me over $1,500 this month," said Magda.

"How long does it take to write a letter? I'm sure there's time enough to do that and decorate the house for Christmas."

"It's Daddy! They got Daddy! He's home!" shouted Rob Jr. at the window behind the Christmas tree. The three older children went scrambling to the door, and even Jessica Ann squealed with excitement and tried to push down from her grandmother's lap.

"Oh, my hair!" Kimmy ran down the hall to the bathroom and slammed the door.

The sound of stomping on the porch was followed by the throwing open of the front door and the children throwing themselves at their father in a frenzy of happy Christmas joy just like a Hallmark movie. Viv and Josh stood on the flimsy wooden steps that led to a platform that passed for a front porch. Lilith Ann didn't move from her seat.

"Aren't you going out to meet him?" asked Magda.

"Let him have his moment with Kimmy and the kids. The little ones haven't seen him in five months."

"At least that's five months Kimmy spent not being pregnant."

Lilith Ann didn't even bother calling Magda down for making such a smart remark. She just waited in her chair, her face turning from green to yellow to red to blue in the slowly changing lights of the Christmas tree.

Kimmy came running out of the bathroom reeking of Fancy Love cologne, her hair sprayed stiffly in perfect order, and her lips coated in Maybelline's Fuchsia Flash. She squealed and threw her arms around Robert. He was as tall as his father had been, 6'2". Next to him, she was doll-sized and their children were like toys clinging to his legs. Robert's hair was cut short and he had lost weight, though his body was taut and fit. The pants he wore were too loose in the waist and hung too low on his hips. In her panic that morning, Kimmy had forgotten to put a belt in the bag of clothes she sent with Viv and Josh for Robert's homecoming. She had bought him new clothes with her Target card, including shoes. He looked crisp and foreign in his blue plaid shirt, khaki pants, and lace-up hiking shoes.

"You look so good," squealed Kimmy, hugging him then pushing back to get a look at him, and then hugging him once more.

"Nothing's looked better than home looks to me right now," said Robert, squeezing her. All the kids vied for their father's attention, shouting their greetings and announcements, interspersed with attention-getters of "Hey, Hey! Hey, Daddy!"

"Daddy, we got a Christmas tree!"

"I love you!"

"Daddy, Mama made macaroni and cheese!"

"Uncle Baxter killed a man in the head!"

"I got some new Legos!"

"There's a wolf in the shed and Mama said you were going to shoot it. Can I watch?"

"Mama said if we weren't good we wouldn't get no presents."

"Cody got a spanking for peeing in the trashcan."

"I did not!"

"Alright, everybody get on inside so we can close the door," shouted Robert, moving with the family hanging on his arms, hands, and legs. "Where's Mama?"

"I'm right here," said Lilith Ann, at last standing up to meet him.

"Mama," said Robert, his voice almost breaking. He bent forward to hug his mother, a petite 5'2", in his arms, and the rest of the family fell away.

"I should have whipped you every day of your life," said Lilith Ann into her son's neck. She held him tightly and rubbed his back.

"Wouldn't have done any good," said Robert, laughing.

"Looks like you could use some home cooking," his mother said, feeling his waist.

"Jail food's the worst food you can eat," said Robert.

"Jails, mental health facilities, and public schools receive the same institutional food. It's the lowest quality and has minimal nutritional value," said Baxter. He stood behind Lilith Ann, hands folded over his stomach like a monk.

The room threatened silence, until Robert released his mother and grabbed his uncle in his arms so quickly that Baxter's folded hands became trapped between them. "You saved my family," he said, his eyes welling with tears. "I heard the whole story. You saved my babies."

"I didn't know the gun wasn't loaded. I told the judge," said Baxter.

"I know, man. And that's what makes you a hero," said Robert. "You did what you did even though you thought he could have shot you."

"He was actually pointing the gun at Magda," said Baxter.

Magda, who had not moved or spoken, opened her mouth in surprise.

"Everybody said he had Scott," said Robert, releasing his uncle and suddenly flinching with rage.

"Peevis didn't hurt the baby," said Lilith Ann.

Robert clenched his fists. "If that little, no good, piece of shit had hurt—"

"He's dead," Lilith Ann interjected. "Now let's put that aside. I don't want to talk about that anymore."

"I'm telling you I would have killed him!" Robert shouted.

"Well you didn't have to 'cause Baxter did it for you," said Lilith Ann. "It's nearly Christmas and you're home for the first time since last summer. Your wife has gotten all dressed up in that, that dress, and she's cooked lunch. The trailer's all fixed up and the kids are glad to see you. Let's not talk about unpleasant stuff today. This time let's have a nice holiday where nothing. . .nothing happens. Just for today. You get to go first in line for lunch." She pointed toward the kitchen and waited for Robert to obey.

"Awright, Mama," he finally said.

Everyone fell into line and headed for the kitchen, where the table that was too small for Kimmy, Robert, and their five kids on a regular day was loaded with food. Desserts of banana pudding, brownies, and a cake that read "Welcome Home" lined the kitchen counter. Kimmy's garbage can was stuffed with boxes and bags marked Kroger, and the receipt was underneath it all. Robert's favorite chicken all the way from Pruitt's Barbeque in Gadsden held center stage on the table. Hands reached for spoons and spatulas, and plates were loaded. Cups were filled, cups spilled over, and then they were refilled by more experienced hands. Soon everyone had food and drink and began heading back to available seats or open floor space.

Only Lilith Ann remained empty-handed. "Hold on," she called out. "Nobody eats until we say grace. Viv," said Lilith Ann, nodding her head in a directive to pray.

Viv took her cue, cleared her throat, and delivered an expertly crafted blessing that included thanks for the food and the hands that prepared it (a statement Magda was sure was a jab at Kimmy for buying nearly every dish except the potato salad), thanks for everyone being alive for yet another holiday (something most families did not feel an urgent need to consider), and special thanks for most of the family being present to celebrate (a reminder that Pete-O would never again be a part of the Boyd-Hemper family holidays), and an admonition that all present would stop and call on God's wisdom to prevail before acting on their own judgment in all situations (a directive Lilith Ann was sure was as much meant for Robert as it was for Josh, Baxter, and maybe even Rob Jr. someday). Amen.

"I've got something to add to that." Everyone looked up at Jack, who stood before them waving an envelope in the air.

"If it ain't the wayfaring stranger," said Viv. "Nobody heard you come in."

"You pray so loud Viv, a herd of cattle could come in here without anybody noticing." Jack unbuttoned his coat.

"I'm not taking that as a compliment," said Viv.

"We weren't sure if you were coming. Grab a plate." Lilith Ann pointed at the table.

"I have an announcement," he said, waving the envelope once more.

"I bet you're joining the Army!" said Kimmy. She licked some potato salad off her fork and grinned at Robert.

"Nope."

"That's a State of Alabama Correctional Institute seal on that letter," said Baxter. The whole family took a collective breath, and Viv screeched, "Oh my god, you're going to prison!"

"Viv, shut it. They don't send you a letter telling you you're going to prison," said Magda.

"Well it can't be good if it's from the state," said Viv, and everyone joined in a cacophony of opinions, declarations of revenge, outbursts for God to have mercy, and one request for banana pudding.

"Will you all let me talk?" shouted Jack.

The noise petered out after a few more insults from Robert to America's sovereignty.

"The letter is from the state. Pete-O is scheduled to be released from prison February 14."

Silence froze the room. Not even the toddlers made a sound. Lilith Ann steadied herself with one hand on the dining room table. Mouths hung open in stunned amazement. Only Baxter remained expressionless, a plate of macaroni and cheese clenched in both hands. "Will we give him a welcome home party, too?" he asked.

Chapter 5

The Hemper-Boyd families were known all over Rayle county and even into neighboring Etowah County for a variety of reasons. The biggest reason was Pete-O, the second biggest reason was Baxter, and then came Robert and Josh. Despite the work that Viv, Lilith Ann, and Magda (when she was pushed to participate) did for the First Baptist Church of Drayton, their contributions to the community did not tip the scales in the favor of righteousness. The notoriety of the men in the family had fueled Magda's break-up letter business. Word had gotten around that the value of her letters was bound to skyrocket eventually, when another one from the Hemper-Boyd clan committed a felony. A few bets were on Robert because he was known for flying off the handle at the slightest of provocations, and if there was a weapon present, he would surely do something to put the Hemper-Boyd name on the front page of *The Gadsden Times*. Again. Expectations had also been placed on the youngest Boyd, Rob Jr., after word of his erratic classroom behavior was set loose by his classmates and a few teachers outside of school. But he was only eight, so it would be years before he reached potential felon status.

Even Daryl, Pete-O's dog, had become a recognizable member of the community, and, despite his dubious human patrimony, everyone had a treat for him or a pat on the head wherever Jack took him around town. Daryl went everywhere with Jack, except to Walmart, of course. The warm brown dog was the only Hemper-Boyd everyone in the community looked forward to seeing and welcomed unconditionally.

Kimmy was a Boyd by marriage and a Hemper by close association, but she had earned her own reputation back when she was nineteen-year-old Kimmy Trissie Holcombe, and it was rumored that she was a fringe member of the "Gadsden

diaper party scandal" of 2002, which involved three deputy sheriffs, some local girls, two members of the city council, along with two transgender strippers from Birmingham. Robert met her when she was twenty-three and starting her first semester of the nursing program at Gadsden State Community College. He was the only person who knew the facts, or as many as Kimmy would give him, and he married her anyway. Magda insisted he married her because she was pregnant with Rob Jr. Kimmy didn't even make it as far as mid-term exams before she and Robert ran off to Trenton, Georgia, got married, and spent the rest of her pregnancy living in the back room of Robert's parents' house. Two weeks after Rob Jr. entered the world, Robert's father died, leaving Robert as the patriarch of the family whether anyone thought it was a good idea or not. He swore to his mother that he was turning over a new leaf and would be a responsible son, father, and husband, but since it had been only three weeks since he had been brought home passed-out drunk in the back of Cosby Claiborne's pick-up truck, his mother had her doubts. For a year and a half, during which time Kimmy got pregnant with Matthew, Robert kept his word. He got a job as a loader for UPS with high hopes of being promoted to driver, and he was able to move his family into a trailer on the east side of Drayton. But after a confrontation with his supervisor, which culminated in Robert getting in the man's face and calling him a "jack-ass sumbitch," the job ended.

On four separate occasions during their marriage, Kimmy insisted she was going to return to nursing school, and each occasion resulted in a new pregnancy. After Jessica Ann's conception was announced, Magda suggested it was too bad Kimmy had to drop out of nursing school right before the chapter on contraception, a statement that prompted Kimmy to lean over the Sunday dinner table and slap her sister-in-law right across the mouth. For once Magda was taken completely by surprise, and the only thing that fizzled her fast-spinning plan for retaliation was Lilith Ann's long lecture about how Kimmy's whole life was going to be eaten up by raising kids, cleaning house, and trying to make ends meet, and all the while she would be wondering what her life could have been. She could only dream of having the opportunities that Magda was sure to have coming her way. Kimmy would never be more than Robert's wife and the mother of a herd of kids, and Lilith Ann made no excuses for what kind of husband her son made.

Lilith Ann was more right than she knew about Kimmy. That night after everyone left Robert's welcome-home party and Kimmy lay next to her sleeping, sated husband, she counted up in her head the days until the bills would come due, and she thought about what Robert had said earlier about trying to get his delivery job back at Cintas. He was going to talk to Mr. Nunez just as soon as he finished meeting with his parole officer. Both meetings would happen in three days, the day after Christmas. There would be the Target bill listing all the presents she had purchased for the kids in addition to the new leather jacket for Robert. Then the other Visa bill, the one showing all the groceries for the party, some new makeup, a space heater to replace the one Jessica Ann had stuck a nail file into and shorted, two new tires for the van, gas, cigarettes, even though Kimmy swore she was quitting just as soon as Robert came home, one nail treatment she had splurged on the day after the Thanksgiving crisis, and a pack of diapers. The other bills would be coming from Sears, MasterCard, TJ Maxx, JCPenny, and there were others she couldn't remember the names of. It was easy to fill out applications in the stores to be given immediate credit or receive the cards in the mail and max them out in only hours.

And then there was the biggest and scariest bill of them all, the one she kept pushing out of her mind: The bank payment on the trailer. She had paid half of it the previous month, but the notices were beginning to trickle in. She kept telling herself Robert would be home soon, he would get his job back, and

they would pay off the bills in just a few months. She hadn't bought herself a thing for Christmas except for the dress and the shoes, but those were really for Robert because she couldn't greet her husband at his welcome home party looking like a frazzled mother of five who'd been pulling her hair out trying to hold a household together all by herself on nothing but grit, hope, and credit. She had needed credit cards to make that miracle happen for five months while her husband was in jail because he was a fool with a gun even if nobody got shot. She had to be worth coming home to, and that took funds and effort, and nobody seemed to understand just how hard it was for her to make that party nice for Robert. Magda and her smarmy looks at the food. Even Lilith Ann just sat around like somebody had knocked the air out of her. Usually she could count on Lilith Ann to ride herd on the kids and give her a break, or take over in the kitchen to make sure the cooking was done on time. This year her mother-in-law hadn't so much as offered to bring a dish, an oversight Kimmy couldn't remember Lilith Ann ever making, even after her own husband died.

The more Kimmy thought about it, the more wide awake she became. Robert's arm lay heavily across her chest and she longed to push it away so she could slip out of bed and go smoke a cigarette in the bathroom. She'd been telling herself she would quit, but it would be a waste of money to not smoke the rest of the pack. She'd just bought it that morning. She would definitely quit when she smoked the last one, especially since Robert would halt the spending of every last penny when he found out about the bills. She hoped that she would still have a cigarette to smoke when that day came. She counted on her fingers how many she could smoke each day to stretch them out to the arrival of the first Visa bill, which was coming in nine days unless Christmas delayed the billing. She had already smoked two, so that left her eighteen, a meager two cigarettes a day. Shit, she might as well just smoke them all at once. Who could make a single pack of cigarettes last nine days, maybe more? Robert snorted and stirred, but he kept his arm in place. Kimmy slowly pushed his hand down from her shoulder and onto the mattress and slid quietly off the bed. Robert rolled to his side, making heavy breathing noises and finally settled back to sleep again.

The house buzzed with the near silence of a sleeping family. Kimmy stepped into the two bedrooms to check on the children. In one, Rob Jr., Matthew, and Cody were still and breathing quietly. In the other, Jessica Ann snorted in her sleep like her father, while Scott slept peacefully in the twin bed next to her crib. Kimmy tucked the loose blanket around Scott's form and slipped off to the bathroom.

Opening the cabinet door above the sink, she took out the round, plastic case and recounted the days even though she had already done it that morning and again when she was doing a last-minute lipstick and hair-fluffing for Robert's arrival. Screw that smartass Magda. She would not be getting pregnant again, and it didn't matter how much the pills cost. She would shoplift them if she had to. That was, if she could figure out how to get to them. Maybe she'd go down to the county clinic and see if she could get them free. Surely if she hauled all the kids she already had with her to the office and plopped them all down in a row in those plastic waiting room chairs, the clinic would take pity on her and give her a grocery bag of birth control pills.

She would do without cigarettes, without getting her nails done, without new tires for the van. She'd use cloth diapers on the kids. That was what washers with hot water cycles were for. She'd let Magda's friend Laney cut her hair. Laney had gone to cosmetology school for a whole year and would probably be glad for a few extra dollars. In fact, Kimmy would let her cut all the kids' hair. Or maybe she'd just do it herself. They were kids. They didn't give a damn how their hair was cut. At least the littlest ones wouldn't. Rob Jr. might protest, but she'd set him straight and Robert would back her up when he realized she was trying to save money. Kimmy closed the toilet lid and sat down. She put a hand over her eyes and let her head rest there a moment. The cigarettes were in the closet, hidden behind the towels on the top shelf. If she smoked one now it would be one less she'd have the next day. Sighing, she took one out of the pack, put it between her lips, and fired up the lighter. The first inhale was glorious, like a hand of relaxation rubbing itself over her hair and down the back of her neck. She inhaled deeply, watching the orange glow of the cigarette's tip brighten and then soften. Almost half of it was gone when the door slowly opened.

"What you doing up?" asked Robert.

"Couldn't sleep," said Kimmy, waving the cigarette out of embarrassment and guilt.

"I thought you were quitting."

"I am. This is my last pack. I promise." She put a hand up in a Bible-swearing gesture. "I just needed to chill a minute."

"Yeah, okay." Robert leaned against the doorframe and scratched at his elbow. He was shirtless, the way he always slept, and Kimmy noticed how thin he was. Gone was the round not-quite-a-gut belly; in its place was the concave stomach of a teenage boy. Robert's jowls and neck were tight and high like when they had first met. He had just bought a Jeep truck then, and he was working for a construction company doing framing. He was learning plumbing on the job, and he told Kimmy the first night he took her out that he wanted to learn about every part of renovating a house so that he could open his own company someday. Robert was a man with prospects, good ones, and he had a fire in him that attracted Kimmy. Robert was a man who, despite his lack of college education and pedigree, was going places. Because of that fire, he would be someone who always came out on top. That had been what Kimmy hoped ten years ago, but so far that fire had gotten him canned at least four times and in jail three times.

"I think it'll be fine when I talk to Mr. Nunez. He likes me.

I'm his best worker. He knows I'm fast. I'm like two of his other guys, just boom, boom, boom onto those trucks. And I was learning how to do the filing right before I got sent away. See, if you can do the grunt work and the paperwork, then you can really move up. Anybody with a good back can load, but they're looking for people with smarts to move up in the company." He pointed to his head. "If they'll just take me back on."

Kimmy's cigarette was little more than a stub, and she looked at the burning end between her knuckles, sadly watching it go. When there was nothing left, she raised her behind, lifted the lid beneath her a few inches and flicked the stub into the toilet.

"What if," Kimmy stopped. The air was tense with his fear and her doubt. Leaning against the door, illuminated by the sparse light from the window above the shower, Robert looked deflated. What would they do if Cintas didn't have a place for Robert? There was no guarantee the company would rehire a man who'd lost his job because he'd been in jail for five months. A man who'd been intoxicated and refused to surrender his weapon to the police, and had assaulted his brother in the front yard (this last offense an incident that had happened enough times between Robert and Josh over the years to make it a bad habit more than a crime). There were fifty men, a hundred men, out there who could do all the work Robert had done and didn't have criminal records hanging over their heads. Cintas could replace him with any one of those men and most certainly had months ago, but Kimmy dared not voice that. There would be other places Robert could try. Or maybe they could move. Maybe they could go to Atlanta or Knoxville, or even farther away. Florida! Florida was filled with old people, and real estate developers were always building places for more old people. Maybe she could even go back to nursing school—at night, of course. If Robert could watch the kids at night she could start classes again, maybe become an LPN and get a job at one of those old people's homes. Kimmy smiled.

"What you thinking about?" Robert asked.

"Just thinking about our future," Kimmy said, almost in a whisper.

"I know." Robert looked away, down the hall a second, and then he turned back. "Hey, there's something I wanted to talk to you about. Something Mama mentioned tonight. I hadn't thought about it before, but I guess we kind of owe it to him."

"Owe who what?"

"Mama wants us to take Baxter in when he gets released from Stoney Brook. It's just for a few weeks, until he gets on his feet again and gets his own place. Definitely not more than a month. Mama thinks—"

"Where are we going to put him, on the ironing board? Robert, we got three kids in one room and two babies in another."

"I was thinking we could put a cot in the laundry room. He was in the Army, so that'd be just like home for him. And you know Baxter, he doesn't complain about anything. Hell, you could put him on an ironing board and he wouldn't say anything about it."

"Robert, we don't have enough food in the house for our own kids. How are we going to feed your uncle?" Kimmy reached past Robert and flipped on the light switch. Both squinted in the harsh, sudden light until their eyes adjusted. "Why would your Mama think it was a good idea for her brother to stay in our house with seven people in three bedrooms, when she's got at least two empty bedrooms in her own house?"

Robert pushed his hand through his hair as he searched for the right words. "Mama, she's worn out with everything that's happened. She just needs some space, you know, to sort things out."

"'Some space?' Your mama needs space to 'sort things out'? Where did you learn that kind of language? Did you watch a lot of TV in jail?"

"Come on Kimmy, let me explain," said Robert.

"Tell me something I don't know. Like, tell me how we can afford another person when you don't have a job yet."

"That's the best part." Robert closed the door and turned to Kimmy. "Uncle Baxter could pay us five hundred dollars for our trouble."

"Five hundred?" Kimmy's mouth fell open, and she began mentally recounting the Visa bills. "He said that?"

"He can afford it for a month. Hell, he could afford it for two or three months. He's got that Army pension."

Kimmy crossed her arms over her stomach and leaned back against the sink. Robert cocked his head to one side and gave her a closed-lip smile, eyebrows upraised. She'd seen that look before. It was practiced, as if the real Robert was somewhere down inside, hoping that what he was showing on the outside would fool her. It was the face he had used when she accused him of fooling around with the chubby receptionist at the lumber yard where he'd once worked, the woman who wore platform shoes and had a pouncing tiger tattooed around her ankle.

"This isn't your Mama's idea at all, is it?"

The face fell away and Robert put his hands up in defeat. "She agreed to it. Look, she knows we need the money. Just until we get on our feet again, too."

"Looks like everybody needs to get back on their feet," said Kimmy, shaking her head. "I'm still surprised he'd agree to come here and pay all that money. Wouldn't he rather stay at Lilith Ann's? I know I would if I was him."

"You know Baxter. He never argues with anybody. Once Mama told him that's the way we were going to do it, he just said okay. I bet if we told him we were going to put him in the shed out back he'd just go on out there and not say a word."

"Five hundred dollars," Kimmy said, nodding her head. "Can he move in now?"

December 27, 2013

Dear Shubie,

So far things are working out as scheduled. I'm still expecting to be released in February. The date keeps getting shifted a little bit, but I will let you know just as soon as a specific time has been set. I guess you'll get this letter around early February anyway, so I may actually be out of prison and back home as you read this. That's sort of funny if you think about it. That means the next letter you get may be the one with your "release" date on it. That's a play on words, in case you didn't figure that out. I'm still working on the details, but it will be soon. Early spring is what I am shooting for. And shooting for is another play on words. It means it's the date I am hoping to get you on a plane. Shooting doesn't have anything to do with planes, so don't worry.

I am glad to hear that your father is getting better. You are lucky to have a good doctor in your village. Remember what I said about getting Vaper-rub if you can find it. It would be good for his cough. In America we have many doctors but unless you have lots of money, lots of insurance, or the government pays for it, you don't get to go to the doctor if you are sick. I am lucky because the government pays for my medical care here in prison, but it's not very good. We have a new insurance our president is making everyone buy, but it's screwing up the entire medical system and it's one of the things that is running our country into the ground. It's too complicated to explain in a letter, like I've said before. America has many problems. I guess I'm not doing too good of a job selling you on coming here, am I? Okay, let me tell you some more good things. Here's the next restaurant that I wanted to tell you about it's called Golden Coral. It's my favorite steak place because they have a chocolate fountain. It's a real fountain with chocolate that comes out the top

and you can hold a strawberry in it and have a chocolate covered strawberry. Then there's the buffet with all kinds of vegetables and of course steak and chicken and a big desert table. My favorite is the pies. They have rubarb and blueberry. If you haven't had those, you will really like them. They have a machine that you can get ice cream out of just by pulling a handle down and letting it fill your cup. I know you asked me if there was a place to get noodles. There's a Chinese restaurant over by the Walmart shopping center, but it's not a place I'd want to go.

Tell your family again not to worry because I am working hard to get things taken care of. I know we've been at this a long time, but I will make it happen. I look at your picture every night before I go to sleep. I still can't believe how lucky I am that you are so beautiful and soon you will be my wife. My family will be amazed when they see you with me, and I know they will all love you when they get to know you. You will have a good life here. Tell your family that, and tell them about the restaurant, not the medical part. When you get to America we can go to the Golden Coral and you can have one of those chocolate covered strawberries. Tell your nephew I have not forgotten our agreement. I always keep my word.

Yours truly,

Pete-O

Chapter 6

Whenever *rain fell over the Murphrey Prison building, it* made black bloodlike streaks between the slits in the gray walls until there were enough to make the entire place blend into the same death gray. For the past seven years, Pete-O had never seen those outer walls, but Jack had visited his uncle enough times to know that the sight of those enormous streaks made his stomach turn. He kept his eyes down as they rolled Pete-O out through the gate. His truck bed was plenty big enough to hold Pete-O's wheelchair, but getting Pete-O into the cab in the rain took two guards, neither of which looked very happy about lifting a legless felon who could not be bothered to thank either one. All the necessary papers had been signed, and life on the outside began once again for Pete-O. His posture relaxed visibly the farther away Jack drove them from the razor wire front fence and those darkening rain-soaked walls.

A stop at the Taco Bell drive-thru put Pete-O in a much better mood. He leaned over Jack and yelled into the speaker. "I'll have a steak gordita and a Mountain Dew. Hell, I'll have a steak, a chicken, and a beef gordita and a Mountain Dew." The voice in the speaker repeated his order and Pete-O laughed heartily at the sound of it. "That sounds good, doesn't it?" Jack pulled the truck around to the pick-up window, where the bag of hot fast food was ready within minutes. "Mmmmm," said Pete-O, opening the bag and breathing in the aroma. "That's about the best thing I've smelled in I don't know when. You sure you don't want any?" Pete-O asked without waiting for an answer. He wolfed down the chicken gordita before they made it back onto the interstate.

Jack let him focus on his food in quiet, listening to his chomping and chewing, which culminated in a moan of

pleasure at the last bite of the chicken. Pete-O's entire being was focused on the bag, and Jack remembered how his uncle loved to eat fast food. How many pleasures were left to a man with no legs who had sat in a prison for seven years? Jack felt the weight of such an idea pressing on him, and he looked out his window just to hide his face from his uncle. Pete-O was noticeably thinner, and gone were his slack, sausage-shaped arms from lying in bed day after day after losing his legs. Pete-O was now dense and compact, like one of Daryl's dog food bags.

The green tips of daffodils peeked above ground through brown grasses around fence posts and in clusters in pastures. The world passed by as they sped down the highway: strip malls, overpasses, trailer parks, fast food, gas stations, forests, roads that led to new subdivisions, churches, car lots, billboards, two forlorn dogs standing idly in a pawn shop parking lot, and mountains far, far away. They were so far Jack could not even make out the trees, just blue-green rises in the earth. All a world Pete-O had not seen in seven years and did not seem to be interested in now. The bright cold sun of February made the day seem hopeful, and Pete-O smiled as he ate.

"You know Mama's got food waiting for you at your house," said Jack. Pete-O's top lip was smeared with taco sauce, and Jack turned his attention back to the road so he wouldn't have to look at it.

"I can always eat again," said Pete-O. He peeled the paper from the steak gordita and bit the sandwich half in two. He stared at the side of Jack's face while he chewed, and then suddenly reached out and punched Jack hard in the shoulder, taking him by surprise. "Man, look at you, all grown up and driving me around."

Jack resisted the urge to rub his shoulder, which surely was bruised. "Well, you know. I'm the one with a truck."

"Yeah, I bet they were all arguing about who the lucky person was who'd have to come and pick me up."

"You know Mama would have come, but she wanted to get

your house ready," said Jack. "Magda's car's not big enough, and Josh is at work."

"You don't have to go down the list," said Pete-O.

"Robert's parole officer wouldn't let him go on account of you both being felons." Jack shrugged a gesture of apology, but Pete-O just laughed it off.

"I don't know what those parole officers expect us to do when at least three of us in the family is felons. They expect us not to talk to each other?" Pete-O wadded up the last piece of wrapper and slurped down the rest of the Mountain Dew. "Damn, I shoulda kept a bite of that for Daryl."

"Daryl can't eat that stuff," said Jack.

"Daryl loves Taco Bell."

"He might love it, but it gives him the squirts," said Jack.

"He used to eat anything I put in front of him," said Pete-O, rolling down his window and tossing the bag out.

"He eats Hill's," said Jack.

"Heels?"

"Hill's," said Jack. "It's a dog food."

"I figured that. What is it, one of those expensive kinds?"

Jack shrugged again. "We gave him the cheap kind for a long time, but he was always getting the squirts, so I finally talked Mama into trying some good dog food. He's a lot healthier now." Pete-O gave him an annoyed look, so Jack added, "It's just 'cause he's getting old. He's nearly nine. That's old for a dog."

"All I know is he used to gobble up anything I gave him, and he never got the squirts when he was with me."

"I know. He's just old," said Jack. "You'll see."

"Yeah, you said that." Pete-O folded his arms across his chest, leaned back in his seat, and closed his eyes.

Daryl had been Jack's dog for the past seven years, and because Pete-O was not supposed to get out of prison, he was supposed to remain Jack's dog forever. At first it was hard, losing Pete-O to prison after losing his own father to death, but he had Daryl, who never left his side throughout the trial

and slept with him at night until Pete-O was found guilty and given a twenty-year sentence. After Pete-O was incarcerated at last, Jack's mother put her foot down and demanded that the dog be put on a chain in the back yard and live in his own doghouse. She offered to buy Daryl the best one Walmart offered. After a week of daily fights over the dog, Jack gave in. On the first night, he dutifully took Daryl to his doghouse with the scrap carpet lining and the pillow with a picture of a bone on it, both courtesy of Josh and Viv, and the boy and his dog crawled inside for the night. No amount of coaxing or threats from Lilith Ann could convince Jack to separate from Daryl, and he swore that if Daryl had to sleep outside in a doghouse then he would, too. After three nights of fighting that got so loud by the end the neighbors called the police, Lilith Ann relented. From that night on, Daryl slept on the foot of Jack's bed and parted from him only long enough for Jack to go to school. When Jack started sleeping at Pete-O's house at the age of sixteen, he took Daryl with him, and the two of them slowly made a comfortable if not Spartan home that Jack thought he could be happy in forever.

Four months before Pete-O's release, he announced during one of Jack's visits that the prison was releasing thirty offenders because of overcrowding, but Jack didn't believe his uncle could be one of them. Pete-O was a cold-blooded killer at whom the Assistant District Attorney had pointed her finger in court and insisted should never see the sky again. The state had agreed, but after seven years of medical expenses for a legless, diabetic inmate in a wheelchair that the government was legally obligated to care for and accommodate in a private handicap-equipped cell for another decade or more, the system decided maybe Pete-O could be trusted on the outside after all. Pete-O's elation at being set free brought the sinking fear to Jack that he would have to give up Daryl. For four months, just the thought of not having Daryl at his side had given Jack a pain in his chest like someone had punched him. Jack felt that punch once more, and he felt a little sick.

The sun sank lower in the sky as Jack and Pete-O headed southwest on I-59. When they got to the outskirts of Drayton, Pete-O told Jack to stop at Best Buy because he needed something. The thought of going into a store with his uncle made Jack a little sick in the stomach, but all Pete-O did was buy a remote-control airplane. Jack wondered why the heck Pete-O would buy such a thing, but then there was no telling what small things a man who'd spent seven years locked up might miss, so it was best to keep his judgments to himself.

Jack was breathing easier by the time he pulled onto the road where Pete-O lived, or would live. Parked in the yard were his sister and mother's cars. Small reception, he thought as he shook Pete-O's arm to wake him. Of course Daryl would be inside, oblivious and no doubt sleeping on the sofa on the left side, pressed up against the big green pillow, the spot he had made his permanent afternoon bed long ago.

Pete-O lifted his head from the headrest and took a long look at his old house. Jack had rebuilt the wheelchair ramp and painted it gray to match the shutters. The ramp began at the front porch, extended into the driveway, and then made a hard left where it settled onto the gravel where Jack stopped the truck. The porch had been painted as well. On the porch were two rocking chairs, pristine white and separated by a spool table that Jack had painted with more of the gray paint. The broken window screens had been replaced. Bushes had been newly planted in front of the porch.

"You do all this?" asked Pete-O.

Jack kept his eyes straight ahead. "Uh-huh."

Pete-O nodded, taking it all in. "Looks good. I wanted it to look good."

"I'll get the chair?" asked Jack.

Pete-O snapped to and reached for his door handle while Jack stepped to the back and lifted out the aluminum chair. He unfolded it and set it up on the gravel next to Pete-O's open door, and immediately regretted having not pulled the truck in backwards so that Pete-O would be closer to the ramp. Taking hold of the grab-handle above the door with his left hand, Pete-O swung himself in a circle toward the chair, grabbed it with his right hand and landed in the seat.

"Damn, Pete-O, how'd you learn to do that?" Jack held onto the chair handles, amazed at his uncle's athleticism after letting the guards do all the work at the prison.

"You learn to take care of yourself real quick if you want to survive," said Pete-O. "Let's go and see what your mama's got cooked."

There was no screech of welcoming family voices or gathering of smiling faces when the front door opened and Pete-O rolled himself inside. Daryl leapt off the sofa and barked at the stranger bound up in rolling metal inside his house. Lilith Ann and Magda were in the kitchen preparing chili and cornbread, and when Pete-O entered they turned around and just stared.

"Uncle Pete-O's home," Jack said quietly. He snapped his fingers at Daryl, who came to his side but kept his ears perked up in danger mode. Jack's hand protectively covered Daryl's head.

"Well. Hello there, Pete-O," said Lilith Ann. "You hungry?"

"I could eat," said Pete-O. He turned his attention to Daryl, who kept his place pressed against Jack's leg. "Come here, boy. Come here and let me take a look at you."

"It's all right," whispered Jack, still holding Daryl's head. "Go on and see Pete-O. Go on, buddy." When Daryl refused to budge, Jack held his hand out toward Pete-O and snapped his fingers until the dog took a few reluctant steps forward. He sniffed and stiffened, not wanting to go closer to the man in the metal chair with the smell that was not the smell of his home. His claws clicked on the kitchen floor as he scrambled backwards to Jack.

"Daryl, don't you remember me?" Pete-O patted his stumps.

"He hasn't seen you since he was a puppy," said Magda. "He'll come around." There was an awkward silence as Daryl remained on full alert next to Jack. He licked his lips and sat down, staring at the man in his house.

"He'll come around," Lilith Ann repeated and turned back to her dish washing. The kitchen was too hot and the air was filled with the smell of simmering chili. Something was wrong, off all around, as if someone had died and no one wanted to talk about it. Lilith Ann's hands moved in slow circles, drying the inside of a mixing bowl. She leaned over and placed the bowl on a low shelf in a cabinet. She rose slowly and kept her back to Pete-O. Magda leaned against the oven door, focusing on Daryl instead of her uncle.

"Well," said Pete-O, turning his chair away from Jack and the dog, "I reckon it's good to see everybody."

"It's good to see you, too, Uncle Pete-O," said Magda.

"I can't wait for a good, long soak in the bathtub," said Pete-O. "I'm gonna sit in the tub until the water turns cold, and then I'm gonna fill it up with hot all over again and sit until that turns cold."

"Reckon who's going to clean the ring?" asked Lilith Ann.

"Oh, I've got that covered," said Pete-O with a sneaky grin.

"We were all so surprised. . ." Magda motioned uselessly with her hand towards him. "I mean, nobody thought you'd ever come home."

"I'm full of surprises," he said, smiling. "Let's eat, 'cause I've got one more I want to tell you." He positioned his chair at the end of the table where he'd last eaten over seven years earlier.

Lilith Ann turned around and flipped her drying rag back on the counter. "Before we get into that, we need to talk about how you're going to get on. I don't want Jack working as a nurse for you. He's going to start classes at the junior college in the summer."

Pete-O's eyes turned hard. "What makes you think I need a nurse? I never asked anybody to nurse me, and I sure hadn't asked Jack to."

Jack was taken by surprise at his mother's words. They had

never discussed who would care for Pete-O, and she had certainly never mentioned her concerns about Pete-O expecting him to do it. His decision to attend school had been left at nothing more than an agreement to look over the majors offered at the junior college, something he hadn't bothered to do yet. The look on Pete-O's face told him a show-down was about to happen. The only person he knew of who ever came out a winner in such a situation was his mother, but her resolve over the past few months was not what it once was. Jack locked eyes with Magda for any hint of direction but received nothing other than his own anxiety mirrored back at him.

Lilith Ann pulled out the chair opposite Pete-O and took her time sitting down. She put her hands flat on the table, in the same position as her brother sitting across from her. "Pete-O, you're my brother, and because you're family I will never turn my back on you, no matter what stupid things you may do. You've never been a cook. You've never cleaned your house even when you were able to do it, and you've never done a decent job of managing your diabetes. If you had, then you wouldn't be in that chair. Now this is just the way things are, and you've got to face it. If you want to have any kind of life, then you'll consider what I'm saying and take a long hard think about how you're going to live from here on out. You're going to have to either make some serious changes or you're going to have to get some hired help. Jack can stay here for a couple of nights to help you get settled in, but after that you're going to have to make do for yourself."

Pete-O just sat back and gave his sister a big smile. He slid his hands onto his lap and kept on smiling at her. "I swear," he said, shaking his head. "You ought to be one of those CEOs running some corporation. You've got a plan for everybody."

"That's just it, Pete-O. I don't have any plan for anybody," said Lilith Ann. Jack furrowed his brow in confusion, because apparently she had a very definite plan for him. It was just Pete-O she wasn't prepared for.

"You may be surprised to know that I have already made plans for myself."

Lilith Ann cocked her head to one side and waited.

Pete-O put his hands back on the table and leaned forward. "I'm getting married."

Lilith Ann's face dropped and Daryl peered up at Jack, sensing some new tension in the air.

"That's right. In two months I'll have a wife who'll be taking good care of me."

"Is she in prison?" asked Lilith Ann.

"No, she's not in prison. She's never been in prison. Her name is Liu Peng, and she's coming all the way from China."

"China! How are you getting a wife from China?"

"It wasn't easy. I been working on it since they first told me about the release nearly a year ago."

"How do you know she's real? Maybe she's one of those scam artists who's just trying to take you for all your money." Lilith Ann was suddenly full of alarm. "Has she asked you to send her money?"

Pete-O reached into his shirt pocket, took out a photograph, and slid it across the table to his sister. Magda and Jack jumped to her side to see. The photograph, folded and dog-eared, was of a woman little more than a girl with shoulder-length black hair and bangs cut straight across her forehead. Her eyes were upswept and small and her smile was shy. She wore a dark blouse with a lace collar encircling her slender neck. The young woman looked only a few years older than Jack and was beautiful in a simple kind of way. While the three of them leaned in to get a good look at the head-and-shoulders figure, Pete-O grinned at his victory.

"She has an uncle who knows the right people in the Party," he said proudly. "You add a little money to that and you can get things done."

"Party? What party are you talking about?" asked Lilith Ann. "You said you didn't send her any money."

"I didn't send it to her. I sent it to her father. He got it to the right people," said Pete-O, giving a shrug like a gangster pretending to be innocent. "And the right people are going to get her here to me."

"But Uncle Pete-O, you can't send money when you're in prison," said Jack.

"Aw hell, you people don't know anything," said Pete-O. "You people act like you think I'm stupid or something."

"So now we've become 'you people'," said Magda, sliding the photo back across the table.

"If you people would shut up and listen a minute." Pete-O took the photograph carefully between his thumb and index finger and slid it back into his pocket. "About five years ago I met up with a fellow named Gary T. Thomas. He was a lawyer serving time for larceny, but he'd lived in China a few years before that because he worked for this other guy who was in business with this other Chinese fella." Lilith Ann, Magda, and Jack sat in rapt attention, waiting for Pete-O to connect all the dots. "So, Gary gets out about two years ago, and he's back in business, but not back in the lawyering business because of that larceny conviction. Gary's got a wife that he got in Guangzhou, that's a city in China, see? He met her while he was working there back before he got sent up. Anyway, Gary knows all the ways of the money handling and is taking care of all the paperwork, all the red tape. I just sign what needs to be signed." Pete-O made a dismissive gesture with his hands, but no one spoke. "Do you get it now?"

"You're sending all your money to a convicted felon who used to be a lawyer, who is now in business but not the lawyering business, who just gives you stuff to sign. Is that what we're supposed to get?" asked Magda.

Pete-O pointed a finger at his niece. "I know what you're trying to do. You're trying to make it sound like I'm some kind of naïve dumbass who's going to get taken, but let me tell you, it was Gary who came through for me in the joint and made sure I got my accommodations when the state didn't want to get me the equipment I needed for the shower. And he was the one helped me file suit against the state when the COs started making it a habit of forgetting to take me to the infirmary for my insulin until four hours after I needed it. I didn't see any of you people coming up there to help me with none of that." He now pointed the same finger at his sister. "You come up there the first Christmas and then one other time on my birthday with Jack, and Viv who chomped my ear off reading Bible verses. The only person who ever showed up regular was Jack when he got old enough to drive. So don't you give me some smartass lecture about who I can depend on, because you all made that plain enough seven years ago."

Lilith Ann gave Magda a look before turning back to her brother. "What'd you say her name was?"

"Liu Peng, but I call her Shubie," said Pete-O.

"You do, huh?" said Lilith Ann. "What do you want us to call her?"

Pete-O looked a bit flummoxed for a second. "I reckon you all can call her that, too. She doesn't speak much English. Her nephew has to read her all my letters and he writes hers for her. I promised to send him one of those remote-control airplanes for all his trouble."

"Did you know about any of this?" said Lilith Ann to Jack.

"This is the first I've heard about it," said Jack.

Lilith Ann gave a long sigh and seemed to pull something together in herself, to reach some resolution. She and Pete-O had always been like two cats who randomly lunged and spat at each other but most of the time simply ignored each other. Being six years older than her brother, she had witnessed his flailing against the system his entire life. When Pete-O was thirteen, he threw a rock through a window of Ned's Bait and Tackle in Centre followed by four M-80's. The ensuing chaos brought two sheriff deputies and a fire truck to the scene. Pete-O did not bother to run, hide, or even deny that he had

done the damage. He was standing on the sidewalk next to the broken glass, the cigarette lighter still in his hand when the first deputy arrived. At the sheriff's office before his father arrived to pick him up, he told the sheriff he had wanted to see how many vehicles would come, and frankly he was disappointed that it had been only three. The story made the second page of the newspaper the next Sunday. Lilith Ann, who had just graduated from high school and was engaged to be married in November, was so embarrassed by Pete-O's run-in with the law that she asked their father if her brother could be excluded from the wedding. Pete-O's embarrassments grew over the years until Lilith Ann decided to acknowledge them as little as possible. After her husband died, Pete-O showered Jack with attention, something she no longer had the energy to do. Life had wrung her dry by that point, and she was often so depleted that she provided few boundaries for her youngest son. Pete-O's final humiliation of the family came when he made himself known as the Walmart Shooter. After her first few visits to prison, which she made because Jack begged her to go, Lilith Ann had resolved that she was rid of her brother forever (and between herself and God, had declared it a blessing). In his kitchen now, looking at him sitting in his wheelchair across from her at the table, the tiredness flooded her limbs and she was sure she had not felt that exhausted since his first day in court all those years ago. She hoped the Chinese girl who had, for God only knew what reason, promised to marry her brother was tougher than she looked. Clearly, the girl was feeble-minded, it was an arranged marriage, or both, and money was certainly what had arranged it. Lilith Ann looked over at the chili on the stove and then turned back to her brother. "I reckon we can give her a wedding shower when she gets here."

Chapter 7

The photograph in the newspaper didn't have Robert in it, and Kimmy gave a sigh of relief. He was long gone by the time *The Gadsden Times* sent a reporter to the school to cover the story. The photographer had taken a rather boring shot of children's lunch trays in a line on the metal bars of the buffet, careful not to show any of the children's faces. The heading of the article read: "Angry Parent Confronts School Cafeteria Worker."

"If they'd put the reason he confronted them, it wouldn't sound so bad. I swear," said Kimmy, throwing down the newspaper Lilith Ann had brought in, "nobody ought to throw out kids' school lunches just because we're behind on paying their fees."

"I'm not saying he was wrong," said Lilith Ann. "I just wish he'd have let me go down there and set that old biddy straight that runs the cafeteria. Then Robert wouldn't have gotten his name in the newspaper. That boy's got to stop flying off the handle."

"Throwing children's lunches in the garbage because we forgot to pay is just over the line, and any other dad would have done the same thing," said Kimmy, picking up Cody. Cody had a hacking cough and runny nose, and Kimmy took a paper towel off the kitchen counter to wipe his face. Baxter had folded up his sleeping cot and pushed it against the wall in the laundry room. He sat at the table quietly facing Kimmy and Lilith Ann. Kimmy had grown accustomed to his silences, and sometimes she rather liked having an adult in the house to talk to who would rarely say anything back, let alone disagree.

"But other dads don't have felony records, and if one of them had he probably would have called that cafeteria manager a dried up old bitch, too," said Lilith Ann.

"It was mean is what it was," said Kimmy.

Lilith Ann didn't know if Kimmy was referring to what Robert had called the manager, or to the manager throwing Rob Jr.'s lunch in the trash. If only Robert had told her, she could have gone to the school with a twenty-dollar bill and straightened the whole thing out long before it came to Robert's early morning trip to the school to chew the woman out.

Kimmy sat holding Cody, who for once didn't have enough energy to be squirming all over the place. He leaned against his mother, and Lilith Ann could hear a slight wheeze coming from his chest.

Kimmy's eyes went to the cookie jar on the counter, where she put all the bills as they arrived. When they were paid, she marked them with a capital "P" and moved them to the flour jar. The cookie jar was full, while the flour jar had a few slips of paper in the bottom. After she had finally summoned the courage to tell Robert about the credit card bills, the payments on the trailer, and other debt that had accumulated over the past months, he disappeared into the woods behind the trailer. She braced herself for a blow-up, but Robert's three-hour disappearance frightened her more. When he returned with bits of tree bark in his hair, she knew where he'd been hiding. That moment was the first time she had ever looked into her husband's face and seen fear. The pounding feeling descended in her stomach and was worse than any yelling she had ever heard from him. Even the fight the year before that landed him in jail had frightened her less than this.

Robert's first job was on the clean-up crew of a Shoney's almost a month after he returned home. The job was a temporary position that ended when the manager's nephew returned from a month-long mission trip in Lithuania. After that, Robert found a position as a night clerk in a Jet Pep but was fired after a week for refusing to sell beer to a man whom he claimed acted "like a terrorist." Most recently, Robert had found work at Delaney's Tires, but only because the manager attended Josh and Viv's church, and Viv had insisted Josh keep visiting the manager and begging until he agreed to hire Robert.

Tom Delaney had hired convicted felons, juvenile delinquents, and once a former prostitute to do the janitorial work, because he was a man who believed in giving second chances to folks who were down on their luck and willing to work hard for the $7.25 per hour he paid. But he was not a man who gave third chances.

Robert had just finished fixing a flat when his morning break began. He wiped his hands on a rag and then tossed it onto the work table in the garage. "Hey Randall, I'm headed to the lounge. You want a Coke or anything?"

"Nah, I'm good," said Randall, returning his attention to the removal of a damaged rim.

The lounge was where the customers were invited to wait while their repairs were being done, and it was the only place in the shop for employees to get a drink or snack. Employees were allowed to use the machines only if their hands were properly washed. Robert shoved his in his pockets as he passed the check-out counter where Mr. Delaney stood sorting through a newly arrived box of oil. The lounge smelled of tire chemicals, and was at its most concentrated in the lounge because there was a display of new tires lining either side of the entrance, and no air flow in the lounge except for one anemic vent on the wall above the television. For the past three days Robert had gotten his drink on his break and carried it to an old truck seat that propped against the back of the building, where he had exactly seven minutes to sit and drink without the inconstant sounds of air compressors and drills puncturing his peace.

A woman who looked to be in her eighties stood a few feet in front of the machine with her hand deep in her purse, fumbling for quarters amidst the spent tissues, lipsticks, and keys. She gave Robert a quick smile and kept searching. "I know I've got another coin in here. I had three quarters in my little coin purse, but I think I've got some more down in here somewhere." Her gaze returned to her purse, and she pushed aside an expired coupon for toilet paper.

Seven minutes.

"I've always got some money down in here. I think I'm out and then, lo and behold, the Lord takes care of me and I find a little something down in the bottom." Robert stepped to the side and she followed his movement with her own sidestep, blocking the coin slot with her body as her fumbling continued.

Six minutes.

"Oh look, here's one," said the woman, holding up a quarter. "Now I need one more to get myself a Fanta. I always like a Fanta when I get tired out. They sure give a pick-me-up."

Robert fished in his pocket for an extra quarter, but he had exactly six, enough for his Coca-Cola, rationed out from the tight pocket that had become his household budget. Kimmy had suggested he get a 2-liter from K-Mart and keep it in the refrigerator with his name on it, and drink from that each day because it would cost so much less per serving than getting an expensive bottle from the machine, but there was something satisfying to Robert about sitting down with his own fresh bottle, alone. He didn't want Coke that lost its fizz after three days or to have to pour it in a Solo cup that he had to wash each day and then hide so it didn't get thrown out. That Coke was his private luxury. He was sure the cost of his daily Cokes did not even approach the amount of money Kimmy spent on nail polish each month.

Four minutes.

"Well maybe I don't have another quarter," the old woman finally said, shutting her purse. "I sure thought the Lord would put just one more little quarter in my purse for me to get a drink."

"Right now the Lord wants you to step out of the way so I can get a Coke," said Robert, reaching past her to feed his first coin into the machine.

Three minutes.

"Well I never!" the old woman gasped.

"You don't look like you have," Robert snapped.

"There's no reason to speak to me like that," said the woman, stepping closer to Robert and dropping one of her coins. It bounced and rolled underneath the machine, out of reach.

"Right now I've got about two minutes left on my break because you blocked the machine while you were looking through your purse for quarters from Jesus," said Robert, leaning over to take the chilled bottle from the open mouth of the machine.

"Young man, you are being very rude," said the old woman.

Robert whirled around and took his Coke out the side door and headed to the back of the building. He didn't even get to finish it before Mr. Delaney appeared at the corner with his hands on his hips. "Boyd," he called. "You'll not push an old woman out of the way and knock her coins to the floor just so you can get your drink ahead of her. If she were my mother you'd be picking yourself off the floor about now!"

"I never touched that lying old biddy."

"Off my property, right now!" Mr. Delaney pointed a finger at the parking lot. "And don't bother coming back for your last check. I'll mail it."

Robert wanted to toss the Coke bottle at the building, except all he could think about was when he was likely to get another one. He also wanted to tell old Mr. Delaney what he could do with that last paycheck, but he didn't dare. For a split second he considered decking the manager right where he stood, but he knew that would end in his speedy return to jail as soon as his parole officer was notified. Robert pushed past Delaney and saw the old woman just outside the roll-up doors, holding her two-quarters-short-from-Jesus pocketbook in little clutched fists. She looked up at him, her face twisted in a satisfied smirk. It would feel so good to back his Chevy into the front of her Acura as he was leaving, but her car was safely inside the garage on jacks, as Randall installed new Firestones.

There was no one to punch, shoot, run over, or even smack talk, and he was out of work again. Robert let out what began as a groan but arched into a yell as he passed by Delaney. Every muscle in his chest strained against his flesh, and he began tearing at the blue work shirt with the Delaney's Tires patch over his heart. Buttons popped off and one of the sleeves tore as he jerked it off his body.

"That'll come out of your last check," Delaney shouted.

Robert threw his work shirt at the fuming manager and stomped to his car. Everyone from the garage watched him get in and speed away.

Chapter 8

*L*iu Village was home to about seven hundred people, and most of them were related. When people in Pete-O's country were dumping tea in Boston Harbor and attempting to annihilate the indigenous peoples of what would become the United States of America, Liu Peng's ancestors were rooted in their central Chinese village, growing their own tea.

Peng, her father, mother, and grandmother lived with her brother, his wife, and their son in a house with two bedrooms and no bathroom. The cooking was done on an open fire in the courtyard next to a shed where their two mongrel dogs were kept. A coal burning stove under the stairwell in the house provided a place for boiling water to make noodles and tea. Peng's parents and grandmother slept on the floor of the main room, where the family gathered for meals, and Peng slept on the floor of the grain storage room, which was built onto the back of the house. The toilet was a cement trough in the pig pen, and the sink was a spigot outside the pen, with a bar of soap suspended on a thin string that ran through a hole in the middle and attached to a nail on the dog shed. This was where Peng helped her sister-in-law, Huirong, wash the dishes after they cooked the meals in weather that ranged from sweltering to freezing. It was Huirong who had commandeered the hardback suitcase for Peng to take to America. A neighbor had thrown it out because her son, a young man attending college in a city far away, had declared it old and insufficient. His mother retrieved the old valise to store things in, but the son discovered it and scolded his mother for embarrassing him with her traditional ways, and threw it out once again.

Peng scoured the outside of the suitcase with a rag until it was clean, and stitched up the torn lining inside. She folded her clothes and placed them at the bottom, first one way and

then another. She wrapped her second-best shoes in a plastic shopping bag and placed them on top of the clothes. Huirong had given her a jacket in bright blue with white birds, but Peng had no idea if it would be fashionable in America. She had paired it with a black skirt and boots to wear on her trip, the thought of which made her stomach jump each time she imagined it. Peng's grandmother, nearly blind and deaf, kept trying to give her a quilted coat that she had worn when Peng was a girl. Peng took it with grateful hands and yelled her thanks to Grandmother's face, before carefully hiding it away on a high shelf with no intention of taking something to America that only old ladies and tourists still wore in China. Her brother gave her a tea bottle, new with a plastic lid and insulated body that she could take on the long train ride to Beijing. A jade bracelet and earrings from her mother, money from her father, and several drawings of giraffes and dogs from her nephew, one set of quilted pajamas, one set of chopsticks and a bowl, carefully selected letters and photographs that Pete-O had sent to her over the years, and her personal grooming items completed her collection of belongings. Though Peng knew no one in her family could read English except her nephew, she couldn't stand the thought of the remainder of the letters from Pete-O lying on a shelf in her house after she had gone, their personal words and intimacies potentially exposed. There were so many; a boxful remained even after she had selected the ones she wanted to take with her. Late one night the week before she was to leave, she had burned them over the cooking fire in the courtyard, witnessed only by their two perplexed dogs awakened in their shed.

In a smaller bag were dried dates and jujubes, oranges, sunflower seeds, and other snacks that Peng's mother and sister-in-law had packed for her trip. Peng took the wooden brush from her suitcase and ran it through her hair again, feeling the sleekness against her fingers as she trailed the strokes with her other hand. Her skin was clean and she'd scrubbed her teeth thoroughly with soda. She looked down at her clothes, flicking away bits of lint. He could not say no. He would not send me back. This is my last chance. Oh god, no, don't let him turn me away when he sees me.

Peng put a hand on her stomach until the shiver passed, and then she reached into the pocket of her suitcase and took out the photograph. Pete-O's eyes were blue and his hair was thick and golden blond. He must have been very happy on the day this photograph was taken because he was not just smiling, he was laughing. Soft furry hairs on his forearms caught the light, and Peng imagined he must feel like a bear. Pete-O was such a strong man. The person taking the picture must have been small or sitting on the ground; the photo was angled upward on Pete-O, who stood next to a tree with his feet planted firmly in green grass and his laughing gaze on something in the distance. He wore pristine white pants, something that confounded Peng each time she looked at the picture. She had never seen a man wearing white pants, and she had certainly never seen anyone wear any pants that were so bright and clean. He must have a clothes washing machine, Huirong had said, giggling at the very idea. Maybe he will take you to Disney World, and they both had squealed at such a glorious possibility.

"It is time to go." Her brother, Jia, stood waiting in the doorway of the house. Tears welled up in Peng's eyes and her hands began to shake. "Come, come! You must hurry!" Jia called.

"I am coming," Peng said, shutting her suitcase with trembling hands.

In the courtyard, her family was gathered around the three-wheeled cart her brother would use to drive her to the bus station. There, she would board a bus that would take her to the train station, where she would board the sleeper train that would deliver her fifteen hours later to Beijing. The train was called a sleeper because it ran all night, but there would be no sleep for her as Pete-O had sent enough money only for a hard plastic seat in the regular car. She had not expected more. In

Beijing she had to take the subway to the airport, a task that put terror in her heart each time she thought about it. Her uncle who had made the arrangements had also written pages of instructions for her, and Peng had read them so many times she had memorized them. There had been talk of sending Jia with her until she got to Beijing, but the two-day round-trip of trains, buses, and subway rides was too expensive, and in the end her father had said no. Peng knew she could understand the directions all the way to Los Angeles, California, in America, but beyond that the trip became more complicated. Her instructions said she was to find a "Chinese flight hostess" who could tell her which way to go when she got off the airplane. She would recognize the hostess by her jaunty V-shaped hat, neckerchief, and elegant amber-colored uniform. Peng had seen flight hostesses once on the television at her neighbor's house, all beautiful, young, and harmoniously matching.

"Follow what you are told by your new husband's family. Do not bring shame to our family," her father said, but Peng could only hear the words he left off, "ever again." She lowered her eyes until all she could see was her father's shoes. She never saw the quivering of his mouth as he stared at the top of his only daughter's head. Peng's mother was next. She laid her hands on Peng's shoulders. "You be a good wife. No running away." Peng's heart fell and she shook her head. "No, no running," said Peng. "Pete-O will be a good husband." Huirong pushed a paper sack of fried dumplings into the food bag and Peng began to cry. "Your new husband will take you to KFC and to see movies," said Huirong, trying her best to sound cheerful. "You will have a cooking stove in your house and hot water all the time and he will take you to New York City for ice skating. I saw this on the television. I am so jealous! I think I will go and you will stay here," cried Huirong.

Even though Peng was ten years older than Huirong, they had been as close as sisters for the five years Peng had lived in the house with her brother's family. The women said more goodbyes and Jia put his sister's bags into the back of the cart. Peng stepped into the cart and sat on the low, fold-out stool that was to be her seat for the forty-five minute ride to the station. Facing backwards, she waved to her family and watched her village, the only home she had ever known, disappear house by house as her brother wheeled the cart down the dirty lane. Her nephew ran after her, waving and shouting more goodbyes. He followed them to the end of the street and was finally left behind as Jia turned the corner and sped down the main road. The road passed through the forest of stumps that had been a grove of trees when Peng was a child. The stream that had run next to it, once blue and full of fish, was now a dead ribbon of sludge, thick with thallium, cadmium, and a hundred other toxins from the town's two factories.

Peng saw it all growing smaller as her cart sped away. The factories with the twenty-four-hour smoking pipes and rings of trash around their perimeters. The cliffside of garbage where the entire village tossed its trash. The dry, barren riverbed punctured by holes where villagers had poled out the rounded boulders they sold to landscaping companies from the city. The crumbling rubble of the cement buildings of the village. The herd of goats rambling through the alley with the grandmother pushing them on from behind with her stick. Squatty, half-wild dogs darting down alleys and around broken cement blocks pushed against houses. Four red-faced children in quilted winter suits poking sticks through the thin icy sheets atop puddles. Everywhere, people dotted the road, walking toward and away from the village, carrying bags and baskets, smoking, pushing carts, holding babies, leaning on canes, limping, herding animals. And at the edge of the village were the fields, the winter brown fields that would soon be green with new plantings of corn and peanuts, the place where the village farmers went with hoes and planting sacks each spring. The fields hurt her heart most of all, and as they passed, she wrapped her arms around her knees and shut her eyes to those memories.

Chapter 9

Before Pete-O went to prison for murder, at least one person had always saluted him everywhere he went, or shook his hand and thanked him for his service to America. Since his release, he was leaner and eight years older, and had become a hero of epic proportions with his high and tight haircut, freshly pressed navy blue shirt adorned with an American flag pin, and clean khaki pants sewn neatly shut at the knees, as Lilith Ann and Magda wheeled him through the Hartsfield International Airport to meet Liu Peng for the first time. He was saluted and applauded three times before they made it to the arrivals gate. A young man in a Glenn Beck T-shirt was headed toward Pete-O with his hand outstretched when Magda intercepted. "It was diabetes, okay?" The young man dropped his hand and slunk away.

"Just look at those fellas there," said Pete-O, looking at two dark-skinned men in turbans who were loaded down with suitcases and bags. "I hope security checked out those bags real good."

"Yeah, I think I see some C-4 sticking out the top of the shorter one's bag," said Magda.

"You make a big joke out of it, but it's no joke when it's one of those sleeper cells sitting behind you on a plane. And don't you tell me it can't happen," warned Pete-O as he shot a finger at his niece. "Middle East foreigners ought to be checked, and I don't give a damn what those libtards whine about profiling. A lot of these foreigners hate America, but they'll come here and stick their hands out to get all the government money they can get."

"Either that or they're here to work in their uncle's falafel restaurant in Five Points," said Magda. "Geesh, Pete-O, you sound pretty irate about foreigners for a guy who's sitting here waiting to meet your foreign Communist fiancée."

"Shubie's not a Communist," Pete-O said in a low voice. "I already told you that, so shut it. If you were as smart as you think you are you'd know that China is a Socialist country." His nerves had made him sweat profusely. Each time he pushed his fingers through his thinning hair, it became more and more damp until he looked as if he had just come from a bath.

Magda shifted her bag to her other shoulder. She was already tired of waiting and desperately wanted to sit down, but the only seats she could find were bolted to the floor far away from the arrivals area. Each time a new wave of people came through the doors, Pete-O became erect in his chair and scanned the faces. A few times he opened his mouth to call his future wife's name, but the face never turned out to be the right one. Magda had gone to the only Chinese restaurant in Drayton and asked the owner, Mr. Chen, to letter Liu Peng's name in English and Chinese on a cardboard sign as a surprise to Pete-O, but Pete-O had folded the thing in half and tossed it on the kitchen table as soon as he saw it, saying he would know Shubie as soon as he laid eyes on her and he wanted to approach her himself. Her insistence that they stop at a Kroger's and purchase a bouquet of pink carnations was met with equal vehemence, but this time Lilith Ann put her foot down and made Magda pull into a grocery store parking lot. She told Pete-O that he must not have the sense God gave a monkey if he didn't know greeting his future wife with flowers in hand was the least a man could do. His protest that he was "gonna get her a ring" was cut off by Lilith Ann's exit from the car and slamming of her door. For the three days leading up to Liu Peng's arrival, Pete-O's behavior had been a source of confusion to everyone, even Baxter, who was waiting behind with Jack at Pete-O's house for the welcoming party. Lilith Ann overlooked his brother's eccentric behavior with the excuse that he was just nervous, but the incident with the sign had left Magda and Pete-O at odds for the entire four-hour trip to Atlanta. Now, Pete-O sat with the flowers in his lap, their stems mostly broken and limp from his sweaty grip.

"Magda, go check the board again," said Pete-O.

"We've checked it three times, Uncle Pete-O. Her plane landed a half hour ago. Maybe she's lost. Maybe she missed her connecting flight in Los Angeles."

"She didn't miss her flight." Pete-O licked his lips and strained to see into the sea of faces passing him by.

"How could you possibly know that?" asked Magda, but Pete-O didn't answer.

Dozens of Asian faces had passed them since they'd arrived, but not one had belonged to the young woman in the photograph Pete-O carried in his shirt pocket. A few looked lost, even frightened. Most happily met up with families or drivers holding signs, and some went to taxis patrolling outside the doors, but not one had approached Pete-O, Magda, and Lilith Ann.

"Do you want me to page her?" asked Magda. "I could find somebody who speaks Chinese."

"I want to find her myself," said Pete-O. "I want to be the first one she speaks to."

"Even if you don't see her, it just seems weird that she isn't finding you. There's not one single other person here in a wheel-chair. That's hard to miss, and it's why I'm thinking she wasn't on that plane," said Magda.

"She was on the damn plane," said Pete-O.

Magda's eyes widened, and she looked over Pete-O's head at her mother. "Did you send this woman a picture of yourself?"

"Of course I did," Pete-O said, not taking his eyes from the passing people.

Lilith Ann caught on and quickly turned to her brother. "Does she know you got no legs?" Her voice was high and loud, and a few people turned to look.

Pete-O flipped his hand up to dismiss her words, but he wouldn't look at either Lilith Ann or Magda.

"Did you tell that woman you're in a wheelchair or not?" Magda asked.

"I sent her a picture of me, and no I wasn't in my chair," Pete-O said, keeping up his scan of the crowd. "I was in Florida with Bert on a fishing trip."

"Bert went fishing with you back when Jack was in kindergarten!" said Lilith Ann, looking as if she might slap her brother. "No wonder she doesn't recognize you. There's some Chinese woman wandering around here looking for a forty-something-year-old man standing on two legs. Does she know you were in prison?" Lilith Ann whispered the last word. Magda burst out laughing and more people began to stare. "That's not funny, Magda, now shut the hell up," said Lilith Ann.

Magda clamped her lips shut and turned her face away. A short, black-haired woman with crow's feet framing her red face and wearing a wrinkled jacket paused and looked at her before disappearing into the masses, dragging her suitcase.

"She knows all about that and she doesn't give a damn. She's from China. Half the people there have been in prison for one thing or another," said Pete-O.

"What if she saw you and she turned right around and got on another plane heading back for China?" said Lilith Ann. "Did you ever think about that?"

Pete-O picked up the flowers and slammed them back down in his lap. "She's here somewhere, and she didn't get on no plane back to China because I bought her a one-way ticket! She's stuck here with me whether she likes it or not."

"At least she's getting a man who's a romantic," said Magda.

This time both Pete-O and Lilith Ann told her to shut up. Magda wandered a few steps away and took the folded-up sign that she had retrieved from the table before they left that morning. She held it up while Lilith Ann and Pete-O continued their tirade, and in a couple of minutes that same petite Asian woman in the wrinkled blue jacket stopped in front of Magda. Running up one side of the woman's tired face, all the way to her left ear, was a fine, pink scar. Hers was the only suitcase with no wheels, and Magda was sure it must be an antique. Tilting precariously to one side, the woman slowly placed the suitcase on the ground and stared at the arguing woman and the man with no legs in the wheelchair behind the young woman who held a sign with her name written both in Pinyin and Chinese characters. Her breath moved rapid fire in her chest, and her mouth trembled so badly she could hardly form the greeting she had practiced with her nephew. "I am Liu Peng." And then she collapsed to the floor.

Chapter 10

*P*eng had ridden in cars before. When she went to the next village to take nursing classes twenty years earlier, when one of her younger brother's friends bought a car and took the family for a ride, and the time before that when she was taken by the police for what happened to her husband. Peng lay with her head against the seat and the wind blowing in her face. Magda had rolled the window down for her because she hadn't known which button to press. Peng kept her eyes closed so that she would not have to look at any of these three strangers in the car with whom she could say little more than hello and goodbye. Looking down at the place where Pete-O's legs should have been, the strong man's legs from the photograph, made her dizzy and tremulous. *I should have known it would all come back to me somehow even after all these years. This is my punishment.*

In the back seat next to Peng, Pete-O sat white-faced and silent in a combination of anger, stunned amazement, and confusion. At first he hadn't even wanted to take this woman with them and insisted that she was an imposter who had done something to the real Liu Peng. He had even refused to refer to her by Shubie, the pet name he had given her. He resigned his protests in disgust when Magda managed to get Peng to show her government identity card, which featured her photo and name in the same Chinese characters that Mr. Chen had written on the sign. Wrangling a flight attendant from Air China who had a layover in Atlanta, they were able to unravel the mystery from a tearful and trembling Liu Peng. She had sent photos not of herself but ten-year-old photos of her sister-in-law when she was a young potential match that her parents were considering for Jia. Peng hadn't started out lying to Pete-O. The first few letters that her nephew wrote for her were genuine. It wasn't until Pete-O started asking

what she looked like that she realized she could never keep his attention if she sent a photograph of herself. She didn't even have a recent picture of herself. If Pete-O had seen her for what she was, a widowed, scarred forty-seven-year-old farm woman with no chance of remarriage in her village in China, he would never have moved heaven and earth and spent nearly all of his money getting her to America.

Peng had not understood any of the words that passed between the three Americans after the young woman from the airline company said her ride was waiting and she had to leave. She could tell that the younger woman who had held up the sign with her name on it somehow thought the occasion was funny at first, but the older woman, whom Peng figured out was Pete-O's sister, yelled at her and finally the young woman's face became serious. Peng decided the woman must be a neighbor because no daughter would laugh at her mother the way this woman did. Pete-O glared at Peng until she thought she would faint again.

The plan to stop and eat at a Golden Corral restaurant was scuttled, so Lilith Ann told Magda to stop at a McDonald's.

"I believe I'll sit right here," said Pete-O, his arms crossed defiantly over his chest. "You can take whatever her name is inside and feed her something if you want to."

"I don't know, Uncle Pete-O. You know those foreigners. Can't trust any of them. She might try to steal some fries or something," said Magda.

"That's not helping one bit, so shut your mouth," said Lilith Ann. She turned to her brother and pointed a finger close to his face. "You better listen to me and listen good. You were just as much of a liar as she was when you sent her those pictures of you standing up on two good legs. So what that you're not getting a pretty little young girl who's gonna be your nursemaid for the rest of your life. You can bet she realized she was getting a raw deal just as much as you did when she got a good look at your sorry ass, so you'd better buck up, take the cow you bought, and appreciate the milk."

Lilith Ann held what was left of the flowers in her lap after Pete-O had dropped them on the floor of the airport and backed his wheelchair over them. She snapped her fingers at Peng and pushed the four remaining intact buds at her. "These were for you. From Pete-O." She poked her brother to make sure Peng understood.

Peng searched for the words a few seconds before she remembered. "Thank you," words she had learned from her nephew.

"Well, she knows thank you. Now we'll teach her please and shut the hell up, Pete-O, and she'll get along fine," said Magda.

Inside the McDonald's Magda ordered a cheeseburger, fries, and a Coke for Peng, the first McDonald's food Peng had ever tried. She wanted to scrape off the yellow plasticky goo, but she dared not and managed to down most of the meal.

"She's got a nice figure," Lilith Ann said, wiping her mouth after finishing her Quarter Pounder. "Can't be more than five feet tall either. She's got some miles on her, but she's kinda cute."

"She's not a used car, Mama," said Magda

Lilith Ann leaned over the table and tapped her fingers on it to make sure Peng understood she was talking to her. "We think you're cute," she said loudly.

"She's not deaf either," Magda added. She smiled and gently patted Peng's shoulder.

"She ain't no puppy either," said Lilith Ann. "What do you think, Pete-O? She's not so bad, now is she?"

"Yeah," said Magda, "we could put a little concealer on that scar and you'd hardly notice it." She reached out to touch Peng's face and Peng shied away. "It's okay," said Magda quietly, "pretty face." She made a circling motion with her hand around her own face to try to convey her words, but all Peng understood was that this woman was noticing her scar and saying something about how she looked. She must be telling Pete-O and his sister that she was ugly. Pete-O's expression had softened,

but he still had nothing to say to her.

"You know," said Magda, first looking at Pete-O and then at Peng. "This may be the best thing that could have happened for you. You were worried she might reject you when she saw your missing legs. I don't think that will happen now, do you?"

"I reckon not," said Pete-O. He finished the last bite of his fries and drank his Sprite to the bottom of the cup. He pushed his cup toward Peng and then pointed at the soda spigots on the wall next to their table. She looked at the cup in confusion.

"Oh no, you didn't," said Magda.

"She's the closest one to the machine," said Pete-O.

"You are not going to treat this woman like she's some kind of servant. She's not even married to you yet, and even if she was she shouldn't be jumping up and getting you drinks," said Magda.

Lilith Ann put a hand up to silence her daughter. "It won't hurt for you to show her how to work the machine. She might want some more for herself, too." She pushed Peng's cup toward Magda. "Go on and help her."

Magda's mouth fell open. "I can't believe you two." She snatched at Peng and Pete-O's cups. "Come on, Peng. Massa wants you to fetch him another drink." Peng responded to her name and followed Magda to the wall of soft drinks.

Lilith Ann took the opportunity to speak to her brother alone. "They'll all be at the house waiting for us to get home. Viv wanted to do a little party for Peng, so my advice to you is to not act all bent out of shape over this since you've got no room to talk."

Pete-O seemed to think over what Lilith Ann said. He scratched his chin and sighed as he watched Peng pull at the handle and then give a little smile of delight when she realized that she could get unlimited amounts of Coca-Cola from the spigot. In fact, she could try them all if she wished, even Powerade Mountain Berry Blast, which she didn't seem to enjoy. Magda laughed and showed her that she could pour it into the drainage area below the spigots and try another. Peng poured a splash of Hi-C Lava Burst next.

"You know I couldn't have sent her a picture of me like this," said Pete-O, his voice low and sad.

"And she had enough sense to know that it's the young and pretty girls that older men want, especially when they're paying out money to buy them," Lilith Ann said. "I don't even want to know what this cost you, but whatever it was, just think about the fact that it cost her something, too. She looks like somebody with a history, and before you get too curious about that, keep in mind that you've got one, too. Whatever it is that she may have left behind, she probably wants it to stay that way."

"Since when did you become the Dr. Phil of the family?" asked Pete-O.

Lilith Ann pushed her tray to another table and searched around for a clean napkin. "I've seen too much in this family not to get some smarts over the past few years. Now let's get you back home."

Daryl and Tebow did not get along. Daryl was a good host who even let Tebow eat from his bowl, until Tebow jumped onto Daryl's blanket on the sofa and growled when Daryl tried to reclaim his space. This caused a minor scuffle that sent Viv flying from Pete-O's kitchen to retrieve her dog.

"I told you we should have done this at Lilith Ann's," she screeched. Jack sat down next to Daryl and rubbed the dog's ears. Tebow growled in Viv's arms. "You put two dogs in neutral territory and they don't act as bad," she said.

"The only dog that's acting bad is Tebow. Daryl's willing to share, aren't you boy?"

"That dog is spoiled is what he is," said Josh, pointing at Tebow. Viv carried him back to the kitchen and put him on the floor, where he crawled underneath the table and lay down. Viv was reaching for the Five Spice powder when her cell rang. Lilith Ann spent the next ten minutes explaining what had happened at the airport and followed it up with a commentary on the guilt of both parties. Viv spent much of the phone call with her hand over her heart, punctuating the conversation with an occasional "Lord have mercy" and "Land sakes." Lilith Ann was rounding up the call with a reminder to check the bathroom to see if the guest towels were set out when Kimmy, Robert, their five children, and Baxter came trailing through the door, creating such a ruckus that Viv didn't hear Lilith Ann's request or her final statement that they were ten minutes away.

Tebow erupted into a new round of barking with the children cavorting through the house, and Robert headed straight to Pete-O's cabinet for beer. Kimmy looked defeated as she watched her husband claim a Pabst Blue Ribbon from a high shelf and then pop the top to take a long draw of the room temperature beer.

"You drinking 'em hot now, Robert? I think that one's even got a little dust on it," Josh quipped.

"Don't start with me," said Robert.

"Honey, let's have a nice dinner with little Shupeng," said Kimmy.

"Her name is Liu Peng," said Baxter. "Liu is her family name, so it comes first."

"You a Chinese expert now?" asked Josh.

"The library has books on these things," said Baxter.

"You should get yourself a computer instead of going to the library every day," said Viv. "Everything you want to read about is online nowadays."

Baxter watched Cody and Matthew trying to ride Daryl, who lay lifeless on the floor in front of the sofa. "I like going to the library."

"'Specially since he can't go back to T&A's," said Robert.

"That place is one of Satan's playrooms," said Viv. "I sure hope you're not going out there."

"Yeah, that's a rough place, even for you," Josh added.

"I haven't seen you in church since you got home, Robert. I

know you don't want to see Mr. Delaney, but you ought to be back in church if you want to stay on the right path," said Viv.

Robert pulled a chair out from the table and sat down. He wanted to tell Viv off so badly he could taste the words on his lips, but he had promised Kimmy that he would cause no family squabbles. Not this time. Kimmy saw the frustration rising in his face and jumped around the table next to Viv. "I found the cutest jacket at the Goodwill and I got it for, what's her name again?"

"Peng," Viv and Josh both said.

"Yes, I was going to give it to her at the wedding shower, but I already got her a cookbook for that. This jacket was only three dollars and it had a little stain right here on the collar but it came right out in the wash, clean as a whistle."

"Well Kimmy, I don't know if we should be giving this woman used clothes. That might ins—"

"Aw, she probably won't know the difference," said Josh, interrupting Viv, who gave him a look of confusion, and then, finally, understanding. "I bet she's used to having stuff like that since she's from a Third World country. She'll be tickled to be getting something to wear whether it's new or not."

"Oh, well yes," said Viv. "I'm sure she'll appreciate it very much." She turned back to the oven to check the casserole. "This is done. I made a chicken casserole with bamboo shoots in it because, you know, I wanted to fix something with Chinese food in it."

The kitchen was filled with talking and the smell of cooking food. The grocery store cake on the counter was lettered with Welcome to U.S.A. Lou Ping, the misspelling crisis averted after Jack reminded Viv that Pete-O's fiancée could not read English anyway. In Pete-O's bedroom, Rob Jr. was jumping on the bed and slapping at the grips that were suspended from the ceiling to help Pete-O pull himself into his wheelchair. Jessica Ann crawled under the table to reach for Tebow, and the other children were still gathered around Daryl, who endured them stoically. The early warmth of summer weather began to heat the crowded little house, so Jack stepped outside to the porch for a breath of fresh air in the dimming afternoon light. He would be back at his mother's house when this new woman and Uncle Pete-O were married. Lilith Ann had relented and let him stay with his uncle over the past two months. Pete-O hadn't been as difficult as Jack remembered him being the first year he'd lost his legs. If anything, Pete-O was more pensive, more resilient, and much more private. He talked about his new life with Shubie often. Living as thriftily as possible, he had added up his pension checks over the coming months and made a budget to make it all work. He would first take Peng to Kell's Jewelry Store and let her pick out a ring. He had already alerted Mr. Kell about which case he should show Peng so that her choice wasn't too expensive. They would take a three-day vacation to Myrtle Beach for their honeymoon and stay at the Beachcomber Motorcourt. In the fall they would take a day trip to Memphis and see Graceland. Her twenty-fifth birthday was on November 9, so he would first take her to JCPenney and buy her a new dress, and then surprise her with a riverboat cruise on the Coosa River. At Christmastime he would go to Big Willie's, Drayton's finest pawn shop, and buy a big screen TV, a gift he readily admitted to Jack was as much for himself as it was for Peng, but he calculated that by then her English would be good enough for her to enjoy watching television with him. He would drive her to the hair salon twice a month and to the discount grocery store once a week. They'd go to the Golden Corral now and then to give her a break from cooking, although she would learn to cook American-style food soon enough. She would keep up their modest house, and Pete-O would treat her like a queen, or as much like a queen as he could on a Republic Steel pension and social security. He was finally going to enjoy the life he had always thought he deserved, and he was going to enjoy it with the woman he had been dreaming of, the beautiful and demure young woman whose letters had gotten him through five of the last of the seven years he'd spent in prison. Jack smiled as he envisioned a future in which his uncle would finally be a settled member of the community who wasn't going to shoot any more innocent store managers.

Magda's Honda eased into Pete-O's special parking spot and Jack launched off the porch to retrieve his uncle's chair from the back of the car. His mother yelled as soon as she got her door open. "Jack, use your manners and come open the door for Liu Peng," except when she said the name, it came out "Lew Ping."

"Pete-O just calls her Shubie," Jack said, opening the trunk.

"But her name is Peng, not Shubie," said Magda. "Shouldn't we call her by her name? It's not like it's hard to say Peng." She took Peng's suitcase from the trunk.

"All Chinese have an English name that they use with their Chinese name," said Pete-O out his window.

"Shubie's not English. You made it up. You said so," said Magda.

"She likes for me to call her Shubie," said Pete-O.

Magda opened Peng's door and leaned in toward Pete-O. "Really now, is that so? Has she ever heard you call her Shubie? Ever?"

Pete-O was about to swing his body around to move into his wheelchair, but he stopped. "I've been calling her Shubie for four years. You don't know anything about her."

"Apparently none of us knows much of anything about her, except the fact that her real name is Peng, not Shubie, because that's what it says on her ID card," said Magda. Peng looked helplessly from Magda to Pete-O as they repeated her name, and then she stepped out of the car to follow Magda, who was holding her suitcase.

"So, do we call her Peng or Shubie?" asked Jack, as Pete-O settled into his chair.

"We'll let Shubie be Uncle Pete-O's name for her. The rest of us can call her by her real name," said Magda.

The family had gathered on the porch to welcome their soon-to-be newest member, and to get a good look at this foreign woman who could speak only a few words of English. The children stared blankly at her exotic face and night-black hair. "Her eyes sure are squinty looking," said Rob Jr.

"We talked about that," Kimmy warned. "Now shut your mouth."

Viv spoke out of the corner of her mouth to Josh. "See what I told you? Lilith Ann said on the phone she was twice as old as she said she was in her letters." Then she turned on her smile and threw up her hand in a big wave. "Hey there, Peng, honey. Welcome to America! Welcome to your new family."

"Helloo," said Peng, smiling up at everyone. Her English greeting brought a round of cheers.

"Oh, isn't that sweet!" Viv clapped her hands. "Come on in. We have food for you," she said in long, slow, loud words. Peng nodded and waited for Magda to make a move. "Why are you bringing that in here?" asked Viv upon seeing Magda with Peng's suitcase in hand. "She's to stay at your house until they're married. We talked about that." She whispered the last words.

"Just put it back in the car," said Lilith Ann.

Peng followed Magda and her suitcase back to the car. "It's okay," Magda tried to explain. Peng reached for her suitcase and spoke in a rapid and clear voice, but no one could understand her. After Magda took her hand and tried to explain, Peng still did not understand, but after a few minutes of haggling she allowed herself to be coaxed into the house based on nothing more than the minuscule amount of faith she had in Magda. As soon as Peng set foot through the door, Tebow and Daryl both began barking, and Tebow punctuated his welcome by lunging at Peng. She jumped backwards out the door, stepping on Lilith Ann's feet and shrieking as she tried to escape. The excitement spurred Daryl to put his paws on Peng's chest, which nearly made her faint again.

"Jack, get this dog off Peng right this minute," shouted Lilith

Ann.

"He's just trying to be friendly," said Jack. Taking Daryl by the collar, he pulled the dog back. Peng was shaking violently and refused to move through the door. She wiped away a tear of fright. "Come on now," said Lilith Ann soothingly, "it's just a dog. He won't hurt you."

Inside, Jack held onto Daryl, who wagged his tail at the curious little stranger coming into his home. "You just wanted to be friends, didn't you boy?" Jack buried his face into Daryl's thick brown neck fur and smiled.

"Keep them outside, why don't you?" said Lilith Ann, and then she added, "both of them. Take them for a walk."

"Daryl doesn't like Tebow, Mama. Put him in the back bedroom."

"He'll shit on the floor. Now take him out. We've got enough noise in there with all of Kimmy's kids. I just want to get through this dinner without Peng crawling out a window and running back to China."

Jack mumbled consent, pushed past the women and onto the porch. He continued on into the yard and whistled for Daryl and Tebow to follow. Soon, the three of them were heading down the trail behind the house and into the woods.

In the kitchen, Peng wiped the tears from her eyes with a ratty tissue she had pulled from her pants pocket. Her face was pink from fear, homesickness, lack of sleep, and now terror of Daryl and Tebow. She mumbled her terror of dogs and pointed at the door, but no one understood.

"Now I know you won't remember any of this, but let me tell you everyone's names," said Viv. "You've already met Magda and Lilith Ann." She pointed to each person as she spoke. "This is Robert and Kimmy and their kids. I won't bother with their names because you'll never keep them all straight until you learn more English."

"Viv, good grief, tell her the kids' names," said Kimmy. She rolled her eyes and rattled them all off to Peng, who seemed

amazed that there were so many children and that they all seemed to be from this one small woman.

"And this is Pete-O's brother, Baxter," said Viv. She was about to move on to Josh, but Baxter broke in.

"*Nihao, wo jiao* Baxter," he said. "*Qingwen, ni jiao shenma?*"

Peng's eyes grew wide and she giggled a little before she responded. "*Renshi ni Bakser hen gaoxing.*"

"*Wo ye hen gaoxing*," said Baxter.

The rest of the family stood agog at the exchange that had just taken place. Peng put her hands over her mouth and kept giggling.

"What the hell was that?" said Pete-O, rolling his chair closer to Peng.

"That was all the Chinese I learned from a library book," said Baxter.

"What did she say?" asked Lilith Ann. "And what did you say?"

"I said hello. I told her my name and that I was glad to meet her," said Baxter. "I think she said she was glad to meet me. I'm not sure."

"What if she said she needed to use the bathroom, something like that?" said Viv.

"If you think she needs to pee, Viv, then show her the bathroom," said Lilith Ann.

More gesturing from Magda and Viv and they were able to lure Peng down the hall and into the bathroom, where they waved at her before leaving her behind the closed door.

"My stars!" Viv mouthed to Magda. "She's older than me. How old do you think she is?"

"She looks to be about Pete-O's age or close to it," said Magda in her normal speaking voice. Viv tried to shush her, but Magda reminded her that Peng couldn't understand a word either of them was speaking.

"I think it's poetic justice, considering what Pete-O did to her," declared Magda when they returned to the kitchen. "Did you tell everybody what Mama told you on the phone?"

"Didn't have much of a chance to tell it," said Viv. "How's he taking it?" She motioned toward Pete-O, who sat in front of the TV, flipping through channels. "Guess he didn't get the little china doll he thought he'd get."

"I'm not deaf, Viv," said Pete-O, startling her.

"You're still going to marry her, aren't you?"

The room fell silent.

"We'll see."

"You made a deal," said Magda, "and you signed all those papers."

"I agreed to marry a twenty-four year-old." Pete-O flipped through three more channels before settling on a fishing show.

"And she agreed to marry a man with two legs," said Magda. She put both hands on her hips and stepped around the table to face her uncle. His eyes were on the television. "That woman back there came all the way around the world because you promised to marry her, so if we have to have ourselves a shot-gun wedding then that's what we'll do."

"Lord have mercy, you sound more like your mother every day," said Viv.

"I don't think she looks so bad," said Kimmy. "Cuter than most women your age."

"He didn't want a woman his age," said Magda. "Wanted himself a young thing half his age."

"Twenty-four's more like a third his age," said Kimmy. "He's sixty-three now."

"He's got to marry her no matter how old she is. She can't just live at Lilith Ann's indefinitely, and he can't send her back," said Viv. "He can't, can he?"

"Of course he can't," snapped Magda. "He got a lawyer to handle everything. There's a contract."

Pete-O suddenly threw the remote control at the wall. Then he jerked his wheelchair toward the women around the kitchen table and made a fist in the air. "All of you shut your damn

mouths. I swear, if I'd known I was going to have a bunch of women chortling around my house and telling me what to do I would have stayed in prison. I said I'd marry her, so I'll marry her just to shut all of you up."

"Yay," Kimmy clapped her hands. "There's going to be a wedding."

"I ain't wearing no suit again for a wedding," said Rob Jr. from his place on the den floor, where he lay watching a fishing show on the TV.

"You don't have to, hon. This will be a Justice of the Peace wedding," said Lilith Ann.

"They call it a Magistrate now," said Pete-O. "I had it already set up for next Friday, and nobody needs to be there except two witnesses. Jack can do that and," he looked around the crowd, "I reckon Baxter can go. He's the only one of you who can keep quiet."

"You mean the rest of us won't even get to go? That's not fair," Kimmy said with her lips in a fake pout.

"We'll do a reception at the church," said Viv. "We can do the shower at the same time, and if we can find somebody who can speak Chinese we can discuss getting her baptized."

"Oooh, that'll be fun. I can fix a pineapple upside-down cake," said Kimmy.

"Hey, she's been in the bathroom a long time," said Magda. "Don't you think we ought to check on her?"

"What are you looking at me for?" said Pete-O. "Junior, go and get me the remote back."

"I think you broke it," said Rob Jr.

"Then get me the pieces and I'll fix it," Pete-O snapped. When he had the pieces in hand, he looked back at Magda. "You going to stand there or you gonna see about Shu—Peng?"

Without further discussion Magda and Viv headed down the hall and Magda knocked on the door. "Peng, you all right?"

Words of reply that no one could understand came from the bathroom.

"She's conscious, so she must be okay," Viv whispered.

"Peng, do you need anything?" Magda rolled her eyes at the uselessness of her question. There was silence for a minute, and then the door handle turned and Peng stood before them looking embarrassed, a wad of toilet paper in her hand.

"Oh honey," said Magda, "that goes in the toilet." She led Peng back to the toilet, which had mercifully been flushed. Magda pointed at the paper in Peng's hand and then down at the toilet. Peng shook her head "no" and clung to the paper. Magda tried to push her hand toward the toilet, but Peng pulled it back up, pointed at the floor around the toilet and spoke.

"How do we get her to throw it in there?" said Magda.

"I don't want to touch it," said Viv, recoiling from Peng's hand.

Magda finally had the idea to pantomime the actions of what to do with toilet paper. She took a piece from the roll, wadded it up, dropped it into the bowl, and then flushed. Peng gave a startled protest at first, but finally dropped her own in and flushed again.

"Pete-O is in for it," said Viv, a big smile on her face.

Chapter 11

L ilith Ann's house was three times as big as Pete-O's, yet no one lived in it except for Lilith Ann and Magda. Peng was given a room on the second floor, and it had its own bathroom with a shower, a toilet, and two sinks. The room was even bigger than the KFC restroom in Xinzheng. Towels hung on a wall rack next to the sinks. A bottle of soap sat on the counter between the sinks, and the place smelled of flowers. When she stood at the sink to wash her hands and face in water that surprised her with its warmth, her feet were on a thick yellow rug that felt like a chick's down under her bare toes. Pete-O's bathroom did not have a rug, and she did not know if his house had hot water like Lilith Ann's, because she never figured out how to turn on the faucets.

The bed she slept on that first night was so soft and high, she woke up several times afraid she would fall off during the night. Finally, around 4:00 a.m., she pulled her pillow and the comforter off the top and slept on the carpeted floor until the sounds of the house awoke her at 7:00. Peng combed her hair and pulled on a pair of pants and a simple blouse underneath her jacket. Lilith Ann was in the kitchen, one that was even bigger than the kitchen in the restaurant in Peng's village, preparing eggs and cooking strips of meat. Bread baked in the oven, and the kitchen table held jars and small plates of more food. Coffee brewed in a machine on the counter, a drink Peng had tried a few times but never much liked. There were no dogs around that Peng could see, and she was relieved.

Before she left home, she feared that Pete-O would find out about what had happened and change his mind. Any man would if he knew, her father had warned her, and she spent several of her last nights in her brother's house back in China crying herself to sleep with worry and fear. Part of her worried that Pete-O would back out of their arrangement, and another part of her worried he wouldn't. Staying or leaving: both possibilities brought a future of what Peng could see only as misery without her family or misery with her family. She found no peace, and the three hours she spent sleeping on Lilith Ann's plush floor that morning, with the thick blanket covering her body, had been the most solid rest she'd had in a month.

"You ready for some breakfast?" asked Lilith Ann, spooning eggs onto two plates. "Magda's run off somewhere early, but she didn't say what for. She does that sometimes," Lilith Ann said, shaking her head. She placed two slices of bacon on each plate and slipped an oven mitt over her hand. "I don't know if you've ever had a biscuit before, but I think they're about the best things God ever invented." She pulled out the cookie sheet of golden brown biscuits and slid it onto the stove top. Using a metal spatula, she scooped up two biscuits and popped them onto Peng's plate, followed by two for herself. "Since you don't know how to do this, I'm going to put some butter on one biscuit and jelly on the other. Then you can decide which one you like better and next time you can choose how you'd like it." Lilith Ann carried the two plates to the table and put one down at her place and one down for Peng. She sliced through the middle of each of Peng's biscuits. Filling one biscuit with a pat of melting butter and the other biscuit with jam, she told Peng what each was, and Peng tried to repeat the words butter and jam. "You'll need to know those words soon enough," said Lilith Ann. She poured two cups of black coffee and sat down at her seat.

"We pray before we eat around here to thank the Lord for what he's given us. I guess since you're an atheist then you don't know about that sort of thing, but I know you can't help it. I don't reckon Pete-O does it before he eats either, so you'll be alright on that count. But Lord help you if you ever go to Viv's place and you don't bow your head. Now, hold your hands together like this in front of your face and close your eyes."

Peng watched her in befuddlement.

"Like this," said Lilith Ann, demonstrating.

Peng held her prayer hands together and stared at them.

"Like this," said Lilith Ann, taking Peng's hands between her own.

Peng felt the calloused, dry warmth of the other woman's flesh. There was something in that comforting touch that made her feel for an instant that she would cry. Lilith Ann's eyes were closed, so Peng closed hers as well.

"Dear Lord, we thank you for this food, and we thank you for getting this woman here safely to America. We thank you that she is now in a Christian nation where all are free to worship your Son, our Savior Jesus Christ, and not have to live in the dark clouds of being an atheist in a heathen land. Amen." Lilith Ann opened her eyes and saw that Peng kept hers closed. "You can eat now," she said, patting Peng's hands before releasing them.

The bread with the yellow sauce tasted heavy and oily. The one with the sweet, fruit-flavored spread was better, but she ate the first one as well to be polite. Peng had eaten eggs many times before, but it perplexed her that Lilith Ann did not know to put tomatoes in them. "Good?" asked Lilith Ann, and Peng repeated it to her. "Good."

"Well now, so far you've learned *butter*, *jelly*, and *good*. I'd say we're having a productive morning," said Lilith Ann. "You've got four days before you marry Pete-O. We'll make the best of it while we can."

"Good," Peng repeated, and the two women laughed.

The rest of the morning was spent learning how to use the washing machine and dryer. Lilith Ann preferred hanging her clothes on the line in the back yard, but Pete-O did not have a clothesline, so for Peng's sake she used her dryer for teaching purposes. While they waited for the machines to finish their cycles, Lilith Ann took out her broom, but Peng needed no instructions for that. She had the entire kitchen swept clean before Lilith Ann washed up the breakfast dishes. Peng was a quick study, and the last two loads of laundry she did on her own, turning the knob to the exact position Lilith Ann had showed her and adding the detergent to the line that Lilith Ann had pointed to on the plastic cup. Peng was pleased with the clean smell the clothes had when she pulled them, still hot, from the dryer as soon as the buzzer went off. They folded the clothes from the dryer and Lilith Ann showed Peng where to put the clean towels in both bathrooms. There was no end of things to look at in Lilith Ann's house. So many rooms had soft carpeted floors, and each room had pictures on the walls. Some were photographs of family members, and some were paintings of flowers or bridges or old houses that looked like pictures Peng had seen of America many years ago when it was a young country. The house had so many beds, six that she counted, and each bed was covered in many blankets and comforters and pillows. Some even had small pillows that were much too small for any real purpose other than to be pretty. In one room, while Lilith Ann talked, Peng caught her using the word, "Magda," the name of the woman who was her daughter, so she figured out that it was the room where Magda slept. They entered with the purpose of hanging some of her freshly washed jeans in the closet. Lilith Ann talked almost constantly, and while she pulled out hangers from the closet and put her daughter's jeans on them, Peng looked at the photographs and postcards that lined the big mirror atop a small table. She gasped with recognition when she saw that one of them was of the Great Wall. She'd never been to the Wall herself, but she knew the place, Badaling, from studying photographs in books. Lilith Ann reached down to Magda's bed and began smoothing out the sheets and rearranging the pillows. Peng couldn't hide her amazement at Lilith Ann's work for her daughter. Why wasn't Magda doing all this work for her mother? Magda looked to be at least twenty-five. Why wasn't she married and with babies by now? Was there some secret in her past, too? Peng could not think of why this woman, who was nearly to her prime marrying age, would still be at home with her mother, who still washed her clothes and straightened her bed. Something terrible had to be wrong with her.

"It's nearly time for Dr. Phil," said Lilith Ann, checking her watch. "You don't know who Dr. Phil is, but I never miss him. He sets people straight. I wish this family could go and see him about some things." She waved a hand in the air and gestured for Peng to follow. "Come this way. I'll get us some Cokes."

The show with the bald-headed man was mostly talking between angry people, except the man whom Lilith Ann said was called Dr. Phil never got angry. He pointed his finger a lot, and the other people shut up and listened to him when he did. The people in the audience seemed to like whatever Dr. Phil said, because they applauded after he talked, even when the people on the stage sitting around him began to cry. Peng was sure he was not trying to say cruel things to them; he often touched them gently on their hands as if he were a firm uncle or father deciding who would be punished. She was also sure that the punishment, which was not carried out on the television, was not very bad because some of them even smiled through their tears and nodded, accepting what he pronounced.

But the best part of watching the television was the commercials. Peng saw many products that she wanted to try. One was for M&M's, which she had eaten before and liked very much, and another was for American toilet paper, which she imagined must be very soft. Her favorite commercial amazed her. In it, a woman rubbed herself all over with soap in a shower just like the one Peng had in her bathroom upstairs. Peng had taken only baths, and the water had to be heated up over a fire. This woman in the commercial stood in steaming hot water that poured over her, and she smiled as she slowly rubbed the soap from a bottle over her arms and shoulders. The soap must have smelled wonderful; whenever the woman rubbed it over her skin, cartoon flowers sprouted from her flesh. She was clearly enjoying this experience as if it were a magical gift, and Peng could not wait to try the shower upstairs. Pete-O had a bathtub, but she had not noticed if there was a showerhead on the wall above it. She hoped there would be. She made up her mind that she would not be afraid of it if there was.

"Hey there," Viv's voice called from the front door.

"We're back here watching Dr. Phil," Lilith Ann called out.

"I hope I'm not interrupting anything important," said Viv, coming in and dropping her purse on the floor. She sat down next to Peng on the sofa.

"It's almost over," said Lilith Ann. "This seventeen-year-old girl wants to marry a boy who's been in prison and hasn't got a job, and her parents tried their best to talk her out of it. That's sort of funny, isn't it?" Lilith Ann raised her eyebrows at Peng, who was focused on the show. "Dr. Phil asked her if she would go to a store and buy a defective product on purpose, but she's got her mind made up. There's just no talking to some people."

"I got everything set for the reception," said Viv. "The girls in my Sunday School class promised to come and they're going to give her a little wedding gift."

"Don't let them give her anything from the church box," said Lilith Ann.

"They won't do that. They took up a collection last Sunday, and it'll be something nice. Lisa's doing the shopping, and she works at Walmart, so it'll be fine."

"Oh good grief, don't let it be a gift certificate. The last thing we need is Pete-O driving her up to Walmart," said Lilith Ann.

"They know," said Viv. "They'll get her something she needs, like some cleaning supplies." She shook her head in Peng's direction, but Peng was studying a commercial with a woman mopping a floor. "Do you reckon she knows about why Pete-O went to prison?"

"He said she knows all about it," said Lilith Ann.

"And she still wanted to marry him?"

"What choice does she have now? Poor little thing," said

Lilith Ann, reaching for her Coke. "She's pretty sharp. I showed her how to use the washer and dryer, and she can sweep a floor like nobody's business."

"Well, no disrespect, but they teach those little retarded people at the training center how to do that kind of stuff, too."

"She's not retarded, Viv. I'm just saying she's a hard worker and she seems to want to please." She allowed an appropriate pause and then added, "I taught her how to pray, too."

"Oh, you did not!" Viv's face lit up and she clapped her hands. Peng turned to see why the horse-faced woman with the bleached hair was so happy.

"We did."

"Can she actually say a prayer?" asked Viv.

"Not yet, but she knows what it means, and she knows that we pray before we eat."

"That's the first step," said Viv, holding up her prayer hands. "The Lord has plans for this woman. I just know it."

"So does Pete-O. I just hope they don't clash," said Lilith Ann.

No one in the Hemper-Boyd family was the right size to loan a dress to Peng for the wedding. Lilith Ann, Viv, and Magda were too tall. Kimmy was too thin. Since Pete-O refused to spring for a new dress, Lilith Ann ended up taking Peng to Goodwill and buying a simple blue dress that needed to be hemmed, but otherwise it fit the slightly thick-hipped, five feet tall Peng just fine. Lilith Ann turned up the sleeves so that they hung evenly at Peng's wrists. "I can fix that," she said. Peng considered herself in the mirror outside the dressing room. Her dress was light periwinkle, and she found herself holding her breath as she looked. She tentatively touched the shoulder as she smiled and said a shy "thank you." When they got the dress home, Lilith Ann took Peng to the room with her sewing machine, a windowless cubicle a little bigger than a walk-in closet, on the second floor next to Peng's bedroom. Peng immediately took the scissors from the sewing machine and began cutting off the bottom three inches of the dress. Lilith Ann let her continue, and soon Peng had threaded a needle and was hemming the dress by hand.

"I was going to do that on the machine for you." Lilith Ann leaned over to watch Peng's fingers move and saw that her stitches were evenly spaced and straight. "I'll be doggone. Somebody sure taught you how to sew." Peng smiled and tried to explain something to Lilith Ann. Then she made some motions with her hands, but the meaning was lost. Finally, she just smiled again and resumed her stitching.

"I'm sorry we haven't been able to talk. You just need to learn some more English, and then we'll be able to share stories and such." Lilith Ann took hold of the scissors, picked up one of the sleeves and began cutting it about an inch below the fold she had made in the hem at the Goodwill. Pulling a needle from the pin cushion atop her sewing machine, she took the spool of thread that Peng had used, and focused on the tiny objects through her bifocals. After a few unsuccessful tries, she threaded the needle, pulled the sleeve inside out, and repositioned the hem. She didn't normally hand-sew anything, but Peng's handiwork inspired her to fold under the raw edge and then whipstitch around the sleeve, the way her mother had taught her to do and the way someone, certainly Peng's mother, had taught Peng to do.

"I tried to teach Magda how to sew, but she didn't get much past cutting out the pattern, and that was only after I pinned the pieces down for her. Some girls just don't take to doing housework, but I always loved to sew. I made all of Magda's dresses for her up until she decided she had to have store-bought stuff. I saved them all, thinking I'd have a granddaughter someday to pass them on to. I've got Jessica Ann, but Kimmy doesn't know how to wash and press things the way I always did Magda's Sunday dresses. They'd probably be a raggedy mess if I let her take them. At one time I even made the crocheted lace that went around the neck. Mmmm, I used to make little collars, and once I even made a brimmed hat for Magda to wear on Easter. She must have been about four years old. They don't argue with you when they're four. Unless they're Kimmy's kids. I guess I was thinking that maybe you and Pete-O would maybe have a little girl. I mean, that's what I was thinking before I saw that you were, you know, as old as you are."

Peng stopped her stitching, and for a moment Lilith Ann thought maybe she had understood what she'd said.

"I don't mean to criticize you. It's just that, we were led to believe, well, we were told that you were twenty-four years old."

Peng held the hem of the dress in her hands and watched Lilith Ann carefully.

"I'm not blaming you one bit for any of what happened. It was just a surprise, that's all. We really don't care how old you are. I reckon Pete-O might, but he's going to marry you. You know, get married?" Lilith Ann pointed to her ring finger on her left hand. "Tomorrow, you'll be Pete-O's wife." Lilith Ann looked down at the sleeve in her hand and felt a wave of sorrow flow over her so fast and hard that her eyes filled with tears before she knew what hit her. She pulled her glasses from her face and wiped her bare forearm over her eyes, spilling tears onto the periwinkle sleeve that lay across her lap. Peng sat frozen and embarrassed. She didn't know what move she could possibly be expected to make on such an occasion. Lilith Ann must have remembered something terrible, something that had hurt her tremendously. She'd been saying Magda's name, so maybe she had been talking about whatever was wrong with her daughter who was not married. Maybe Magda had a secret like hers, one that everyone around the family knew, and she was trying to tell her what Magda had done to bring so much shame that not a single man anywhere would want to marry her, so Lilith Ann was forced to keep this husbandless daughter under her roof, the daughter who was honor-bound to take care of Lilith Ann and not the other way around. Peng put her head back down and continued with her sewing. Lilith

Ann took a few deep breaths and wiped the remaining tears from her eyes. Then she sniffed and picked up her sleeve, and the two women kept working on the dress in silence.

Chapter 12

*L*ilith Ann *knew more about Pete-O than anyone else alive. She* didn't know the things he used to talk about with Jack, when Jack hung around with his uncle after school, and— God forgive them all—the day of the shooting at Walmart. She remembered Pete-O from the day he was born. She was the oldest of the family, followed by Norva, who died while Pete-O was in prison, then Baxter, and then just over a year later Pete Othel came into the world establishing himself as the new royalty of the Hemper household. Baxter was a quiet child, sometimes saying absolutely nothing for days. Pete-O had expected to be waited on and catered to from the time he was born. He was a bully, but he was a helpless kind of bully who badgered Lilith Ann into taking care of him because he genuinely did not seem to know how to do it himself at no matter what age. Baxter was just over a year older, but Pete-O treated him like a younger brother. They ran together, but all the kids knew Baxter "wasn't right," which meant he was usually the one who was put up to committing whatever mischief Pete-O thought up.

In 1963, Birmingham, Alabama was already securely on the map thanks to Martin Luther King Jr., and the 16th Street Baptist Church bombing was the latest embarrassment for a city torn by hate and fear. Drayton was an hour to the east, and the people of the town, like most every other Southern town, processed the news with a broad mixture of horror, anger, glee, shame, empathy, indifference, amusement, and rage. People expressed disgust that four young girls could be murdered in their church, a place of God's refuge, and still others said it was a necessary act to keep "those people" in their place. Pete-O's family was not openly racist in their views, but like most Southern white families they kept prejudice polite and

secured snugly under the mantle of "Christian standards." Robert Chambliss was the man who had planted nineteen sticks of dynamite in the church, but Pete-O didn't know this until almost fifteen years later when he saw a photograph of Chambliss being taken into custody, and there was something in the cocky way he looked that made Pete-O want to be like him. Holding a cigarette in the corner of his smiling mouth and reaching into his pocket for a lighter, Chambliss moved like a man headed for his car after a hard day's work to go out for a beer with friends.

As a child, Pete-O had no real understanding of the depth of the calamity, but as an adult he was determined to make his mark in this movement of social change that was sweeping over his community, stripping his world of the order that white people had held fast to for decades. In his first act of destruction that could have altered the course of local history, Pete-O decided he would bomb the Drayton AME Church; and because he was unsuccessful in recruiting Tybee Norris, his best friend, to help, he had no choice but to enlist Baxter. In 1963 Alabama, if a family had a child who was "not right," as the family liked to say of Baxter, they didn't talk about it, and they certainly didn't seek help. Baxter was usually compliant when Pete-O duped or pressured him into mischief, but he could also be unreliable and contrary, a risk Pete-O was going to have to take.

The problem Pete-O ran into first was that he didn't know where to lay hands on dynamite. When he did find a place, a local construction company, he discovered that it was locked up tighter than Fort Knox. So, he settled on a different plan. He would burn the church down.

Getting gasoline wasn't difficult at all. His father kept gallons of it in their shed to power the lawn mower. It was October, and the mowing season was nearing its end, but two gas cans remained. Pete-O's plan was to break out a church window and send Baxter through it with instructions to open the side door near the pastor's study. Pete-O would carry the gas cans inside, saturate the floors, light the match, and then he would make Alabama history.

Pete-O had to wait until his parents were gone to put his plan into motion. He got his opportunity in early November when they were invited to a birthday party for one of his father's co-workers. Lilith Ann was left in charge of her brothers, and Norva planted herself in front of the TV. Pete-O told Lilith Ann that he and Baxter were going to play in the treehouse in the back yard. He knew she was loath to go to check up on them, since the treehouse was a precariously attached piece of wood high up in a sycamore tree at the rear of their property, ringed in pine cones, sticks, and hidden swampy patches. They could be gone away up in that treehouse for hours and Lilith Ann wouldn't come near it.

The ride to the church was just over three miles, but the full can of gasoline hanging from the handle bars, bumping against the front wheel of his bike, slowed Pete-O down considerably. When they arrived, the yard was dark and the white clapboard church sat in blissful calmness next to an open pasture. From somewhere down the road a dog barked huskily in the open night air, sounding ominously loud.

The parking area in front of Drayton AME was no more than a dirt lot. Pete-O got off his bike and began pushing it through knee-high weeds around to the back of the church. Without a word, Baxter followed. They leaned their bikes against the side of the building, and Pete-O loosened his belt to release the wrench he had secured underneath. The windows were higher than he had calculated on trips down Maney Branch Road. Pete-O raised his arm and smacked the wrench against the glass, but it didn't break. He muttered a curse under his breath and looked around for something to stand on. "Damn niggers ain't even got any cement blocks or nothing around here." Baxter stood behind him, staring across the pasture and into the darkened woods, where twinkling

lights shone through the trees like fireflies.

"Baxter! Are you listening to me?" Pete-O slapped his older brother's head from behind. "See if you can find something for me to stand on."

Baxter set off around the church, his eyes on the brightening stars, while Pete-O kept up his whacking on the frosted glass until it finally gave and the bottom broke away with a crash on the hardwood floor inside. "Baxter! Baxter, I got it. Come back!" But Baxter was on the other side of the building, standing at the edge of the field staring off at nothing that Pete-O could make out. Pete-O grabbed his brother by the arm and led him back to the window with no more sound than their sneakers rustling through the weeds. Hoisting the much lighter Baxter onto his shoulders, he leaned against the white clapboards.

As Baxter pulled himself over the window ledge, his palm grazed a piece of glass Pete-O had missed. He dropped down onto the shard-covered floor inside and clinched his bleeding fist to his chest.

"Remember what I said do? Go to the side door and unlock it," Pete-O called up to Baxter's disappearing form.

Pete-O ran to the side door and waited for the sound of his brother's footsteps. He put his head to the door and listened.

Inside, Baxter sat down across from the broken window and let his eyes adjust to the dim interior of the church. The wooden pew was cool and smooth under his legs, and he let his body be enveloped in the darkness and safety of that place. On the wall above the pulpit was a wooden cross, rough-hewn, the way Baxter imagined Christ's would actually have looked. It rose fifteen feet up the back wall, and the crossbar stretched across the choir loft like two comforting arms. Baxter stood and stepped lightly across the floor and up onto the platform where the choir normally sat. He went down the center aisle of short pews and stopped in front of the cross and laid his bleeding hand upon the wood. When he drew his hand away, there was the print of his palm shining in the moonlight from the windows.

"Baxter, you sumbitch, open that door!" Pete-O was yelling into the broken window. "I'm gone kill you if you don't open that door right this minute!"

Baxter caught sight of a moth fluttering against a different window, a rapid shadow hitting the glass in its feeble attempt at escape.

"Baxter, somebody's coming! A car's coming into the parking lot! You'd better hide!" In a minute Baxter heard a car door slam and then a woman's voice calling his name. He thought it odd that someone would be calling him in this silent, darkened place, but he didn't want to leave. He liked it inside the church at night. There was no reason to leave.

There was a rustling sound outside, and then the clear shrill voice of Lilith Ann. "Baxter, we've all got to get out of here now. Come on out the side door and let's go before anybody sees us."

Baxter stood up and walked to the window. Down below, he saw his sister, and Pete-O stomping the ground and flinging his fists as if he were looking for a fight. "This has gone far enough, Baxter. You come on out of there and let's get your bikes in the trunk of the car. We're liable to get ourselves lynched if somebody from this neighborhood happens by here," said Lilith Ann.

"Only white people lynch," said Baxter.

"Well, this white sister is going to lynch you if you don't do as I say and get out here to the car!"

Baxter unlocked the side door from the inside and, taking one last look around the Spartan interior of the church, slipped out. The dog with the ominous-sounding bark from earlier started up again as the brothers hoisted their bikes and the gas cans into the back of Lilith Ann's Ford. Pete-O was surprised to see Norva in the front passenger seat. Lilith Ann ordered him and Baxter to lie down in the back. Everybody knew a car full of white people traveling down Maney Branch Road was up to no good, which made the Hemper kids fair game

for somebody's shotgun. Lilith Ann pushed the Ford down that bumpy gravel road, throwing up dirt and pebbles as they headed toward the highway. She was determined to get her brothers home before their parents arrived.

"How'd you know where we were?" asked Pete-O.

"You know good and well Tybee can't keep his mouth shut. All I had to do was threaten to tell his Mama about those magazines you and him were looking at and he started singing the whole story," said Lilith Ann.

"And boy did he sing it," said Norva. "He even told us about you stealing money from the church collection plate on Easter."

"He took a dollar, too! I'll kill that sumbitch Tybee Norris."

"You'll clean up that dirty mouth or I'll tell Mama about what you did tonight," said Lilith Ann.

"No you won't, 'cause you don't want Mama to know you weren't keeping your eyes on us," said Pete-O. This gave Lilith Ann cause to reassess the situation. She knew that Pete-O had her nailed, and almost as bad, she knew that he knew it, too. She needed to come up with another offense to threaten turning him in for. There were so many.

"I'm still bleeding," said Baxter.

"What?" Lilith Ann cast a quick glance over her shoulder. "My hand."

"Holy moly! He's cut," said Pete-O.

Norva turned in her seat and held up Baxter's hand to the light, making him wince. A fresh line of blood ran from his palm and dripped onto the seat, and Lilith Ann nearly screamed. "This looks bad," said Norva. "We need to get him to the hospital."

"We could tell them he cut it on a saw blade," said Pete-O.

"Why in the world would anybody be messing with a saw blade at night?" asked Lilith Ann. They reached the highway and she made a right turn onto the smooth road, relieved to be driving on familiar ground.

"We could stop and get drinks and say he broke his bottle,"

said Pete-O. "Say he tripped and fell and broke it in his hand when he hit the ground."

"There's blood all over the place, Lilith Ann. We've got to do something," said Norva.

"Alright! Let me think a minute." Lilith Ann drove on silently while taking quick glances in the rearview mirror and thinking about Pete-O's idea. She was in trouble for being out at night with her brothers and sister in the car no matter what she did at this point, and if she didn't get Baxter to a doctor she would be in even more trouble. "Alright, fine then," she said, succumbing to the inevitable. "Pete-O, give Norva a dime and let her get a Co-Cola soon as we can find a place."

It took Pete-O three tries to break the bottle. As the sugary liquid spilled out onto the pavement, he regretted passing up the opportunity to take a few swigs. He grabbed up the pieces and jumped back into the car.

"Gimme your hand, Baxter. We've got to put some blood on this bottle."

Baxter let Pete-O rub the broken bottle pieces against his hand until they were smeared with his blood. Within fifteen minutes, Lilith Ann was parking her Ford at the Drayton Medical Center, a sleepy little hospital barely big enough to earn the name. Everyone jumped out of the Ford at once and Pete-O charged ahead, pushing through the ER door with a bloody, broken bottle piece in the air. He thrust it at the first nurse he saw. "My brother cut his hand on this Co-Cola bottle and he needs stitching up."

Before she could ask where the brother was, Lilith Ann led Baxter through the door, his wound now a crusted over mess down past his wrist. "Well Lordamercy, why didn't anyone think to wrap a towel around his hand? And get rid of that nasty Coke bottle," chided the nurse, leading Baxter toward an examining room. Lilith Ann, Norva, and Pete-O with his broken bottle sat on the vinyl chairs in the waiting room. Lilith Ann whispered to Pete-O that if he ever tried to set any building on fire again, be it a church or a doghouse, she would take that blood-smeared Coke bottle and slice his throat with it.

Baxter's hand took six stitches, and when they all got home their parents gave them a half hour of scolding for riding around at night when they were supposed to be home. Two days later there was a two-inch column in the Sunday paper about a shattered window and a bloody intruder desecrating the cross in the Drayton AME Church.

Chapter 13

L ilith Ann leaned into the car. *"Are you sure you don't want me to come along and help?"*

"Help what?" quipped Pete-O from the passenger side.

Lilith Ann didn't bother answering. In the back seat next to Baxter and looking small and frightened, Peng held a bouquet of cornflowers and white daisies that Lilith Ann had bought for her off the sale rack at Kroger's the night before.

"All right, Jack, no speeding. I want my car back in one piece. And don't be late to the church. Viv's got half of Drayton coming." Of course that wasn't even close to true. Viv had strong-armed a few friends into coming to the reception, and a few others just wanted to see who was marrying Pete-O. Jack waved his mother off and the wedding day began.

"One of these days you're going to buy her flowers your own damn self," muttered Lilith Ann to the back of her brother's head as the car pulled away.

The Rayle County Courthouse was not an attractive site and certainly not the place any bride dreamed of having her wedding. The front of the building was constructed like any government administration building in the seventies, with lots of burnished chrome and painted bricks. The place could have been anything from a recreation complex to a Social Security office to a dialysis center. Once Pete-O got his chair through the front doors that Jack held open, he caught the stares from the two women at the reception desk who knew everyone in town, especially ex-convicts, housebreakers, juvenile delinquents, and lawyers. Pete-O gave them a smirk as he passed. On the third floor, Pete-O, Jack, and Baxter sat quietly outside the magistrate judge's office, and they waited their turn to be let into the chambers to be married. Two other couples were already ahead of them, and the time it took Pete-O to process the necessary paperwork filled the near hour they had to wait for their turn. Peng signed her name wherever Pete-O told her to. When Judge Beckman's secretary called them in for the ceremony and Pete-O entered the chambers, he gave a snort of derision. Judge Beckman was a woman.

"I believe I know who you are," she said.

Pete-O gritted his teeth. "I'm here to get married."

"Yes, I gathered that. And you're Baxter. I know your story as well." Baxter gave her a slow, shy nod.

Judge Beckman was a slight woman in her early fifties and dressed like a person who thought regularly of running for office. "I suppose this is our bride." Judge Beckman reached out to Peng and clasped her hand easily, holding it a few seconds before releasing it. She turned to Jack. "And you are?"

"Jack Hemper, Pete-O's nephew." He self-consciously shoved his hands into his jean pockets before the judge had a chance to offer hers.

Judge Beckman's face lit up with recognition. "Ah, you have grown up so much since you were in the papers. Well now," she said, quickly getting to business. "Let's see your paperwork." She took the thin folder from her secretary and expertly perused the first few pages. "You are Peng Liu?"

Peng looked at the judge and then at Pete-O. "You say the last name first," said Pete-O. "Liu Peng. That's the way you say Chinese names."

"Can't she tell me that?"

Pete-O rolled his chair a few feet closer and for a moment Jack was afraid his uncle was going to do something foolish. "She doesn't speak English more than a few words."

"I see," said Judge Beckman, her bleached teeth showing widely. "Peng? Can you understand what I'm saying?" Her voice was gentle and feminine in a way that seemed to offer comfort and support. Peng smiled back but said nothing.

"I said she didn't speak English."

"I'm sure you're right, but that leaves us with a problem. If she can't speak English, then she can't confirm that she is here of her own free will to get married."

The tension in the air sucked all the goodwill right out the window. "Take a look at her. Does she look like anybody's forcing her?" asked Pete-O.

Judge Beckman's eyes dropped their kindly expression, and her voice became clipped and firm. "I'll be the judge of whether anyone in my courtroom is acting out of free will or something else. Melba, get Mr. Chen on the phone and ask him to come down here right away, please."

The secretary grabbed the phone and hit two buttons.

"You don't even have to look up his number?" asked Pete-O.

"We order a lot of Chinese," said Judge Beckman, her smile returning, but not as brightly as before.

Pete-O, Peng, Jack, and Baxter returned to the waiting area and sat while a very pregnant young woman and her soon-to-be husband passed into the chambers next. Twenty minutes later they came out smiling and being congratulated by a stern-faced man who was certainly the young woman's father. Not long after, Mr. Chen, the owner of Drayton's only Chinese restaurant, came huffing up the stairs. He reeked of cigarettes and his forehead was covered in sweat.

"Hi there, Mr. Chen," said Jack, "you could have taken the elevator, you know."

"No elevator," said Mr. Chen. "Makes me nervous."

He nodded his hellos, looked curiously at Peng, and then went into the court chambers without even knocking on the door.

"Reckon some folks has got free rein with the right government officials," said Pete-O, stretching his back against his chair. "It's amazing what a little free General Chow's chicken will buy you."

In a few minutes Melba stuck her head out the door. "Miss Peng, can you come in here?" She made exaggerated motions for Peng to come forward.

"It's alright," said Jack. "They just want to talk to you." He touched Peng's arm and motioned for her to follow Melba. Still clutching her flowers, Peng went inside.

"I guess some time today they might let the rest of us in there. Or maybe that judge will just marry Peng to Mr. Chen and be done with it," said Pete-O.

"I thought you were going to call her Shubie," said Jack.

"I planned on it, but then I changed my mind."

"Peng is a better name," said Baxter.

"I guess it's best to be called the name you were born with," said Jack. Pete-O was staring a hole in the door of the judge's chambers, and Jack was trying his best to keep the conversation light.

"When Peng was born, Chinese babies were not named until their one-hundredth day celebration," said Baxter.

"Why was that?" asked Jack.

"No one knew if they'd live," Baxter replied.

Several minutes went by and no one spoke. Finally, Melba reappeared. "Okay," she said, "let's get this show on the road."

Inside the chambers, Peng stood next to Mr. Chen, and she was smiling. "Mr. Hemper," said the judge, "you come next to Peng, and you two stand behind." Baxter and Jack moved to their positions, and Baxter stood with his feet apart and hands behind his back like a Boy Scout at attention.

"Mr. Chen will translate for Peng," said Judge Beckman. She kept her eyes on Pete-O as she spoke, and in less than ten minutes, Pete-O and Peng were husband and wife.

Chapter 14

When Lilith Ann congratulated Viv on using such nice blue-themed decorations for the wedding reception, she didn't know the decorations were leftover from Kimberly Diane Redman's sixteenth birthday party, which never happened because Kimberly ran off with a Pizza Hut manager just three days before the party was scheduled. Mrs. Redman left all the tablecloths, paper plates, napkins, table decorations, and other flotsam in the kitchen closet where it had sat for the past three months. The only thing Viv didn't use was the silver and blue banner that said, "Sweet Sixteen."

The gathering at the church applauded when Pete-O rolled in with his new wife walking beside him.

"Oh Peng, let me put those flowers in water for you," said Viv, taking the bouquet from Peng and disappearing in the kitchen. The fellowship hall was lined in mostly empty chairs. Members of Viv's Sunday School class darted about, arranging the sparse gift offerings and setting out more cookies. The only person not helping was Mrs. Redman, who sat dabbing her eyes. All of the Hemper family was present, including the grandchildren, three of whom lingered near the cake table.

"We should cut the cake," said Viv, returning from the kitchen and managing the reception with the confidence and expertise of a movie director. She took up a long knife and began cutting into the sheet cake on the center table. "Magda, could you start pouring the grape juice?"

"God, we're drinking grape juice?"

"This is the Lord's house and you will not use that language," said Viv in a low voice.

"I can't say God in the Lord's house?"

"Not in that tone."

"This is not the time," said Lilith Ann to Magda, before she

could make her retort. "Now get to pouring the juice."

People began to trickle in. A tall man with frizzy hair and wearing a Tears for Fears T-shirt ambled into the room and looked around nervously. Following him was a woman in tight white pants that revealed a horrific thong. She was clutching an oversized lime bag. The pair stood near the entrance, sizing the place up. A man on crutches with a grimy cast on one leg and a woman wearing sweatpants with a monkey face on the rear edged in next.

"Are those Baxter's friends?" asked Kimmy, sidling up next to Viv.

"Oh good Lord, those people are from the AA meeting downstairs," said Viv.

"Not in that tone," mocked Magda.

Viv was clutching the knife from the cake, watching the man in the Tears for Fears T-shirt as he skirted the gift table with one finger in his mouth, the woman in the monkey pants tagging behind.

"Hey there!" called out a cheerful voice. A young woman appeared carrying a gift wrapped in shiny white paper.

"Oh my goodness, one of them's brought a present," said Kimmy.

Large gold hoop earrings almost touched the young woman's shoulders, and a blue skirt stretched tightly across her behind. The Boyd women reacted with a mixture of horror and amusement at seeing her march straight up to Baxter and begin a lively conversation. After a brief exchange, she delivered her package to the gift table and entered the line for a piece of cake.

"Uncle Baxter, is she a friend of yours?" asked Magda.

"We met last year," was all he offered.

"And? Where'd you meet her?"

Baxter turned to Magda and observed her carefully, until she began to feel uncomfortable, which was something she had never felt before from her uncle. "Baxter?" she said quietly.

"Her name is Janeeca. She worked at the T&A Lounge, but

she got fired."

"The T&A Lounge," said Magda, not loud enough for Viv to hear. "How do you get fired from a crappy dive like that?"

"She was supposed to keep me tied up, but she let me go. The manager fired her. I wasn't taking my pills then. I had a gun."

"Oh geesh, don't say that word out loud around Mama and Viv. Or Kimmy. Or anybody else for that matter," said Magda, leading Baxter to a chair and ignoring the food table with the half-finished glasses of grape juice. Baxter told her everything, including how he had spent the rest of that night sleeping in a deer stand before walking the remainder of the way home at first light. "She works at the Jolly Lolly Day Care Center behind the church. I invited her."

"Do they know she was a stripper? The people at the day care center?"

"She's not a stripper anymore," Baxter said.

"That's good but, well, it doesn't matter."

"She doesn't have a father. She wants to be an organic gardener and a nurse," said Baxter.

"You seem to know her pretty well," said Magda.

"We had doughnuts once. She talks a lot."

"Wow, Baxter." Magda considered her uncle in a way she had never before. He sat calmly, his pale hands resting on his khaki pants, his graying hair falling thinly over his skull. She knew of one other time when he went off his meds, when she was a teenager, and they got a call from a homeless shelter in Birmingham saying they had a man there who fit the description of the missing person report Lilith Ann had filed weeks before. Pointing out that he couldn't possibly have entered any town in the center of Alabama by ship due to a lack of sea water did not deter Baxter's insistence that he'd arrived in an oil rig and needed to report back to his commanding officer before he was declared AWOL. When Magda and her parents arrived to pick Baxter up, he'd gone, but they found him a short way down the interstate trying to hitchhike to Georgia. He was carrying

a trophy with a tiny plaque that said Miss Tri-Cities Rutabaga Queen. Magda displayed the trophy for years on her dresser until she tired of it and sold it in a yard sale. Baxter's demons had always turned him inward, and they frightened him more than he ever frightened anyone else. Magda put her hand on his and squeezed it. "You've had yourself some real adventures."

"I don't mean to," said Baxter.

"Come on. We should go congratulate Pete-O and Peng. And you can introduce me to your friend."

The crowd around the cake table had thinned, and most of the AA members had finished their helpings and departed. Peng was opening gifts while Pete-O watched. A variety of objects from blankets to towels to vases populated the table. "That one's mine," said Magda, pointing at a lavishly wrapped box on the end. "It's a wok."

"I gave her socks," said Baxter, staring ahead at the boxes.

"Socks?"

"Yes."

"Um, I could have gone shopping with you if you didn't know what to buy."

"I knew what to buy. I bought socks."

"But, people usually give things for the house for the bride and groom to start their lives, like cooking utensils or towels, something like that," said Magda. "A pair of socks is not really the best choice."

"I bought fifty-five pairs." Baxter pointed toward a box even bigger than the one concealing Magda's wok.

"You bought Peng fifty-five pairs of socks?"

Viv was handing Baxter's box to Peng, who by now had become adept at pulling the paper off. Her face was pure delight when she saw what was in the box. She began holding up socks, all bound around the middle with various wrappers. There were ankle socks, knee socks, footlets, and calf-high socks in every color and in prints and solids.

"Well I swanee," said Viv, "somebody gave Peng a big box

of socks. I wonder who that could have been." She looked right at Baxter.

In one hand, Peng held up a green pair with hopping frogs. In the other hand, she held up a pair of thick light pink socks. With each new pair she pulled out of the box, she grinned and laughed. Before she put the box away she had removed and inspected every single pair, and no two were alike.

"Baxter, you never cease to amaze," said Magda.

"They were made in China. All of them. I checked," said Baxter. He had an expression that was almost a smile.

"But why? Why socks?"

"My feet get cold at night. When I lived at Stoney Brook I had only two pairs of socks. Everyone should have plenty of socks."

Magda wanted to put her arms around her uncle and tell him she was sorry for his life, for all the unfair, damaged cells in his brain that would make him hitchhike to Birmingham or get tied up at dive bars or hang around with strippers at doughnut shops, but she didn't know how to tell him. How could she find words that would touch any of the places in him that hurt? All she knew how to find were words that whipped and cursed the readers of her letters, and suddenly she felt hollow and small.

A young woman tugged gently on Baxter's arm. "Thanks for inviting me."

"Hello," said Baxter. There was an awkward moment while Magda waited for her uncle to make an introduction, but he was watching Peng open the wok.

"Hi," she said. "I'm Magda, Baxter's niece."

"Oh, your uncle was really kind to me. He bought me a whole box of Dunkin' Doughnuts when I lost my job, and he listened to me for two whole hours when I felt like nobody in the world cared about me. I love doughnuts, and he's a good listener. I mean, he just really listens. Sometimes he leaves doughnuts on my front stoop. Every now and then when I

leave for work in the morning there's a big old box of doughnuts right there in front of my door. He never knocks, but I
know they're from him. And I know all about that, you know,
that terrible thing that happened last Thanksgiving. I mean,
everybody does, but I know that your uncle was only trying to
protect the family. I got interviewed on TV at the courthouse
because I came to see the trial. But it's like I was saying, that's
the kind of person he is. He'd do anything to help people. He'd
even bash somebody's head in to help other people if it needed
doing. And it was real nice of him to invite me to this wedding
party. I was off work today anyway, and I just live a few streets
over, so I was glad to come. I bought placemats. That's my gift."
Janeeca was smiling as if she were being interviewed for the
Miss Alabama pageant. Magda was fast concluding that if she
hadn't worked as a stripper but been a doctor's daughter and
maybe been given braces at the right age, Janeeca might have
had a shot at the title. She was pretty enough.

"Baxter was right about you," said Magda. And then she
added, "he said you were really nice."

"Oh," said Janeeca, gushing. "You are, too. I read one of your
letters last summer."

"My letters?"

"It was for a friend of mine. Her boyfriend hit her. I mean,
the letter wasn't really nice because he didn't deserve anything
nice, but it was nice for you to write it for her since she can
hardly, well…she needed help. She's dyslexic. That's when you
can hardly read because the letters keep flipping around in your
eyes," said Janeeca, making letters in the air with her fingers
as she explained the last part.

Magda searched her mental list of break-up letters from
the summer before and came up with only one person who
had claimed abuse, a detail that had made writing the letter
exceptionally easy. She had suspected the woman was perhaps a hooker or involved in some type of drug production
because of her bad teeth and her nervous habit of chewing at

her fingernails even while she spoke. Magda hadn't liked her, but the connection had been made through Laney in a kind of "friend of a friend" arrangement. The woman had called herself Randy, and the bruises and cuts were still fresh.

"Oh, and just so you know, I've decided to use my real name now. Fanny."

"Fanny?" said Magda. "Your real name is Fanny?"

"I know, I know. My dad said before I was born that he was going to name his son Frank after himself, but there I was and I was a girl, so he named me Fanny. I started calling myself Jan in sixth grade, and then later when I started dancing at T&A, I changed it again because nobody wants to see a Jan or especially a Fanny," she said. "So, here I am. Fanny."

The more Fanny talked, the more Magda liked her. Fanny said whatever entered her mind, and soon Magda began to see her as a kind of filtered version of what she herself could have been like without a mean streak.

For the first half of the reception, Pete-O sat off to one side, disinterested and barely responding to wishes of happiness on his nuptials. Jack remained next to him, but neither one said much. When Robert arrived, the two of them retreated to a corner away from Jack and began an animated conversation in low voices that continued from the opening of the first gift to the tossing of the bouquet, a ritual which Viv first had to mime for Peng so that she would understand the ritual of throwing perfectly good flowers into the air, backwards and over her head, for strangers to fight over until someone caught them.

Robert left and Pete-O returned to his silence next to Jack. Soon the reception ended, and Jack began hauling gifts to his truck for the drive to Pete-O's house. Now Pete-O and Peng's house. Baxter began helping, and soon the truck bed was filled with towels, fifty-five pairs of socks, a wok, placemats, assorted vases and candle holders, one bright blue pocketbook, one blanket, two sets of sheets, one set of carpet cleaning products, a chicken and rooster salt and pepper set, a juicer, a set of potholders decorated with pictures of farm animal heads, a quilted cat stuffed with potpourri, a cheese knife and cutting block, and something in the shape of a rabbit wearing a long pinafore dress that went atop a vacuum cleaner so that when the closet door was open there would be a three foot tall rabbit dressed as a pioneer woman staring out.

"Should one of us talk to her?" said Magda to Viv, when everyone was in the parking lot saying their goodbyes. Magda winced a little as she smiled at Peng, who stood next to Jack's truck holding a plastic container of leftover cookies. "She's married to Pete-O now."

"Jack said the judge called in an interpreter, that Mr. Chen from the Chinese restaurant," said Viv.

"And she did it anyway." Magda sighed and headed for her car.

Chapter 15

*J*ack tried to unload his truck single-handedly at the place now to be called Pete-O and Peng's house, but Peng could not be stopped from grabbing boxes and hauling them inside, earning both amazement and respect from Jack. She balanced the box of socks on her shoulder and carried it without stopping all the way to the bedroom. As soon as all the gifts were safely inside, Jack nodded his goodbyes. Peng gave him her thanks and wished him a safe trip to wherever he was going, but she knew he didn't understand her, just like Pete-O didn't either. After such an adventurous day, she was sorry to see it end.

Mr. Chen had been a surprise at the wedding ceremony because he was the first person she had been able to talk to in days. The words had poured out of her. She told him all about her trip and how she saw that the Pete-O she would be marrying was not the Pete-O she had thought he was, but it was okay with her because she couldn't go back to China. The shame of doing such a thing would be far worse than whatever she was to face in a life with Pete-O. She told Mr. Chen about the years of letters translated for her by her nephew. Once a month for three years she had sat with her nephew to tell him what to write, and then she would take his paper riddled with Chinglish to the post office and mail it off for its month-long journey to Alabama, America. For a long time it was exciting and fun, hearing kind and loving words read aloud to her by her nephew from a man who had no idea what she had done, had never heard the story of her first husband and how he had died. In almost every letter she considered telling Pete-O the full story, but fear stopped her every time she sat down to dictate her thoughts to her nephew, who knew the entire story along with every other person in her village and beyond. For a few minutes, talking with Mr. Chen, Peng considered telling him as well, but then she shivered at the danger of possible

consequences. He asked her again if she was completely sure she wanted to marry Pete-O and she said yes, so the ceremony went on and her secret remained a secret. Mr. Chen seemed to understand her position. He had grown up in the next province, Shandong, so he knew the kind of life she had come from. He had brought his two sisters from home to work in his restaurant, young women who had once worked in the fields like Peng. He told her to come to his restaurant anytime and he would give her a free dinner of sour vinegar cucumbers and mutton as a wedding present.

To Peng, Pete-O's house remained simply Pete-O's house. She could not yet declare it in her own mind as her house, too. The box of socks was hers, a wonderful wedding ritual she had not known about before. There had been no firecrackers, which made Peng feel a little like the wedding was not yet complete. She had never seen a wedding without the exciting *Pop! Pop! Pop!* for the bride and groom to begin their new life together. The silence after the wedding ceremony had been confusing, as if no old doors had been slammed shut behind her the way she expected they should be. She wasn't entirely sure she was married when the judge announced that the two of them were husband and wife. At Mr. Chen's directive, she leaned over to let Pete-O kiss her, and he gave her a quick kiss on the lips. The ceremony had left her with some sense of relief, some assurance of her safety. He could not send her back now. She knew it was against American law for him to deny his responsibility for her once they were married. She would resign herself to be a good housekeeper and learn to cook the foods he liked, and maybe her life would unwind peacefully and she could finally put her past to rest. She would close her eyes at night and hope that she would not cry for the memory of her father, mother, brother, sister-in-law, and nephew, the people she loved most in all the world and whom she would probably never see again. She had given her father what he wanted, and now she must be strong and live out her life as the wife of Pete-O Hemper, the man who had promised to show her a fountain of chocolate.

The wedding night ritual was fast and unceremonious. It took Pete-O a good fifteen minutes to ready himself, and he motioned Peng away when she tried to offer assistance. The consummation of their marriage reminded Peng of a man scratching an enormous itch. When Pete-O was finished, the whole event, which lasted only about five minutes, ceased abruptly and without any subsequent communication. Pete-O rolled over and was soon fast asleep. Peng sat up in the darkness and slipped out of bed to wrap herself in the fleece robe Lilith Ann had given her. It was well-worn and smelled of Lilith Ann's washing powder, a new comfort for Peng, like mangos and fresh grass, two rare scents that she had never smelled together. She pulled the robe around her and tied the thick belt in a loose knot. Her feet were cold, and she grinned at the idea of putting on a pair of her wedding socks. They were from the man who was Pete-O's brother. He had spoken mispronounced Chinese to her at her arrival, and his tones were so off she had barely been able to make out what he was saying, but as poorly as he spoke, his words were the first she had heard in her language from any American. He had said almost nothing else to her since that day, but he had always been kind. Once he had been over at Lilith Ann's house to fix a pipe underneath her sink. Peng watched him from the kitchen door as he kneeled at the open cabinet, smoothly reaching for tools from a box that Lilith Ann kept in the special room where she had a washing machine. He worked for nearly an hour, and when he was finished he put Lilith Ann's toolbox back on the high shelf it had come from, told Peng goodbye in her own language, and then left. Lilith Ann was smiling and speaking rapidly, so he must have repaired whatever had been broken. He did not own a car, something that everyone around her seemed to have. Pete-O had a big van, but it was very old and it smelled funny. She had seen him looking at pictures of big vehicles in a magazine and making phone calls,

so she assumed he was planning to buy a nicer one. He was always on the phone during the times she had been around him.

The older son of Lilith Ann, the one married to the skinny blonde woman with all the children, was usually sitting and talking to Pete-O away from the others. If anyone came near, they stopped talking—anyone except her. Peng's presence did not alter any of their conversations. Pete-O seemed to like the fact that she understood nothing. He had become agitated when Mr. Chen arrived at the ceremony, but he tried hard to keep it to himself. Peng had quickly learned some of Pete-O's moods, a skill she knew was requisite for her survival. There was so much to know, so many new things to master; the thought of all of them made her sigh in dismay and loneliness. None of these people knew her at all. They were kind in their strange and foreign ways, all except for Pete-O, who just seemed distracted and annoyed much of the time. She knew how to make herself hidden, mostly invisible, a skill that bode well with her father after the terrible shame. That secret was so heavy she wanted to extract it from her mind and leave it locked away in some place where no one could find it. Peng put her hands on either side of her head and covered her ears to shut out the sounds, but they were locked inside, and nothing she could do would make them go away. She pinched her mouth shut to keep from crying and held her breath until she could calm herself. Wiping away tears, she dried her hands on her robe and reached into the box of socks. In the darkness she could not see but she could feel the softness of so many socks. Her fingers found a thick pair with short tops and she pulled them onto her feet. Her toes stretched luxuriously in her wedding socks as she eased herself onto a padded chair in the corner. It was comfortably used and molded perfectly to her body.

Peng let her head relax against the back of the chair. Pete-O's snores were not so loud as her brother's had been when she lived in his house in Henan and slept inside the thin-walled feed storage room at the back. The winter air in that room was always frigid. Peng could lie on her cot and see the moon through the small, high, open window above the stacks of fertilizer, a small white dot of snow in the blackness of the universe. She had often wished she could fly to the cold moon, especially in the early days before her brother married Huirong. She would lie very still, hoping the ancestors she was sure were looking in at her would not know she was there if she just refrained from moving even a single muscle. Peng felt the tightening in her chest come again, and she made herself very still.

"I will tell you my story," she said in her own tongue, with the quietest voice she could whisper. "I will tell you everything this one time, and you must never speak to me of it again and never tell another soul." Pete-O didn't stir, and in whispers she began to unravel the tale.

"I was nineteen when I went to the hospital to learn to be a nurse. It was not a hospital like the kind we have today. This hospital was only a few rooms and did not have fancy equipment. This was many years ago when you watched, you learned, and you did it with your own hands if you wanted to do something. There was no university nearby where we could learn. The hospital was in my village. It had two doctors and five nurses. Three of the nurses were longtime workers at the hospital, and two of us were learning. The other young nurse's name was Dandan. We were both very nervous but we were hard workers. We had to do what they told us to do, the doctors and the nurses who taught us. The work was hard and dirty, but I learned fast, faster than Dandan. She was very strong, but her heart was not.

"When the babies were born, sometimes, you see, this was many years ago, sometimes the parents did not want it because it had some problem, and sometimes there were other reasons. There were so many reasons why. It was the job of the old nurse that we called Nai Nai Shu to take the baby. Sometimes she used a bucket full of water, but most of the time she did it with her hands. Nai Nai Shu was fast with her hands and the baby did not feel anything that way. You must understand, she was not a bad person. This was her job. Dandan could not do this work even with her strong hands, because of the softness of her heart. She tried once when the nurses told her she must learn to do it, but she was clumsy and the baby began to cry. The mother, a young girl who already had another daughter at home, began to scream. It was horrible until Nai Nai Shu stopped the sounds from the baby with her quick hands, and then the mother turned over and could not breathe. I told her she must breathe and to be strong for her other daughter, the older one waiting for her at home to come take care of her. I held the young girl's face and looked only at her so that I would not have to look at Dandan's red eyes and shaking body. I was always afraid Nai Nai Shu would make me learn to do this thing, but she scoffed at me and said my arms were too small and that I could never learn it. I was glad. But this was just the beginning. It was later that the terrible thing happened.

"I became a good nurse because I learned to not be afraid, and I was quick to help the doctors. I never cried or said I could not do something. Once there was an accident with a bus and many people were hurt. We worked through the night taking care of the injured people. The doctors had to do surgeries for some who were badly wounded, and I helped one of the doctors remove a man's leg because it was so mangled we could not repair it. The doctor saved his life. This was how I learned. I watched the doctor with the saw, and I learned.

"When I was twenty-two, my father said that I must marry. He made arrangements for me to marry a farmer's son named Kong. I wanted to keep my job, but I could not argue with my father. I quit my job at the hospital, married Kong, and we lived in a small house and worked the fields with Kong's parents and their two young daughters. Kong was a good man and soon I came to love him. Many months went by and then a year passed. We were happy for that time. We grew peanuts in the big fields behind our house. Kong and I grew a small garden and had plenty to eat from our hard work. Soon I forgot how much I missed learning to be a nurse at the hospital. I think that if I had been a rich man's daughter I could have gone to university maybe and become a real nurse in a big city. But that was not my life. Kong did not like for me to talk about my work because he had never been to school beyond the lower grades to learn anything. He could read but not very well.

"The accident happened one day far away in the fields. Another farmer named Ju was driving a tractor that cut down the dead crops while we were preparing the fields for burning. Every year in autumn we burned the fields to ready the soil for planting the following spring. I don't know how Kong got so close to the tractor. Maybe he just wanted to take a look at it because he had always admired Ju's tractor and wanted to drive it himself. He would not talk about it afterwards. But on that day he got too close to the blades and one of them sliced his leg badly. I thought that he had died because there was so much blood, but I knew what to do. I tore the cloth from my jacket and wrapped his leg up as best I could to stop the bleeding, and we took him back to the village to see the doctor at the hospital. He sewed up Kong's leg and I took him home. He could not walk at all, the cut was so bad.

"Kong lay on our bed for a week, but the wound did not seem to get better. His mother and I made poultices for it and I fed him broth, but in a few more days Kong developed a fever and his leg turned dark. I tried to clean it the way I remembered from the hospital, but you must understand, we did not have the clean water and towels and medicines that we used when I worked at the hospital. Days went by. I did the best I could, but his leg became much worse, and it began to smell bad. I begged Kong's father to help me take him back to the hospital. He was a stern man and very poor, but he did not want his son to die, so he and some friends put Kong on a cart and we took him to see the doctor. When the doctor

saw Kong's leg, he was angry. At that time I thought he was angry at me for not taking good care of Kong. He was one of the doctors from when I was a nurse, and I was sure that he expected me to know how to properly care for Kong. I guess I knew when we took Kong to the hospital what had to be done. His wound was festering and the leg was rotting because of it, but the doctor did not want to perform this expensive surgery. We were not like the rich man who had been injured on the bus so long ago. Kong and I had no money, and neither did his father. The doctor gave us some medicine to give to Kong and told us to take him home and make him comfortable. He said the medicine would help him rest and that he would soon be better. I did not believe him, but I did not argue. Kong's father argued with the doctor, but this made the doctor angry that he questioned him and he told us to leave the hospital.

"That night Kong's father and mother stayed with us for a while. His mother helped me change the bandages that stank, and I could see tears in her eyes as she turned away to take the cloths outside. His father sat rubbing his knotted hand back and forth across his chin and fretting uselessly. I made up my mind then what I would do. I told him that the doctor was right and that the medicine would make Kong better if we just let him rest. I made myself smile and lied to the old man saying that I had seen many men, dozens of men, get better in only one day after they took this very medicine. Our house was small with no comfortable place for them to sleep. Why don't you go home to rest and in the morning you can come back and see Kong sitting up and feeling much better, I said. Kong's father argued at first and said they would sleep on the floor next to Kong, but I told him they should be in their own place. I would take care of Kong and in the morning he would be ready to see them.

"After more resistance, they finally agreed that this would be the best plan, but that they would be back after sunrise to see their only son. As soon as they were safely down the road,

I gave Kong more medicine, as much as I thought he could safely take, and soon he was almost asleep. I knew this would not be enough, and I hated myself for what I had to do next. I rolled up a small piece of the cleanest cloth I could find and set it aside. Then I started a fire. The blade had to be as clean as I could make it. The doctor had used a chemical to clean his blade, but I did not have the medicines or a clean place for Kong. He was asleep but he stirred and coughed when I opened his mouth and put the wad of cloth inside. I cried all the way until the moment when I put the small knife to his flesh and muscle to make the skin flaps that I would later sew together. Then I took the saw to his fetid flesh. Before I pushed it into his leg, I made myself remember what I was, who I had been at the hospital. I made myself remember the concentration that I had learned with Nai Nai Shu and how the doctors could depend on me to know what to do. The way to ease suffering was to work efficiently and quickly. Half-measures caused more pain. I shook my head and told myself that I was a nurse saving my husband's life. I would not let myself cry. Kong would die if I did not do this.

"I will never forget what it was like to put the blade to my husband's leg, not ever. The sound the saw made against his bones still makes me tremble to think of it. Kong cried out at first but in a few seconds he passed out from the pain, so I worked fast to wrap up and tie off the arteries with strong thread. I had made the cut above the knee because I wanted to be sure that all of the rot from the wound would be gone. I began sewing the pieces of flesh together the way I had seen the doctors do with many injuries. My work was not very neat, and there was so much more blood than I remembered from the hospital. At one point I became afraid that I could not finish, and my hands began to shake. My heart began to beat very hard as I began to realize that I was not skilled enough to do this thing for Kong, but it was too late. There could be no stopping or he would certainly die.

"I was frightened for Kong. He opened his eyes and looked at me but he could not speak. I sat beside him and tried my best to comfort him and tell him that he would be fine, and in the morning he would see his father and mother. I tried to smile the way we had been taught to do for sick patients to show them there was nothing to be afraid of. He was hot with fever, so I put cold cloths on his forehead and gave him more of the medicine from the hospital, but all it did was send him into a fitful sleep. Hours went by and I could not hold my eyes open any longer. It was almost morning when I lay down next to Kong to let myself rest just a little. I did not mean to sleep, but I did, and soon I awoke to a strained voice calling from above. I thought I was dreaming, that I was hearing the voice of a crow calling out Kong's name, the voice was so strange and high. For a few seconds I saw Kong's father as a large black crow cawing before me, but then I awoke and there he was standing in the room over us. I tried to rise up from the floor, and then I felt that my chest and arms were heavy with blood that had pooled underneath me from Kong's wound after I fell asleep. Next to me, my husband was dead.

"Later that morning I was arrested, and the police said I had murdered my husband. I told them one thousand times that I had tried to save his life, but they would not listen. One of them said I was a murdering monster and he beat me with a splintered stick. That is how I have this scar on my face. Some said I would be put to death for what I had done. I sat alone in a jail cell for seven days before my father and mother would come to see me, their shame was so great. If I could have found a way to die in those days, I would have taken my own life. I no longer cared if they executed me. I would have done the thing again and again in an attempt to save him, no matter what they did to me afterwards. My great regret was not in cutting off his leg, but in not being a good enough nurse to save him afterward. This is what I told the judge when they took me to my trial. I told my story about how I had been studying to be a nurse and about the time I had watched the doctor remove an injured man's leg. I told everything about the day Kong had been hurt and how the doctor would not do the surgery because we had no money. I told the judge the name of the medicine the doctor had given him that did almost nothing except numb the pain and make him sleepy. The doctor was there at the trial, sitting in the front row with his legs sprawled out, smoking one cigarette after another. Kong's father sat behind the doctor all throughout the day, and when the judge called the doctor to give his story, he did not tell the whole truth about the surgery. He claimed he had offered to do it but I had said no because we could not pay him. He made me angry with his lies, but I kept my eyes on the floor and let my tears fall onto my lap.

"Kong's father also told his story of how he came into the house and found me lying in Kong's blood next to his body on the floor. He said that beside me lay a bloody blade and next to it lay Kong's leg, blue and foul. I had planned to take Kong's leg outside and bury it. No one believed that I could do such a thing, leave my husband's leg there, but I could not leave him, even for a moment. I was blind with fear and so tired, more tired than I thought a person could ever be. I could see only Kong before me, until my eyes became so heavy that I saw nothing.

"The judge asked my father-in-law if he thought I meant to kill Kong, but Kong's father looked at the floor and began to cry. His thin body shook so hard I was sure he would fall over dead himself. He said only, 'My son is dead, and she lay in his blood.' He could not answer the question. Maybe his heart was too broken from telling his story, because when he tried to talk his pain overtook him and no words would come. He just kept sobbing, and it hurt my heart to look at this old man who had lost his only son. It was then that I stood from my chair and said I had tried only to save Kong. I was going to say more, to tell him I loved his son and would have given my own life for his, but the policeman who had brought me there pushed

me back into my chair and threatened me. The judge ordered me not to speak again, so I sat silently. I was sure I would die. I had brought shame to myself, my family, and Kong's family. No one would ever welcome me at their door again.

"I don't know what made the judge decide to set me free. Someone said later he had a son who died from illness after his wife left him, and maybe he was thinking that if she had stayed and tried to help him, maybe he would have lived. I thought that story was not likely. Maybe he did not like the lying doctor for his arrogance. Maybe he did not want to see another person die. Maybe he believed me when I told him I had tried not to hurt Kong but to save him. I have thought of a thousand maybes to explain why he told me I should go home to my family and never marry again. People in our village were angry, and some said they would kill me themselves before they would let me come back into my father's house. I did not care if they did. Without Kong, I did not want to live.

"My father and mother took me home quietly, and I lived in the back of their house, not going out the front door for one full year. When I did finally go out the front during the day, it was to work in the fields, and though people did not forget what I had done, they did forget saying that they would kill me. I had no friends, but people mostly left me alone and my heart began to heal. My parents knew no one would ever marry me again. No one would marry a woman who had cut off her husband's leg, even if it was to save his life. The children made up stories about me and called me names. They said that I sneaked into houses and cut off the fingers of children who stole things, and when they saw me coming they ran. Some women said I cut off the private parts of men who cheated on their wives, threatening their own husbands with my name if they behaved in this way.

"I learned to live in the shadows. I moved quickly, just a gray shape. Years passed, a decade passed, children grew up, and people noticed me less and less. One day my brother decided to get married, and he chose a beautiful girl from a far village who had never heard of what I had done. She was Huirong, and she became like a little sister. She was the only person who was truly kind to me besides my own parents. It was Huirong who put my name on the list that the man showed you, the list of women who would be friends with Westerners. Only, when she told me what she had done, I added the photograph to the man's list, but it was of Huirong. The picture was a lie, and I'm sorry, but yours was a lie, too. Can you imagine how I felt when I saw you, the man I was going to marry, and your legs had already been cut off?"

Chapter 16

The coffee cup *Kimmy placed on the kitchen table was only half-way on the placemat.* Baxter stood up from his seat, stepped around to Kimmy's chair, slid the coffee cup so that it was exactly one inch from the top and right-side edges of the rectangular placemat, and then took his seat again. He could never understand why it was so hard for people to put things in the right place. A woman named Linda at Stoney Brook knew where to put the cups, plates, and silverware. She had shown Baxter how to put together a place setting, and when he saw how perfect it was, the symmetry, the rightness, the order of it all, he knew that each dish, cup, glass, fork, knife, and spoon had its own place, and that putting all of those pieces in their proper places would calm the energy in the room. He could see each piece on the table fitting into its slot, as if the table were covered in the shapes of perfect place settings. In his mind he could put each piece down into its own three-dimensional shape, and it would all sink down into the table and become one with it. Why was this never clear to anyone else?

"Dang, Baxter, you ought to be working at one of those fancy restaurants as a butler or something," said Robert.

"The cup goes on the placemat," said Baxter.

Robert and Kimmy exchanged looks but said nothing. Kimmy took Scott from his high chair and wiped the oatmeal from his face. The children were always a source of disorder to Baxter, but he kept that to himself, along with many other things. Lilith Ann had insisted that he remain with Robert and Kimmy until Robert could get his feet on the ground, as Lilith Ann had put it repeatedly. They needed the rent money, she would say, and then she would promise Baxter that it wouldn't be much longer. She said that at least once a week lately. Baxter drank the coffee that Kimmy had made and kept his eyes on

the place setting before him.

"If you've got something to say, then go ahead and say it," said Kimmy. Baxter thought she was talking to him, but when he looked up at her, he could see that her eyes were only on Robert.

"Is there something I missed?" Robert pushed his cup so hard, coffee sloshed onto the placemat. Baxter cringed.

"No, I think you about covered everything there was to say last night," said Kimmy. Baxter thought the conversation would end since Kimmy announced there was nothing more to say, but apparently this was another one of those things that people said when they, in fact, meant the exact opposite. He wanted to put the placemat in the washing machine, or at least blot up the coffee, but Robert did not move from his seat. "Or maybe you thought of some other names to call me," Kimmy said.

"I could have called you a lot of things," said Robert, his voice low for the sake of Scott and Jessica Ann, the only two children not old enough to get on the bus for school.

"I reckon 'Irresponsible' is a name we can both share," said Kimmy, adjusting the buttons on Scott's sweater, even though Baxter could clearly see they were all snapped shut.

"I told you I was going to take care of things," said Robert.

"It's the *how* that worries me," said Kimmy.

Robert flicked his eyes on Baxter a second before speaking. "I told you I was going to take care of things, and that's all you need to concern yourself with."

"Well fine. I'm going to need money for groceries," said Kimmy. "Unless you want to give me one of my cards back."

"We're done with the damn credit cards. I told you that," Robert said.

"Well I guess we're done with milk, bread, and diapers, too," Kimmy snapped.

"Fine, I'll sell the fu—" Robert clamped his mouth shut and banged his fist on the table. "I'll sell the lawnmower."

"How're we supposed to mow the lawn this summer, huh?"

asked Kimmy.

"You want to eat or cut the grass? Make up your damn mind," Robert said.

Kimmy shot a look at Baxter, who was focusing on his placemat. "Baxter?" Now her voice was sweet and soft, not the way it had sounded when she was speaking to Robert. "Do you think you could do us a favor and help out with some groceries? We could just call it an advance on your next month's rent."

"Next month?" asked Baxter. "I pay my rent on the tenth of every month."

"I know, but we're really tight for money. The house payment is due. Again. And the kids are—the kids are going hungry," Kimmy said, leaning closer to him.

"I pay my rent on the tenth of each month."

"Well, couldn't you just pay a little of your May payment today?"

"It's April 12," said Baxter.

"Aw hell, Kimmy," said Robert.

Kimmy waved him off and focused on Baxter. She was close enough for him to smell the cigarette on her breath that she had sneaked before Robert got up. "If you'll give me a hundred dollars now, I'll make you lemon squares."

"Lemon squares don't cost a hundred dollars," said Baxter.

Kimmy sighed hard, and pushed a strand of hair out of her eyes that had fallen from its trap of hairspray. "Baxter, it's just this one time. You pay me a little bit today, and then next month you deduct it from your rent. It doesn't cost you anything, and it would really help us out until things get back to the way they were." She put her hands down on the table in front of Baxter and let her voice drop. "You don't want your little nieces and nephews going hungry now, do you? They are hungry children, Baxter, and you can feed them."

"Well set my shit afire, Kimmy." Robert rocked his chair backwards on its back two legs and balanced with his hands on the table. "Why don't you start doing commercials for starving children in Africa?" Robert threw his head back and laughed, and Baxter was sure his nephew would fall. One of his back teeth showed, dark and deep in his mouth. Baxter had seen a tooth like that in a man's mouth at Stoney Brook. He had been assigned to the room across the hall from Baxter, and at night he used to scream horrible cursing phrases that included his mother, Jesus, and his ass. The man's words had made little sense, and Baxter despised hearing them. Sitting there with Kimmy's face so close to his and Robert's blackened tooth showing in the back of his roaring mouth, Baxter realized he hated being in that house. He did not want the early morning sounds of the children squealing near him in the kitchen as they slopped their spoons in cereal and dribbled orange juice from plastic cups onto the table. He wanted to go back to Lilith Ann's house where he had a bed, a real bed, not a cot in the laundry room that he had to fold up against the wall each morning so that Kimmy could get to the washing machine. He wanted to sleep in a real bed in a quiet upstairs room at Lilith Ann's where he could close the drapes and lie in the darkness listening to cars pass on the highway in the distance. "I have to go," he said, and headed for the front door.

Chapter 17

Peng did not know how fat Pete-O had been before he went to prison. No one had wanted to take any pictures of him after his amputation surgery, so his pre-prison physique existed only in the minds of Pete-O and his family. Seven years of learning how to cope on his own while locked up without the patient care of his sisters or home health nurses had made him not quite lean enough to be called stalwart, but no longer the slothful man who took pot shots at cans placed atop fence posts from his van window.

When his parole officer came for a visit, Pete-O was watching the news, while Peng was in the kitchen trying to make dinner from the refrigerator full of foods she mostly could not identify. The eggs were familiar, and so was a bundle of carrots she found at the bottom, but the jars and bottles of sauces and dressings all smelled and tasted foul. Peng had gone to Kroger's with Pete-O in his smelly old van with the special controls that let him drive even with no legs, but she had hardly been able to catch her breath in the store with so many boxes and cans; she did not even know so much food could exist in one place. She had tried to put a bag of rice in the cart, but from the angry gestures of his hands, Pete-O made it clear he wouldn't have it. They went home with bags of food items that made no sense to Peng unless she could figure out the picture on the label or recognize the unpackaged food itself. She chopped the carrots into pieces while Pete-O talked to his parole officer, and by the time he left, she had found a package of noodles and put a pan of water on to boil. When the officer's car got to the end of the street, the smile that Pete-O had occasionally shown the man was gone for good.

Within a half hour, Pete-O was settled in the bathtub with a beer pushed in the corner behind his head and his radio

tuned to his favorite talk show. Jack had removed the radio from the window ledge years ago and stored it away. He tried to talk Pete-O into getting an iPhone so he could take his music everywhere he went, but Pete-O wanted nothing but his fifteen-year-old radio returned to its spot in the bathroom. Jack gave up trying to convince Pete-O of how dangerous it was to have a radio so close to the tub, but Pete-O said that he was sick to damn death of everybody in the family trying to take away every last little bit of relaxation and enjoyment he had left. Jack swallowed his fury and finally set the radio back up on the window ledge above the tub, but this time he secured it with a nail driven into the wooden frame to ensure the radio didn't tip and fall into the water. From his comfortable perch against the back of the tub, Pete-O could just barely reach the knobs to adjust the channel. The bathtub was his favorite place to be, next to the driver's seat in his van. He loved being able to move himself long distances with wheels that were not attached to a chair. With his parole visit over, this evening he was enjoying a soak in the bathtub.

The family members had finally gotten used to Peng opening the door, so when Robert knocked he said a polite "hello" and looked around for Pete-O. She pointed to the hallway and said, "Bah-tub." Robert could hear the voices on the radio arguing over baseball scores.

"That you, Robert?" Pete-O called from behind the closed bathroom door. "Go on and get yourself a beer." For a moment, Robert considered Peng's presence in the sacred space of the kitchen, before sauntering past her to get a Budweiser from the refrigerator. He nodded with polite deference as he stepped by her, and she immediately dropped her eyes to the floor.

The door was lined with nothing but beer, a sight that had convinced Peng the space was reserved for this special drink. All cans were turned with their labels facing outward on all three shelves. Robert admired the cans for a few seconds before breaking up their perfect symmetry by taking one. Peng immediately grabbed another from the stash under the sink, re-filled the empty spot, and closed the door. "I wish Kimmy'd do that," said Robert to the uncomprehending Peng. He pointed at the full door. "Nice."

Peng said nothing, but returned to her place at the kitchen sink where she had been washing dishes. Robert pulled the top on his beer and tried to think of something to say. He watched Peng dip her hands into the hot water and slowly rub a soapy sponge around the rim of a cup. She dipped the cup in rinse water and carefully placed it into a drain on the counter, then reached for the next dish, repeating the motion. Her hands moved as if she were laying tiny babies in baskets, and it became clear to Robert that someone must have spent a considerable amount of time showing Peng how to use a kitchen sink. He assumed at once that it was his own mother, who had surely washed tens of thousands of dishes in her lifetime, and had initiated all the women in the Boyd family with her dishwashing procedure.

Robert raised his beer to her in a kind of salutation, and then headed down the hall. His knock was three short raps. "Uncle Pete-O?"

"Come on in," said Pete-O, but the radio made it hard to decipher his words. Robert pushed the door open and stuck his head in, but he didn't look directly at the tub.

"You said I could come by. Want me to wait until you're done?"

"Nah. Come on in. Just taking a Epsom soak. My back gets damn sore from sitting in that chair all day."

Robert glanced over quickly at the figure in the tub and dropped his eyes to his beer can. The transfer seat that Pete-O used to get himself from his wheelchair into the tub was pushed up next to the wall, and the wheelchair was in front of it, leaving Robert only a cramped space in front of the door to stand. He slipped inside and kept looking at anything except his uncle lying comfortably with his back against the sloping end of the tub and extended in front of his body, two stumps. There was something unsettling about his missing parts, like a photograph taken with an arm or the top of a head cut off at the margins. You know it's there, even though it's not in the picture. Pete-O's extremities stopped well over a foot from the end of the bathtub, and they floated there, pink under the water. For Robert, there was something obscene about his uncle lying there in the water, his body hazy beneath the surface. Robert had the crazy thought that maybe he could squeeze his eyes shut a few moments, open them, and make the rest of his uncle's legs appear. Sort of like a grown-up game of hide-and-seek, except Pete-O's legs would never come out of hiding. He willed himself to look at his uncle's face.

"What's that you wanted to talk to me about?" A static-filled commercial about a muscle-warming ointment blared at a volume at least a step louder than the show had been, but Pete-O made no motion to turn it down.

"Hey uh," Robert scratched his head, trying to think of a way to begin the conversation. "Where's Daryl? I haven't seen him around here in I don't know when."

"Didn't Jack tell you? Had to let Daryl go back to him. Peng about pissed her pants every time that dog came near her. She'd go off crying in the bedroom and wouldn't come out until I put Daryl outside. I never seen a woman so scared of dogs."

Robert muttered agreement and then motioned over his shoulder toward the door. "You sure she can't understand anything we're saying?"

"Nothing except 'beer' and 'sandwich,'" said Pete-O, "and she's still not too clear on the sandwich part."

"Looks to me like you got it made," said Robert, "with having a wife who don't ever complain about anything, you know? Hell, sometimes I wish Kimmy didn't speak English. Maybe just 'beer' and 'sandwich.'" Robert tried to follow up his comment with a laugh, but Pete-O didn't join him. Pete-O's only response was *hmmmph*. He reached upward for the radio, and

Robert thought he was going to turn down the sound, but he adjusted the tuning knob enough to eliminate the slight static in the voices and lie back down again. He began scratching at the chest hairs that protruded from the water's surface and Robert looked away in barely-concealed disgust.

"I told Kimmy I was going over to Sam Meeks's place to see about a generator," said Robert.

"What you gonna do with a generator?" asked Pete-O.

"Well, nothing, but she don't know that."

"She must have you by the short hairs." Pete-O almost gave a little laugh.

"I don't want her getting suspicious about nothing. The last thing I need is her sniffing over here looking for me. Hell, it's all I can do to keep her from riding my back about work. She don't know what it's like. You work your ass off for $7.25 an hour for some asshole thinks you're there to listen to every sack of shit who walks through the door expecting you to jump up and wait on them hand and foot and get them what they want even if they don't know what it is," said Robert. He began shifting his beer from one hand to the other. "Went by that new grocery warehouse off the highway seeing if they were hiring, and they said no, they didn't have nothing. I didn't even get out the door when some fella look like he was from India or Iraq, some place like that, come in with a job application in his hand all filled out already. I looked to see what they'd say, and they took it just like he was going to be the next manager of the company or something. Shit. Might be he was a Mexican." Robert took a long drink of his beer and shook his head. He was nervous and had a habit of flexing his fingers to ease the stress. Just thinking about his latest firing put a queasy feeling in his stomach.

"Most fellows would be going off to see some woman if they're lying to the one they got at home," said Pete-O. "And here all you're doing is sneaking off to your uncle's house to drink all of his beer. What gives?"

"I told you she thinks I'm at Sam Meeks's."

"Ain't much difference, I guess," said Pete-O, casting a long suspicious glance at his nephew. "I can tell you got something on your mind. You didn't come over here to ask me where my dog was."

Pete-O folded his hands over his belly as if he were going to give Robert a speech or a scolding, but instead he called out loudly to Peng. "Go on and watch yourself a little TV if you want to," he said. Then, in an uncharacteristically kind voice, he added, "I'll call you when I'm ready to get out of the bathtub."

"Bathtub out?" called Peng from the kitchen.

"No! I'll call you. No bathtub out."

After a thoughtful interval, Peng's clear voice sounded from the kitchen. "Ookay, Pete-O."

"She fixed some noodles for dinner with chicken and vegetables. Not too bad." Pete-O was nodding his head, as if the possibility was an entirely new thought that had just occurred to him.

"Thought you said she couldn't understand anything," said Robert.

"She knows 'TV.' That's not even a word anyway." Pete-O knew that while he sat up late at night watching shows in the den about ducks and guns and sometimes fishing, that she watched the TV in their bedroom, shows of people sitting on sofas and talking. Unseen in the kitchen, Peng wrapped a dish towel around the hot bowl of food and quietly took it down the hall.

"It'd drive me crazy not to be able to talk to anybody," said Robert.

"She talks to herself sometimes. Woke me up the one night a while back across the room whispering to herself. I never went back to sleep," Pete-O said.

"Women like to talk, that's for sure," Robert added.

"They never stop," said Pete-O. He mumbled it in the way people reply when they're just looking for something to say to fill the empty spaces of a conversation.

Robert came farther into the room and slumped down on the closed toilet lid. He feared his uncle's reputation as much as the actual man who sat before him in the water. Even without legs, Pete-O was a man who could make things happen, and not in a good way. Since Robert was a boy no older than in first grade, his uncle Pete-O knew how to make him feel small, like someone who has said something stupid at the worst moment. Robert was never quite sure if he actually had.

"So," said Pete-O, casting another long look at his nephew. "You here to ask for money?"

"Hell no, I ain't here to ask for money," said Robert, shifting uneasily. His reply forced a clear look in his uncle's eyes. "Have I ever asked anybody for money?"

"You asked Baxter."

"That was rent money because he's living in our house, and anyhow that was all Mama's idea. And Kimmy's."

"So you're not here for a loan or nothing."

Robert put his beer on the bathroom counter, leaned forward to make sure Peng was not lingering in the hallway, and then lowered his voice. "I know a fellow who used to work for Alton."

"You mean Alton Sanders? Guy who has that strip joint?"

"He's part-owner." Robert hesitated. For a moment, he considered asking his uncle to turn the radio up to disguise their voices.

"I'm listening."

"Well, remember when we was talking at the wedding reception about making some things right? About how some things need to be set back the way they used to be?"

"I remember," said Pete-O.

"I've been thinking of one way to help do that."

"At a strip joint?"

Robert felt his frustration rise, the burning anger that always made him lose his cool when he was talking but nobody was

taking him seriously. He caught the flicker of condescension in his uncle's eyes and it almost made him want to tell Pete-O to fuck off. "I said…"

"You said you know someone who used to work for Alton." Pete-O's eyes narrowed just enough to make him look like he was suffering from a bad headache or he was trying hard to look mean.

"That's what I'm trying to tell you," said Robert, still trying to keep his cool.

"How long's it been since he was on the inside?"

"Well, that's the thing," said Robert. He swallowed another mouthful of beer, belched, and found his courage once more. "He's got a girlfriend who works there. Gets his information from her."

"She one of the strippers?"

"Uh-huh."

"And you're putting all this on the word of some guy's stripper girlfriend?"

"She saw it. They keep the boxes in the basement. They're shipped out on Fridays before the place opens."

"Boxes? Boxes of what?"

Robert snickered confidently with his new upper hand. "Boxes of meth, man. Everybody knows about it. You been out of the loop a long time."

"I don't go hanging around strip joints and meth labs. I'm a respectable man now. Got a wife. Started a new life," said Pete-O. He jerked his head a little toward the back of the house, where Peng had gone. "I wouldn't know about dens of iniquity and shady characters."

Robert's mouth quivered a little and his smile faded. Pete-O was joking, or he was jerking him around. Robert couldn't tell which. He picked up his beer again and took a sip, waiting for some cue from his uncle.

"Last I heard about Alton," said Pete-O, a little cautiously, "he was dealing a little weed. But I don't go in for that junk."

"Well, I don't either," Robert said, a little too quickly. "I got a family."

Pete-O looked at him a little quizzically, but said nothing.

Robert pushed a hand through his hair before picking up his story again. "A van comes by around six o'clock and unloads boxes of beer at the kitchen around back, and then some of Alton's guys bring up a couple of old beer boxes from the basement, and they're filled with product. They load it in the back of the van and it all just looks like Alton's recycling. All we do is get hold of the delivery and I take them a load of beer and let them load it up and then we leave. It's so easy it makes me wonder why nobody else has thought to do it," said Robert. He was trying not to smile, but it was nearly impossible for him not to show how delighted he was in himself. He took a sip of beer and waited for his uncle to tell him what a damn genius he was.

Pete-O let a smile creep over his face. He raised a dripping hand from the water and pointed it at Robert. "The reason nobody else has thought of it is because that's the damn dumbest plan I ever heard," he said. "You believe that story? People just load up boxes of meth into a van at six o'clock in the damn afternoon out the back of a bar where the police are liable to raid any time they damn well please, and they're all just standing around like it's some pizza delivery business? Oh, and you think you're just going to 'get hold' of the delivery van. How the hell do you think you're going to do that? Hell, man," Pete-O said, shaking his head and staring off away from Robert, "I thought you were smarter than that."

Robert felt the rage rising again and he pointed a finger back at his uncle. "Tell me something. You think they're going to have some underground fancy hideout like on the TV shows? Shipping it out in the daytime like it was nothing is exactly how they do it under everybody's noses. This is Alton and TP we're talking about. They don't exactly run a cartel. I'd be surprised if Alton's got anything more than some punk kid with a shotgun standing by the door when the stuff goes out."

"You don't even know?" said Pete-O, suddenly sitting up and making waves in the water. "You come up with this half-assed plan and you don't even know who he's got standing watch when the goods go out?"

"It wouldn't be hard to find out. All I have to do is go by there one night, ask a few questions, maybe get one of the girls to talk, tell me what she knows."

"You think some stripper's going to tell you? Do you think she's going to spill the beans about their operation? Do you think those girls even know what's going on?"

"People hear all kinds of things you think they don't know about," said Robert. "When I was working at Shoney's I over-heard these two Mexicans talking about meeting up with a guy named Mave later that night to sell him some pot, and I know damn good and well he's a cop 'cause there's only one guy in this town named Mave and that's not a name a guy could make up. But I didn't say nothing to those two because if they sell him some pot and he's Mave Job, the guy I know, then those guys'll get their asses sent back to Mexico before you can say 'illegal immigrant.'"

Pete-O's face turned serious once more and he adjusted himself back down in the tub. "First of all, if they're breaking the law, then they'll get put in jail, American jail, and we get to support them with our tax dollars until they get out, and then they get sent back to Mexico. And second of all, none of what you just said about being a one-man deportation department has anything the hell to do with what we've been talking about. All it means is that you listen in on people's conversations when you're cleaning tables."

Robert's face burned with anger and embarrassment. His uncle had done it again, making him feel like an errant teenager who could not get the attention of the adults and has to be put in his place. For an instant, Robert wanted to push Pete-O's head underneath the water and drown him right there in his own bathtub. "If you're not interested, I can do it myself. All I needed from you was a van."

"What are you planning to do? Load it up in the back seat of your Toyota by yourself?"

"What did you think I was gonna do with your van?"

Pete-O chuckled a little, but then his face quickly fell serious. He pulled himself forward with the bars on either side of the tub and reached for the hot water knob. He turned it all the way on and a steaming rush of water fell from the spigot. "Look, Robert. I know you want to make a big score, but robbing a meth lab by yourself in broad daylight is a suicide mission. TP and Alton might be a couple of knuckleheads, but you mess with them and they're going to shoot you, drag what's left of you to the club in the front, call it a robbery attempt, and let the police haul your bleeding ass to jail. Find yourself a business that doesn't have drugs or guns on the front counter if you want to make yourself some fast money."

"Like what? Walmart?"

Pete-O's eyes went hard. "That wasn't about money."

"No, you popped a cap in a guy and you didn't get nothing for it except seven years in the can."

"A lot can change in seven years," said Pete-O, waving his hands under the water to spread the heat.

"Yeah, and I reckon one of 'em's you." Robert stood up and crunched his empty beer can between his hands, dropped it on the bathroom counter, and walked out the door.

Chapter 18

Sam Meeks's cabin perpetually smelled of mold, but it was worse when the weather was warm. When he pushed the door open, the air inside hit Robert like the scent of an old boot somebody had left in the back of a closet. "Sam? You in here?" he called out before stepping inside. A woman with straw-colored hair and a suspiciously ugly sore on her chin sat up on the sofa. She blinked her eyes open, but said nothing. From the other side of the room, a silent television cast colors on the woman's face, but she seemed unaware of it. "Will the Circle Be Unbroken" wafted from the radio, a mismatched audio stream to the image of a sleek blonde woman talking soundlessly on a news program.

"Sam around?" Robert asked.

The woman on the sofa turned her head a little but still didn't speak. She was watching the newscaster.

"He's out back," a man's voice said. The man in the doorway of the kitchen didn't look directly at Robert. His hair was stiff and black, and it was covered in some kind of gray film. To Robert it looked as if someone had sprayed it with Christmas snow. A quick shake and the white would have fallen right off the man's head, but he didn't seem to notice or care that it was there. Robert cocked his head at the man and stepped farther inside. "He coming back?"

The man nodded his head slowly. "I reckon. He's just getting a hammer."

Robert waited for an explanation but none was offered. "Mind if I wait?"

The man said nothing but motioned to a chair. "Suit yourself." Robert decided the powder in the man's hair looked like sheetrock dust; if it was, maybe the man could clue him in on a job. Even if it was part-time it would be better than nothing.

The man ambled over to the sofa and took a seat next to the sedate woman with the ugly chin. Robert didn't sit down. He was too nervous, too full of energy after his wasted proposal at Pete-O's. At first he pondered how difficult it would be to learn to hang sheetrock, but he soon abandoned it as being not profitable enough. His thoughts returned to the meth lab idea, and he considered telling the whole shebang to Sam so that he could enlist his help. Maybe Sam could even get a couple of other guys to join them so they wouldn't be outnumbered if things got messy. Suddenly Robert's stomach got jumpy and he thought he might be sick. Something told him he should keep his mouth shut. He rarely listened to his instincts when they told him to keep quiet, but this time he held his tongue and waited for Sam to reappear. The news show played itself out, and a show about pawn shops was just coming on, when Robert heard a door open from the back of the house.

"Liked to never found the damn hammer," Sam called out from the door before he made it into the room. He headed straight for a framed picture leaning against the wall to the left of the TV that Robert had not noticed until then. The picture faced the wall so that Robert could not tell what was on the front. The wire across the back was new and tautly wound, but the wood it was attached to was stained; the blackened hairy thread of a spider's web hung from the left side. Sam pulled a nail from his shirt pocket, eyed the wall hastily, and without bothering to measure the height or find the center of the space, he began hammering the nail. It sank into the sheetrock after no more than three blows. Sam whisked the picture from the floor and centered the wire over the nail. When he let go of it, the picture listed to the left. It was a poster copy of the U.S. Constitution in an unpainted wooden frame that left a two-inch-wide strip of exposed cardboard backing on either side. The picture had the yellowed look of the document along with the tears and wrinkles.

"Told you not to pull that wire so tight," the other man said.

"It can't catch in the center unless you give it some slack."

Sam tugged downward on the picture and then let it go once more. It listed even farther to the left. He jerked the picture to the right, tugged it downward once more, hard, and the nail popped out onto the floor. Sam caught it just as it fell. The wall now had a powdery hole and a chipped piece of sheetrock where the U.S. Constitution had hung for all of thirty seconds.

"Damn," said Sam. "Ain't nothing right about America no more."

"Ain't America, Sam," said the woman, laughing. "It's your hammering that's crazy as shit."

"Shit," quipped Sam. "Cheap wall is what it is. If I'da made it myself it wouldn't be falling apart like some dadgum junk shit." He propped the frame back up against the wall.

"You don't know how to build a wall," said the man with sheetrock in his hair.

"Don't nobody know how to build a wall anymore," Sam said. "These days all we get's falling apart shit like this. That's just America now." Robert noticed that Sam's face was pale and covered in a sheen of sweat even though the temperature outside was in the forties. Sam's hands shook, and he waved the hammer in his right hand as if it didn't weigh anything.

"You're an American, Sam. Is that why you can't hang a damn picture?" The woman snickered but didn't take her eyes from the TV show. Sam picked up the Constitution once more and looked it over, but Robert could see that his eyes moved too quickly to be reading anything. Sam looked at it the way a child would look at a picture of something he had never seen before.

"Won't you just take the Constitution out of that frame and tape it on the wall?" Robert suggested. Sam jerked his head toward him, and Robert wondered if Sam was just now noticing him.

"Tape it? You fucking kidding me?" Sam's voice was explosive, and Robert could see the spittle that flew from his lips from across the room. "You don't put fucking tape on the

Constitution."

"S'already got holes in it from when you had it on the bedroom wall with thumbtacks," said the woman.

At this the man burst into laughter, and the woman covered her mouth with her hand to hide her uncontrollable snickering. "You had the United States of American Constitution on your bedroom wall? What you got in your bathroom? The Bill of Rights above your toilet, so you don't forget all those amendments?"

"Amendments are in the Constitution, dumbass," said Sam. "If you read anything besides a potato chip bag and an unemployment composition application, you'd know that." Sweat ran down Sam's forehead, and to Robert he looked pasty white. Sam had always seemed pretty healthy, but now he looked like a man either sick or high. Robert had known Sam since junior high school and they'd hung out together off and on since they graduated, but not so much after child number two was born to Robert and Kimmy, and none at all after number three. Except for catching a glimpse of Sam at a Christmas party the previous year, Robert hadn't seen him since Rob Jr. was no more than three years old.

Sam didn't seem to recognize Robert at all, but what was stranger was that Sam didn't seem the least bit concerned that there was someone was in his house that he didn't know. Robert had been watching Sam's shaking, sweating form ponder the fate of his pocked, faded U.S. Constitution for nearly twenty minutes, but no one had asked him his name or his reason for standing there.

"Sam? You remember me?" Robert asked.

Sam stared at the frame before him and then looked up at the wall with the gouged-out hole.

"We went down to Orton's Lake back when we were in high school, and you jumped in with all your clothes on and damn near drowned. Clint Jack Hoffman pulled you out. You remember that? It must have been forty degrees that night," said Robert.

"Oh, I remember that," said the woman on the sofa. "Him and Clint Jack both was drunk as Cooter Brown. I was worried to death that both of them was gonna drown." She pulled a cigarette from some hidden recess in the top of her blouse and lit it.

"You were there?" asked Robert. The woman's face didn't stir up any names, and she looked a good ten years older than Sam. Her hair was a dried-out bristle that had faded to a garish top layer of blonde over gray. He hadn't been nearly as drunk as Sam had been that night, but he still had no memory of anyone dragging his spindly old aunt along.

"Sure, I was there." She gave him a smile. Only three of her front upper teeth were still in her mouth. "Have you forgotten me?"

"There were a lot of people there that night."

The woman snorted and leaned forward to tap the ashes from her cigarette on the ashtray on the coffee table. "Shit. You were the one brung me to Orton's Lake that night. But you weren't the one took me home." She grinned and stuck the cigarette back between her lips, letting the smoke curl up and into her hair.

Something cold and small dropped down in Robert's stomach. Gemma Penderton had been his girlfriend for nearly two months when he was a senior in high school. She had had long curly blonde hair and Robert always thought she looked a little like a pointy-nosed version of Jennifer Aniston. The person who sat before him on the sofa was a wrinkle-mouthed, gray-haired, pock-faced, saggy-skinned old woman. She had been the girl he screwed in the seat of somebody's pick-up truck. Robert gave an involuntary shudder at the memory.

"You remember who took me home?" she asked.

"Who what?" Robert shook his head back into reality.

"That night Sam almost drowned. Do you remember? Of course you don't," she said, looking more amused than angry.

"That was a long time ago," said Robert, trying to smile.

"Yeah, it was." Gemma didn't offer an answer and instead turned her attention back to the TV, their conversation seemingly at an end.

"She's my wife," said Sam. His entry into the conversation took Robert by surprise. "Well, we was divorced two years ago, but she never left, so I reckon that makes her still my wife."

Robert wasn't sure if he should congratulate them or change the subject. He chose the latter. "What do you know about TP and Alton's operation out off Piedmont Highway?"

This time all three of them stared at Robert for several seconds, before Sam gave an abrupt answer. "They got themselves a good strip joint."

"What you wanna know about Alton's place for?" asked Gemma. The man sitting next to her was staring straight ahead at the TV, but he perked up when Robert mentioned Alton.

"I was looking for work. Thought maybe they could use a bouncer," said Robert.

Gemma and the man exchanged glances. Her eyes tried to catch Sam's but he was finally interested in Robert. "I gotta take a piss. Come outside with me," he said.

Robert followed him onto the porch, where Sam stopped for a few seconds. Robert thought he was going to do his business right off the edge into the bushes, but then Sam motioned for him to follow. Sam stepped down off the porch and headed toward the boat dock. He moved like a person being chased, his elbows flapping, and his head turning from side to side to take in everything around him. At the end of the dock, Sam stopped and lit a cigarette; he put his hands on his hips, and peered down into the water.

Robert halted a few steps behind him. "A man ought not to pee where he fishes," said Robert.

"You interested in doing business with Alton?"

"I ain't interested in being a stripper, if that's what you mean."

"There's some folks that might pay to see what you got."

Robert laughed out loud, but quickly stopped when he saw that Sam wasn't laughing. He wasn't even smiling. For a half second, Robert entertained the thought of knocking Sam backwards into the water, but before he could make up his mind, Sam put up a hand and began shaking his head. "If you think you want to get a piece of what Alton and TP's got going on out there, you got to get yourself a connection with somebody on the inside."

"And I reckon that would be you."

Sam took a draw on his cigarette and seemed to think a minute before answering. "How much you wanting to buy?"

The question took Robert a little by surprise. He scratched his chin and appeared to think. "How much they got to sell?"

This time Sam did laugh. "What? You planning to open up a drug store?"

For a second Robert considered giving a flip answer, but he changed his mind and went in another direction. "I reckon they got a lot of money."

Instead of looking suspicious or shutting down, Sam brightened up and began nodding his head. "Damn right, they's a lot of money in that place."

"And it's a cash business, 'cause you know they can't exactly put that money in the bank. They gotta have a big vault in that place. A feller gets his hands on that vault and he's a rich man."

"Oh yeah, they got a vault alright," said Sam.

"Is that where they keep the uh. . . the drugs?"

"I don't know."

"I heard the lab was downstairs in the basement. You seen any of it? The lab?"

Sam scratched his head. "No, but they've probably got the drugs stored away down there in between shipments. But I know they got the money. Hey, you thinking what I'm thinking?"

Robert looked out across the water at the soft shards of moonlight shimmering on the surface. This was the last moment to back out before it was too late. If he spoke the

words, he would be stepping across a line he'd never crossed before. He'd been in trouble for minor infractions like fighting, drunken and disorderly conduct, and then there was the thing that happened at the Pizza Hut, but this was a whole new level. Robbing the T&A would give his family the money he had not been able to provide for them on his minimum wage shit jobs, or it could leave him dead or in jail. He decided to play coy and let Sam think it was his idea. Robert shook his head at the thought, but Sam took it for a no.

"Think about it," said Sam, and suddenly it was Sam trying to talk Robert into doing what he had come there to talk Sam into. "All we have to do is get into the back when they're closed and get the safe out the door. I got hand trucks. We back my truck up to the dock out back, we move fast, we get it loaded, and we haul ass fast and quiet."

"How do we know that safe's not bolted down to the floor? We don't even know how big it is. Or where it is." Robert held both arms up in desperate surrender.

"You know it's in TP's office. Where else are they gonna put it? The stripper's dressing room? They put it where TP and Alton can keep an eye on it."

Robert shook his head. "We know the drugs are in the basement, and they're not heavy as hell."

"Yeah, but then we'd have to unload it. Drugs ain't worth nothing unless you're selling it. Or using it."

"I don't know." Robert sighed and stared at the water. The whole idea somehow sounded easier when it was just an idea, a fantasy that he could mull over in his mind like it was some television show that he could play out any way he wanted to. The thought of actually doing it, of pulling off a heist of drugs and cash in a strip joint loomed dangerously large in his head. If he got caught he wouldn't be serving time in the Rayle County jail, he'd be in prison, and Kimmy would be at home with five kids. "I'm thinking we need to case the place," said Robert. "Do we even know if they've got anybody watching things after closing?"

"Hell man, we can go out there in the daytime to see what the back looks like and then go back at night and see if anybody's watching."

"Don't you know what it looks like in the back?"

"Why would I know that? I always park in the parking lot out front with everybody else."

"But I thought you, uh," Robert searched his words. "I thought you was buying from them."

"Who told you that?"

"Nobody. I just figured."

The air was still for several seconds and neither man spoke. Somewhere in the thick grasses that lined the riverbank a bullfrog began to croak, startling Robert. The thought of it almost made him laugh. Jumping at the sound of bullfrogs. His mother would have thought that was funny. When he was no more than four or five he would catch frogs in the bushes around the house in the summer and put them in a shoebox to show to Lilith Ann. Remembering it made his stomach feel loose somehow. His mother would be furious with him for what he was thinking of doing.

"Hey Sam," called Gemma from the front door of the house. "Got a phone call. I think it's Jimmy Swain." She coughed twice and then let the screen door slam shut.

"Don't you have a cell? Man, who's got a phone in his house these days?" said Robert.

"I ain't carrying no cell phone that the government can track me with. You know they can follow you everywhere you go on a screen 'cause there's a GPS tracker in every phone these days. They got a place in Anniston where Fort McClellan used to be. Got computers where they can type in your information and they can find wherever you are just by tracking your phone. You're just a dot on the screen. You get in your car and drive across town and the government can see right where you go." Sam moved his head in slow conspiratorial nods.

Robert whistled in amazement and his hand naturally went to the phone in his back pocket. He wondered if they could see that he was out here next to the river at Sam Meeks's cabin, just a single dot standing next to the water because Sam didn't have a phone. If they went to the T&A, he was leaving his phone at home.

"Let's go out there Saturday night. See what we see. Awright?" said Sam. He took off back toward the house and waved over his shoulder at Robert who remained next to the water, listening to the bullfrog.

Chapter 19

Lilith Ann had never been able to get past the tiny leap she felt in her stomach whenever the phone rang. This affliction began when her own kids were little, and it had escalated with the next generation. At the sound of the telephone ringing, in a millisecond her mind ran down the long list of names of family members who might be in trouble. The grandchildren were first. One of them had swallowed poison. One of the older boys had fallen out of a tree and broken an arm. Or one of them had been kidnapped by a gang in the parking lot of Dollar General, while Kimmy had been bent over trying to get them all snapped into their seats. Things had been safer when they didn't have to fool with those seats.

Next in her line of fear were her own children. Viv and Josh were probably fine, although with the way Josh put back the fried chicken and Pepsi, he was due for a heart attack at some point relatively soon. Robert was the one she most feared for. His temper, his impatience, his downright stupidity made her wonder when the next disaster would hit. The only physical calamity that ever befell Kimmy was that she got pregnant once a year. Baxter, himself, never called when he was in trouble. The phone calls referring to Baxter always began with a request for confirmation that she was Lilith Ann Boyd followed by another question: "Are you the sister of Baxter Hemper?" Then the person would identify himself or herself as either law enforcement, mental health, or medical personnel. The most recent person on her list to be concerned about was Pete-O. For seven years she worried that someone would call from the federal penitentiary informing her that her brother had been stabbed, or perhaps had stabbed someone else with one of those prison-made weapons that they carve out of toothbrushes. She had learned all about them on a public television

documentary that Magda had insisted they watch. They never did call, but she never ceased feeling that momentary fear inside at the sound of the ringing. At one point she'd even considered having her telephone disconnected, but the idea of something happening without her knowing about it immediately was even worse than having to know about it immediately.

Magda stuck her head out of the bathroom door. "Are you going to answer that?"

Lilith Ann snapped back to the present. She was standing above the small table in the hallway, quaintly known as the "telephone table," staring at the ringing phone. "It's probably nobody."

Magda stepped into the hallway from the bathroom where she'd been brushing her hair. "You're right, Mama. There's a ghost on the other end of the phone." She muttered to herself and headed for the phone, but it stopped ringing before she could get her hand on it. "I don't know why you can't get a cell. Then you'd know who was calling, and if you didn't want to pick up then you wouldn't have to."

"I don't have to pick up now."

"Yeah, but you don't know who it is you're not picking up on. Somebody might need to talk to you."

"If they do then they'll call back and I'll answer it then." Lilith Ann headed back toward the kitchen.

"What if it's just one of your friends wanting to chat?"

"I don't want to chat with anybody," called Lilith Ann. "If they want to talk to me so bad they can come over here and talk at my kitchen table."

"Did it ever occur to you that they're calling to ask you if they can come over and chat with you at your kitchen table?"

Lilith Ann was momentarily silenced. "Well," she said, but nothing followed. Magda didn't hear her because she was already back in her bedroom. Her cell phone rang in her purse and she caught it on the third ring. It was Jack.

"We're on our way to the ER," Jack shouted over the wind

blowing through his open driver's seat window.

"What? What happened?"

"It's Peng. Pete-O thinks she broke her leg. Maybe both legs."

"What the hell happened?"

"Uh." Jack was distracted by Pete-O's voice from nearby, but Magda couldn't make out what he was saying. "She fell in the bathroom as best we can figure. Pete-O heard a loud noise and she was on the floor. Both of her legs are messed up. We're on our way to Rayle County Regional. I tried to call Mama, but nobody answered. Is she home?"

Magda ignored the question. "Hand the phone to Peng," said Magda. "I want to talk to her."

"What for? She can't understand you."

"She knows my voice. I want to let her know that I know she's hurt so she'll know we're coming."

"Uh, she can't talk anyway. I can't get the phone to her."

"Why not?"

"She's in the back of the truck."

"What?!" Magda shrieked. "What do you mean she's in the back of the truck with two broken legs? Why didn't you drive Pete-O's van?" Lilith Ann was standing next to Magda trying to pull the phone out from her daughter's ear to hear the conversation.

"Flat tire. Take too long to fix it."

"Well of all things," said Magda. "Still, in the back of the truck?"

"Where was I going to put Pete-O? He can't get in the back," said Jack.

"Why didn't you call an ambulance?"

"An ambulance?" said Jack. From the side of the truck Pete-O yelled, "Ambulance costs eight hundred dollars!"

Magda held the phone out from her ear and put a hand over her eyes in maddened frustration. She didn't protest when her mother took it from her hand. "You got that woman in the back of a pickup truck hauling her to the hospital?" said Lilith Ann.

"It's not like that," argued Jack. "I lifted her in there real gentle in a big blanket sling. She's right up next to the cab on a bunch of blankets and pillows. I couldn't leave Pete-O. He told me – I–I didn't know what else to do." His voice cracked a little at the end, and so Lilith Ann felt a pang of sympathy for Jack caught in the middle of the entire mess.

"Alright son, alright. We'll meet you at the hospital. Drive slow and don't take the turns hard, alright?"

Lilith Ann had to tell Magda to shut her mouth three times on the way to the hospital because she was counting all the ways she was going to bless out both Jack and Pete-O for putting Peng in the back of a pickup like a hog on the way to market. Magda was so busy working up her retaliation she wasn't the one who thought of the idea to call Mr. Chen to meet them there so he could translate. This idea from Lilith Ann finally distracted Magda enough that she dropped her tirade against her brother and called the restaurant with a request for Mr. Chen to come to the hospital. At first he didn't know who Magda was and why she would ask him to leave his restaurant during their lunch prep time, but when she said Peng's name, he agreed to meet them at the ER.

The hospital personnel were not nearly as surprised as Magda thought they would be at seeing an injured person sitting in the bed of a pickup truck. She pulled into a parking space, just as Jack wheeled his truck into the ER entrance and a weary looking nurse came out to help extract Peng from the back. "Grab her wheelchair first so we can put her down in it," the nurse said, pointing at the chair lying next to Peng.

"It's not hers," said Jack, motioning to his uncle, who sat in the passenger's seat awaiting his chair to be delivered to his open door.

"Oh. They usually bring the disabled ones in the back," the nurse said.

"Who is 'they'?" asked Magda, coming up fast behind her.

The nurse took a quick look at her and returned her

attention to the diminutive Asian woman with windblown hair who looked so frightened sitting with her back up against the cab. "At least you put blankets under her. They don't always think to do that," she said.

Jack shoved the wheelchair into place beside his uncle and then ran around the back of the truck to retrieve Peng. As he lifted her from the truck bed, two EMTs were suddenly there to help ease her down to a wheelchair at the rear of the truck. Peng spoke in a rapid, shrill voice and pointed a finger violently at the EMTs as they worked. When she was safely in the chair, they began wheeling her through the back entrance where Pete-O was already leading the way. Lilith Ann brought up the rear. "I reckon we've got a wagon train," she said over Peng's panicked chatter.

Once inside, the group parked at the check-in desk, where a heavily made-up woman with a nametag that read "Linda" pushed papers at Pete-O to sign. "Sir, do you speak English?" she asked.

"Course I speak it. Do you?" Pete-O shot back. He grabbed a pen from the cup on her desk.

"Are you the responsible party?" Linda asked.

The look Pete-O gave her was so venomous Lilith Ann decided to step in. "Yes, he's responsible. He's her husband." Lilith Ann spoke with a kind of stiff pride in the fact, and pointed to Peng, who was still talking and reaching for her ankles.

"What language does she speak?"

"Asian," Pete-O said.

"She speaks Mandarin," said Magda.

"Do any of you speak Mandarin?" Linda asked. She was already reaching for the phone on her desk.

"You know Mr. Chen at the Chinese restaurant?" said Lilith Ann. "He's on his way and he's going to be the translation."

"The what?" Linda looked at Lilith Ann as if she had said they were bringing in a bucket of crawdads to the ER. Peng interrupted the moment with a dreadful moan. She had the bottom of one pant leg pulled up in her hand, and Magda gasped when she saw the side of Peng's red, swollen leg. "Oh, that looks awful. Can't you give her something for pain?"

The nurse began giving orders to one of the EMTs; in seconds, Peng was wheeled through a pristine set of chrome swinging doors and into an examining room. Pete-O was told to wait outside, and he protested with minor resistance. When Mr. Chen arrived minutes later, however, and was ushered through the swinging doors, Pete-O launched into a series of threats to the hospital's legal team. "Pete-O, you'd just be in the way. Let them see about her," said Lilith Ann. "They'll let you back there as soon as they get her fixed up." She ushered the group to a row of blue plastic chairs at the rear of the ER waiting area. Lilith Ann didn't say anything more about Peng, but she knew the likely reason Pete-O wanted to get back there was to make sure they didn't perform any drastic procedures on his wife that would cost him a lot of money. The thought of her brother being such a cheap-ass over Peng, when his own medical needs had been costing the taxpayers and Medicare a wad of money for nearly ten years, made Lilith Ann want to slap him.

Jack suddenly sat up in his chair and looked fearfully at his mother. "What if she's in a wheelchair now for good?"

The small group fell silent, and Magda finally spoke. "She'll be fine."

"It looked bad. I was scared to death to put her in the truck," said Jack, casting a quick look at Pete-O.

"They might have to keep her a while, but she'll be all right," said Lilith Ann.

Pete-O sighed and banged his hands in disgust on the arms of his chair. "Blood suckers'll charge me $2,500 a day for her to lay up in this place."

"Pete-O, she's really hurt," said Magda. "It's not like she's faking being sick so she can get a few days off from cleaning and cooking for you."

"Let's just worry about taking care of your wife," said Lilith Ann. She rose a little from her seat and directed a hard stare at Pete-O. The venom was barely concealed in her voice. "Do you remember when you broke your arm?"

"That was different."

"You fell. You broke a bone. What's so different about it?" asked Lilith Ann.

"I was playing football in the state play-offs. She fell down in the bathroom."

"It doesn't matter if she was ice-skating for a gold medal in the Olympics."

"Breaking her leg is not going to cost her a football scholarship," said Pete-O. His voice had become loud enough to concern Linda at the front desk; by now, she could have no doubt he spoke fluent English. She craned her neck to get a better look at the disruptive family in the waiting area.

"Psshaw," said Lilith Ann. "You tell that story like Bear Bryant hisself was watching the game waiting to sign you up."

"He had scouts there before the playoffs," said Pete-O. "They were looking right at me and that other guy."

"And it was the other guy they signed. The black one, Henderson."

Pete-O gave a dismissive wave, as if the memory was still painful.

"High-Five Henderson?" asked Jack, suddenly interested.

"His name was Clarence Sheffield Henderson. Quit Alabama after only two years. Just wasted himself." Pete-O focused on something far across the waiting room and pretended to lose interest.

"You don't have to tell me who he was," said Jack. "High-Five got thirty-four rushing touchdowns in twelve games his second year at Alabama. I didn't know you knew him," said Jack, smiling admiringly at his uncle.

"Knew him? Hell, I played with him since he was in junior high school. He got a scholarship to the best school in the country, and I got a broken arm."

Lilith Ann looked away and sighed hard in disgust. Pete-O had been telling that story for nearly fifty years, but she knew the scouts had never even looked his way. Lilith Ann had been waiting to pick up her brother from practice when he was grandstanding and strutting every which way on the field trying to catch their attention, but the only acknowledgment he got was when one of them pointed a finger in Pete-O's direction and commented on how fast High-Five "passed that clumsy guy on the right." She never told anyone, especially not Pete-O. She was sorely tempted to tell him right now just to shut him up, but looking at him in his wheelchair, such a pathetic and angry old man, made her perish the thought.

When Mr. Chen entered the examining room, he gave Peng an encouraging smile. He smelled of garlic and cooking oil, a combination that would have pleased Peng in any other situation, but she was shaking with pain and terror. Mr. Chen spent the next fifteen minutes explaining to Peng what the doctor told him to say about how badly her ankle was broken, and the surgery that was required. At the word "surgery," she tearfully asked if they would be removing her leg, and Mr. Chen smiled. "No, your leg will be all right, but it must heal. It is a very bad break."

Peng burst into hysterical tears. "I will always be punished," she cried into an already-shredded wad of tissues.

"You are not being punished," said Mr. Chen, trying to sound reassuring. "You had an accident. Tell me how it happened."

When she finished her story, Mr. Chen's face was a mask of amusement and horror, and Peng was terrified all over again. Many years ago one of his workers, a young second cousin from Shaanxi, had been doing the same thing, but she hadn't broken her ankle. His wife had opened the unlocked restroom door and seen what the girl was doing. When Mr. Chen heard his wife calling the girl "a backwards dog," he thought something terrible had happened; but he was too afraid to come closer to the two women over something that originated in their employee restroom. He waited behind his office door, listening to his wife explain in exasperated tones that in America toilets were not like in China. A person did not squat atop a Western toilet with her feet balanced on either side of the seat. Western toilets were seats, like a chair. A person sat down on the hole to do business. It was this same explanation that Mr. Chen gave the stupefied Peng. When he finished telling her that she must sit on the seat and not climb on top of it, she was so shocked she was no longer crying.

"Like on a horse?" she asked in a whisper.

"No, face this way." Embarrassed, Mr. Chen bent his legs in a seated position. "You see the room in front of you, like this." He straightened up and began telling the doctor and two shocked nurses how Peng had climbed up atop Pete-O's handicap-accessible toilet and slipped. One leg went through each of the two metal curving bars on either side and twisted, trapping and breaking her ankles as she hit the floor backwards on her shoulder.

"How can a person not know how to use a toilet?" said a nurse with her hair in a tight ponytail. "Dang, where's she from?"

Mr. Chen tried to explain, but shook his head after a brief description of the Chinese toilet.

"Doesn't she watch television?" the nurse asked.

"They don't show people sitting on toilets on the TV," another nurse said.

"They do on mine," replied the nurse with the ponytail. "She ought to be watching *Orange is the New Black*. Every week they've got some woman on a toilet, seems like."

Doctor Banerjee was filling out a clipboard. When Peng spoke, she didn't bother looking up. "We're going to get somebody from Occupational Therapy to show Mrs. uh," she looked at the paperwork, "Mrs. Hemper how to use a toilet."

In the waiting area, everyone stood up as Mr. Chen approached; everyone except Pete-O. Mr. Chen gave them all

a broad wave as he slipped through the wide sliding door. "Where's he going?" Lilith Ann took a step toward his departing figure and stopped. "Where does he think he's going?" she repeated. Mr. Chen was heading toward a small brown Honda. "We called him to come out and translate and there he goes."

"I think I can interpret everything pretty well," said a voice from behind.

At hearing the doctor's voice, Magda turned and asked, "How's Peng?"

"We're prepping her for surgery. She has a broken fibula in her right leg and both the tibia and fibula are broken in the left."

Lilith Ann waved an impatient hand. "When can we talk to the doctor?"

The doctor gave a small sigh that indicated she had had this conversation many times. "I am the doctor. Doctor Banerjee." She briefly held out the name badge that hung around her neck before dropping it, and launching into an explanation of everything Mr. Chen had told her about how Peng had broken her ankles. The story brought the same round of astonished gasps from the family as it had from the nurses. Doctor Banerjee gave an overview of the surgical procedure that was to begin in less than an hour. At the mention of the word pins, Jack gave an involuntary shiver; Lilith Ann shook her head and quietly invoked God's intervention. Pete-O listened carefully as he tapped an impatient finger on the arm of his chair. The doctor finished and put her hands in her pockets. "Do you have any questions?"

"Where are you from?" asked Pete-O.

"Tennessee."

"Before that."

Doctor Banerjee forced a tight little smile and began her ready speech. "I was born at Parkwest Medical Center in Knoxville, Tennessee. I got my medical degree from Johns Hopkins. My father was an oncologist at Parkwest until he retired four years ago. He was born in Parawip and my mother comes from Puri. Those are cities in India," she said, pushing the last word out the way her parents spoke. "Eenndya."

Pete-O nodded his head as if something important had just been settled in his mind. "All right then. My wife is from China. How long will she be put up?"

"Put up?"

"Out of commission. Not able to get around and do stuff."

The doctor opened her mouth to speak, but hesitated. She studied Pete-O for a second. "She won't be able to walk for at least ten weeks, and she'll need to use a wheelchair," she said at last, "for at least six weeks. She'll require someone to wait on her."

"Yeah, yeah." Pete-O took in a big breath and then began the nodding again. Finally, he looked up and gave the doctor a serious look. "You take good care of her, awright?"

"She's in good hands. We'll call you as soon as she's out of surgery," Doctor Banerjee said, turning to go.

Pete-O's eyes followed until he saw the doctor's long black hair disappear through the chrome doors. "So that's why there's always footprints on the toilet seat," said Pete-O. "I thought she was trying to reach the towel shelf up over the tub."

"That toilet must be as high as her waist," said Lilith Ann. "She might have killed herself falling off that thing."

"I knew she didn't know how to drive a car or use a coffee maker or a toaster or turn on a vacuum cleaner," said Pete-O, shaking his head. "I have to show her everything, but I sure as hell thought she knew how to pee."

Magda's mouth dropped open. "She didn't know how to do any of that? Seriously? Good-night! This woman needs some help."

"This is a new mess alright," said Lilith Ann.

"She won't be in a wheelchair forever, and when she does get on her feet again we need to make sure she knows how to work stuff. And I mean everything," said Magda, pointing a finger in a circle at the family.

"You're going to have to get a home nurse," Lilith Ann said to her brother.

"Nurses are expensive."

"You can't afford not to have one," said his sister, looking fiercely down at him. "Your wife is going to need help just like you do now." Lilith Ann tried to suppress a smile.

Chapter 20

To Peng, who watched Pete-O from her wheelchair at the kitchen table, he had the face of an ugly dog with a pushed-in snout that had run with a gang of dogs around her village that she remembered from when she was a girl. She had feared those dogs, especially the smashed-faced leader of the pack. He had eventually been eaten.

Peng had been home from the hospital for three weeks, and her ankle still hurt if she was clumsy and bumped it against something when she was trying to maneuver her chair. Pete-O was much more adept at navigating the space than she was. Once, a few days after Peng came home, she had accidentally run into him as she tried to turn her chair around the kitchen table. The pain had been so great it had brought tears to her eyes. Pete-O had yelled something, and rolled past her on his way to the den to watch television.

He seemed annoyed at her all the time now, and spent most of his time out in his van going places; this was fine with Peng. When she heard his van door shut in the morning, she gave a little sigh of relief that she would likely have a little time to herself. Alone time was now a rare luxury, because a young woman had started coming to their house each morning at 9:00 a.m. She stayed there all day long. At first Peng didn't like her because she seemed to take over the kitchen and did all the cleaning. Peng suspected that Pete-O had decided to take on a second wife. The possibility didn't bother her terribly because having another woman in the house who was younger would take some of the responsibility for cooking and cleaning off of her. After all, she was Number One Wife and always would be. But she abandoned that idea after only a day when she considered that she was in America, a place where second wives were not allowed, and anyway, the young woman left each day as soon as she washed the dinner dishes. Pete-O paid little attention to her when he was home, and it was clear to Peng that he didn't like her cooking from the way he poked at the food on his plate.

After a few days, Peng grew to like the young woman, who called herself Fanny, a name that Peng had heard in a movie musical they watched on television. That was what they did much of the time Fanny was there. They watched television, except Fanny didn't watch so much as she had conversations with the characters on the shows they watched. When one of the people on the TV got angry or yelled or cried or showed any kind of extreme emotion, Fanny would gesture and point at them, and seem to give them advice. Sometimes Fanny would point at Peng and repeat words so that she could learn them herself. After about a week, Peng could put together simple sentences that Fanny had taught her.

That woman is a witch. He's so impossible. Can't trust him. She has plasic-surgee. How ridicalus is that? Coca-Cola is deleeshursh. Donnal Trum has bad hair. Let's have ice cream. I need to use the bassroom.

She also learned the words for her new favorite American foods like *hambuguh* and *roase beef*. Fanny cooked roast beef with vegetables in the pot. And she used such a big piece of beef! Peng secretly wondered how they could afford such expensive meat for everyday eating. Maybe Pete-O was wealthier than he had let on. The only time her family offered so much meat at the table was on Chinese New Year, and that was when they slaughtered a pig they had raised that year just for the occasion. Peng loved the scent the meat, carrots, potatoes, and onions gave off when they were nearly done. She often rolled her chair to the table near the stove where Fanny was cooking and talking. She waved her hands a lot when she talked, and sometimes Peng was as caught up in her movements as she was with her words. Fanny smiled almost all the time. Even when she seemed to be upset about something, her face was smiling. This was reassuring to Peng because this was the way of Chinese people. Keep your face happy, even if your stomach is tight with anger.

As much as she tried, Peng could not get entirely comfortable with Fanny's insistence on helping her with the toilet. She had suffered through an hour with the woman at the hospital who demonstrated how to use the toilet The American Way, and even made Peng go through the motions herself to show that she understood. She had no idea what this woman's job could possibly have been at the hospital, because no nurse would do such silly work. The hospital had managed to find an interpreter, a young college student, female of course, who stood uncomfortably next to the hospital woman and spoke for her as she explained how to sit on a toilet, use the paper, and most disgustingly, drop it in the toilet. What a repugnantly dirty business it all was. Her body was touching the same surface that other people's bodies touched when they did their toilet business. The flushing handle took it all away, which Peng did like about this Western contraption, but toilets took up so much space and they used water like a clothes washing machine each time she pulled down the flushing handle. Westerners were such wasteful people.

At least twice a day, Peng made the announcement that Fanny had taught her. Fanny never made her wait or appeared irritated that she had to help her with this most personal act. Once she helped Peng get herself seated safely, she stepped outside the door and waited for Peng to complete the steps all the way through flushing. Peng would then call out, "I am finish." Fanny would return and assist Peng with her clothes and support her under the arms as she maneuvered herself back into the chair. This necessity never stopped embarrassing Peng, but Fanny did the work with kindness and cheerfulness that made Peng ever more determined to get strong enough to do it by herself soon. Pete-O could do it with ease, and he didn't even have legs. Peng vowed to herself that as soon as she recovered from this broken leg she would never again be so helpless that she would need others to help her perform the most basic bodily functions. Despite Fanny's unfailing selflessness and patience, Peng determined she would rather die than ever feel so weak and dependent again.

Fanny was particularly worked up this afternoon about something they had been watching on the television news. Some people had been killed by someone with a gun, but Peng could not tell which person on the television had done the killing. She knew what it meant when pieces of long black plastic were strapped over the stretchers and the men who carried them were in no hurry to load them into the back of the ambulance. She had watched enough television shows about police to know all about these terrible scenes, except this was different because the ones on the news were real. The news reporter interviewed a man with dark glasses and a hat pulled low on his forehead. The hat had a picture of a skull and a pickup truck, and Peng was sure that he must have been the killer because he was too ashamed to show his face. He talked slowly, and Peng understood the word "dead." He may have been confessing his crime because he kept looking down and shaking his head as he spoke, but if that were true he was showing little remorse. The police in the background did not even seem to be in any hurry to arrest the man. Fanny was taking out a pot from a lower cabinet when there was a knock at the door.

"Hey! Anybody home?" Viv stuck her head around the door.

"Hello," said Fanny.

"Sorry we're late." She stepped in the door and then called out behind her. "Josh, you planning on growing a beard out there? Come on inside. And bring Peng's cushion." She stepped into the kitchen and dropped three video tapes onto the table. "You must be Fanny. Lilith Ann said Pete-O had found somebody to help out while Peng is under the weather. Are you with a temp service?"

"Oh no. I'm a friend of Baxter's."

"Oh," said Viv, suddenly eyeing Fanny with suspicion.

"You and I met at the church. Remember?"

Viv forced a little smile. "I met so many of Baxter's friends that day. So, are you in the. . . care business?"

"I have home care experience," Fanny said. "I tended to my great aunt when she was sick last year for three whole months, but she died."

There was an uncomfortable pause which Fanny seemed in no hurry to dispel. "Well," said Viv, "we stopped at Red Box and got these for Peng." The covers all featured angry, grimacing martial arts practitioners in varying degrees of punching and kicking positions. "They were the only ones we could find that had Chinese subtitles. We figured it would help her to learn the English if she could see what it meant in the subtitles while they were talking."

"How ridicalus is that?" said Peng. Viv's eyes bulged in shock at Peng's words.

"She's speaking English!" said Viv as Josh bustled into the house carrying a cushion with three terriers wearing red bow-ties on one side.

"I know. She's getting pretty good. We've been working at it since I got here," Fanny said proudly.

"Where's Pete-O?" asked Josh, holding out the cushion to Viv. "He's supposed to be here."

Fanny looked confusedly at Viv and then at Josh. "He doesn't usually get here until after I leave."

"I talked to him on the phone last night and told him we were coming to take him and Peng out to dinner. He said he wanted to go to Golden Corral," said Viv.

"Well, I don't know what to tell you. He didn't leave any note or anything, and I was just about to put on some hotdogs for dinner."

"Oh goodness," said Viv, waving her pink-nailed hand at the pot Fanny held. "We told Pete-O we were going to treat

Peng to dinner at the Golden Corral since she's been cooped up in the house for three weeks. I just feel terrible about not getting over here to see her before now, but I've had a million things going at work and with the yard sale at the church. You reckon he's going to meet us there?"

Josh shrugged his shoulders. "I don't know. You were the one called him."

"And you know how he is," Viv said in a voice only slightly above a mutter. "You come with us, too," she said to Fanny. "You and I need to get to know one another. You can tell me all about how you know Baxter."

The parking lot of the Golden Corral was packed, but Josh pulled the Ford right into a handicap spot even though he didn't have a sticker. Viv had called every member of the family with a phone which was everyone except Baxter, to ask if anyone had seen Pete-O and no one had. She was about to give up in frustration when Robert's car pulled in behind them and he honked the horn.

"Oh for crying out loud," said Viv. "There's Robert. Josh, if he badgers you about that job at the plant you tell him it's filled."

"Viv, he's my brother," said Josh.

"Uh-huh, and he embarrassed the stew out of both of us over that job with Tom. I am tired of apologizing for him all over town. You burn enough bridges and after a while you just get to sit yourself down on the other side of the river."

Robert was waiting to hold the door open for Peng as Josh wheeled her into the restaurant. Fanny felt that same hard man's stare that she was accustomed to from her days at the T&A as she passed him by on her way into the restaurant. When they got their plates and settled around the handicap-accessible table she noticed that he made a quick turn around the corner to sit next to her.

"Robert, I was going to sit there," said Viv.

"You can sit next to Josh."

Viv sighed and put her plate next to Josh's. Peng's chair

was pushed against the table on the end and in front of her Viv had placed a plate with a spoonful of everything from the buffet. Food was heaped up in a pile in the center. Peng was astonished to see that it was enough to feed her and both of her parents back home.

"I cut your steak for you," said Viv, raising her eyebrows at Peng, who showed no understanding. "And I went ahead and got you a piece of pie. Once the A&M lets out down the road they'll all come in and swarm the food like there's no tomorrow. Lordamercy those people love pie."

"Pete-O coming," said Peng, looking toward the door. Pete-O rolled around the corner of the dining room to the opposite end of the table from Peng, taking everyone by surprise.

"There you are," said Viv. "I thought you must have forgot."

"Got tied up," said Pete-O. His face was red as if he'd been outside, and he smelled like something that had been burning.

Viv crinkled her nose a little at his proximity. "You're here just in time. We were about to give thanks. Robert, you can put down your fork for just a minute. Look at that, even Peng here knows to wait for the prayer."

"Oh, that's because I forgot to give her the chopsticks," said Fanny, fishing them from her purse and handing them over to Peng. "She hates forks."

Viv pursed her lips with annoyance before bowing her head and thanking God for the food and for allowing everyone to live in a country where the current White House executive administration had not taken their freedom to bow their heads in restaurants and pray to God without fear of being arrested, put in jail, or otherwise persecuted for their religious beliefs. Amen. Before they could reach for their forks Fanny chimed in, "And thank you for providing a good job with good people." Amen.

"You know she can't understand you," said Pete-O to Viv.

"It's important for her to know how lucky she is to be in our country," said Viv. "When she sends letters back to her family, don't you want her to say good things about America?"

"Oh, she loves it here," said Fanny, nodding at Peng. "She really likes the flowers Jack planted around the house. She said so."

"She said that? Well, I'll be doggone," said Josh.

"Well, she said something and pointed at them," Fanny replied.

"And we're glad you're grateful for your job," said Viv. "In fact, we're anxious to get to know you a little bit better." She turned to Pete-O. "Lilith Ann said you'd hired somebody to do the nursing for Peng. We didn't know it was one of Baxter's friends."

"He gave me her name. That don't mean they're friends," said Pete-O.

"We're friends," said Fanny. She held an ear of corn limply in one hand and a kernel stuck on her lip as she chewed.

"Did he meet you where you used to work?" Robert asked. "At that place?"

At this Fanny's chewing slowed. "What's that supposed to mean?"

"I hear things," said Robert. "But it doesn't matter to me how you met." He was smiling at her, but it was a smile that made her stomach quiver.

"So, where did she work?" asked Viv, looking at the two of them.

"She worked at the day care center over behind the church," said Pete-O. "Hellfire, what does anybody care where she worked?"

"We're just getting to know her. After all, she's there all day with your wife. Alone. Don't you think we ought to know something about her?" Viv's mouth twitched a little.

"Do you not think I have enough sense to check people out when I hire them? I know where she's worked. How much money she made. Where she went to school. What kind of grades she made. Who her family is. What kind of car she drives. Whether or not she's ever had a traffic ticket. If she's been arrested. What her credit rating is. I checked it all out better than any of you would know how to do, so just stop worrying about stuff that's none of your business. And that means you, too, Robert. You don't need to be asking her questions about stuff that you ought to just stay away from and forget the hell about 'cause she doesn't have nothing to tell you about nothing."

Everyone at the table sat in shocked silence. The server came by the table and hesitated before placing a basket of yeast bread on the table. When she was gone, Pete-O reached into the basket and took a roll.

"Well now Pete-O, nobody was trying to give her the third degree," said Viv. "But I guess since you've covered everything then we'll just not concern ourselves."

"Good," said Pete-O. "Did you show Peng the chocolate fountain?"

"Uh, it's broke," said Josh.

"Broke?" Pete-O exclaimed. "How does a chocolate fountain break?"

"Everything breaks, now don't it!" said Robert. "Things just break down. That's what America's come to." Several people at the next table turned to stare.

"I wanted Peng to see it," said Pete-O.

No one spoke.

"Choco-lit," said Peng.

Pete-O pointed a finger back towards the buffet. "Yeah, that's right. Chocolate fountain. Remember? I told you there was a fountain where chocolate flowed down it." He made a gesture of something overflowing with his hands, and then his hands dropped to the table. "I really wanted her to see that."

"Why don't you buy her one? You can get the table top ones for $24.99 at Walmart," said Josh, but he didn't catch his mistake before Viv kicked him under the table. "They got them on Ebay, too."

"Hey! Waitress!" Pete-O was snapping his fingers at the server who was passing with a tray of drinks. "What happened to the chocolate fountain?"

"I'm sorry, sir. It's out of order."

"Out of order? Darling, it's not an elevator. Can't somebody around here fix it?"

"I'm sure they've called somebody to repair it, but it's not working right now." She tried to walk away, but Pete-O wasn't finished with her.

"This here's my wife down at the other end of the table." He pointed at Peng, who looked up from her plate at the commotion at Pete-O's end. "She came all the way from China to see that chocolate fountain, and now she's got a broke leg and we're both in wheelchairs. It's just a shame that she can't get herself a chocolate-covered strawberry at that fountain."

The waitress sagged under the weight of the drinks. "I could put some cake icing on some strawberries."

Pete-O shook his head. "That's just not the same, now is it?"

"Pete-O, there ain't nothing the poor girl can do," said Josh. "They'll get it fixed and we'll come back another time." He motioned to the waitress to go on her way and she backed away quickly.

Peng watched the ensuing conversation unfold. The words were a mystery, but the tone, the expressions, the rolling eyes, the bulging neck of her husband, his fist smacking down on the table, and the disgusted exhales from Viv told her there was some unpleasant communication going on. Pete-O didn't seem to be pleased with the service because he wasn't eating anything, and he had raised his voice to both the young girl serving the food and to Viv. She'd heard it many times before and was glad to be seated so far away.

"I just get tired of things not being like they promised," said Pete-O, smacking a fist down on the table and jarring his drink so that it nearly spilled.

"Nobody promised you a chocolate fountain," said Josh.

"I promised Peng one."

Viv raised her eyebrows at Pete-O. "It sure is nice to see

that you're concerned about keeping your promises to her. But Jesus doesn't even promise us a tomorrow, so we should thank him when we get it each day."

"I didn't ask for tomorrow. I asked for a damn chocolate fountain. You'd think that Jesus could provide something as simple as that."

"I won't have you blaspheming our Lord," snapped Viv.

"It's the little things that get to me." Pete-O pointed at Peng again. "She's been wanting to see this for two years, and on the one day I take her to see—"

"You took her? You weren't even home. We're the ones who brought her here and got her supper," said Viv, turning in her seat to face Pete-O more fully.

"He is so imposs-ble! Let's have ice cream," said Peng. The table erupted into laughter, all except Pete-O, who looked at Peng as if he was hearing the first words ever out of her mouth. Fanny clapped her hands and made excited whoops of joy.

"You are SO RIGHT!" Viv shouted. "Let's get this gal some ice cream." She jumped up from her seat at the same time Fanny moved from her own. Viv led the way and Fanny pushed Peng's chair.

As soon as they were out of earshot, Pete-O pointed a finger at Robert. "I meant what I said about you not talking to Fanny. I know who she is. Baxter told me all about it, and I don't need you dragging her back down. I need her to keep looking after Peng until she gets back on her feet."

"I wasn't going to drag her down anywhere. I just wanted to ask her a few questions about stuff," said Robert. "She might be of some help."

"Where'd this girl work?" asked Josh. "The Pentagon?" Robert and Pete-O ignored him.

"I said it was a bad idea," said Pete-O, "and I still think it is. It's dangerous."

"Talking ain't dangerous."

"Asking too many questions is dangerous."

"I sure liked you better before you went to prison," said Robert.

"When I left for prison you were still riding around in a pickup truck bird-dogging chicks."

"'Chicks?'" said Josh, laughing. "I haven't heard anybody say that word since I was a kid, Pete-O. You getting old, man." Josh continued to laugh, and they continued to ignore him.

"It doesn't have anything to do with you, Pete-O, so don't worry about nothing, alright?" Robert picked up his fork again.

"It's not me I'm worried about," said Pete-O. "You go messing with my nursing care and I'll never hear the end of it from your mama."

Josh raised his eyebrows. "Is this girl a hooker?"

"Hell no, she ain't no hooker." Pete-O would have said more, but the women were headed back to the table. Fanny carried a tray with ice cream and strawberries coated in chocolate icing.

"Lookit at what we got," said Fanny. "Chocolate-covered strawberries. We fixed them ourselves."

"That wasn't what she wanted," Pete-O said.

"You mean it wasn't what you wanted," said Viv. "Peng's tickled pink to be getting chocolate-covered strawberries whether the chocolate came from under a fountain or got spooned on at the dessert bar." Peng licked the chocolate off the tip of a strawberry and then put the entire thing in her mouth. In a second, she pushed the stem out with her tongue, dropped it on her plate and picked up another strawberry. She ate nine strawberries this way until she could hold no more. Fanny finished off the last three. The two of them maintained a bits-and-pieces conversation that Pete-O could not follow from his end of the table. He eyed the two of them throughout the remainder of dessert until everyone was clearly sated and then Viv announced it was time to go.

"We'll take Peng and Fanny back to the house," said Viv.

"I can give Fanny a ride," said Robert.

"What for?" asked Viv. "We're taking Peng back anyway."

"I got to stop by Pete-O's for a minute anyway," said Robert. "I can give her a ride and your car won't be so crowded."

Viv eyed him suspiciously. "What have you got to do at Pete-O's?"

"That's between me and Pete-O," said Robert.

"Viv, it doesn't matter who rides with who. We're all going to the same place," Josh said, pushing up from the table. Viv gave him a murderous stare and stood up from her seat.

"Well, don't you think Fanny should decide which car she wants to ride in?" asked Viv. Robert reached into his pocket for his keys. "Kimmy must be wondering when you're going to get home."

"I told her I was going to Pete-O's tonight after we had dinner," said Robert. "Come on, Fanny. I'll drive you back. Got to go there anyway, so I won't take no for an answer."

Eyes shifted uneasily and Fanny spoke up. "Well, if it's no trouble." Robert flipped the keys around his finger and headed for the door. "Not one bit," he said. Fanny tucked her pocketbook under her arm and followed.

Viv's tirade on the ride back to Pete-O's began as soon as the car doors were shut. Why in the world was Robert so heckfire anxious to get that woman alone? What did he think that woman was, a hooker? And what questions did he want to ask her? What in the heckfire samhill did he think she had to tell him about? And why did Pete-O get so upset when Robert said he wanted to talk to her?

Josh kept trying to shush Viv and rolled his eyes to Peng in the back seat, but Viv was on fire to know the secret of why everyone was so sensitive about Fanny. "She must know something," she said, motioning with her eyes at the rearview mirror to the image of Peng, who sat in the back watching the scenery pass by. "She's spends her days with that woman, so she knows more than she's letting on. I'm telling you there is something very strange going on. I'm of a good mind to call Kimmy right now and tell her that Robert has run off in his car with a woman we hardly know a thing about."

"You'll do no such thing!" snapped Josh, and his sharp tone made Viv's mouth fall open. "Don't you go lighting fires that other people are gonna have to put out. There's no trouble he can get into with that woman in a five-minute drive from the restaurant. The last thing you want to do is crank Kimmy up over nothing. Girl's got enough problems without thinking her husband's up to no good."

"Robert's been up to no good most of his life," said Viv, but Josh's speech had managed to snuff out much of her anger. They pulled into the driveway in time to see Fanny making a beeline from Robert's car to her own. She didn't even wave good-bye. "I told you there was something going on," said Viv, and she got out of the car before Josh could speak. They all watched Fanny back out into the road and pass Pete-O's van as it neared the house.

While Josh and Viv got Peng settled inside the house, Pete-O helped himself to a beer. Viv stood between his chair and the entrance to the den. Keeping her voice calm, she asked, "Are you going to tell me why Robert is so interested in that little nurse you hired?" Pete-O took a drink of his beer and sighed hard. In the next room he could see the television. Josh and Peng sat watching a kitchen full of angry women with lots of hair who were yelling at one another. Pete-O wanted to retreat to his bathroom and soak in a tub of warm water and Epsom salts to ease his tired back and forget the world, especially his family. Surely Viv would not follow him if he turned his chair around and headed down the hall. "I'm not leaving until I get an answer," she said in a voice just above a whisper.

Pete-O shook his head in frustration. "He's got this idea she knows something about this job he thinks he can get."

"What job is that?"

"She doesn't know anything, and I told him so."

"You said she worked in a day care center. If Robert's all of a sudden decided he wants to look after little kids all day, he doesn't have to look any further than his own house."

"Robert doesn't know what the hell he's doing."

"Did you see how Fanny jumped in her car and left without so much as a 'thank you for dinner, see you later'? Whatever he was asking her about must have got her mighty upset."

"I'll talk to him."

"You'd better hope he didn't run Peng's nurse off," said Viv. "You know how hard it is to find good help these days. And Peng seems to really like her."

"I said I'd talk to him."

"When?"

"Tomorrow."

"Well, all right then. Do it before he does something stupid," said Viv. "Something else, I mean."

Chapter 21

As *soon as the door shut behind Viv and Josh, Peng reached* for the remote and turned the channel away from the yelling, ugly-faced women. She wasn't sure what names they were calling one another, but the TV sound was riddled with beeps that came so often and so long it was impossible for her to make out any words she knew. Peng flipped through the channels until she found a movie that looked old because the color was black and white. She liked the old movies because there was a lot of talking and most of the time the faces were filmed close-up, making it easier to tell what they were saying. The people were always beautiful with pretty clothes and hats, and sometimes the women even wore gloves. She had never owned a pair of gloves.

Peng's stomach was a little uncomfortable from the big meal she'd eaten at the dinner. Viv had put too much food on her plate, but Peng ate as much as she could so as not to appear rude. She needed to use the toilet, but Pete-O had occupied the bathroom right after Viv and Josh left. They seemed angry, or Viv had. She'd snapped at Josh as they were going out the door, and for the second time that evening, she heard Josh snap back at Viv. That had never happened before, at least not that Peng had heard. She made out the words "go" and "tomorrow." There was always anger in this family, always loud words. It was better when Fanny was there with her during the day. Her words were so gentle and kind, and she was anxious to learn Chinese. Peng taught her as many words in Chinese as Fanny taught her in English. The two of them managed to keep up tiny conversations with lots of pointing and laughing. Peng had been able to take a few steps with the help of crutches, but she was in no hurry to show Pete-O how fast she was healing. He'd surely get rid of Fanny as soon as he knew Peng could get around on her own, even if it were no more than hobbling on one foot with crutches.

Pete-O had been in the bathroom for nearly an hour, and the movie was ending. She enjoyed listening to the quick cadence of the English, although she'd been able to make little sense of it. A woman named Hiddy argued with a man, but somehow neither one looked very angry, as if the two of them were making a game of it. She strongly suspected they were really in love with one another. She'd never seen a movie with so many people talking so loudly and so rapidly. They kept picking up and talking into what were obviously telephones, or what served as telephones in America when this movie had been made. So absurd-looking, a table littered with at least a dozen upside-down, wooden cups on wires attached to posts that the characters kept grabbing and yelling into before sticking the cups back on. It was during this scene, near the end of the movie, when the lights flickered. Later, Peng would realize that this must have been when it happened. The electricity didn't go out completely. Everything just dimmed, as if sizzling, for a couple of seconds, and then the lights and the television illuminated normally again. Music began to play as the ending movie credits rolled. She didn't hear anything over the music, if there had been anything to hear. They said that there likely hadn't been much noise, that Pete-O would have been too stricken to cry out.

Usually Peng would go to bed early, but she needed to get into the bathroom first, and Pete-O was still in there. Soaking in the tub while listening to his radio for an hour or more was nothing unusual for him. When he did, she could hear a man's voice coming from the radio, a voice that sounded much like Pete-O's in rhythm and tone, an angry voice that rattled on in a series of high-pitched rants before calming down again. Peng could always tell when the commercials were coming because the same music played before the breaks from the man talking. Pete-O often tuned in to this same radio show when they went places in the van. She never talked during the show because he still didn't know enough words to maintain a conversation with him. She always wanted to ask him to turn it off, the angry talking that never stopped except for commercials. Why did Americans on the radio have to be so angry all the time?

Another half hour passed, and Peng watched a man on the cooking channel demonstrate how to cut up a fish, something she already knew, but this man made the fish look very nice on the dish with his fancy cuts. By the time that show ended, Peng's discomfort was growing, and she was feeling desperate. She didn't dare use the toilet while he was just two feet from it in the bathtub. She had never done such a thing. It was time for Pete-O to free up the bathroom. She rolled her chair down the hall and stopped in front of the door. "Pete-O? You want sandwich?" No answer. "You want beer?" There was no answer, and no sound, not even the radio. She knocked again and called his name. Still nothing. A small fear rolled over Peng, and she hurried her chair back to the kitchen. Holding a hand over her chest, she took deep breaths of air, and tried to calm the panic she was beginning to feel. "It's okay. It's okay," she whispered to herself in English. Peng turned her chair once more, this time bumping her injured leg against the kitchen table. She flinched at the momentary pain and proceeded down the hall, back to the bathroom.

"Pete-O?" She called his name three more times, but there was no answer. Peng pushed the door open and looked inside. Pete-O lay very still in the bathtub. "Pete-O?" Her voice was now a hoarse whisper. She rolled her chair a few feet inside and saw his face nearly submerged in the water. All that remained above the surface was his eyes staring straight up and open wide at the ceiling and the tip of his nose. In the center of the tub, wedged between Pete-O's stomach and the side of the tub lay his radio, still plugged into the wall. The room stank of something burning, and around the wall socket was a blackened circle extending about six inches around the plug.

Peng could not remember how to breathe. She gasped for air as she backed out of the bathroom and hit the hall wall behind her with her chair wheels. She had to focus hard to make her hands work at moving her chair forward. Back in the kitchen, she continued to gasp to bring in enough air and calm herself down. Peng had never wanted to run away so badly in her entire life, even more badly than when Kong was dying. She would have sacrificed her own two hands if she could have just run right out that door and hidden herself somewhere, anywhere. She could not have two dead husbands. The police would never believe that she did not kill Pete-O. In another village in China, she had heard of a woman who drowned her husband in a washtub in their back yard, and she was sentenced to death. Now with Pete-O dead, this would mean her end. No one would believe that she had not done it. She would be arrested, tried, and sentenced to death in a strange country. There could be no escape this time. Peng wiped her face with her hands and was thankful that this time her family would not be there to know about it. No one in the family except Pete-O had their contact information, and now he was dead. She could accept her fate and be sentenced to death as long as her family did not know about it. She took a deep breath and sat up straight in her chair. She would face the future with dignity. It was time to call someone and tell them what had happened. She would then wait for the police.

Peng had to lean on her good leg and stand a little to reach the wall phone in the kitchen. Pete-O did not believe in cell phones, and the yellow push button phone next to the kitchen door was their only communication with the outside world.

She looked at the emergency phone numbers written on the paper taped to the wall and thought about which one would be best to notify first. She knew the shape of "V" was for Viv's name, but she did not want to talk with that woman. Lilith Ann started with the "L" shape, and there was only one name that began with that character, so she punched in the numbers and listened as the phone rang. She heard the sounds five times, but no one spoke. Peng was about to hang up the phone, when there was a voice on the other end. It was Magda.

Peng cleared her throat before finding her words. "Pete-O is bad."

"What?"

"Pete-O. Pete-O is bad."

Magda gave out a little laugh. "Well, we know that."

Peng swallowed a little cry and said it again. "Pete-O. Is. Bad."

There was a long pause and then Magda said, "Peng? What did he do? Did he hurt you?"

"Peng? Can you hear me?" Lilith Ann yelled into the phone, and Peng had to pull the receiver away quickly before her ears were assaulted again. "You tell me what happened." There was more talking from Magda and then Lilith Ann came back on the phone. "Let me talk to Pete-O. Put him on the phone."

Peng clutched at the receiver a moment, trying to think of what she wanted. She understood only Pete-O's name. Lilith Ann said something else and then the phone went dead. Soon the police would arrive and Peng would have to say good-bye to the American life she had. There would never be a fountain with chocolate for her now. It hadn't been as bad as she feared it would be when she first saw Pete-O at the airport. They'd actually reached a kind of comfortable truce around one another. He didn't say much, and as long as she provided food for him and kept the house clean, he rarely complained. He had fulfilled his promises to her regarding a ring and a nice house. Occasionally he drove her to town and she got her hair fixed at a hair salon that smelled to her of fake flowers. The ladies there chatted with her a lot and laughed when she tried to talk to them, but it was never a mean laugh. She didn't care for the way they did her hair, all puffy and stiff with little flip curls around her forehead, but Pete-O requested that style specifically so she didn't dare complain about it. They'd been to the

salon just the day before, so her hair was still neatly in place. That was good, she thought, since her time was so limited, and she didn't want to look disheveled when they took her away. On the television she saw that there were always television cameras on the criminals when the police arrested them. She and Fanny watched a show every week about people getting arrested, and the cameras were always focused on the person as the police put on the handcuffs and then put him into a police car, the officer always pushing the criminal's head down with his hand as he entered the car. Sometimes women were arrested, and many times they screamed and acted rudely. Peng would not be rude. She would hold her hands out in front of her so that they could easily slip on the wrist bracelets and she would say nothing at all when they took her away. Later, after they executed her, she hoped they would remember that she was a dignified person and say how brave she was when the police came for her.

Her need to use the bathroom was now at a critical level, but she didn't dare enter the bathroom with her husband's dead body in there. She had to go before the police arrived because there was no telling when they might give her the opportunity to use a toilet. Hers was an impossible situation, and she knew she had only minutes before someone came. The decision brought tears to her eyes as much from terror as from the pain of having to relieve herself. She rolled her chair to the door of the bathroom and called out to Pete-O in Mandarin. She asked his forgiveness for what she was about to do, but under the circumstances she had little choice. She positioned her chair next to the toilet and turned her face toward the door as she stood up and took hold of the silver arched bars on either side. Pete-O's body was in her peripheral vision, but she refused to turn her head his way. Peng could feel him there, floating, his waxy body pale in the cloudy, cold tub water. She was so nervous she nearly fell onto the seat with her pants still up, but she righted herself and pulled her clothes to her knees. Easing herself down on the toilet, the relief came quickly and she let out a little involuntary sigh when all was finished. In seconds there were headlights in the driveway and she fumbled to finish her business and get back in her chair. She almost forgot to flush the toilet, and when Lilith Ann's furious knock sounded on the door the toilet was still filling with water. There was no time to wash her hands, so she pushed the wheels of her chair hard and headed for the front door.

"Peng? Pete-O? Somebody open up or I'm coming in!" Lilith Ann called through the pane of glass.

Peng pulled her chair sideways to the front door and began unlocking it. There was movement outside the window and she could see that there were two people, but she couldn't see who the second one was. Lilith Ann pushed the door open as soon as she heard the lock disengage, almost ramming it into Peng's chair. "Tell me what's going on," Lilith Ann said, even before she stepped inside.

Peng lifted her chin and pointed back to the hallway. They would soon take her away, and she had to be brave. "Pete-O," she said, but she began to cry softly.

Magda and Lilith Ann bumped into one another as they launched toward the hallway to the bedroom. "Pete-O?" Lilith Ann called out.

"He's not here," said Magda. "What the hell?"

Peng rolled her chair to the end of the hall. "Bassroom!" she cried.

Magda and her mother came trotting out of the bedroom and both women gave out a shriek when they spotted Pete-O in the tub. "We need an ambulance," said Lilith Ann. She took two steps toward the kitchen, turned back and stopped.

"What? What?" said Magda.

"You're the one with a phone," Lilith Ann said. Magda fumbled in her pocket and took out her cell. In seconds, she had a 911 operator on the line and asked for an ambulance. She gave the address and then said, "We think he's dead, so maybe you should send a hearse, too." Magda clicked her phone off without saying good-bye.

"Peng, what happened?" said Lilith Ann. Peng sat quietly at the end of the hall, wiping her eyes with her sleeve.

"Oh, shit, I forgot to ask for an interpreter." Magda flipped open her cell once more. "I'll call Mr. Chen." When he answered the phone and Magda identified herself, his tone changed.

"You people never run out of problems. I have a restaurant to run. Hire one of the Chinese girls from the college," said Mr. Chen.

"It's her husband. He's dead," said Magda.

There was a pause. "Why don't you call an ambulance?" he said.

"We did, but he was, the way he was killed. She needs your help," said Magda.

There was something about her choice of words, *the way he was killed*, that made Mr. Chen change his mind. "I'll be there," he said. Magda gave him the address and hung up.

"You don't think she had anything to do with it," said Lilith Ann.

"No, I don't, but you know how the police are."

"He was her gravy train. She wouldn't hurt a hair on his head." Lilith Ann paused. "And you thought the same thing I did when she called. You thought it was the other way around, you know."

"I know, I was ready to brain Pete-O with a stick, but I never expected this," said Magda. The siren sounded from the end of the road and the three women were in the den waiting when it pulled into the driveway. A police car followed close behind, and in minutes the small house was full of men and women in black uniforms with guns and bags of equipment. Lilith Ann gave Peng a paper towel to dry her eyes with, and in minutes it hung in wet shreds.

The tiny bathroom was quickly filled with people taking

photographs and then lifting Pete-O's corpse onto a gurney. Officer Dugas was anxious to question Peng and his loud voice brought nothing but an even more stricken look on her face. "We've got somebody that speaks Chinese on the way, so just hold off a minute," said Lilith Ann, waving the officer back with her hand.

"She can't speak any English?"

"Not unless you want a sandwich," said Lilith Ann. Officer Dugas put his notepad back in his pocket and went back to the bathroom where the EMTs were rolling out Pete-O's body. When the covered gurney came into view, Peng let out a long wail and scratched at her face. She began screaming words that no one could understand, for which she would later be quietly grateful, because Peng had shouted out that she was a killer who deserved to die.

Mr. Chen arrived, still in an apron, just as the doors closed on the ambulance. Peng began talking rapidly as soon as he set foot in the door, and even he had to tell her to slow down because he couldn't understand her. The police officer told her to stop talking until he could ask the questions, but Peng kept up her wailing and Mr. Chen tried again to calm her down. Lilith Ann pushed him back, kneeled down in front of Peng, and took the terrified woman's face in her hands. "Peng, honey, now shut up. Just shut your mouth, okay?" Lilith Ann took a deep breath and blew it out, gesturing for Peng to do the same. Slowly, Peng relaxed and began to breathe with Lilith Ann. "You're upset because your husband just died. You're grieving. Any woman would, but dying's just one of those things we can't help. You hear me? Nobody could help it. Everybody here knows that he was the light of your life, and you two loved each other like a couple of teenagers. We know how you adored Pete-O and you never harmed a hair on his head. It was all just an accident, and everybody knows it. Okay? So you just answer this nice officer's questions, and then they'll all go away and leave you alone, okay?"

"I thought you said she couldn't understand any English," said Officer Dugas.

"She can't," said Lilith Ann, standing up and taking a seat on the sofa. He pushed his pen up underneath his hat and scratched his head a moment, thinking about Lilith's words before taking out his notepad once more.

Mr. Chen knelt down and spoke softly to Peng. His eyes met Lilith Ann's a few times as he spoke, and she nodded back. As he spoke, Peng's face relaxed a little. He smelled of fried chicken and peppers, a scent that comforted her.

The four of them took seats around Peng, and the interview went on for over half an hour. Mr. Chen interpreted each answer from Peng carefully, but he left out her pleas for mercy because he knew it would sound as if she had done something wrong. Sometimes as Peng answered she would reach out for Mr. Chen's hand and squeeze it, but her actions were desperate, unconscious. He knew the feeling of desperation that she was accustomed to when dealing with police in China. For a woman as poor as Mr. Chen suspected Peng had been, if someone higher up thought you were guilty of something, there was little a person could do. He tried to tell her that America was different, that she would be treated fairly, even if he didn't entirely believe it himself. He saw on television what they did to innocent people, especially people who were not white. His nephew had spent a weekend in jail two years earlier, and he told tales of how he was cursed at, called "chink" and worse while being kicked by a police officer. Instead of telling her the reality of the police, he repeated the line that immigrants comforted themselves with when they arrived in America, the one about how everyone had freedom and the police could not throw you in jail for no reason. This woman was certainly innocent, a terrified, tiny woman in a wheelchair who could speak barely any English. She told her story of how she had found Pete-O in the tub, dead. She did not even understand that it was the radio falling in the water that killed him. She thought he had fallen asleep and drowned. Mr. Chen repeated all that she said, or almost all of it, for Officer Dugas barely looked up to ask questions as he wrote on his pad. At the end of the interview, Mr. Chen stood up and gave Officer Dugas a big smile. "She needs rest, okay? You let her stay?" Lilith Ann and Magda waited next to him with expectant faces.

"Yeah, sure." Officer Dugas was writing something on his notepad. When he flipped it shut, they were all watching him intently. "Accidental death. Looks like he was trying to change the channel, maybe adjust the volume or something and the radio fell in the water, electrocution. Maybe a heart attack. Coroner's office will tell us for sure in a few days." He held up a plastic bag with a nail inside that no one else had noticed he had in his possession. "EMT found this in the water and there was a big nail hole in the window sill that looked like where the radio sat. From the looks of how that hole had been rocked out, I suspect he was in the habit of reaching up and maybe pulling on the radio a little bit to reach the knobs when he turned it on and off since he, you know, he couldn't stand up to do it. After a while that nail got loose with all that pulling against it, and then he did it one too many times and—" He made a motion of something going splat with his hands. "There it went, down in the water. Terrible accident."

"Oh yes, a terrible accident," said Lilith Ann. The relief in her voice was a little too obvious.

"My condolences to you, ma'am," Officer Dugas said. He made a brief tip of his hat to Peng, who sat hunched low in her chair. To him she looked like a broken child, like one of those pitiful, skinny children with Muscular Dystrophy that he had to stand next to when the department participated in the fundraiser each December. He felt a little sorry for her, and hoped it would be the last time he had to deal with any Hempers for a while.

Mr. Chen had to shake Peng's shoulders to get her to look up at him. He began speaking rapidly, and then the shock on

her face was clear. Her mouth fell open and she began crying again. She reached for the policeman's hand, but Mr. Chen stopped her. He repeated a half dozen thank-yous as Officer Dugas headed for the door. Peng watched him leave, her trembling hand now over her beating heart.

"Looks like we've got a funeral to plan," said Lilith Ann.

Chapter 22

On the day that Pete-O was laid to rest, North Alabama was having unusually warm weather. The funeral procession ended at the First Baptist Church of Drayton cemetery where the infamous Lattie Kay McMoreland was buried, a woman who had axe-murdered three members of her family just after World War II. Locals referred to her as the "Alabama Lizzie Borden." This fun fact was not lost on *The Gadsden Times* reporter who wrote an article pointing out how Pete-O would be joining the likes of McMoreland in the hereafter. The headline read: "Walmart Shooter Dies by Electrocution." This unfair allusion to an electric chair and Pete-O's past once again drew attention to the Hemper-Boyd family, and once again reporters and nosey people started hanging around his house, trying to get a glimpse of anything they could. When word spread around that there was a grieving widow inside who was an "immigrant," another wave of indignation rose because Pete-O had married "one of those Mexicans." The next morning Lilith Ann and Magda retrieved Peng and kept her at their house for two more days until it was time for the funeral, and all the family gathered for the service. For this special occasion Lilith Ann had sent Magda to JCPenney to buy Peng a proper funeral dress; no second-hand Goodwill frock for the grieving widow. When they arrived at the funeral home with Peng in the back seat, she wore a navy blue silk dress with JCPenney's best imitation pearl earrings, a luxurious accessory that Magda had to convince her was necessary.

At the cemetery, Pete-O was laid to rest three spaces from his parents, and one row up from Lilith Ann's husband. Peng had expressed the wish to attend the funeral on her crutches, but the family consensus, plus Fanny's input, was that she should remain in the chair. When the graveside service concluded,

Baxter pushed her chair over the bumpy grass under the tent to Pete-O's casket where he plucked a single carnation from the spray of flowers and handed it to her. Peng assumed this was some Western ritual of death and some reciprocation must have been expected of her, so she stretched her arm up and pulled off a palm leaf, the only greenery within reach, presenting it with two hands to Baxter. With great ceremony, he accepted it, also with two hands, and placed it in his coat pocket where it splayed out so tall and wide it covered his chin and one shoulder.

Peng wondered why Pete-O's casket still rested on a frame underneath the tent that covered the hole into which it would clearly be lowered. Leaving the cemetery before he was securely in the ground seemed oddly disrespectful. She leaned over and whispered to Baxter, "Bury Pete-O now?"

Baxter looked at his brother's casket, down at the hole, and then finally at Peng. His eyes moved with slow deliberation, as if someone were telling him which direction to look in next, and for how long. "Yes," he said, "I expect they will."

Behind her, there was a commotion that did not belong in the tranquil atmosphere of a cemetery. Several people were walking quickly in a group toward the funeral site. Walking front and center, dressed all in black, was a small woman not much bigger than Peng, with her wren-colored hair sprayed tight and unmovable. Two large young men walked on either side of her, and as they drew closer Peng could see that each one was holding the woman by an arm. They were either forcing her to walk through the cemetery, or they were propping her up. Peng couldn't tell. When the little woman was close enough for Peng to see her face clearly, she saw that the woman had been crying, and the young men were trying to be gentle with her. Other people walked behind, but it was clear the attention was on this fraught woman. The Hemper-Boyd family turned as one and faced the crowd as they came within a car length of the funeral tent and stopped.

For a moment no one spoke. The woman took a deep breath

and it was clear she was willing herself not to cry. One of the young men whispered to her and she shook her head adamantly. He spoke again, and she pushed a few steps away from him.

"I just had to see for myself," she said.

Lilith Ann cocked her head a little to one side and took a few steps to meet the woman halfway on the one-lane, asphalt path. Magda followed a step behind her. "What is it you came to see?" asked Lilith Ann.

"Do you know who I am?" asked the woman.

Lilith Ann studied her face and shook her head. "I'm afraid I don't."

"Pete-O Hemper shot my husband eight years ago. Shot him dead for no reason and left two little boys without their daddy." She pointed a shaking finger at the coffin. "And when I heard he was dead, I had to see for myself that justice had finally been done."

"I don't reckon justice can ever be done when somebody kills a man." Lilith Ann's words seem to deflate the woman's anger just a little, but she pressed on.

"I wanted to see," she said, letting her voice rise a little for effect, "how the Lord gave him the death penalty after all. If he wasn't to get the electric chair for killing my husband in cold blood, then he got justice from the Lord with electrocution in another way."

Magda approached her mother from behind and spoke up. "If you want to give somebody credit for electrocuting Pete-O, then give it to Rush Limbaugh 'cause that's who the EMTs said he was listening to when he decided to turn up the volume."

"You hush up and stay out of this," said Lilith Ann in a low voice.

The young man on the woman's right stepped up next to his mother. "Seven years wasn't near long enough for him to pay for what he did to my daddy," he said. His move made Magda close the space between herself and her mother. The four of them stood a few feet from one another, the son and Magda like soldiers next to their generals in a stand-off.

"No son, it wasn't, and nothing can bring your daddy back. I'm sure sorry you lost him," said Lilith Ann.

"Is that his wife there?" asked the woman, tilting her head toward Peng.

Lilith Ann looked back at her sister-in-law who sat perplexed in her chair, watching the events unfold. "That's his widow. She didn't have anything to do with what happened back then. She didn't even know him."

The woman ignored Lilith Ann and walked to Peng under the tent. She studied the diminutive, crippled woman in the wheelchair and started nodding her head. "Now you'll see what I've been feeling all these years. You'll know what it's like to lose the man you love, and your heart will hurt like—" The woman choked up and could not finish her words. The young man who had spoken rushed to his mother's side and put his arms around her shoulders. The other young man followed and stood next to her, touching his mother's back. Neither of them was any older than Jack, who remained next to Viv and Josh near the last row of chairs under the tent. For several seconds the only sounds were the woman's light sobs. Then something happened that changed the tension in the air completely. With both hands, Peng lifted up the pink carnation that Baxter had given her from Pete-O's casket. The offering hung between the two women and Peng said, "Sorry. So sorry." The woman's breath caught in her throat and she stared down in disbelief at the flower. She took it from Peng's hands and held it in front of her as if it were a delicate bird. She opened her mouth to say something, maybe "thank you," maybe something else, but she couldn't get the words out. She held the flower in her fist and turned to walk back to the crowd, her sons gently guiding her away.

"Well now I wasn't expecting that part," Lilith Ann said to Magda.

"I wasn't expecting any of it," said Magda.

"I'm beginning to think that woman understands a whole lot more than anybody gives her credit for."

Chapter 23

The church normally offered a covered-dish meal after a funeral, but Lilith Ann declined the offer in lieu of a simple family lunch at her own home. That would ensure no members of the media would be lurking around. She could not order them out of the church, but she could tell them to get off her property. Two members of her Sunday School class volunteered to coordinate the meal on Lilith Ann's behalf, the only time in her life, including her own husband's death, when she allowed anyone else in her kitchen to be in charge of food.

When the Hempers and Boyds arrived at her home after the service, Lilith Ann dropped into a kitchen chair, resting her forehead against her fist. Two of Robert and Kimmy's children pulled at her dress and asked her questions, but she didn't pay them any mind. She didn't even notice which ones they were.

"Come on now, leave Grandmother alone," said Viv. Lilith Ann heard footsteps and whining as they headed down the hall. She remained in a fog, as if she had just awakened from a nap too late in the afternoon. Throughout the meal she heard comments about banana pudding, the woman who "crashed the funeral," how hot it was under the tent, how much those boys had grown since the shooting, the fact that the tea provided by Emma Cochran was "too damn sweet," and a dozen orders from either Kimmy or Robert for one, two, or all of the kids to quiet down and eat their lunch. When Lilith Ann finished her meal, she was looking down at an empty plate and it was then that she realized she had no memory of filling it with food. Someone, probably Viv, had fixed it for her. She must have been hungrier than she thought. Peng sat at the far end of the table next to Baxter. The two of them were the only ones neither talking nor looking at anyone. Peng picked through green beans, mashed potatoes, and chicken while different family members caught glances at her and then exchanged uncomfortable looks with one another. When the last slice of pecan pie and chocolate cake had been consumed, the table grew quiet, and Viv got up to close the door to the kitchen.

"Kimmy, why don't you take the kids in the yard so they can play?" asked Viv, although it didn't sound like a question.

Kimmy made a feeble protest, but got up and barked for them all to follow her. Carrying Jessica Ann on her hip, she led the chattering children out the door. The house became silent except for the sound of hot water filling the sink in the kitchen where the Sunday School members were washing dishes. "We may as well talk about this now while everybody's here," said Viv.

Josh lifted his hands and then folded them on the table, the gesture so dramatic it got everyone's attention. "Hon, let me do this." Lilith Ann sat up a little higher in her chair and willed her mind to clear itself enough to pay attention. "Now that Pete-O is gone, there is the question of where Peng will stay. She can't talk. She can't walk, and she sure can't live by herself in that house. She can't stay by herself anywhere."

"I don't like the sound of this," said Magda. "She can talk just fine. We're the ones who can't always understand what she's saying, and she'll be walking in no time."

"She can't work anywhere in the shape she's in," said Viv. "What we were thinking is that she might be happier with her own people now that Pete-O isn't around."

"Are you saying we just send her back like she's some barbeque grill that we're returning to the store? We are her people now," said Magda. "Mama? Don't you have anything to say about this?"

Lilith Ann pushed her plate aside and tried to think of a response. "We don't have to decide anything right now. Pete-O's grave doesn't even have grass growing over it yet."

"Nobody wants to go pushing her out anywhere before she's had a chance to heal," said Josh. "But—"

"Nobody's going to push her out at all," said Magda.

"I was gonna say," said Josh, his tone annoyed and short, "that she is welcome to stay here with the family for as long as she needs to, but when she's over her grieving, it wouldn't be right of us to expect her to stay in a place where she feels isolated and so far from home. She doesn't have any of her own family that she's known her whole life. She's known us since last spring, and she's never had a conversation with anybody in this room."

"She never had a conversation with Pete-O either, but none of you had a problem with letting her live with him for the rest of her life," Magda said.

"She's getting a check, isn't she? Or she will be pretty soon. Survivor's benefits?" asked Robert.

"She's not going to live with you," Magda replied.

"It's too early to be having this conversation," said Lilith Ann. "We shouldn't even be discussing the rest of her life when she can't even understand what we're saying."

"We just thought it was important to open a dialogue," said Viv. "When she's ready to tell us how she feels about things, we can get one of those girls from the college to come out and interpret for her and then we'll decide what the next step should be for Peng."

Hearing her name, Peng looked up at Viv, and a little scowl came over her face. Baxter put his napkin next to his plate. He placed both hands on the table in a formal gesture, like a man about to declare war or announce he is going to commit murder. "The next step is in the Bible."

"What are you talking about?" snapped Viv.

"The Bible is very clear. We will have a levirate marriage," said Baxter. "I am Pete-O's next brother in age and I have no wife. I will marry her."

No one knew what to say. Even Viv, who was the family authority in giving biblical answers for complex questions, was stammering. "Now, Baxter. Now you. I don't think this is what anybody had in mind."

"I want to hear what he's talking about," said Jack.

"Deuteronomy. Twenty-fifth chapter. Verses five through nine. I looked it up yesterday," said Baxter. Josh was already heading to the den for the big, white, show-off-to-guests Bible that Lilith Ann kept on her coffee table.

Viv turned to her sister-in-law and said, "Lilith Ann. Aren't you going to say something about this?"

Lilith Ann sat back in her chair and threw up her hands in frustration. "You're the one opened up this can of worms, Viv."

"Baxter," said Magda, leaning close to her uncle and putting a hand over his. "It's not that I don't think you would make a good husband, but do you understand that we don't have to follow Old Testament laws anymore despite what people like Viv may say?"

"I know," he said. "But it would be a kind thing to do."

"Taking in stray kittens is kind," said Magda.

"I got it right here!" Josh came back into the room holding the enormous Bible in both hands. He pushed the dishes aside to make room and placed it on the edge. The book was open to Deuteronomy and he placed his index finger on the page as he began.

"Hey, can we come back in?" Kimmy yelled from the front door. "The kids are melting out here and so am I."

"Yes, come on in," Magda yelled back and then stopped Viv before she could protest. "Viv, no. They may as well come on back in and vote, too. Everybody except Peng seems to be getting a say in this." Kimmy and all the kids began swarming back into the house.

"Ya'll listen now," said Josh. "Here's what it says in verse five. 'If brethren dwell together, and one of them die, and have no child, the wife of the dead shall not marry without unto a stranger: her husband's brother shall go in unto her, and take her to him to wife, and perform the duty of an husband's brother unto her.'"

"Well, that settles it. It says if they dwell together, and Baxter didn't dwell with Pete-O, so that verse doesn't apply," said Magda.

Josh put up a hand to hush her. "'And it shall be, that the firstborn which she beareth shall succeed in the name of his brother which is dead, that his name be not put out of Israel.'"

"They're not having any babies, Josh. Mama, why are you just sitting there letting this go on?" said Magda.

"What are they talking about, Mama?" asked Rob Jr.

Kimmy snapped her fingers at her son and pointed to an empty chair. "We're having Bible time, now sit down and hush."

Josh continued with his scripture. "'And if the man like not to take his brother's wife, then let his brother's wife go up to the gate unto the elders, and say, My husband's brother refuseth to raise up unto his brother a name in Israel, he will not perform the duty of my husband's brother. Then the elders of his city shall call him, and speak unto him: and if he stand to it, and say, I like not to take her. Then shall his brother's wife come unto him in the presence of the elders, and loose his shoe from off his foot, and spit in his face, and shall answer and say, So shall it be done unto that man that will not build up his brother's house.' Well," said Josh, "Baxter's the one brought this up, so I reckon he's willing to 'build up his brother's house.'"

"We don't live under Sharia law," said Magda. "You don't get to decide who Peng marries."

"Nobody's making anybody do anything," said Josh. "We're just getting the Lord's perspective on this whole situation. We live by His rules."

"Yes, Josh, I know we do, but this is different," said Viv. "I'm inclined to agree with Magda on this one."

"How is it different?" asked Jack.

"It's just—it just is. Now Baxter, I don't mean any offense, but you've had your problems."

"I don't know," said Jack. "She could do worse than marrying Baxter."

"She did. She married Pete-O," said Robert.

"She married Pete-O without ever having met him," said Magda, "and when she did meet him he wasn't what she thought she'd signed up for. This time around she deserves to know what she's getting into before she signs on the dotted line, so to speak."

"They could get to know one another," said Kimmy. "You know, like go on some dates, see how it goes."

"Baxter doesn't go on dates," said Viv, her eyes wide.

"How do you know what Baxter does and doesn't do?" asked Robert.

Viv smacked her hands down on the table, rattling the dishes around her. "Baxter is not right in the head! He can't go marrying Peng. There'll be no end to the trouble that causes!"

Voices exploded around the table, and one of the women from the kitchen stuck her head in the door just to see what the ruckus was about. Lilith Ann stood and held her hands up, yelling for everyone to shut up. "All right, all right now! Let's stop right here. If Baxter wants to take her to a movie and out to supper, then that's their business. They are adults, and not one person in this room is going to say anything about it. And later, if Peng decides she wants to marry Baxter then Peng will marry Baxter, and nobody's going to push her one way or another."

"Now, Lilith Ann—" Viv began.

"I marry Baxter," Peng announced. A gasp went around the room, and the Sunday School member who had been looking around the doorway shrank back into the kitchen pulling the door shut behind her.

"Peng? Did you say you want to marry Baxter?" asked Lilith Ann.

"I marry Baxter. Shut up now. I marry Baxter." Peng nodded and looked up at Baxter, whose expression had not changed throughout the entire discussion. Whether it was from nervousness or amusement, several of the children began to snicker.

"I reckon that's enough television for her," said Magda.

"Baxter," said Lilith Ann, "this green bean casserole's been cooked longer than your brother's been in the ground. Don't you think we can at least go through a decent mourning time before having another wedding?"

"It's customary for a widow to wait at least thirty days, according to Jewish law," said Baxter.

"How do you know all this stuff? Besides that, nobody here is Jewish, so I don't see why we're paying credence to all these Jewish customs," said Viv.

"We don't have laws about things like that," said Baxter. "We're Baptists."

"Peng's not Baptist," said Kimmy. "Is she?"

"What difference does it make?" asked Jack. "Pete-O wasn't Baptist either. He wasn't nothing."

"We have to follow the next best thing," said Baxter. "That would be Judaic law."

Magda leaned over the table, rested her chin in her hand and sighed in defeat. "Nobody better wear polyester and cotton to the wedding."

"Well, if this is going to happen I'd feel better if she was baptized," said Viv.

"Really, Viv? Why would that make you feel better for somebody who has not one clue what it means to get dunked under water behind the choir loft while a man in a robe recites stuff over her?"

"Magda, stop that right now," said Lilith Ann. "Baxter, later this week I'm driving you and Peng out for dinner at Chen's place. I'll bet if you're eating in his restaurant, Mr. Chen won't mind doing a little Chinese talking for the two of you." She caught Peng's eye and said slowly, "Dinner. Mr. Chen's restaurant. You."

"*Chi. Mintian*," said Baxter.

Peng nodded yes.

Chapter 24

The job at *Bates's Roofing Company ended two days earlier* than the foreman had promised Robert. It was only a three-week gig, but the money had provided enough for him to edge up to two months behind on their mortgage instead of three. Jessica Ann had been sniffling and coughing for days, and Cody was coming down with the same symptoms. Robert had taken one day off to attend his Uncle Pete-O's funeral, a day of missed work and missed income. Now it was nearly two weeks later on Saturday night, and Robert sat on the front porch slapping at mosquitoes that buzzed his head.

The night was getting cool but the mosquitoes didn't seem to have anywhere else to go. The moon was not quite full, sort of lopsided, Robert thought. From down the street the sounds of a sitcom laugh track joined the animated voices of the movie inside the house. There was no place to go for quiet. Suddenly, Robert wished he could disappear to the river's edge at Sam's place. Sit outside on the dock and close out the relentless noise of creditors, banks, and a hundred different "no, sorry's" when he asked about work. Then there was Kimmy's voice cutting through it all. Kimmy yelling in that high-pitched, whiny voice of hers about how they were going to lose the house if they didn't "do something." Sometimes Robert wished he were back in jail where he had the perfect excuse for their misfortunes. She felt sorry for him then, couldn't wait for him to get home, and now that he was home it seemed he couldn't do anything good enough.

Kimmy and the children were in the house watching *Ratatouille* for the umpteenth time. He'd made the mistake of complaining when Kimmy put the movie on, and Rob Jr. said if he didn't like them watching it so many times then why didn't he go buy them some new movies? The question got Rob Jr. a whack across the butt with Robert's bare hand, a punishment the kids were accustomed to from Kimmy but almost never from their dad. Robert had stomped outside to the porch and no one dared follow. He hadn't moved from his lawn chair seat. His head throbbed. Whenever he tried to think of a way out of his predicament his thoughts went in circles. His conversation with Fanny about the T&A had been largely a waste of time. To make matters worse, she had thought he was hitting on her that night they all went out to dinner. If his Uncle Pete-O hadn't died, he was sure Fanny would have said something to him eventually, and then the whole family would have been down his throat about it.

The Hemper-Boyd family didn't know a damn thing about keeping their mouths shut about anything. It seemed like everybody had some idea about some place he ought to apply for a job. Go to Walmart, his mother had said, and when Robert reminded her that the Drayton Walmart was never going to hire anybody with Hemper or Boyd for a last name, she just said that it was time somebody gave the family a good name for a change. But Robert knew it wasn't going to be him. Maybe Magda could get a job there, or even Jack, but one look at his criminal record and Robert would be given the we're-not-hiring-right-now excuse that he'd heard so many times; he could tell when it was coming just by the expression on the face of whatever down-the-line clerk he was talking to. Try the Grease 'N Go, suggested Jack, but the manager had already caught wind of Robert's customer service skills from Tom Delaney. Besides, he knew Pete-O, the kiss-of-death of all references. Magda said he should apply for the landscaping crew at the elementary school, but his felony conviction eliminated him from even being considered. Even the fast-food places weren't hiring, or that's what Arby's, Wendy's, McDonald's, and KFC told him when he stopped by to apply. Damn, thought Robert, *what's the world coming to when you can't even get a job flipping burgers?*

Pushing a sweaty hand through his hair, he sighed hard

and then smacked another mosquito dead on his arm. "Yeah," he muttered as he flicked off the bloody smear with his index finger, "nobody wants you around, and if they notice you, you get smacked down deader than shit no matter how hard you try." Inside the house he could hear the voice of his oldest son. He was saying something about how far he could throw a ball, bragging about how he was stronger than the other boys in his grade. When Robert was his son's age he was just as much of a handful, probably more. Lilith Ann spanked him more than Jack and Magda put together, but it didn't seem to make much difference. It was funny though. He had forgotten what he'd done to get most of the spankings in his life, but it was a night when he didn't get a spanking for getting into trouble that he remembered most clearly.

He'd been about ten years old. It was summer time, August, and the church was having its annual revival, with a traveling guest preacher wailing behind the pulpit every night that week about how they must all drive the devil from their midst no matter if he took the form of demon drink, hellcat whores, the wiles of gambling, the loathsome slothfulness of laziness, or the vile dripping tongue of gossip. All were roads that led to an eternity in the pits of hell. Robert's parents had taken him, Magda, and Jack, who was a baby at the time, to the service each night to be warned of the dangers that befell them each day of their fragile lives. Josh had been spared because he was off at Boy Scout camp. Magda had busied herself with an ink pen and some scrap paper drawing doodles of princesses holding wands that shot out fire, while Robert squirmed on the hard wooden pew in the August heat. The decrepit air-conditioning unit in the sanctuary had broken hours before the first night of the revival began, leaving many parishioners whining and wilting, but they received no sympathy from the visiting preacher. "If you can't take a little heat in the Lord's house," he cried, pacing back and forth in front of the pulpit, mopping up the sweat from his face with a pristine white handkerchief,

"then you sure can't withstand the flames of hell that await you if you don't turn your soul over to Jesus! Can I get an amen?" Lilith Ann and Linden dutifully repeated the amens as they were requested. They endured the heat along with everyone else, and bemoaned the fact that the church did not have the $12,000 replacement cost for the air-conditioning unit. This was the predicament each night until the culminating baptismal service on Friday, when the lucky penitents who had turned their souls over to Jesus that week would get a merciful and soul-saving dip in the gloriously cool waters of the baptismal pool at the rear of the sanctuary.

Robert had endured nightly smacks on the back of his head from his mother when he kicked the pew in front, or bent over onto the floor out of boredom and sweaty misery. His idea to bring a thermos of ice water had been met with an unusually pious response from his mother, proving to everyone how much she had been affected by the words of the revival preacher. "Do you think anyone's going to give you a single drop of ice water in hell, even if you beg for it?" Lilith Ann had said. Later that night, Robert fumed in the back of the car all the way to the church.

The baptism was to take place during the last half hour of the two-hour service. Robert lay with his head against the back of the pew, breathing the humid air. Lilith Ann fanned herself with the program, the single respite from the heat she permitted herself in the midst of so many other miserable people. Since her outburst at Robert earlier in the day, a thread of guilt had been working its way through her psyche, but she didn't dare admit it to either Robert or his father. She held the sleeping infant Jack against her chest, a hot bundle of flesh that left her arms slick with sweat. She showed her sympathy for Robert by turning her fan on him, which sent a tepid breeze over his sweating face.

"Mama, can I please go to the bathroom?" Robert whispered.

Lilith Ann nodded and said, "Hurry back."

At the end of the hall, Robert pushed open the men's room door and stood over the sink, letting the water run cool over his hands. After splashing his face, he wiped his sleeve over his eyes and the idea came to him. Smiling in the mirror, he made up his mind. There was one place to get cool in the church that night. He didn't put any thought into the consequences that would certainly befall him afterwards. He never did, and that was why he never stopped getting into trouble.

At the rear of the sanctuary behind the baptismal pool stood seven newly-saved souls draped in white cotton gowns. Most wore their clothes underneath, but Robert saw that one of them, a high school boy who went by the name of Teeny, wore a swim suit underneath his wrinkled, white gown. Teeny stood nervously at the top of the plywood staircase that led up to the back of the sanctuary and then down into the baptismal pool. The rest milled around on the floor, except for Randy Nichols, a dubious candidate who lingered at the back door, smoking a cigarette in the night air. This part of the sanctuary had no windows and was several degrees cooler than the heat-baked rows of pews, where Lilith Ann sat growing suspiciously worried about what might be keeping Robert. Time was running out, and Robert knew if he didn't make his move he would either lose his nerve or his mother would come looking for him and he'd never get his chance.

The visiting revival preacher, Brother Bovee, was just stepping into the pool to begin his scripture reading for the coming event. "Now friends, we're turning in our Bibles to Romans chapter six, starting with verse three. 'Know ye not, that so many of us as were baptized into Jesus Christ were baptized into his death? Therefore,'" and his voice boomed at the word *therefore*. He raised up his left hand and continued. "'Therefore, we are buried with him by baptism into death: that like as Christ was raised up from the dead by the glory of the Father, even so we also should walk in newness of life.' Can I get an amen?"

The congregation echoed its tired refrain and he asked again, louder. "Can I get an amen?" This time he raised his Bible over his head and clapped his hand against it in a powerful smack that made some people jump in their seats. If he hadn't been thrusting his Bible so high in the air, when Robert leaped past Teeny and landed in the baptismal pool, it would have doused not only the preacher's seersucker suit but his Bible as well. The water was much colder than Robert had imagined it would be, and the shock was like a glorious heavenly bath. "Amen!" Robert shouted. "Amen, amen, amen! Jeeeesus amen!" He dropped under the water and then rose up, flinging his hands straight up in the air over his head. "Whoo! Whoo! Amen! Whooee!" He shook his fists in triumphant jabs above his head, still shouting, "Whooee! Jesus!" Brother Bovee recovered himself, placed his Bible safely out of the wet zone and joyfully joined the shouting. "This boy's on fire for Jesus! Washed clean! His sins are washed away!" He clapped his hands after each sentence and then he placed one on Robert's head, which was just about to duck under the cooling waters once more. "This young man has the spirit just a-surging through him tonight!" Robert was momentarily held in place by the preacher's meaty hand; it clasped his skull more tightly than it looked to Lilith Ann, who sat with her mouth hanging open. "I baptize you in the name of the Father, the Son, and Holy Ghost!" At the last word, Brother Bovee placed his other hand over Robert's nose, dipping him backwards and then back up again so hard and fast his feet flew up and his arms flailed at his sides. Robert came up spewing a mouthful of water in the air. "That's right, son. You spit that foul sin out and breathe in the clean air of Christ!"

Lilith Ann sat still and clasped Jack tightly against her chest. Next to her Linden sat frozen in place, his eyes about to pop out of his head. Several voices around her sounded enthusiastic amens, and a few began clapping as Robert stepped gingerly out of the baptismal pool and out of sight. "That's what I like to see, folks," Brother Bovee said, his hands still in the air, "a young man who is excited about getting baptized. Yessiree, crying a joyful noise unto the Lord." Teeny stepped hesitantly to the pool's edge, his momentum now stunted in the events of the past few minutes.

When Lilith Ann realized it was her Robert jumping in that baptismal pool, her first thought had been to smack him silly; but as she watched the reactions of Brother Bovee and the surrounding parishioners, she swallowed her rage. Linden flicked his eyes over at her, and in that moment the two of them were allied in a pact of self-preserving silence, at least until they all got home.

In the parking lot after the service, they received countless hugs, handshakes, claps on the back, and "Lord Bless yous." By the time they all piled through the door of their house, all Lilith Ann had left in her was the squinty-eyed threat that if he ever did anything like that again she'd "bust his butt from now 'til next week." All Robert remembered of that night after they returned home was that he didn't get a whupping, and the next year his mother did not make him attend the summer church revival.

Robert grinned at the memory and took his cell from his pocket. He glanced over his shoulder, around the corner and through the screen door into the trailer. He scrolled through his numbers until he found the one he wanted. Inside, Kimmy held Cody and Jessica Ann on her lap, her hand absently stroking the girl's forehead. The flickering light from the television played over the children's faces, and Robert's stomach twisted in love and anxiety. They were frozen blue in the light from the box in front of them. The cell rang five times, and a voice finally answered.

"Nyep," said Sam.

"Sam?"

"Uh-huh."

Robert pushed the phone closer to his ear. "Hey, man, it's

me, Boyd."

"Oh yeah, man, hey, I'm real sorry about your uncle," said Sam, his voice sounding more clear and attentive.

"Thanks. Hey, remember that conversation we had a while back? Let's you and me get together and talk about that some more."

The line was silent for a few seconds, followed by something that sounded to Robert like sniffling or maybe a thwarted sneeze. "Uh, what was that we were talking about? I forgot."

Robert switched the cell to his other ear and stood up, taking a step farther away from the front door. "I got a lead on this place, remember? The T&A? I told you I heard they got a lab going down in the basement and they're cooking—"

"Shut it, man," Sam said, becoming suddenly lucid. "Don't talk about stuff like that on the phone. You know they're listening."

"Who's listening?" said Robert, whispering.

"Damn, don't you pay attention to anything that's going on?"

"I don't know what the hell you're talking about. I just know I've got to get my hands on some cash. I can't find work, and I got kids," said Robert. He was using those three final magic words that are supposed to make the bad guy in the movies suddenly refrain from killing the hapless victim, or excuse any crummy behavior committed by a character who's trying to get out of trouble.

"Don't say nothing else," said Sam. "If you want to talk then let's meet some place. You can't come over here because we're redecorating."

Robert almost laughed, but there was silence on the line and he realized Sam wasn't joking. "Sure, alright. Let's meet at the Waffle House."

"No good. Cops hang out there."

"Well you can't come here," said Robert. "My wife's here and I got kids."

"Yeah, you said that. Look, come by the Tomahawk in

Anniston tomorrow morning. You know it?"

"All the way out in Anniston? That's a half-hour drive." Robert was actually thinking it was a six-dollar round trip of gas, but he kept that part to himself.

"Not as many people know me over there. You neither," he said. "You got to get smart about these things, you know? Meet me there at 7:30."

Robert sighed and said, "Alright, man. I'll be there." He clicked off his cell. He was going to make things happen by this weekend even if he died trying.

Chapter 25

For several days following Pete-O's funeral, Lilith Ann fell ill and did not come out of her room. Peng had initially thought she was so saddened over her brother's death that she could not get out of bed, but there was no crying, only the sound of sneezing and coughing from Lilith Ann's bedroom. She had brought Peng to spend a couple of days at her house, with Fanny there to look after them both. Peng was constantly baffled at the assortment of women who came and went at Lilith Ann's house, with no seeming order in their hierarchy. Mothers seemed to look after everyone, daughters didn't look after anyone, and women who weren't family members came in to care for her and Lilith Ann. Even the irritating wife of one of Lilith Ann's sons, Viv, came over with soup a few times, but she left quickly and rarely even tried to speak to either Peng or Fanny.

She saw Baxter only once during this time. Actually, she didn't see him, but she knew he was at the door because she heard him talking to Magda. He had brought a gift for her, but it seemed that he made no effort to come inside. Magda brought the gift to Peng, who soon figured out it was a game of some sort, but she was not entirely sure what to do with it. Tiny English letters engraved on plastic squares about half the size of the Bakelite tiles of a MahJongg set were gathered in a cloth bag. There was a board covered with squares in perfect rows, and it was clear she was supposed to put the little letters on the board, but in what order? She played around with words in a list down the board, the ones she had learned easily from the television: Ford, Dodge, Ajax, clean, good, hot, America, attorney-at-law, choice, spicy chicken, and the hardest one of all, erectile dysfunction. After she listed all the words she had memorized, she began forming other words from the cover

of a magazine that Magda had tossed on the coffee table featuring a picture of a minimally dressed woman. The woman looked much the way Magda did most of the time, angry and bored. Peng studied the words around the picture, and added the new ones to her list on the board: vogue, satisfy, strategy, penis, adore, and embarrass.

Peng ached to get on her feet and do some cooking, or at least use the washing machine to help with the laundry, but each time she attempted to rise from her lounge chair in front of the television, Fanny shooed her back down and shoved more tea and triangular pieces of toast coated in disgusting yellow butter at her. Being waited on like an empress had become an exhausting bore.

Peng knew she was supposed to be in mourning, but she often forgot out of fear that the police would come and arrest her for Pete-O's death. Several times over her first few days at Lilith Ann's house, Fanny or Magda found Peng wiping her eyes; what they didn't know was that Peng had seen a car pass by—one of the dark-colored vehicles driven by the men in dark uniforms and big hats, she was sure. Once Peng had spotted a black and white police cruiser moving down Lilith Ann's street so slowly she had to put her hands over her mouth in shock and terror. When the days came and went in casual order, with nothing more than an occasional bowl of soup or casserole from a neighbor for Lilith Ann's mourning household, Peng began to relax. Apparently, the entire household had no trouble relaxing. Magda was always laughing about something, and when Lilith Ann felt like coming out of her bedroom she sat down in a chair, blew her nose a lot, and drank cups of hot liquid that Fanny brought her. Lilith Ann laughed until she snorted at the television antics of a very fat woman with a daughter who was always getting into some kind of trouble. This lasted almost five days, but Peng was relieved to see Lilith Ann finally getting back to her old self and begin doing things she seemed to enjoy, like baking the bread that Peng liked and cleaning the bathroom, Peng's favorite room in the house. It was about this time, nearly a week after Pete-O's funeral, that Peng finally went on the date that the family had been so interested in.

Lilith Ann drove Peng and Baxter to Mr. Chen's restaurant, then left them sitting silently across from one another at one of the Formica tables with the plastic menu stuck between the napkin holder and the salt and pepper shakers. Peng ended up wearing the same dress she'd married Pete-O in for her "date" with Baxter. The truth was, she had thought the two of them were getting married that day, and it seemed the sensible thing to do to get more mileage out of the dress, especially since it was a gift from her sister-in-law twice over. But apparently there had to be a courtship before the wedding could take place. She'd already been through that process twice before, and felt that at this point in her life it was an unnecessary step. She was most anxious to get the ceremony behind her and the marriage certificate safely stored away in the box she kept for important papers because the more of them she had, the more she felt insulated from the possibility of either being sent back to her parents or possibly to jail.

The food at Mr. Chen's restaurant, which was called simply Chen's, was terribly expensive, much more expensive than meals in China. One dish cost almost six dollars! American custom- ers had more money than the people she knew back home, so perhaps it was normal for restaurants to charge so much. She had no idea how much money Baxter had in his pocket to pay for their meal, so she ordered the cheapest three dishes on the menu, speaking in Chinese to the young girl who came to the table. Baxter didn't look like a man who could afford a six-dol- lar dish, but then again neither had Pete-O. No matter how much a meal cost, Pete-O had always complained about how expensive it was, pointing at the menu, shaking his head and waving a hand around as if he would be sent onto the streets to starve if he had to keep paying such high prices to take his wife out to eat; however, he always ordered those higher-priced dishes and ate them down to the last spoonful.

Baxter did not blink at having someone else order the food, and Peng felt a mild sense of pride. For once, she was the person who knew how to say what she wanted, and her companion was the one who had to wait for her. She smiled a little to herself and Baxter caught it. He must have thought her smile was for him, because he gave her a little one back, a small and friendly smile, a real smile, the kind of smile she had never seen on Pete-O's face. The two of them sat there like that, silent and unmoving until the food came out. When the waitress turned the corner with Peng's order, a bowl of noodles, vinegar cucumbers, and a tofu/carrot dish, Mr. Chen was right behind her with another larger tray of dishes. Peng thought he was headed for a table of four people on the other side of the restaurant, but he stopped at her table, smiling so widely she was sure he must have just won a prize or found some kind of treasure. He began placing dish after dish on the table. There was steamed fish, special eggplant in the "snake" style, pigeon eggs, roasted duck with garlic and greens, mutton and onion, tomato and egg soup, and a tray of steaming-hot tender dumplings no bigger than a baby's ears. Peng's shock was so great she had trouble getting her words out, even in her native Mandarin.

"What is all this? I didn't order so much food! It's a mistake!"

Mr. Chen waved his hand and continued placing the dishes on the table. "No mistake," he said.

"No, no, no! It's too much. You are too generous with your food."

"I insist," said Mr. Chen, also speaking Chinese. "I never got to give you a wedding present, so here it is." Peng's shock and embarrassment were so great tears sprang into her eyes. She could not bring herself to look at Baxter or Mr. Chen. "No, no, no, no. This is too much. Too much," she kept saying, waving her hands over the food and trying to push the dishes back at Mr. Chen.

"Ah, no need to be embarrassed. You're in America now. I know about everything," he said, keeping his voice low so the wait staff could not hear. "I read in the paper that your husband had died, so…." Mr. Chen waved his hand over the food. "Your sister-in-law called yesterday and told me all about the new arrangements. No sense in waiting around. You're very smart to accept a good offer." He gave a little nod of acknowledgment to Baxter. "You'll be okay. Everyone knows Baxter. He doesn't talk much."

"Thank you," said Baxter. Peng wasn't sure if maybe he had understood the Chinese they were speaking, or if he was thanking Mr. Chen for all the food.

"You're welcome," Mr. Chen said to Baxter. "Enjoy." And he was gone.

Peng gave Baxter a shaky smile. "This is so much," she said one last time, sighing over all the steaming dishes. Baxter sat with his hands in his lap, waiting for her. When she saw that he would take no food before she did, Peng nodded her head as if she had finally reached an important decision. "We eat," she said softly, in English.

"We eat," repeated Baxter.

Speaking no more, Peng began spooning a palm-sized bowl of tomato and egg soup for Baxter. She slid it close to him using both hands, placing a ceramic spoon inside the bowl. He nodded, took a sip of the soup and said, "*Hen hao.*"

"Yes, very good," said Peng. She helped herself to soup as well, and the two of them slurped delicate sips until their bowls were empty and it was time to partake of the mutton and onion, Peng's favorite when she could get it. She tried to remember why Pete-O had never taken her to Chen's restaurant, but there had never been a clear answer. She had asked to go, or tried to ask with her limited English. She could easily say "Chen," and she was sure he had understood her. Anyone in town knew that the word could mean nothing other than Mr. Chen's restaurant.

By the time she and Baxter began the Jiaozi, her few remaining mournful thoughts of Pete-O had all but evaporated. She took the bottle of chili oil and poured some onto Baxter's plate to show him how to push the dumpling through it before eating them. He obeyed, emotionless but dutiful, and soon the basket of Jiaozi was empty as well. Baxter liked to eat one food at a time. She had noticed it once before at a meal she had shared with the family. There had been little reason to pay attention, but today she watched his mannerisms, trying to follow his lead as he finished one food and waited for her to choose the next. Peng wanted to eat as her family had in China, reaching into each dish as the flavors led her, but this man was to be her new husband and she, as she had learned from her mother, let him determine the pace and order of the foods they ate at the table.

"Gawd, Baxter, are you doing that weird thing with the dishes?" The voice startled Peng, as Magda strode through the entrance and struggled with an oversized black bag on her shoulder. She huffed, out of breath, and kept looking behind her into the parking lot, scanning the cars.

"I like my foods this way. Many flavors are best perceived in a singular state," Baxter said.

"No, most foods taste better if you eat them with the right other foods like steak and potatoes or bacon and cantaloupe," said Magda. She drummed a finger on the table and looked over her shoulder once more. "Look, I didn't come here to talk about food." She waited a moment, but no one asked her why she came. "I wanted to say I was sorry for like, I don't know, being against you two getting married and all that. It was just a shock. You've never been married, Baxter, and Peng, you've been a widow for something like a day, you know?"

"We know," said Baxter, reaching for a pigeon egg.

Peng cast an uncomfortable glance at Baxter, whose face showed nothing. This woman, the lazy daughter Lilith Ann was always yelling at, was here at their table looking nervous and making some speech that Peng was sure was going to ruin their meal.

"Statistics say I'm more likely to live a longer life if I get married," said Baxter. "Peng will have fewer legal problems. The courts don't seem to like immigrants anymore. It's better for her if she's married." Baxter shook his head, as if remembering something unpleasant, and then put the tiny egg in his mouth.

Uninvited, Magda dragged a chair from a nearby table to theirs and sat down, pulling the handle of the enormous bag. "I can't stay, but I wanted to tell you that you have my blessing if you really do decide to get married."

Baxter stopped chewing for a few seconds as if he had something he wanted to say, but changed his mind and continued eating. Without raising her eyes at Magda, Peng put a large helping of mutton on Baxter's plate and then gave a lesser portion to herself. The food smelled wonderful, and suddenly Magda realized she was hungry. She eyed the plates and bowls of food and picked up the thread once more. "It's just that you've always been a certain umm. . . a certain way to me. You've always been my Uncle Baxter. You used to take me and Robert to the park when you were, you know, when you were feeling okay and when Mama let you. You would stand at the back of the slide when I climbed up the ladder because I was afraid, and then you would wait for me at the bottom when I slid down. Do you remember that?" Baxter's face was pensive but he said nothing. He positioned his chopsticks between his fingers, studying them until they were properly aligned; in one awkward but successful movement he gripped a bit of mutton and onion, raising it to his mouth. Peng, with natural ease, echoed his gesture and they were both chewing mouthfuls of mutton.

Magda pushed on. "I know that none of that is . . . I'm all grown up now, but I guess I was afraid of losing something. I didn't want things to change. I'm sorry. I just wanted things to stay the same."

"I want to be happy," said Baxter.

Magda nodded. "Of course. Of course you do. And...and I want you to be happy." She touched his arm lightly and stood up to leave, hoisting the heavy bag higher onto her shoulder. "I'll see you. I've got to go. I've got to deliver a break-up letter to some gun nut guy. It's a divorce thing." She shrugged her shoulders, took a few steps and then stopped. "Hey, don't tell Mama I came by here. She made me promise not to, but I guess I'm not much good with promises." She almost made it to the door before Baxter stopped her.

"Magda?"

She turned back. "Yes?"

"Are you still afraid to go up the ladder?"

Magda shook her head, at first uncertainly, and then slightly more forcefully. "No, I'm not."

"Good," said Baxter, and he took another bite of mutton.

Chapter 26

Robert had set the alarm for 6:00 a.m., but there had been no need for it. At 4:35 Scott woke Kimmy and Robert with a cough and fever, so Kimmy brought him into the bedroom and placed the child between them, which kept both parents awake until the dawn light started breaking through the bedroom sheers. "I'm going to have to take him to the doctor," Kimmy said, her arm shielding her eyes from the growing light.

"Mmmmm," Robert mumbled.

"You'll have to watch the kids while I'm gone," said Kimmy.

"I can't watch the kids." Robert turned toward her suddenly in bed, and Scott coughed full in his face. "I've got to go to a job thing, a job interview."

"What interview? You didn't say anything about a job interview last night," said Kimmy. She pushed Scott's matted hair away from his eyes.

"Well, I do."

"What time is the interview?"

"It's at seven thirty," said Robert.

"What kind of place does interviews at seven thirty in the morning?" Kimmy asked.

"It's a restaurant."

"What kind of restaurant?"

"The kind that's going to interview me at seven thirty," Robert said, sitting on the edge of the bed and rubbing the sleep out of his eyes. He picked up the alarm clock, pretending to look at the time.

"Does this place have a name?"

"You don't ever eat there."

"That's a funny name for a restaurant," said Kimmy.

"Mommy, go potty," said the sleepy child on the bed.

"Sure, honey," she said, hoisting him off the bed and onto

the floor. "So?" she called over her shoulder as she followed Scott into the bathroom. "I asked you a question."

Robert rummaged in a drawer for a T-shirt. "It's just a short order job. Over at the Tomahawk."

Kimmy reappeared in the doorway of the bedroom without Scott, her mouth open in disbelief. "Are you kidding? That dump has been there since before I was born. How are they even still in business?"

"Dunno," he said, pushing the folded shirts into a heap as he searched.

"Even if they hired you, that's all that way in the next county," said Kimmy. Scott called out her name from behind her, and she disappeared into the bathroom once again. "Are you sure you want to work in a place like that?" she called. Robert didn't answer. When she returned, he was wearing a blue T-shirt with a faded barbeque restaurant logo: The Pit Stop. "Why are you wearing that old thing for a job interview? You ought to be wearing a button-down."

"Shitfire Kimmy, you just asked me if I wanted to work in a place like that and now you're all up in my ass for not wearing a good enough shirt for the interview."

Scott began crying from the bathroom. "Fine," said Kimmy, "wear whatever damn shirt you want to, but you've got to help me with the kids today." She jerked her closet door open and began pushing hangers aside, searching for something to wear.

Rob Jr. stepped into the bedroom and got as far as the bathroom door. "Mommy," he said. "Scott threw up on the bathroom floor."

"Shit," Kimmy hissed. "Just a minute, Scott. Just wait a minute." She pulled a blue blouse from the closet and threw it onto the bed. "I can't deal with five kids at the doctor's office."

"Take them to Mama's," said Robert.

"Your mama's been sick with the crud all week. I can't take all of them over there and have everybody come down with it."

"They're all going to come down with it anyway if Scott's

got it," said Robert. "Just drop a couple of them off. She can't say no once you're already there with them."

"That is just about the most irresponsible thing that's ever come out of your mouth. You want to put your own kids in a place that's not safe for them," said Kimmy.

"Since when is my mama's house not the safest place for the kids besides their own house?" Robert checked his cell to see if Sam had left any texts. There was nothing.

"When? I'll tell you when. Since there was a pole-dancing hooker, a crazy old Chinese woman with a broken leg who can't put three words of English together, your weirdo hate-letter writing sister, and your sick-with-the-crud mama all there in one house!"

Robert gripped his cell hard and then flung it across the room, cracking the mirror over the dresser. "She's not a hooker!"

"Oh, that's all you've got to say? The only person you're going to even try and defend is that hooker from the T&A pretending to be a nurse that your mama's got over there? Yeah," she said, raising a finger to Robert's face, "don't think I haven't heard about that woman. Everybody knows what she's about." She put both hands on her hips and began shaking her head. "If you don't beat all." She took a step away from him and then stepped right back. "Of all the women you could have gone sniffing around you pick something like that."

"What the hell are you talking about? I haven't been sniffing around nobody."

"Don't think you can get away with anything without me finding out about it," Kimmy said, suddenly lowering her voice.

"Mama! Scott's standing in it," called Rob Jr.

"I'll be right there! Scott, don't stand in that!" Kimmy turned her attention back to Robert. "I don't know what you think—"

"Look Kimmy, I don't need this right now. I've got to get to a job interview," said Robert, snatching his wallet from the dresser and shoving it into his back pocket. "I asked her some questions about something is all."

"Questions? About what? Being a stripper?"

"About nothing. Just forget it. I've got to go." Robert headed for the door.

"We're not finished talking about this," said Kimmy.

"I said I've got to go," Robert yelled from the hallway.

"Fine, then take Rob Jr. with you. You can handle one kid, or is that too much to ask?"

"Did you not hear me say I've got a job interview?"

"It's the damn Tomahawk. Half the waitresses there have got as many kids as we do. They're not going to freak out if you bring one inside. And when you get home we're going to finish that conversation about you-know-who." Kimmy brushed past him as she headed for the bathroom, where Scott stood with no pants on and a greenish smear down his shirt. On the floor was a nasty puddle of last night's dinner. "Did you even try to get any of this in the toilet?"

"Pee pee," said Scott, pointing at the toilet.

Rob Jr. was running after his dad out the door, relieved to be out of the house.

Anniston, Alabama was a town known mostly for Fort McClellan, a military base, and an Army Depot, both now closed. The chemical factory, Monsanto, had done its share to make Anniston what Magda called the most toxic chemical dump in America. It, too, had been closed for years, though its legacy lived on. With those industries gone and a steady decline in population for nearly fifty years, the town was now lined in bail bondsmen, massage parlors, fast food, nail salons, and quickie loan companies. The tattoo parlors, as they were known in the days when thousands of servicemen patronized the downtown, were mostly gone. Anniston was known by some as the place where a Freedom Riders bus was firebombed by a mob of whites when it tried to pass through the town. When the bus was ablaze, the mob held the doors shut in an attempt to burn the riders alive, but then some say the fuel tank exploded and the mob dispersed. It was a story Robert had never heard before, and he had no idea it was part of Anniston's legacy. His mother remembered the burned bus, but she never spoke of it to any of her children. This is how the chapters of a town's history begin to die. People just stop talking about the parts that aren't nice, and soon what people claim as their history becomes a rag full of holes.

The town was full of people just like Robert, men who wanted to work but could find nothing more than minimum wage service jobs, and even those were hard to come by. Houses surrounded by lawns dotted with toys, trailers with aging cars parked out front, and shuttered businesses made up much of the landscape. Only the K-Mart and Walmart areas showed enough economic vitality to attract other businesses to their islands.

The Tomahawk was nestled between a check-cashing company and a nail salon. A few doors down was a doughnut shop that had remained in business for thirty years with inexplicable tenacity, much the way a weed grows from a crack in the sidewalk. It was the same way with the Tomahawk, a malt shop in the early seventies, and then a hotdog and hamburger joint in the eighties. Now it was hamburgers and barbeque served by waitresses who called their clientele "honey" and "darling" with thick accents that one hears only in movies and comedy TV anymore. There was a long-standing rumor that Mary Ann from *Gilligan's Island* had once eaten at the Tomahawk right after the place opened, but no one had bothered to take a picture, so the story remained a local folk legend. The one celebrity who had stopped and was photographed was a defensive end for the Saints in 1980 known as "Dogbone" Dickerson. The team turned out to be so bad that year that the owner of the Tomahawk had taken Dogbone's picture off the wall and never put it back. Robert knew none of this about the Tomahawk. He'd never heard of Dogbone Dickerson, and if anyone had told him that Dawn Wells had sat right there at the counter and eaten a hamburger, large Coca-Cola, and an order of chili

fries, he wouldn't have known who they were talking about. Now, local politicians, lawyers, and business owners patronized the Tomahawk, especially at breakfast when one could order the Tomahawk's special sausage, sliced tomato, and gravy biscuit, a local favorite. Despite its lack of panache, the place was comfortable and familiar, so people kept coming back despite the mediocrity of the food. The Tomahawk continued to limp along through the decades, watching Anniston swirl ever smaller and deader for going on forty-five years.

"Can I get something to eat?" Rob Jr. asked as his dad pulled the car into a parking spot on the opposite side of the street.

Robert looked around nervously, looking for something that would explain why he felt so suspicious inside, and then he realized he didn't know what he was supposed to be suspicious about. Who would present any danger to him in a diner? Hardly anyone was on the street at such an early hour, but he found the quiet unnerving. He had been thinking all the way to Anniston about how he would get his son out of earshot while he talked to Sam about the comings and goings of the T&A lounge, but he had less than three dollars in his pocket after putting enough gas in the car to get the both of them home. "No Coke," said Robert, "just a sausage biscuit and water." Rob Jr. mumbled something that Robert couldn't hear as the two of them got out of the car.

When they made it across one lane of traffic Rob Jr. piped up again. "Why you park all the way back there? There's two whole parking spaces over there in front. See?" Robert hadn't even thought to take his son's hand as he crossed the street. Rob Jr. trotted behind and caught up with his dad on the grassy median. "Dad? I said why you park all the way—"

"Your daddy's got business to tend to, so don't be talking my ear off."

Rob Jr. sighed and followed his father across the oncoming lane of traffic until they were at the door of the restaurant. Robert stopped and looked around again before pulling the glass door open and stepping inside.

"Why do you keep looking around?" asked Rob Jr.

"Why do you keep asking so many questions?"

"I dunno."

"Well, quit it."

It took Robert only a cursory glance at the seven people who were having their early breakfast to see that Sam had not yet arrived. He wondered why Sam had even chosen a place like the Tomahawk. It was too familiar for the patrons who ate there. They all knew one another, and when someone new came in, someone like Robert, everyone noticed. What if they remembered him being there with his son? What if somebody came around asking questions about him later? Would they recall a thin man with brown hair wearing a T-shirt with "The Pit Stop" on the front accompanied by a mouthy, eight-year-old boy? Robert determined he'd throw the T-shirt away first chance he got.

"Hey, hon, find a seat." The waitress had two menus tucked under her arm as she breezed past Robert and his son.

"Uh," said Robert, suddenly flustered about how to get his son seated at a separate table. "Yeah, okay."

"Be with you in a minute," said the waitress, giving him hardly any more notice.

"Can we sit by the window?" asked Rob Jr.

"Let's sit in the back. In one of the booths."

"I hate those. I can't ever get out unless I'm sitting on the outside," said Rob Jr.

"Fine, then sit on the outside. When this guy gets here you can go sit wherever you want."

"I can?" asked Rob Jr.

Robert did not answer but headed for a booth in the corner and slid onto the slick vinyl seat. He wished he'd worn a hat so that he could shield his face. He felt as if everyone in the place was trying to sneak a look at him. A few cars passed outside, but not one stopped in front of the Tomahawk.

"Hey Dad, who's coming?" Rob Jr. slid in next to his dad.

"Nobody you know."

"What's his name?"

"I said it's nobody you know," said Robert.

"Then tell me his name and I'll know who he is."

"Go on over there and tell that waitress you want a biscuit." Robert gestured toward the waitress, who was now at the cash register taking money from a portly businessman gripping a toothpick between his teeth.

Rob Jr. squirmed his way to the edge of the seat to get up, and he bumped the table so hard he rattled the salt and pepper shakers on the far end. Robert glanced around to see if anyone had noticed, but no one paid them any mind. Before his son could retreat from the table, the waitress was halfway back to their booth. Without looking up, she slid her pad from the stained apron she wore.

"Sorry, we're short-handed this morning. What you want to eat?"

Robert gave her the biscuit order.

"Want some coffee with that?"

A slight wave of anger mixed with shame rose in Robert's stomach as he muttered a quick "no." She made a final note on the pad and walked away.

"Why aren't you eating?" asked Rob Jr.

"Not hungry," said Robert.

"Mama says we don't have a pot to piss in."

The anger overrode the shame in Robert's gut and he ducked his head close to his son who was standing in front of the booth, kicking his foot at the bar that secured it to the floor. "Well your mama's just mouthing off, so don't you listen to that kind of talk."

"You gonna work here?"

"No, I'm not gonna work here."

"Mama says you're going to get a job here."

The waitress stepped behind Rob Jr. and slid onto the table

a saucer with a steaming hot biscuit sandwiching a sausage and tomato slice. "I brought the boy some milk," she said, winking at Robert and placing the glass next to the saucer. "Boys need milk."

Robert wanted to give a "thank you," but all he could manage was a nod.

"Do I have to eat the tomato?" asked the boy as soon as the waitress walked away.

"Eat it all," said Robert, but then he changed his mind, reaching inside the biscuit to take the tomato slice. He popped it into his mouth and almost swallowed it whole. Rob Jr. grinned and took a bite of the now tomato-free biscuit.

"Why aren't you going to ask them for a job?" Rob Jr. spoke with a mouth full of biscuit.

"'Cause I got better plans," said Robert.

"What kinda plans?"

Robert ducked his head a little closer to his son. "Plans that would make working in a dump like this a big waste of my time. Now I told you before we came in here not to ask me a million questions."

"Mama said—"

Robert snapped his fingers hard in front of the boy's face, and stuck a finger barely an inch from his nose. "Not one more word out of you or I'll give you a reason to wish you'd stayed home with your mama."

Rob Jr. moved his mouth as if he was going to respond, but he thought better of it and stayed quiet.

For the remaining five minutes it took for Rob Jr. to eat the biscuit and drink the glass of milk, the two of them sat silently. A steady flow of customers came into the Tomahawk, and Robert kept up with the number of customers at any given time; it never dipped below eight and never rose above eleven. Each person who passed by the cash register either knew the hostess/waitress by name or she knew them by name, or both. Robert was hoping the crowd would die down eventually, but one thing proved for certain: the Tomahawk was doing a steady business, regardless of the dismal state of Anniston's economy. For a few seconds he entertained the thought of actually asking for a job.

Rob Jr.'s voice almost made his father jump. "Mom smokes in the bathroom."

"I know."

"Smoking's bad," said Rob Jr.

"Yeah, don't ever smoke," said Robert.

"I ain't ever gonna smoke. It stinks."

The door opened and a group of six young men entered. None looked younger than nineteen or twenty, and all were clean-cut, tanned, and wearing shorts and pull-over shirts that looked as if they'd all been chosen by the same wardrobe coordinator on a sitcom set. Each young man was lean and casually handsome in a way that said they'd led comfortable lives and had rarely known a day of desperation that would have driven any one of them to consider holding up a meth lab. Talking and laughing amongst themselves, they took their seats at a large table next to a window; one of them, a blonde-haired fellow in a shirt the color of bathwater, waved for the waitress. Robert looked away, focusing on the wall above his son's head.

"Who are those guys?" the boy asked.

"How should I know?"

"Is one of them the guy you're here to see?" Rob Jr. craned his neck to see them better.

"Why the hell would I want to see some college kid barely older than your Uncle Jack?"

"How do you know they're in college?"

Robert sighed hard and said, "'Cause we're about ten miles from JSU, and they look like a bunch of spoiled college kids."

"Yep, they're wasting daddy's money in the big ivory tower, that's for sure." Sam Meeks's voice made Robert's head jerk up.

"Man, I didn't see you come in," said Robert, taking a deep breath. "How'd you sneak up on me like that?"

Sam pulled his cap off his head and tossed it onto the seat next to Rob Jr. "Come in through the kitchen." He was wearing a jacket even though it was over ninety degrees outside, and his forehead was shiny with sweat.

Robert turned sharply and stared at the kitchen door he hadn't even noticed until that moment. "How'd you? You just walked right in and nobody saw you?

Sam scooted onto the seat next to the boy, forcing him further into the booth. "I had to scout the place first. Check out the back. The alley. See who's in here first, you know. I move like a thief in the night, man." Sam flicked his eyes back and forth, and then reached around behind with one hand, patting the small of his back three times in a weirdly awkward motion as he checked the place out. His eyes were sunken and his pupils were dilated. He kept licking his lips and running his hand over his forehead in a motion that made Robert think of his uncle Baxter when he got off his meds, but in this case it was clear Sam was on all too many. Robert couldn't tell if he was nervous or anticipating what he wanted to eat. Suddenly, Sam noticed the child sitting low in the seat next to him for the first time. He stared at the boy and then began rubbing a finger back and forth over his chin. "You brought your kid?"

"I had to," said Robert. He shifted in his seat, glancing at all the tables in the place. He couldn't send the boy outside, the waitress wouldn't let him take up a booth to himself, and there was only one table left with no one seated at it. "Hey Bud," Robert said, "take a seat over there and let us talk." Rob Jr. had been itching to get up and walk around all the way up until the moment when the mysterious stranger startled them with his entrance, but now he wanted to hang around and find out what business this twitchy man might have with his father. Rob Jr. was pinned in the booth and made no effort to get free. "Hey Sam," Robert said, nodding once at his son, "let the boy out." Sam slid out and stood next to the table, scanning the restaurant anew while Rob Jr. bounced his way out of the vinyl seat until he was standing up. He lingered at the table a few seconds while Sam slid back into the booth and made a coffee-pouring motion with his hand at the waitress three tables over. "Go on, son," said Robert, "I won't be long."

Rob Jr. weighed the possibility of begging for his right to stay at the table and listen to Man Conversation. He was nearly nine, the oldest kid in his family, and he could listen to adult stuff. He heard "shit," "hell," and "damn" all the time, even though his mother always bitched when people used that kind of language around him and his siblings, except for when she forgot and used those words herself. There was something in his father's face, a strange look in his eyes that Rob Jr. had never seen before, as if he was afraid of something, and that made him feel strange. He'd never seen his father afraid—angry many times, but never afraid—and this look gave him a fuzzy feeling in his stomach that he didn't like.

"Go on, son," said Robert, a little firmer than before. Rob Jr. turned away from the two men and headed toward a two-person table pressed between the loud college boys who were now chugging coffee and a coat rack with a forgotten beige raincoat sagging from it.

"You got any more?" asked Sam, poking a thumb toward Rob Jr., now slumped in his seat, watching the college students. Sam made the coffee-pouring motion once more, this time more urgently.

"He's the oldest. I got four more."

"I mean in here," Sam said.

"No," said Robert, a little annoyed. "I just brought him because the youngest one got sick and my wife had to take him and the other ones to the doctor."

Sam made a whistling sound of amazement, rocking against the back of the booth like a person about to have some kind of mild seizure. At this the waitress thought he was getting impatient, and she grabbed a nearly empty pot of coffee and a cup from a tray and headed to their table. She smacked the cup down a little hard and poured it full, but she didn't offer any cream or sugar. "I told you we were short-handed today," she said in a voice barely above a mutter. She turned on her heel and headed for the kitchen door, but Sam seemed not to notice her temper.

"So you can see why I got to make some quick money," Robert said, as soon as she was out of earshot. "You can't get a job anywhere around here that pays shit, and when I get something it seems like there's always some asshole manager with a Ven-Detta against me." He punctuated the "V" and "D" with a finger jab onto the table for each. "Everywhere I go they don't want to hire me because they say I don't have enough experience, or I don't have the right kind of experience, or shitfire, they even say, 'Oh, you're one of them Boyds. I know your family.' And then they don't even want to talk to me when they find out I got a record. It doesn't matter that I did my time. How you supposed to take care of your family when you can't get a job? Everybody expects you to get a job after you get out, but nobody wants to hire you. Shit."

"Shit," echoed Sam.

"Some of them places say you got to have a college degree. Can you believe they want their shift managers out at the John Deere place to have college degrees? Shitfire, you don't need a college degree to run a place that sells tractors and lawn mowers and shit."

"I know it, man. My daddy worked at Republic Steel all his life and he didn't need no degree. He made good money, too." His hand clenched the coffee cup, and Robert noticed that it shook. "Dead now," Sam added.

For a second Robert wondered if he should offer his con-dolences, but Sam didn't seem to even notice he'd said the words. He kept looking out the windows, his eyes sticking to the bodies that passed by as if looking for a lost family member. He didn't look away until they disappeared out of sight on the far end of the window, and then, inexplicably, something

lit up inside Sam and he started up once more. "Damn gooks and chinks took near all our factories. Hell, they can live over there on a dollar a day like they's kings. Damn near it, anyway," said Sam. Robert had heard Pete-O use those names when he was a kid, but he wasn't sure exactly what people each referred to. He knew one of them probably meant Chinese, like Peng, and strangely, the names took on a small ugliness for the first time. He wanted to get Sam back on track, so he jumped in before Sam could get wound up about something else. "So," said Robert, "like I was telling you back when we talked, you know? Before?"

Sam didn't look at him. A man with a cap pulled over his eyes was passing by on the sidewalk, and Sam was trying hard to study his face.

"That idea that I had about the," Robert lowered his voice, "the T&A."

Sam suddenly turned his attention to Robert with a look that was both incredulous and stupefied. "What about it?"

Robert leaned back in his seat, stumped that Sam could be so absent. "That idea about the basement operation," he whispered. "You remember."

"Oh yeah, yeah, yeah, yeah." Sam spoke rapid-fire while nodding his head in recognition. "But you know man," said Sam, "I been thinking about all that. If we go ripping them off, and they find out it was us then, hell you know what'll happen. We'd end up on the bottom of the Tallapoosa all eat up by catfish. That's what happened to Scottie Hooch, remember him?" Sam glanced around again before motioning to Robert to come closer. "You know they start with your eyes. That's what they eat first."

Robert had no idea who Scottie Hooch was, and he shook his head to rid his mind of such an image. "Sam, just listen. I got a plan all worked out. Nobody's going to know anything."

"Why don't you just ask TP and Alton to hire you to work in the business? You said you needed a job."

Robert stared at Sam, incredulous at the fact that he was lucid, even if only for a few seconds. "Working at a meth lab isn't a real job." Robert waited a moment, hoping it would sink in. "What am I supposed to tell my family? Do I tell my wife I'm working for drug dealers?"

"Don't tell her nothing," said Sam, making a dismissive blowing sound with his lips. "Just say you're doing deliveries for a company. Hell, you think I tell my wife anything about what I'm doing? She don't know, and she don't want to know. Know what I mean?" Sam made a tapping motion against his forehead that could have meant any number of things, despite the fact that he seemed convinced his gestures were perfectly clear.

Robert was beginning to wish he hadn't even bothered asking Sam to meet him. He leaned over the table and tried one more time, keeping his voice barely above a whisper. "Look, I can't afford to get locked up again, so the last thing I want is a career job working for two of Rayle County's biggest meth dealers. I want this to be a one-time thing. I got an idea about how we can get in without anybody knowing. Fast in and fast out. Big money, one time, and then I'm done. I don't even care about the drugs. I just want the money. If I get enough, I get some breathing space, and then maybe I can figure out what to do long-term. Maybe when things get better I could find a decent job, a better job. Or maybe I could get that college degree, you know? If I could just get everybody off my back for a while." Robert leaned back hard against his seat, feeling spent at the effort it was taking to get Sam to even concentrate on what he was saying. If Pete-O was still alive, if he had both his legs, thought Robert, but no, Pete-O had thought it was a bad idea, too. The woman, the stripper who had worked at the T&A for over a year, knew all about what was going on in the basement and even she said it was a crazy idea, refusing to talk about it anymore. Robert could find no one who believed in him.

Across the restaurant some noise erupted, but Sam took no

notice. He looked serious, as if he was really thinking about the options Robert had laid out before him and was ready to hear his plan for breaking in. The young men at the table were making a ruckus. Robert could see that they were laughing at one of the group who kept slamming his hand in mock anger on the table next to his plate of half-eaten eggs, bacon, and toast. He was telling some kind of story that all of his friends found hysterically funny.

At the cash register the waitress ignored the table of unruly college boys because she was distracted by someone at the counter. She was shaking her head at a man who stood just inside the door next to the coat rack a few feet from Rob Jr. who was on his knees in his seat, leaning forward in rapt attention at the story being told at the college students' table.

Robert turned back to Sam and tried to ignore the commotion. He was sure Sam needed only a little more convincing. Robert put two fists on the table like bookends facing one another. "If I can get this job done. If we can—" He hesitated, not wanting to actually say the words aloud, but he made himself go on. "TP and Alton are not going to go to the cops if somebody robs them, and if we're smart about it they'll never know who it was. So we're home free. Hell, they're making meth. They've got to be pulling in fifty thou a week, maybe more. They might be making as much as a hundred thousand dollars a week." He paused, letting that figure sink in. Robert actually had no idea how much money a meth lab brought in on a weekly basis, but the two figures were enough to get Sam back in his court once more. As far as Robert was concerned, anything over twenty thousand, after he split it with Sam, would give him enough to get their bills caught up. Be fast, be smart, and don't get greedy. He'd never do it again. Not ever. Especially not with a punched-up addict like Sam. He clenched his fists harder and opened his mouth to continue, but Rob Jr. was suddenly running toward the booth.

"Hey Daddy, that man's got a gun." Rob Jr. slid to a stop. His mouth hung open and his wide eyes were glued to his father.

"What the hell are you talking about?" Robert turned to see over his son's head. Sam sat upright in his seat, fiddling with his jacket.

"That man," said Rob Jr., pointing his entire right arm straight out toward a man in a white T-shirt. The rain coat on the rack partially hid the man's back from view. His red hair hung thinly down to his T-shirt collar, but Robert could see no other part of him except for his right arm. From the back Robert saw a tattoo of some kind, like a turkey or maybe an eagle. The waitress pointed at the door and said something to him, still shaking her head. Robert couldn't make out what she'd said over the din from the students at the table, all now laughing at another story. The red-haired man with the tattoo argued back at the waitress, but Robert could make out only bits and pieces of his words. "It's my right as an American! It's my God-given right!"

"What the hell?" said Sam, sniffing hard. His hands shook and he started to stand up, but then he sat down again. His eyes moved from the man with the gun to the kitchen entrance and back several times, as if his brain was stuck on a loop. "Oh, shit. Oh, shit, oh shit," he kept saying.

The waitress was shaking her head at the man and telling him he had to leave his weapon outside. "The Second Amendment! The Second Amendment," he repeated, getting louder. "Men fought and died for this right. American men! You can't deny me my rights," shouted the man. He put a hand over his shoulder and touched the butt of his gun, a motion that made an older couple waiting in line to pay their bill suddenly shove past him. With his wife running ahead, the older man threw a handful of bills on the counter. Reaching over his wife's head, the man jerked the door back, nearly hitting his wife who was scrambling to exit. The woman's hands flew out as she tripped over one of the legs of the coat rack. It toppled under the weight of the rain coat and fell over the chair Rob Jr. had been sitting in only moments before. The commotion caught the attention of the college students, two of whom bolted from their seats. With nothing blocking the view between Robert and the front counter, he clearly saw what everyone else in the place had just seen. Strapped to the back of the red-haired man was an AK-15, his fingers touching it over his shoulder.

"I told you he had a gun," said Rob Jr., thrilled to be proven right.

"He's gonna draw!" shouted Sam.

Both Sam and Robert were on their feet. The next words that came out of anyone's mouth did not even register in Robert's brain. They were a muffled, inarticulate roar coming from every direction. From the corner of his eye Robert caught the fast but fluid motion of Sam's right hand reaching behind his back, and when his hand whipped back around he was holding a gun. Someone screamed from across the restaurant, and Sam took aim. The red-haired man turned at the same instant, and in a motion, fast and well-practiced, he pulled his weapon around to the front and released the safety. Just as Sam's shot narrowly missed the tattooed man's shoulder, the man fired back at Sam three times. The first bullet hit Sam's left forearm and he crumpled to the seat, dropping his gun. When the next bullet hit Rob Jr., he fell backwards and blood sprayed over Robert, covering his cheeks and eye lids. Robert's arms shot forward, catching his son as they both collapsed to the floor. Robert heard himself saying, "No, no, no, no," in his mind, but it sounded more like someone else was speaking the words. There was a gaping bloody hole in his son's forehead, and the boy's shocked eyes were wide open, staring up blankly past Robert's face.

Cathy Adams   285

The Gadsden Times

Eight-Year-Old Drayton Boy Shot Dead at Anniston Diner

In an apparent shoot-out between a Second Amendment supporter and a restaurant patron in the Tomahawk Diner, a child, Robert Harley Boyd Jr., was shot and killed and one of the shooters suffered minor injuries Tuesday morning in Anniston, at approximately 8:15 a.m. According to Tomahawk employee, Anna Mangum, Daniel G. Kelley attempted to enter the diner with a fully-loaded AK-15 strapped to his back. "He told me his Second Amendment rights guaranteed his freedom to carry his weapon," said Mangum. She then told Kelley he was, "not welcome in the diner with his gun. I said he could leave it in his car, and he started arguing that it was his right."

According to Sheriff Po "Dunk" Williams, Sam Christopher Meeks was seated at a booth with the victim's father, Robert H. Boyd, who had come to the restaurant to apply for a job. Williams confirmed that four shots were fired, one from Meeks and three from Kelley. The shots fired from Kelley injured Meeks and caused the death of the child.

The victim, Robert H. Boyd, Jr., was the son of Robert H. and Kimberly Boyd of Drayton, Alabama. Rob Jr. was a rising third-grader at Drayton Elementary School. "Rob Jr. had lots of friends and he was eager in the classroom. His parents were always at the school what for one thing or another," said Drayton Elementary Principal, Dr. Rick Canard.

According to Sheriff Williams, Kelley has been active in a Second Amendment group based in Glencoe. Kelley and supporters were recently seen carrying guns on the sidewalk in front of the Glencoe McDonald's. Open carry laws in Alabama reserve the right for citizens to carry licensed weapons in public venues.

One witness said he saw the victim's father go without food so that his child could eat. "I seen him counting out the last penny he had so that boy could have breakfast. I wish now I'd bought him some food."

Mangum, employed with the Tomahawk for twelve years, said, "The man was out trying to find a job and his child gets killed. My heart goes out to the whole family."

Charges against Kelley and Meeks are pending further investigation.

Chapter 27

The First Baptist Church of Drayton was not big enough to handle a funeral for a murdered child. News teams stood behind a cordoned-off area monitored by three of Sheriff William's deputies on one side of the parking lot. Rumors had flown all over Drayton for the past three days that the Westboro Baptist Church was coming to protest Rob Jr.'s funeral, but the only protesters that showed up was Kelley's Second Amendment group. All six of them stood quietly in a show of respect "for the family of the slain" and "for the Constitution of these United States," said a woman in a pink tank top carrying an AK-15 with a pink handle; she identified herself to the press as the spokesperson for the Second Amendment Preservationists of Alabama, Chapter 3. Someone in the crowd said she was Kelley's girlfriend.

"Those psychotic assholes," said Magda as she pulled into the parking lot of the church with Baxter and Peng. "I wish I had a gun so I could shoot that bitch right between the eyes."

"They took my gun away," said Baxter, staring across the street at the woman speaking into a microphone that a reporter held in front of her face.

Something about his words made Magda do a double take. "You had a gun?"

"It's broken. They took it from me and smashed it."

"I don't—" Magda sputtered. "When did you have a gun? Who took it away?"

"I promised Peng I wouldn't have any more guns," said Baxter.

"No guns," said Peng from the back seat. "*Meyo* guns."

"Well," said Magda, shaking her head, "I reckon that's the last thing this family needs." She unbuckled her seat belt and they followed suit. Inside, the church pianist was already playing, setting the mood for a rousing come-to-Jesus funeral.

Church members who could not get a seat spilled out the open front doors of the church and into the parking lot and strained to listen. When the congregation began singing "How Great Thou Art," members standing on the church steps all the way to the front row of cars sang along with them, sending the holy hymn all the way to the cameramen who scrambled to capture the haunting sound of the chorus. Inside the church, the family sat in anticipation of their most painful funeral yet.

Since the first newscast announcing the tragic shooting of a child who waited while his father applied to be a busboy at a diner, calls offering jobs to Robert had been fielded by the funeral home, Lilith Ann's church, and Lilith Ann's household. No one had called Robert's house since Tuesday, because Kimmy had ripped the landline from the wall the night of her son's death in a rage of grief. Robert didn't know who had started the rumor about him looking for work that day. He had been in shock when the police arrived, and Sam began firing off a story about how he had just been passing by when he saw his friend inside and stopped in to have coffee. He rattled on, saying that Robert was waiting to ask the waitress for a job application and it was all a coincidence, his being there. Since then, the story had spread to people who didn't know anything about Robert's felonious background or his family history. Businesses as far away as Birmingham and one in Montgomery had offered him positions. He could take his pick of anything from roofer, slaughterhouse assistant manager, strip mall security guard, quick shop night-shift worker, shoe salesman, groomer at a horse ranch, grocery store butcher's apprentice, deliveryman for a bakery, First Methodist Church of Drayton janitor, cabinet maker's assistant, carpet factory line inspector, landscaper, nursing home bus driver, lighting showroom salesman, and night manager of one of Alabama's last surviving drive-in movie theatres. The offers were put in folders and awaited him in a neat pile atop Lilith Ann's kitchen table. Another envelope of checks and cash from across the state, in amounts from a single dollar bill to two-hundred-dollar checks, was held in a locked drawer at Sheriff Williams' office, money given by concerned citizens moved by Rob Jr.'s picture on all the news outlets three nights running. The world had frozen that week for each member of the extended family who, once again, put aside their daily obligations to attend a funeral.

Magda took her seat in the second row behind her mother. She was getting a lot of wear out of The Funeral Dress. She was thinking that if things kept up she might have to invest in a new one just so she'd have some variety for the next funeral. Maybe she'd get a Dog Funeral Dress and a People Funeral Dress, she thought. She shook her head and covered her eyes. When the absolute worst things happened, they brought Magda's most twisted, black strains of humor to the surface. She kept these horrible thoughts to herself mostly, thoughts like: maybe now Kimmy would be able to keep up with how many children she had.

Magda had read somewhere that inappropriate humor was a coping mechanism for stress, like the way some people mean to cry at funerals but laugh instead because the wires in their brains get their emotions all mixed up. Magda wondered if maybe that was her problem. Maybe her psyche was so bent out of shape from funerals and killings and family members entering and exiting prison, that she wanted to scream and cry at the same time. Despite this, the people lost to her were those she was not even fond of or close to. Losing Pete-O was a kind of quiet relief, though she'd never told a soul. But the death of a child was different. How could anyone not feel the most profound grief when a child died, any child? Rob Jr. had been by far her least favorite of all her brother's children, and she told herself that she would shed tears at his funeral even if she had to stick a pin in her hand to make them flow, but she didn't have to use the pin. All she had to do was look at her mother. Gray-faced and shrunken, Lilith Ann sat on the front row of the church, like a person who was melting from the

inside out. To Magda her mother looked ten years older. When Lilith Ann walked to the casket to say good-bye to her oldest grandchild, she looked down at his pale, small face and sucked air into her lungs in little gasps. "Oh, my grandbaby looks like he's sleeping." And then she sank to her knees. Magda had never seen her mother so hollow with grief.

While waiting for the service to begin, Kimmy had stood next to her dead son, her hand rubbing the cool white surface of the casket as if it were a large sleeping animal, while her remaining children squirmed on the pew between Viv and Lilith Ann.

Twice Matthew approached the casket and asked his mother why Rob Jr. was in there, and twice Josh picked him up and returned him to his seat. Seeing his brother get no satisfactory answers, Cody ran to the shiny coffin, gripped the edge, and tried to peer inside. This time Robert picked up his now eldest son and the two of them stared down at Rob Jr.

After a long, contemplative look, Cody asked, "Is he dead?"

"Yes," said Robert, "he's dead."

"My teacher said he was with Jesus, but she's wrong. I'm going to tell her he's right here." He wriggled to get down and Robert let him slide back to the floor. He paid no attention to Cody, who darted down the aisle to find Mrs. Riviera and correct her mistake. Matthew, seeing his brother depart from the family, squawked in protest and stood up in the pew. Viv tried to quiet him, and then Scott began to whine and expressed his displeasure by throwing himself down on the pew and arching his back, making it nearly impossible to keep him upright in the pew. Lilith Ann glanced at the children and made a half-hearted gesture at them to remain quiet.

Magda leaned over and tried to help Viv straighten out the uncooperative Scott, who was now sideways on the pew, flailing his arms. "I told you we needed Fanny in the front row to help with the kids, but you didn't want anyone who wasn't family."

"Can't you give one of them to Peng? She's technically family," said Viv, trying to wrangle Matthew frontward.

"She IS family," said Magda, lifting Matthew up under his arms and dropping him on the pew between her and Baxter. "Zip it and keep still," she said to the boy, and then thinking better of it she added, "Sweetie." For about two seconds he considered his new situation, and for that brief moment Magda thought he was going to quiet down. Matthew turned around in his seat and looked down at his brother, who was already trying to climb onto his feet in the pew. The music took them all by surprise, and the boys were momentarily transfixed by the piano and the movement of the congregation into a standing position. As Kimmy returned to her place with the family, Viv turned one last time and whispered to Magda, "I don't care what Kimmy says. These kids need to be taken out."

Robert stood next to her, his son's face never out of his peripheral vision. He and Kimmy were on the opposite end of the pew from Lilith Ann, leaning onto one another. Viv remained seated on the pew, stroking Jessica Ann's hair and holding the baby in a sleeping position across her lap. Neither Robert nor Kimmy had said more than a few words to anyone since they entered the sanctuary. Robert stared at the wood floor under his feet and heard nothing but the pounding rage and grief that covered every sound around him. Behind the two of them Peng was offering the still-whining Scott a hard candy from her purse. The day of Rob Jr.'s funeral was the first day Peng had been able to walk, and when she saw the child in the casket upon entering she gasped almost as hard as Lilith Ann. Up until that moment, she had thought it was the father who had been shot. Seeing the child, his waxy face drawn in death with the small sanitary-looking hole above his eyes, sent her into such shock she had to be led outside by Magda and Fanny until she could catch her breath.

The service commenced, and there was complete silence as Reverend Giles approached the pulpit. Kimmy kept her eyes on the casket a few feet in front of her, barely noticing

Cody who had returned to his seat and was crawling up onto the pew next to his father. Rob Jr.'s nose and eyes were barely visible, but she watched him, concentrating hard. In place of the unmoving face in the casket she saw her son in the nonstop movement of life. She saw him running past his siblings to get the front seat in the van. She saw him dashing from the table after dabbling a fork around in his scrambled eggs. She saw him taking his shoes and socks off and running across the back yard, his muddy bare feet trampling the petunias she'd just set out. She saw him darting down the hall after she'd told him it was time to take a bath. And she saw him heading out the door Tuesday morning, glad to be able to go somewhere with his father, and no brothers or sister tagging along. Kimmy saw all these images of him threading backward in hopscotch order until she saw the red, scrunched up face in her arms when she gave birth to him four months after she and Robert had been married. His tiny face had been magnificent. So perfect. She never tired of staring at it during the first few days of his life. His head, covered in dark hair, was so small, she could hold the back of it in the palm of her hand and stare down at him, his eyes darting between her forehead and hairline and eyes. Watching that child lying still, Kimmy felt the pain of knowing that tiny face, like an enormous pearl in her hand, was gone from her forever. Then someone touched her shoulder and she heard a voice say, "Time to go to the cemetery." Kimmy did not remember who said the words, but she obeyed.

The only member of the family absent from the funeral was Jack, who swayed listlessly on a tire swing in the back yard of his mother's house because he wanted to get away from everyone: his family, curious onlookers, and news crews. Bending forward, he watched the ground turning beneath him as he kicked at the dirt with his sneakers. Lying in the grass a few feet away, Daryl panted, hot and bored in the humid afternoon air. It would be happening again, the interviews, their faces on the news, the whispers behind their backs, the sympathy, the blame, the judgment, the pitiful faces saying how sorry they all were, the empty offers of "anything we can do." Jack had heard the lines and seen the faces too many times. In little more than five years Jack had said good-bye to his father, his uncle who had been like a father to him, and now his nephew who'd watched three men in the family go in and out of jail, prison, and a mental ward. It was no wonder the boy had held a gun on his own mother.

When all this was over, Jack was leaving. He didn't know which direction he was headed. Maybe west. Maybe all the way to California, or at least Colorado. Or maybe he'd go to Texas to get a landscaping job. He was good at that. He'd planted flowering plants and bushes all around Pete-O's house, once his house, now Peng's house, probably soon to be Baxter and Peng's house. In the springtime, the yard had been almost pretty. But Texas was hot and dry. There probably weren't that many landscaping jobs in a state that was short on water. Maybe he should forget going west and head up the east coast. That was where the money was. He could go to one of those small states, the ones that are so tiny on maps they can't fit their names on the state so they get these little lines drawn out into the Atlantic Ocean with their names written over the water. That's where people with money lived, and if there were people with money, then they had big houses, and if they had big houses, then they had big yards and would pay good money to have somebody keep those yards looking nice. He'd hire on with one of those high-dollar landscaping companies that had all the big contracts, and he'd do alright. He wouldn't get rich, but he didn't care. He just wanted to start anew somewhere else. He wanted to be in a place where people weren't breathing down his neck about going to college or asking him what he wanted to do with his life all the time. He didn't want to end up like any of his uncles or his brother Robert, locked up for all kinds of reasons. He didn't even want to end up like his brother Josh, who was dumb as a box of nails. There was nothing left

in Drayton for Jack.

He felt guilty at the thought of leaving his mother after she'd been through so much heartache, but even she would have to accept that it was time for him to make his own life, one away from all the death he'd seen, all the decay of a dying town, a place where few people were going anywhere. A place that anyone with any sense would want to leave.

Magda was still there. He often wondered what it was that kept her tethered to a town she'd said for as far back as he could remember that she hated. She was always going on about some job opportunity, but the furthest she ever seemed to get was talking about it. He never knew her to apply to any of those jobs. A year ago, she was on a kick to move to some place in northern China for a job teaching English to little kids. She had even bought a book and said she was going to learn Chinese. Sometimes he saw her in the back yard in a lawn chair studying the book, her mouth moving without any sounds coming out. After about a month she stopped going outside to practice, and soon after he never heard anything more about that idea.

Of all their mother's children, Magda was the one who had the best chance of making it somewhere else. Even more than he did, Jack thought. She wouldn't have to take on a day-labor job. She could get a job in a company somewhere doing work that could be done in nice clothes. Magda was smart enough not to get her hands dirty unless she wanted to, and Jack was sure she didn't. He couldn't understand why she had never made that final step and put Drayton, Alabama behind her. Maybe she was as afraid as he was. Leaving the only home he'd ever known. Going to some place where nobody knew you and maybe nobody wanted to.

"Hey, you back there?" Josh's voice called from the back door.

Jack raised his head and returned the call. "Yeah, I'm here."

Josh stood in the doorway, holding the doorknob in his hand as if he were going to say something else, but after a few seconds he backed into the house in silence. He almost had the door shut when Viv poked her head out. She yelled for Jack to come inside as if he were a child being called in from playing when it was dinnertime. Jack stood up from the swing and hesitated a moment. He wasn't about to be taking orders from his sister-in-law, no matter how much older she was, but he knew that today was different and there was no room for family spats. Not today. But maybe tomorrow.

In the house, Lilith Ann's kitchen table and counters were covered in food brought in from neighbors, friends, and members of her church. It was only a few days ago that the family had finished up all the food from Pete-O's funeral. For weeks, Lilith Ann had pulled out casseroles and soups from her freezer. This time no one felt much like eating. Kimmy and Robert sat side by side on the sofa. Someone had turned on the TV, but the sound was muted. The screen flickered with commercials of beautiful people doing interesting things, like jogging in a park or driving sleek cars around curving roads in autumn, flickering pictures of life that were an obscene backdrop to the static solitude of the room.

Jack appeared in the doorway and put his hands on his hips. "What was it you wanted?" he said to Viv.

Viv opened her mouth in a huff. She glanced at Robert and Kimmy, still sitting like two marionettes someone had abandoned, and then back at Jack. "I just thought you should be here for your brother and for Kimmy. They've been through a tragedy and we all need to be here for them."

The two of them barely stirred from their seats on the sofa.

Jack held his tongue a moment and then replied, "Well I'm here, aren't I?"

"I'm sorry your boy die," said Peng from a seat at the dining table far across the room. She and Baxter sat side by side at the table as if awaiting a meal.

Kimmy was shaken to life enough to answer. "Oh, oh, thank you." She looked around, suddenly baffled. "Where are the kids?"

Viv looked stunned. "Kimmy, don't you remember? Mary Pendergast took them with her before we went out to the cemetery."

"Well no, I guess I forgot," said Kimmy. "It's funny. They're always all around me, and then when they're gone I don't. . . it's like I can't even see them in my mind even."

"Well, they're fine," said Viv. "She's bringing them back here after supper." The room fell into uncomfortable silence and remained that way until Lilith Ann broke it with her footsteps from down the hall.

"That was the Anniston News station again on the phone," said Lilith Ann, coming from her bedroom. "They asked if they could come by and get a word or two, but I told them we'd speak outside. Don't worry, I'll do the talking."

"Mama, you sure you're up to it?" asked Magda.

"I can do it."

Kimmy stood up and began rubbing her wrist as if she'd just been tied up. She paced the floor once and then turned around. "I'm just glad those crazy Westboro people didn't show up," she said.

"Dunk wouldn't have let them get within a mile even if they tried," said Lilith Ann.

"Yeah, it's too bad they didn't come around. Maybe those gun nuts would have had somebody to shoot at," said Magda.

Viv tried not to grin. "Now Magda, that's just terrible."

"Yes, that's just terrible," repeated Lilith Ann, but she didn't sound angry.

Josh suddenly stood up from his chair and said, "I wish they could have done something about those people across the street."

"I never thought I'd live to see the day you'd complain about somebody's Second Amendment rights," said Magda.

"Magda, I'll tie your tongue in a knot if you start in with anything today," said Lilith Ann. "I am in no mood."

"Half of those gun nuts are on meth. Or that's what

everybody said," Magda said.

Robert rose out of the trancelike stillness he had been in since the funeral had ended and looked at Magda with a funny expression that made her squirm a little in her seat. "That woman across the street was on meth?" asked Robert.

"That's what they say," repeated Magda.

"Drayton has the highest ratio of methamphetamine labs per capita in the state of Alabama," Baxter said.

"Really? Seriously?" said Magda.

"Yes."

"How would you know a thing like that?" asked Viv.

"There's one in the basement of the T&A Lounge," said Baxter. "And there's one out off I-59 past the flea market that was burned out."

Viv and Magda both sputtered over one another in an attempt to ask questions, and Robert stood up from his chair.

"Hokes Bluff has two fewer than Drayton, or they'd be the number one producer of methamphetamine," said Baxter.

"How could you possibly know how many meth labs there are anywhere?" Magda was on her feet as well. "I mean, Uncle Baxter, nobody knows this stuff. Do they?"

"I hear things," he said.

"Oh, sweet Jesus in heaven, it's the voices again," said Viv, clutching dramatically at her heart. "I thought the medication was going to put a stop to that."

"People talk. Police officers like to talk when they're at the doughnut place," said Baxter. "They must think I can't hear them. They sit there right next to me at the counter and they talk and talk."

"Why aren't they out there arresting those people instead of sitting around eating doughnuts and talking about it?" asked Viv. Her voice was shrill and she looked spooked.

"I liked the voices better. They were kinder," said Baxter. He looked down at his hands and was quiet.

"Lord knows we don't want to go through that again," said

Viv. "So you'd better keep on your pills, you understand?"

"He's not going off his pills, Viv. He's going to get married soon, so he's going to stay on his pills, aren't you, Baxter?"

Baxter kept looking at his hands and said nothing. Peng smiled and reached over to pat his right hand with hers. "Baxter is good man."

"Of course he is," said Magda.

"You people are crazy," said Peng, still smiling.

Viv looked as if she'd been stung by a bee. Lilith Ann just sighed and put her hands on her hips. "Well, I reckon you're right," she said. Magda and Jack burst out laughing.

After a moment Jack's laughter spun itself out. "Where'd Robert go?" he asked.

No one had noticed Robert slip down the hall and disappear into Lilith Ann's bedroom. Kimmy lingered at the front window of the den, rubbing her hands over her arms like a person with an obsessive-compulsive disorder. She looked back at the room, her eyes lighting on one face and then another. "I need a smoke. Will you all excuse me?" She didn't wait for an answer but headed for the front door. She didn't even get the door shut behind her before she was back inside.

"You all right?" asked Magda.

"It's the neighbors. They're just hanging out on their porches trying to spy on us," said Kimmy, rubbing her arms harder.

Magda went to the front window and pulled the curtains back for a look. "It's just old Mr. and Mrs. Haney. They sit out on their porch like that every day."

"That news crew's not back are they?" Lilith Ann pushed up behind her and almost bumped into Magda. Earlier that morning, four or five members of the news media had loitered across the street next to a van with a big satellite dish mounted on top. The Haneys had gone to the street to find out what they wanted and discovered themselves in an interview. "No, the news vans left," said Magda. "They're calling it the 'Second Amendment Shooting,' and it was one of the main

stories online this morning. I googled it, and it was everywhere."
Kimmy seemed to shrink under her words and Magda regretted
them immediately.

Lilith Ann turned abruptly. "You mean it's on the google?"

"They're making it a political thing," said Magda. "It'll die
down." She stopped and regretted her word choice again. "I
mean, people will...." She sighed and looked at Kimmy.

"I don't understand how they got hold of it," said Lilith Ann.
"This is a local story."

"Not really, Mama."

"Can't you call them and tell them to leave it alone?"

"Call who?" asked Magda.

"The google," said Lilith Ann.

"It doesn't work like that," said Magda. "Kimmy, maybe you
ought to go to the back stoop. Nobody'll bother you out there."

"Where'd Robert get off to?" Lilith Ann checked the front
yard from the window again. "I don't see him anywhere. Robert?"
she called. At the end of the darkened hall a line of light shined
at the base of the door, and she began ambling toward. "You
all right?"

There was no response. Lilith knocked softly on the door
and called his name, but there was no sound. She tried the
knob, but it was locked. A trickle of fear rose up her neck and
she took a deep breath before calling his name once more, this
time with a firm urgency. "Robert? This is your mama. Now
open the door so I'll know you're all right."

Magda stole up behind Lilith Ann, almost making her jump.
"What's he doing?" asked Magda.

"Shhh, don't let the others hear you," Lilith Ann said. Her
hand still gripped the doorknob.

"Robert?" Magda's voice was a stage whisper. "Robert, open
the door."

"Robert," said Lilith Ann, her hand clenching over the knob
so hard her fingers were white, "Kimmy needs you to come on
out. Now, don't you hide yourself away like this. She doesn't

need to be alone right now."

From inside there was a creaking noise, one that Lilith Ann recognized immediately. The sound was the creak the mattress makes when a person stands up after sitting on it. She held her breath and let go of the knob, waiting for him to open the door. There was the sound of a hand sliding over the hollow wood on the other side, and then silence once more. "Son, I know you're hurting. Kimmy's hurting. We're all hurting, but let's not do this. Come on and open the door and let's not have any trouble."

"What's going on down there?" Viv called from the other end of the hall. "What's Robert up to?" Lilith Ann flagged her hand violently up and down to shut Viv up.

"Is Robert doing something?" Josh called from behind her. Viv's heels clomped down the hallway, making a staccato beat that raised the tension a couple of notches before she even arrived at the door.

"Everything's fine," Lilith Ann said, speaking in a deliberately loud voice. "He's just taking a little break and then he's going to come out and we're going to all have some cake. Junie Aimes sent us a Mississippi Mud cake and he loves that. Don't you, hon?"

There was still no answer. Viv reached for the doorknob. "Why's the door locked?"

"Maybe he just wants to be alone," said Magda. She put her hand against the door and called to him. "Robert? You want us to leave you alone? Just say the word and we'll go on back to the den, but you really need to come out soon and be with Kimmy. She's smoked half a pack out on the back porch while we've been standing here trying to talk to you. Just tell us you're okay. Okay?"

The unmistakable sound of sobbing made the trio of women turn to one another in mutual expressions of dread and fright. It was Lilith Ann who took the situation in hand. "You two go on back and let me handle this."

"We're going to have cake, Robert," said Magda. "We'll save some for you." Viv was going to speak, but Lilith Ann snapped her fingers and waved them both away.

Robert pushed his hands through his hair again and stared down at his mother's Smith and Wesson 638 lying on the green and yellow afghan folded neatly at the foot of his mother's bed. He'd seen each of his children lying on that same afghan at various times in their lives, usually when they were newborns. As the babies came, one by one, and Lilith Ann served as sitter, she would often wrap them up on cold days, and it was usually in this afghan, knitted by Lilith Ann when Robert was a boy about Rob Jr.'s age. The thought made him cringe, that he could no longer think of his son in the present. Everything about Rob Jr. was now past tense. He had been eight years old. He had been a student at Drayton Elementary School. He had been the eldest of Robert and Kimmy's children. Lilith Ann had had five grandchildren, and now she had four. Robert would go home that night and his son would not be sleeping in his bed in the boys' room ever again. Neither of the other boys seemed to have processed this fact. Early that morning, Scott had thrown a yellow toy gun across the room and it had landed on Rob Jr.'s bed. When Kimmy came into the room to get the boys dressed for the funeral, she had shrieked so loudly at them that Robert thought another child had been mortally wounded.

"Who did this?" she had screamed over and over at the petrified brothers who could not take their eyes from their mother's pink, tear-streaked face. Her finger shook in their faces. "Don't you touch your brother's bed!" she screamed. "Ever! Don't touch it. You two stay away from Rob Jr.'s things."

Robert appeared in the doorway. "Kimmy! Why the hell are you yelling at the kids?" he said.

Cody began to cry, and Kimmy grabbed him up and squeezed him hard to her chest. When Lilith Ann arrived to help get the children ready for the service she found Kimmy

sitting cross-legged in the floor of the boys' room, refusing to let Cody out of her arms until Lilith Ann coaxed her to let him go. Robert and Kimmy dressed the now totally silent Cody and Matthew, who stole glances at the sanctified corner of the room where their eldest brother's possessions lay in neat array. Lilith Ann removed the toy gun and tossed it in the kitchen trash. The two women had moved silently as well, going through motions of pulling arms into sleeves, socks onto feet, and dragging combs across heads. Lilith Ann's hands shook as she tied the laces of Scott's shoes, only to realize they had once belonged to Rob Jr.

The revolver lay so heavily on the afghan that it made a gun-shaped indentation in the fibers, just the way a fancy gift looks lying in a custom box. Robert drew his finger down the handle and then inserted five bullets into it. His mother kept the box of bullets next to the gun that lay in the top drawer. Robert didn't know why he put in five bullets, except that maybe there was something final, something thorough about filling every chamber of the gun. Three bullets were missing from the box, he noticed, and he couldn't help but wonder what his mother had done with them. How many years had it been since his mother had shot a gun? Had she shot it just to get in a little practice? The revolver had belonged to Robert's father, and Lilith Ann had pulled it out of the attic after Pete-O shot that man in the Walmart. Maybe she felt she needed to be able to protect herself after all that had happened. They'd received death threats, the whole family, even little Jack who was just a kid when Pete-O got locked up. Robert tried to picture his mother in the back yard, focusing on a couple of aluminum cans atop a tree stump, squeezing the trigger, probably missing, and then deciding it wasn't important. After all, the only time she was going to shoot her gun was when somebody broke into the house, and at close range accuracy didn't much matter.

Robert picked up the gun and let his finger slide around the trigger. He quickly put it down again. The gun was so small.

How could something not much bigger than a ham sandwich bring a life to a screeching halt, both for the person who was shot and the person who did the shooting? The man who'd killed his son would serve a long sentence, or so the police had assured him. Maybe they'd said that to make him feel better, or maybe they thought Robert wanted to kill the man himself. Who knew what the outcome of the trial would be? He didn't even care. Not at that moment. He was hardly thinking of the guilt of the man who pulled the trigger.

Robert picked the gun up again and rested the chamber against his forehead. He could not bring himself to put the barrel end between his eyes. "Never point a gun at anything you don't intend to kill," his father had told him every time a firearm was near, and Lilith Ann echoed the words just to impress them even deeper into Robert's mind. But he did intend to kill himself, didn't he? The shooting of his own son, it had been set into motion somehow by Robert's decisions. He hadn't pulled the trigger, but if he hadn't come up with his plan to rob a meth lab, his son would still be alive. Crossing that line was what flipped some switch in the universe that brought death to his family. Robert remembered when he had made up his mind to do it, to go through with the robbery. He could hear a voice trying to pull him back from the decision, trying to convince him that the risk was too great, that he'd regret it, but somehow it had been easy to choose, and as soon as he turned his back on the voice, he had silenced it. For a while he thought about the risks, the possibility that something could go wrong; he calculated it all in his head, but not one of those calculations had involved his children in any way. The risk was always directed at him. The worst thing that could have happened would happen to him, and he wanted to take the risk that it would. He wanted to do it for his family, but it had cost them all.

His mother was not going to leave the door. He could hear her on the other side, her breathing, her presence. She had

Cathy Adams 305

never been able to be quiet. Viv and Magda had gone away, but Lilith Ann would stay there as long as it took.

Out the window he could see the back yard, the silent and massive trees that he had played in and under when he was a child. When Robert was ten he had climbed the sycamore tree in the yard after getting a whipping from his dad. He couldn't remember what he had done, but he remembered his father coming after him with a black leather belt and beating him until he had welts on the backs of his legs. Robert sat up in that tree shouting down to his mother, who implored him to come down, that he was going to stay there the rest of the night. Lilith Ann had called up that if he was going to spend the night in the tree, then she was going to sit right there at the bottom in a lawn chair until morning just to make sure he didn't fall asleep and hurt himself falling out of it. She went to the garage and got an aluminum chair with a green woven vinyl seat, not comfortable, but much more so than the branch Robert balanced his bottom on. The standoff lasted an incredible three hours, longer than even Robert thought he could last. His legs were asleep from his awkward perch in the crook of a branch, and his skin was cold and scraped bloody from trying to keep his body balanced against the trunk. Lilith Ann said nothing. She just sat in that chair until long after the sun went down and ignored the mosquitoes that bit her neck and arms. Up in the branches of the sycamore tree, they buzzed Robert's bare arms and face, twice almost making him lose his balance as he released his grip to swat at them. Once his father had come to the back door to ask what the hell they were both doing out there, and Lilith Ann told him to go watch TV, that she'd take care of it. She said nothing to Robert after her initial demand that he come down; she just waited, watching the dusk turn to moonlight and the bats come out for their breakfast. Finally, when Robert's arms began to shiver so badly from exhaustion and cold, he began the painful descent which had been such an easy climb up. Lilith Ann waited at the bottom, saying nothing. Robert let his feet drop to the ground and he stood up, his back burning from discomfort. She folded up her chair and just looked at him, nearly her height at such a young age, and said, "Let's get on to the house now."

Lilith Ann had always been good at letting him suffer from his own choices, all the while saying little. Magda was the one she blew up at, and he had never understood why. His younger sister had been smarter than he was. She'd done better in school, won awards, gone to college, and graduated with a degree in something. He never could remember what. Robert had never aspired to college. He was supposed to be able to find a job after he graduated high school. That was the way it had been for generations. A high school graduate was supposed to get some kind of job decent enough that he could support a family if he was willing to work hard. That's the way it had been for his father and for most of the men in his family. You either went to the steel plant or the tire plant, but those days were long gone. Baxter had trouble getting a job, but that was only because he was "off" as his mother put it. Pete-O never went to college, but he got on at the steel plant after high school and worked there until he quit and went on disability decades later. He complained that they were "bustin' his balls," but everyone knew it was because he'd become too sick with diabetes to keep up.

Just a few years after graduation, Robert found himself on a ball and chain to Kimmy, and the honeymoon was barely over when Rob Jr. showed up. And then the other kids started coming, but the paychecks shrank. Or the jobs dried up like just after Rob Jr. was born and the calls for construction jobs stopped coming. Only the best plumbers or electricians or sheetrock guys got any more work. Robert got nothing. Then the jobs got worse or he was let go for some stupid reason, and soon the only thing he could get was fast-food or delivery truck jobs, stuff like that. He had experience doing a dozen or more different kinds of jobs, but it seemed none of that

experience added up to get him anywhere. He got arrested a couple of times when he was younger, but it was never for anything serious: public drunkenness once and disturbing the peace another time. Pete-O had been the one who bailed him out because his mother had said he should "sit his ass in jail for a night and sober up," or that's the way Pete-O had put it. Drayton was a small town and people had the deadly combination of long memories and unforgiving natures, his mother included. Later, when he was older and got into trouble with the law Kimmy had been none too happy about it, but by the time of his fourth arrest, or maybe it was the fifth, she had just discovered she was pregnant again and was not afforded the luxury of being angry at the only person in her life whose responsibility it was to keep food in her children's mouths and a roof over their heads.

But now everything was winding tighter and tighter. It seemed nobody wanted to hire full-time anymore, let alone overtime or offer any kind of insurance that could take care of the children when they were sick, and one of them always seemed to be sick. Not a week seemed to go by without one of the kids coughing from a cold that threatened to turn into a full-blown respiratory infection. Getting ahead had never been this hard. Getting a full-time job, even one at minimum wage, always seemed to be beyond his grasp. Robert knew some people were getting good jobs, they had to be. But not him, and the frustration of it sometimes made him feel he was losing his mind from the unfairness of it all. It made him want to do crazy things like rob meth labs in the basements of titty bars, and just thinking about how the very words sounded inside his head made him want to wretch with sobs of anger and despair. He saw no way to escape the hopelessness of his future and the guilt of his present. Kimmy had made sure everyone knew he was in that diner looking for a job, and the story had made people feel sorry for him, but it had all been a lie. He hated the lie that brought pity even more than the truth that would have brought condemnation had they known it. Robert bent his head almost between his knees and felt a pressure inside that was so hot and hard it was as if his organs would burst.

"Robert? You have to open up this door right this minute." Lilith Ann's voice made his breath catch in his throat. His mother had always been able to make him feel like a child who had done something wrong, and for much of his life that is exactly what he had been to her, but now he was a grown man who had lost his son. He could not be that child who jumped when his mother called. Robert wiped a hand over his eyes and took a breath. The gun was now hot and oily from his grip. He stood up and, still holding the loaded gun, unlocked the door and then stepped back. Lilith Ann pushed it a few inches, hesitated, and pushed it open far enough to get her head inside. At first she didn't see the gun in her son's hand, but the thought was clearly in her mind. Her eyes took in the red-eyed Robert, and then she glanced at the drawer. It was closed, and for a second she relaxed, but then she saw the open box of bullets atop the dresser. Robert moved his hand from behind his leg and let her see what she feared most. The effort it took for her to calm herself was obvious. She stepped inside the bedroom and gently closed the door behind her, not taking her eyes from the weapon.

"Kimmy's in the back yard, and she's a mess, but I reckon you are, too." She forced herself to look at Robert's face. "Looks like you found the bullets."

Robert moved his mouth just a little but no sound came out. He looked out the window searching for Kimmy but couldn't see her.

"I cannot believe that once again I am standing here in my bedroom looking at one of my own holding that gun."

"Mama, I can't live with what happened. I don't deserve to live." Robert lifted the gun, clutching the barrel in his left hand.

"What happened is all the more reason why you've got to keep going because you can't turn your back on your family

when there's a tragedy. I don't care how much you blame your-self. I reckon I'd be lying if I said I didn't blame you a little myself, but if you go shooting yourself you'll just make every-thing worse."

"It can't get any worse," said Robert, taking a menacing step toward Lilith Ann and waving the gun as he spoke. She pulled her head back a little, but she didn't retreat.

"I've got nothing! Don't you see? I've got nothing for my family. Less than nothing. My son is dead because I went to that restaurant, but I wasn't there looking for no job. Not a job like you think."

"What are you talking about?"

Robert held the gun up in the air and then dropped his hand to his side, lost in how to explain. "I was there to set up a robbery. That's why I was there with Sam Meeks. He didn't just drop in. We were there to work out a plan," said Robert.

"You met at a restaurant to plan a robbery?" asked Lilith Ann, incredulous at her son's stupidity.

Anger and embarrassment flared up in Robert and he turned away, looking out the window into the back yard. "I don't know where people are supposed to go to do stuff like that. There's always kids at my house." He turned back, shaking his head at his confusion. "Damn, Mama, that's not the point! A body's just as dead whether I went there for a job or to plan a robbery. If we hadn't been there none of it would have happened. Rob Jr. would still be alive if I hadn't taken him with me."

"Kimmy said you went there looking for a job. She said you were—"

"Of course that's what Kimmy said because that's what I told her," said Robert, flinging his hand with the gun up in the air. "Did you think I was gonna tell her that I was slap out of luck and the only way we could eat this week and not get the van repossessed or lose the trailer was for me to go to the T&A Lounge and try to steal their drug money? Damn, Mama!" Robert whirled back toward Lilith Ann and smacked his free hand on his forehead. "Do you have any idea what it's been like?"

"I know it's been hard. Why do you think I set up Baxter staying at your house and paying you twice the rent he should have just so he could sleep on an ironing board in your closet?"

"I've had the life squeezed out of me everywhere I go. I get shorted every time I get work, and most of the time I can't get no work. It's not supposed to be this way. It was never supposed to be this way. Daddy worked at the steel plant all those years and everything was fine. What happened, Mama? Why can't things be like they were then?"

Lilith Ann's shoulders slumped down and she suddenly looked older and even more tired. "Things weren't always so easy as you think."

"Daddy always had a job and he had a pension, but look at things now. Everybody's getting laid off. They'd rather send our jobs to the damn Mexicans and Chinese, and if you do have a job you work yourself to death because there's no more retirement."

"What's any of this got to do with you and that fella robbing a place?" asked Lilith Ann, determined to bring her son back on track. "You can go spouting off news headlines all you want, but the fact is nobody made you get yourself into the jams you've gotten into. Your daddy had enough sense not to go around getting in fights and," she started to say that he had enough sense not to drink two six-packs, shoot off guns in the yard, and get thrown in jail but thought the better of it. "Your daddy kept a cool head, and I reckon it's too bad you took too much after me. You and Magda."

Robert waved the barrel of the gun in the air. "Sometimes a man gets cornered and he just has to come out swinging."

"Is that what you're doing now? After what happened to your own boy?" asked Lilith Ann, pointing at the gun.

Robert's face twitched a little but he kept the gun in the air. "A man keeps getting slapped down over and over and he does what he has to for his family. Sometimes he just doesn't

have a choice," said Robert.

"Don't you throw that in my face as a choice! Robbing drug dealers is not a choice," spat Lilith Ann. "It's not a choice a man makes. It's not one your father would have made."

"I'm not talking about that anymore, Mama. I don't have anything left but this," he said, waving the gun.

"What's going on in there?" Viv's voice barked loudly from the hallway.

"Nothing," Robert and Lilith Ann shouted at the same instant.

"What do you mean nothing? I can hear you two arguing," said Viv.

"We're talking, now go on back down the hall," Lilith Ann said. From outside the door there was mumbling and then silence.

Robert put the gun to his temple and when he squeezed his eyes shut, tears poured down his cheeks.

"You better listen to me," Lilith Ann said in a low voice. Robert opened his eyes, and his mother pointed a shaking finger at him. "Don't you make me watch you die. Don't you be so damn selfish that you make your own mother see her son die on the same day we buried Rob Jr. I will never forgive you for that. Never." Her voice came out strained and choking. "I am going to walk out that door, and if you think that this is the best thing you've got left to offer Kimmy and the kids, then you pull that trigger. I mean it. You pull that trigger and you end it if that's what you think you've got to do. But I am tired, I am so damn tired of seeing the men in this family tear themselves up from the inside out and then sit back and wait for me to pick up the pieces. I don't care anymore, I really don't. I'm tired of picking you up and pushing you to get your life together while all you can do is blame everybody else, and I'll bet Kimmy's fed up with it too, so if this is the path you've chosen, then you've got five bullets. You figure out the right thing to do for them." She pointed behind her. "And you do it.

For the first time in your sorry selfish life. Do it." Lilith Ann was so angry her red face shook as if it were biscuit dough. She turned on her heel and jerked the door open. Magda and Viv nearly fell inside when she pulled the handle. She slammed it shut behind her before they could get a good look at the bewildered Robert, who still held the gun against his head. Robert heard muffled shrieks as Lilith Ann pulled the two of them back down the hall with her.

When the door was shut, Robert got up and locked it and then let out a long sigh. He took several sporadic breaths, his head bursting from the pressure of the moment, and then turned around to face the open window into the back yard. He wanted the last sight he remembered to be the big sycamore tree he had climbed so many times as a child. Raising the gun, he took a deep breath and put it to his temple once more, his hand shaking so badly the end of the barrel rattled against his temple. He held it there for ten seconds, then thirty, then a full minute, starting the count over each time he arrived at the number he had determined would be the end. Focusing on the tree, he felt hot tears roll down his cheeks as he remembered his son's face the last time he saw him alive. He began counting once more.

The first shot made Magda and Viv jump from their seats. The remaining four came in rapid succession. "Oh sweet Jesus! He's shot himself to death!" Viv shrieked.

Lilith Ann didn't move from her rocking chair.

"It was five shots! Nobody shoots himself five times," said Magda. She looked to her mother, whose eyes had not changed. Lilith Ann never broke the rhythm of her gentle rocking. Viv, Magda, Josh, and Lilith Ann ran in a jumbled mob down the hall to the door. Baxter took off out the front door with Peng hobbling after him. Josh reached the bedroom door first and tried to open it.

"He's locked the door. Robert!" Josh beat on the door three times.

Kimmy came running down the hall from the yard, still clenching the cigarette between her fingers. "Robert? Robert!"

Viv tried to take Kimmy by the shoulders and push her backwards. "Kimmy, you don't need to see this."

"I'm going to break the door," said Josh.

"I heard gunshots!" Kimmy shrieked.

"It was five shots," Magda repeated, as if citing the number was going to make Kimmy understand.

"Ya'll stand back," said Josh. He lunged hard at the door with his shoulder but failed to break it open. "Jack, come over here and help me."

"It's a hollow door, Josh. Just kick it in," Magda said.

"Shut the hell up," said Josh. Jack rushed past him and kicked the door twice until it popped open and banged back against the wall. No one was there and the window facing the back yard was wide open, the curtains moving lightly in the breeze. The gun, now empty of its five bullets, lay on the floor.

All of them chattered in panicked confusion at once, and after several seconds Jack's voice was heard above the din calling for silence. "Mama's trying to tell us something, now shut up!"

They all turned to see Lilith Ann standing in the hallway, her hands on her hips. "I said, if you'll all shut up long enough to listen, he's right out there." She pointed straight through the room and out the open window. "Baxter and Peng are out there with him."

"Where, Mama?" asked Magda.

"Up in the tree there." Lilith Ann's eyes were on the sycamore tree that towered over the others in the back yard. "Just like always."

"We should have known," Jack said.

"Robert's 'Get Mad Tree,'" said Magda, still shaking from the gunfire.

"Shitfire, I forgot about that," said Josh, leading the way out the bedroom door, down the hall, and through the kitchen to the back door. Peng and Baxter were standing at the bottom of the tree looking up at Robert, who had nearly made his way to the uppermost branches that were still strong enough to hold his weight.

Josh was the first one to get to Peng and Baxter at the tree. "Robert! What the hell, man. Come on back down."

"Leave me alone!" Robert shouted down.

"Robert?" Kimmy's voice was barely strong enough to be heard from where Robert sat. "Honey, won't you come down, please? You're not a kid anymore. I'm scared to death you'll fall."

"I ain't gonna fall," said Robert, calmer than he'd sounded all afternoon.

"Just give him a few minutes," said Lilith Ann. "He'll come down when he's good and ready."

"He always did act like a child when there were problems. He needs to come down and face them like a man," Viv said.

Lilith Ann's eyes squinted and she chewed her lip a moment but before she could think of a response, Baxter spoke up. "Everyone needs an exit strategy. Robert has his tree."

"Yeah, like I said, only a child climbs a tree when there's problems to be faced," Viv said.

"I reckon he's facing them up there for the moment," said Lilith Ann.

"I'm surprised somebody hadn't called the police after all those shots," said Viv, looking around at the neighbor's yards.

"Well, I guess it wouldn't be a family gathering around this place if somebody didn't shoot off a gun," said Lilith Ann.

"Josh, go up and there and talk to him," ordered Viv.

Josh's face fell. "I ain't climbing that tree, Viv."

"He's your little brother and he's...he's up in a tree," said Viv, pointing up at the branches where Robert was wedged between the trunk and a branch that looked too small to hold him.

"I can see that," said Josh.

"What if something happens to him?" Viv cast a side-eyed glance at Kimmy, who was wringing her hands and looking up at Robert.

"Do you think there's something I can do up in the tree that I can't do from down here?"

Viv sighed and put her hands on her hips. "I just think we ought to do something."

"He's a grown-ass man. If he wants to climb a tree then there's not much I can do about it."

"We are doing something," said Magda. "We're waiting for Robert to get himself together and come down. In the meantime, we can just eat some pie."

"Eat some pie?" snorted Viv. "We're in the middle of a crisis and you want to eat pie?"

Up in the sycamore tree, Robert sat with his back pressed uncomfortably against the trunk and his knees drawn up to his chest. He didn't remember the fit being so tight the last time he sat up in that tree, but that had been, how many years ago? He tried to recall the last time he had climbed it. Maybe he'd been a teenager then. It was before he met Kimmy. Way before any of the kids. He looked down and saw her blonde hair, a circle around her tiny head far below. She was focused upward on him, her eyes barely visible from his towering height up in the tree. Viv and Josh had been barking up at him, but he'd stopped listening. Josh had gestured up at the tree several times, but seemed to be looking at Viv when he did it, so Robert figured Josh's concern was more with his wife than it was with him. His mother stood off to one side of the yard, and Jack, bored, leaned against a nearby tree, one hand slowly scratching Daryl behind his ears. Peng and Baxter had pulled out lawn chairs from somewhere and retired close to where Lilith Ann stood. Robert ignored them all for a while and then he noticed Magda enter the house through the back kitchen door and several minutes later return carrying a tray. It was covered in plates of something and soon everyone was eating except Viv and Kimmy. Robert squinted down at the plate Magda held. She looked back up at him and raised her fork in the air. "Come down and have some pie?" she shouted.

Pie. They were eating pie, probably chocolate pie, or maybe pecan. Maybe it was both. Magda loved pie of almost every kind. He readjusted himself to get a better look at his near whole damn family down there eating pie while he sat in a tree after having shot his mother's bedroom floor full of holes. She was going to be pissed when she caught sight of all those holes in her floor. Maybe she already had and that was why she was standing off to the side acting like she didn't care what he did. Robert knew his mother would lie in bed at night thinking about those holes, thinking what a dumbass he was for losing his cool and shooting up her bedroom. Suddenly Robert was sick and sorry for doing such a thing, but he knew if he hadn't shot out those bullets he might have exploded inside.

That was exactly how he'd felt when he emptied his mother's gun and jumped out the window. It was better up there in the sycamore tree. He could breathe easier up high in the branches, and sounds didn't quite reach up there the way they traveled down below. He could make out most of what the people below were saying, but sometimes sounds got blown away on the wind before they made their way up to him. That was one of the reasons he had liked to lose himself high up there since he was a child. His own kids had never even tried to climb that tree. They'd played in his mother's back yard plenty of times, but for some reason the idea of ascending a tree had not occurred to any of them. Maybe they were too young. Maybe they watched too much television and were used to lying around the way kids did these days, but maybe if they had seen him do it, one of them would have been seized by the urge to shimmy up the trunk and learn to love the scrape of the bark against his flesh just like he did. Of course, the one most likely to want to climb would have been Rob Jr. The thought that his son would never get the chance to do that seized his heart again and squeezed, and he felt the now familiar tightening in his chest that made the tears come.

His view extended all the way over his mother's house and

down the street in both directions, and suddenly he wanted more than anything for his oldest son to know what it was to climb that tree and see the views the way the birds did up high near the top of the sycamore. A white van slowed, pulled into the front driveway, and stopped in the last open space in the yard on the far left next to Magda's car. It had to be another one of those news vans that had been parked around the church all morning, but Robert couldn't make out any insignia on the side. The driver's door opened; a woman exited the van and then went out of sight around the other side. Voices like excited birds were just loud enough to reach him. His kids. Someone was returning Matthew, Cody, Scott, and Jessica Ann. He tried to think which of the "church ladies" had taken them home after the funeral. She must have been one of his mother's friends. Several tiny heads were moving into the house, where they disappeared for several seconds before he heard the back door open and saw those little heads darting into the yard to their mother, who had remained at the base of the tree. For a moment, Kimmy and the kids made up a single blob there on the ground, all of the people who depended on Robert wrapped around one another so closely he could not tell them apart in his partial view through the leaves. Then a voice broke through clearly. "Daddy's up in a tree? What's he doing up in a tree?" It was Cody, or maybe it was Matthew. Robert could hardly tell them apart from up above. When you're looking straight down on a body, height is distorted.

"Hey, Daddy! What you doing up in that tree?" Cody's high voice pierced the air.

Robert rested his chin over a branch and watched the dots of his children's heads on the ground, his surviving children. "I'm just taking a little break," Robert called down.

"I want to come up there, too!"

"Me, too," said Matthew. "I wanna climb a tree with Daddy. Mama, let me go, too."

Voices fluttered down below and then Kimmy looked up,

shielding her eyes from the glare with her hand. She looked so thin that far down on the ground with the children circling around her. Her blonde hair was poufed out all around, making her look like a lollipop standing among gummy bears that couldn't be still.

"Robert?" Her voice was tired and so thin it barely made it up to him.

Magda, holding a plate that must have been refilled with pie when he wasn't looking, repeated his name and added her incentive. "Robert, there's pie."

He looked down at them all again, counting the children. Four. He saw only four, and his heart ached that Rob Jr. would never be among them again.

"Robert." said Magda. "If you want to teach these kids how to climb, you've got to come down first. Come on down and eat some pie, then everybody can climb with you. They need you to show them how."

Robert didn't hear Baxter, who had just finished his own slice of chocolate pie and put his paper plate next to Peng's on the grass. "There's always pie at funerals. We have good funerals. The best." He smiled at his future wife and leaned back in his flimsy lawn chair. Together they looked up to see a small white cloud moving far, far past the figure of Robert, who was now descending carefully, cautiously, toward his family.

Acknowledgments

I would like to thank Steve McCondichie for seeing the potential in my manuscript, April Ford for her editing excellence, and the whole team at SFK Press for their exuberant commitment to my book. Joy Bagley for decades of pulling no punches when critiquing my writing. Playwright Kelly McBurnette-Andronicos for creative support since third grade. The late Dr. William "Bill" Doxey for teaching me about great literature. *Steel Toe Review* for publishing the prologue, "Daryl and Pete-O Go to Walmart." Stan Rubin of Pacific Lutheran University's Rainier Writing Workshop and all the faculty members who pushed me to write harder and smarter than I thought I could.

About the Author

Cathy Adams has been writing novels nonstop for twenty-five years, ever since she wrote a play consisting of two characters and five lines of dialogue as a first-grader. Opening up the raw insides of what makes us who we are is the basis for most of her stories—when a plot or character makes Cathy feel uncomfortable, then she knows she needs to write about it. *A Body's Just as Dead* is inspired by an actual event and comes from her desire to understand why someone planning to buy AA batteries and toilet paper at a Walmart could end up shooting another person out of rage. A native of Alabama, Cathy is a Pushcart Prize-nominated short story writer. She currently resides in Liaoning, China.

Photo by Julian Jackson

Share Your Thoughts

Want to help spread the word about *A Body's Just as Dead*? Consider leaving an honest review on Goodreads. It is our priority at SFK Press to publish books for readers to enjoy, and our authors would love to hear from you!

Do You Know About Our Weekly Zine?

Would you like your unpublished prose, poetry, or visual art featured in SFK Press's weekly online literary publication, *The New Southern Fugitives*? A zine that's free to readers and subscribers, and pays contributors:

$60 per book review, essay & short story
$25 per photograph & piece of visual art
$25 per poem

Visit **NewSouthernFugitives.com/Submit** for more information!

CPSIA information can be obtained
at www.ICGtesting.com
Printed in the USA
LVHW041755101218
599938LV00002B/460/P